Avalon

Avalon

Aaron Friedrick

RESOURCE *Publications* · Eugene, Oregon

Resource Publications
An Imprint of Wipf and Stock Publishers
199 W. 8th Ave., Suite 3
Eugene, OR 97401

www.wipfandstock.com

PAPERBACK ISBN: 978-1-6667-4539-9
HARDCOVER ISBN: 978-1-6667-4540-5
EBOOK ISBN: 978-1-6667-4541-2

10/19/22

Dedicated to
Corissa, my "Nya"
and
those seeking hope

Special thanks to
my editor,
Jenny Beckworth

Contents

Introduction

THE FOLLOWING IS A story that follows a young man named Tarro through an adventurous life journey. Set in a society filled with danger and confusion, he seeks to make sense of it all. In the face of adversity, he strives to live with courage, love, and goodness but struggles to do so with mounting feelings of hopelessness and despair.

Serving as an illustration for life in our own chaotic world, this story leads to a message of hope, a hope which exists outside of man.

This hope is expressed in Romans 5:8:

"But God demonstrates His own love toward us, in that while we were yet sinners, Christ died for us."

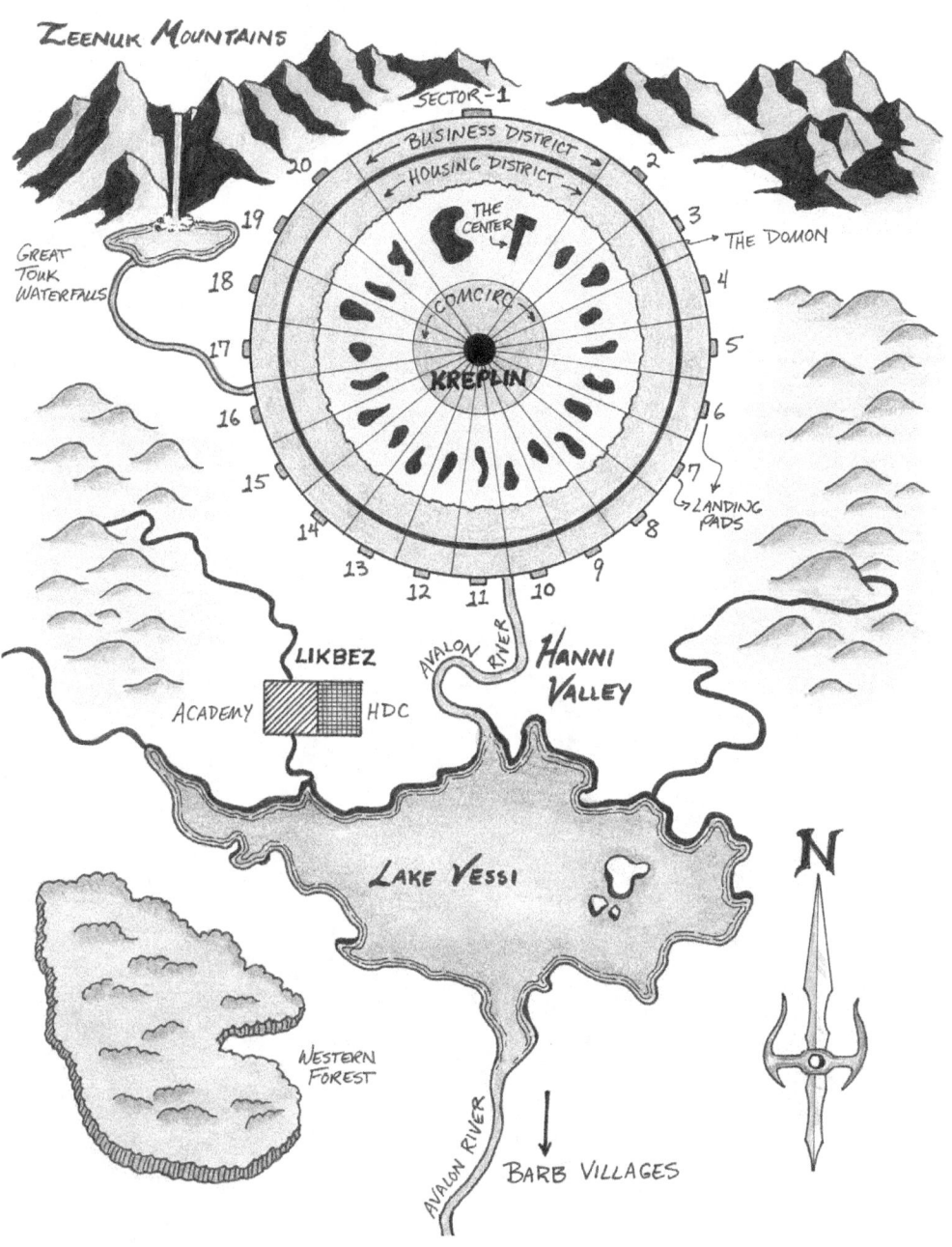

Prologue

Justice Day

THE CITY VIBRATED WITH excitement. Today was July 10th, 2498. Today was also Justice Day, and the citizens of Avalon loved Justice Day. The entire city had come out for the event, gathering in Comrade Circle, the center of the city, most commonly referred to simply as COMCIRC. This expansive circular plaza surrounded the Kreplin, headquarters for the city's government.

The city of Avalon was constructed in a series of concentric circles of beautifully designed spaces spanning twenty miles in diameter. But for all of Avalon's architectural grandeur, nothing compared to the magnificence of the Kreplin, the crown jewel of the city in both appearance and function, embodying both the grand edifice and its elite government.

Peace Officer number 4,365, along with the other Peace Officers of the city, quietly moved about the crowd surveying the energized spectators in COMCIRC. The citizens casually milled about, buzzing with chatter as they waited for the accused to be brought forth and the spectacle of Justice Day to begin.

"Officer 43–65, status report," said a female voice through the Peace Officer's implanted ear chips.

Officer 43–65, otherwise known as Tarro, hated the Kreplin's numbering system. He was one of exactly five thousand Peace Officers deployed by the city's government. To them he wasn't a valued officer, he wasn't even a respected citizen. He was just a number. Tomorrow he might advance to number 4,364, but whether he was 4,365 or 4,364, in the end, he was just a number.

He masked his disdain and responded in a professional tone, "Sector-11 secure."

He'd always wondered who it was that spoke to him. The voice came from the Security Division of the Kreplin called SD-6. He had never met the owner of the voice. He wasn't allowed. No one was. It was the faceless voice of SD-6 who daily directed the corps of Peace Officers and went by "Mother-6." It was always the same, a soothing voice that spoke as if she embodied a happy ray of sunshine and you were her best friend.

The voice responded with dripping sweetness, "Mother-6 copies. Peace and love."

"Peace and love. 43–65 out." Tarro grudgingly gave the requisite sign-off which he loathed. SD-6 monitored every detail and moment of his life through his Bionet, a network of implanted eye, ear, and body computer chips. He hated the Bionet as much as he hated that voice and liked to imagine her as some dour old hag who only feigned a happy voice in order to mask her miserable existence which had been with him every second of his three years of Peace Officer service.

He continued to meander through the crowd, picking his way toward the Kreplin, when the crowd erupted into a deafening cheer. Two massive gold doors leading onto the main balcony of the Kreplin swung open. A man who looked to be in his fifties emerged and elegantly strode to the front of the balcony which faced Sector-11, extending forty feet above COMCIRC. Draped in a crimson robe trimmed with elegant patterns of inset silver braids, he took a position next to a small orb which hovered near his face. The orb slowly circled him, broadcasting large holographic projections displayed at intervals all throughout COMCIRC, so that every citizen could see and hear. The man wore a smile which showcased brilliantly white teeth; a gold cord deftly wove through his long, fine silver hair giving the appearance of a crown.

Next to Tarro, a man with a face plastered in colorful makeup exclaimed to the woman next to him, "Look! Isn't Supreme Confidant Talin's robe just simply divine?"

"It's absolutely stunning!" gushed the woman. Like all the other citizens, she wore her best and most expensive clothes. Her exuberance was as extravagant as the peacock plumes that adorned her head piece.

Supreme Confidant Talin raised his hands to the crowd and said, pausing after each word for effect, "Welcome . . . citizens . . . of . . . Avalon!" His welcome elicited a new wave of cheers from the people, along with a choreographed introduction from the Kreplin. Trumpet-sounding horns blasted Avalon's anthem. All around the Kreplin, brilliant colors flashed in the air like a swarm of vibrant, giant fireflies as thousands of gold and royal blue silk streamers appeared above COMCIRC and began slowly descending, twirling and snaking their way down toward the crowd. The citizens were now in a frenzy, cheering and pointing to the streamers, maneuvering underneath them, attempting to snatch one or two before they reached the ground. Each streamer was very valuable, able to be exchanged to the Kreplin for a hundred Colonnade credits, an amount that would last for an entire month of visits to the Colonnades, the recreation houses of Avalon.

Tarro watched the leader of Avalon whose arms were still stretched out as wide as his smile. Being somewhat distant from the balcony, he shifted his gaze to a nearby holographic projection. The hologram was as clear as if the man himself were standing there in person. Tarro was struck by the blackness of his eyes.

Once all the streamers had been collected, the music stopped and the Supreme Confidant resumed, "Welcome, my friends." He looked left and right, allowing the orb to project his smiling face to the people, all of whom had dutifully taken their places in their respective sectors of COMCIRC. Each citizen lived in an allocated sector, governed by a Minister of Avalon, all twenty of whom were now sitting in a semi-circle at the rear of the balcony behind the Supreme Confidant.

"Today, it saddens me to inform you that we have discovered a traitor to Avalon." The crowd let out a collective groan of disapproval. Supreme Confidant Talin's smile disappeared, giving way to an exaggerated face of sadness. "I love this city. I love you all. I love our way of life. But this city, this life, you yourselves, dear friends, must be protected. This is my duty. But this is my great privilege."

Talin waited for the applause to die down and then began to drone on about his loyalties to the people and the rule of law. Tarro scanned the faces in the crowd, looking for a man assigned to Sector-11, the respectable older man who had befriended him. He was different from the rest. Quite different, in fact.

Tarro soon spotted him standing next to what looked to be a companion droid. They were so human-like, it was often hard to tell if they were droids or humans, particularly from a distance. Tarro made his way closer to the genteel man and saw him clapping politely. Most would not have noticed, but Tarro observed the distinct lack of enthusiasm.

They often met at the man's cafe when Tarro was off duty. Tarro recalled their conversation yesterday when the man insinuated that today's event would not be what it seemed. Tarro had pressed him to explain what he meant by that, but the cafe owner wouldn't go any further.

This morning, Tarro had received a brief report on the accused. The report was concise: "Business owner, age 23, failed to pay lawful taxes to the Kreplin for the last two years. Citizen has defied the sound laws of Avalon and stolen from its law-abiding citizens and is therefore guilty of sedition against the Kreplin."

The crowd burst into another ovation as this rebel was finally revealed. Emerging from the same balcony doors came a young man, a woman, and a female companion droid. Tarro fixated on the woman, wondering how she was to be implicated in this as his briefing said nothing about her.

The three of them walked out to Talin who had traded his gloomy expression for one of amusement. Two Peace Officers escorted the trio, each officer carrying a chivvy, a long titanium rod whose end could discharge a lethal electric charge.

Talin waved his arms with great fanfare as he presented the charges. "This citizen is guilty of not paying taxes. This coward has cheated the Kreplin and has rebelled against our laws, and most scandalous of all . . . has robbed from *you,* dear friends!"

The crowd began jeering and taunting the accused. The young man, who had been looking down until this point, raised his head. Tarro instantly froze upon seeing the familiar face. He couldn't breathe. A wave of panic and anger simultaneously swept over his entire body as he saw the fellow Peace Officer stand there as an accused lawbreaker of Avalon.

Talin's voice continued to echo throughout COMCIRC. "And the most unfortunate part of this sordid matter is that this betrayer is a Peace Officer. Peace Officer 39–88. This officer swore an oath to protect Avalon but instead became a traitor." As Talin continued to lay out the accusations, the balcony detached from the Kreplin building and began slowly circling the towering dome of the Kreplin. As it orbited the dome, it rose upward, elevated by the city's advanced electromagnetic power grid. The orb continued to broadcast the balcony scene.

Tarro felt as if he were going to vomit and it took every ounce of concentration to keep from doing so. He refused to believe the Kreplin's charge against his fellow officer, Klon. Klon was one of the most loyal guys he had ever met, top of his class, highly industrious and motivated, squeaky clean and never in trouble. Though they had graduated in the same class, Klon moved up the ranks as a Peace Officer even faster than

Tarro, who was himself a highly-motivated officer. Klon ran a perfectly legal and successful business on the side and Tarro figured the chances of Klon cheating on his taxes, particularly as a continually monitored Peace Officer, were zero. His right hand began to tremble and he instinctively placed it on his holstered GP-9 Gamma Phaser.

The rising balcony continued to move skyward in its orbit around the Kreplin dome, and Tarro intently watched the nearby hologram. Klon was once again staring down at the ground, slowly shaking his head, silently denying the charges. He placed his finger momentarily to his eye, and Tarro suspected it was to wipe away a tear. The guard next to him would have none of it and quickly struck him in the arm with the non-lethal side of his chivvy.

By now, Talin had worked up the crowd's outrage to a frenzy. "So the question, my dear friends, is this—what shall we do with this traitor, this person who doesn't love me, who doesn't love you, who doesn't love our dear city?" Talin dramatically pointed at the young man and shouted, "What shall we do with this rebel who *hates*?!"

Before Talin could finish the last question, the crowd began chanting for his death.

The balcony finally reached the top of the Kreplin, taking a hovering position directly over the dome's spire—the center of the Kreplin, the center of COMCIRC, the center of Avalon. By design, the climax in this spectacle had been reached. The full weight and power of the Kreplin would be unleashed upon this offender in the name of justice and peace. And love.

Talin raised his hands and the crowd obediently ceased its chanting. "My friends, I hear your demands and your demands are just. But this officer is not the only offender. No. Both the partner and the companion are likewise guilty." Tarro felt a light nudge on his right arm. He looked over and received a brief nod of acknowledgement from the cafe owner standing next to him.

Talin pointed at the woman and the droid. "Sadly, in the name of Avalon and all that is good and decent, these two must face the same fate as this man, for they were complicit in the crimes. They knew of the wrongdoing and did not report it."

The woman, who had managed to hold it together up to this point, began sobbing uncontrollably. Klon remained stoically at her side, but the companion droid attempted to console her. As Tarro's rage began to overpower the nausea he was feeling, he glanced at his friend standing next to him. Surrounded by citizens who had come out to this event to celebrate in their party attire, Tarro noticed for the first time that the older man was dressed simply in all black. Tarro momentarily locked eyes with him and was struck by his expression. There wasn't any anger. Certainly no elation like the mob surrounding him. Just a perceptible, deep sadness.

As Talin announced the guilt of the woman and the droid, the crowd simultaneously came to grips with an unthinkable outcome, the elimination of a companion droid which most of them also possessed. The attitude of the citizens of Avalon quickly pivoted as many began crying out for mercy for the droid.

The female-looking droid, who had been attempting to console the woman, had until now been oblivious to her own death sentence. Picking up on the crowd's chants and beginning to process what was happening, the droid abruptly separated from the woman and faced the crowd. Tarro couldn't hear what the droid was saying, but it was clear that she was playing to the crowd, egging them on with animated gestures to keep the chants coming. Her self-preservation programming was proving to be sound.

Talin seemed to anticipate all this as he calmly silenced the crowd. "So you wish me to spare the companion?"

The crowd shouted its affirmation, and the droid began joyfully clapping her hands over her head and giving thumbs up to the crowd. The woman crumpled to her knees while Klon remained motionless with his head bowed.

SD-6 chirped into Tarro's ear, "Officer 43–65, your blood pressure has spiked. Please advise on your condition." Whatever his pressure was reading, Tarro guessed that the clinically happy voice had just made it jump to even more dangerous levels, dangerous in drawing attention to himself. Knowing SD-6 monitored every aspect of his health, he had learned to control his emotions, particularly his anger, an emotion the Kreplin was not fond of, particularly if directed at them.

Tarro took a deep breath and exhaled slowly. "Mother-6, Officer 43–65 is angry these criminals would dare to commit such treason against our city." He took another deep breath. "You should be noticing my pressure decreasing as my anger subsides, knowing that truth and justice are being upheld. Thank you for your concern."

"Copy 43–65. Please keep Mother-6 advised if you need any assistance. Peace and love. Mother-6 out."

Tarro watched as Supreme Confidant Talin gave the signal. In response, the two officers thrust the lethal ends of the chivvies into the backs of Klon and his wife. The bright blue spark of high voltage signaled their deaths as they instantly collapsed onto the balcony floor.

The balcony quickly began its descent while the droid blew kisses to the crowd. After the balcony docked in its original location, Talin turned with a flourish toward the double doors. He passed through the ornate doors and the two officers followed, dragging the two dead criminals by the feet. The droid brought up the rear, walking backward, still blowing its ridiculous kisses to the already dispersing crowd. The balcony doors closed, and the lucky citizens who had captured streamers nearly ran to collect their Colonnade credits.

SD-6 broke into Tarro's trance. "Officer 43–65, congratulations on your promotion. You are now Peace Officer 43–64. The Supreme Confidant sends his regards."

Tarro was shocked and didn't respond.

"Officer 43–64, do you copy?" After another moment of silence, SD-6 repeated herself with more volume, "Officer 43–64, do you copy?"

Tarro composed himself and uttered a raspy response, "Roger, Mother-6. 43–65 . . . I—I mean . . . 43 . . . 64 . . . copies."

He stood motionless for several minutes. Never had he envisioned a promotion would come though the execution of a fellow Peace Officer. Surrounded by beautiful people and a magnificent city of incomparable technological advancements, he glared angrily at the opulent Kreplin. Soon, blinding rage gave way to a new clarity, a new purpose in life. *I will work my way into the belly of the beast*, he thought. *And then I will end it. I will end it all.*

Part 1

The Academy

Chapter 1

Academy Life

5 Years Earlier . . .

IT WAS AN ENGINEERING marvel. The city of Avalon rotated effortlessly like a slow spinning plate almost a mile above the earth's surface, affording its residents a three hundred sixty degree view of the earth below. With the Zeenuk Mountain Range to the north and the Hanni Valley to the south, Avalon was surrounded by extraordinary natural beauty.

The Great Touk Waterfalls in the Zeenuk Mountains cascaded over a thousand feet, pouring into the Avalon River which passed under the city and eventually emptied into Lake Vessi in the southern valley. A tall wall surrounded Avalon's perimeter, interrupted at intervals by towering spires. Inside the wall, along the perimeter of the city, the tops of various buildings of all shapes and sizes could be seen from the earth's surface, each possessing unique architectural design. Emanating from the wall was a translucent force field dome, called the BioDome, which blanketed the city, barely discernible to the naked eye.

"Bravo 3–58, would you care to join us?" The gruff voice of Tarro's Academy instructor jolted him out of his daydreaming. He took one last longing glance at the distant city through the classroom window. He loved this assigned seat. The window was small and high, but on most days he could see the glorious city. The drawback was the inevitable daydreaming which was frequent, for this was his least favorite instructor and least favorite class. *Advanced Physics* with Instructor-5, one of the oldest and grumpiest instructors at the Academy.

"Bravo 3–58!" shouted Instructor-5, with a biting tone. "Perhaps you would care to regale us with your incomparable knowledge and answer the question!"

Tarro tried to hide the annoyance felt from his lost daydream. "I'm sorry, Instructor-5, can you repeat the question?"

The instructor glared at him as if attempting to bore two holes into his forehead with her fierce eyes. She folded her arms across her chest to visually enhance the disgust she wore on her craggy face. "The question was . . ." she said slowly as if she were talking to a toddler, "what type of energy powers the generators on the earth's surface, the generators that produce the electromagnetic forces needed to keep the city of Avalon suspended above the surface?"

Tarro stood at attention next to his desk, the required posture for speaking in class, and stumbled through a disjointed answer. Happily, it contained enough factual content to get the instructor off his back. He disliked her intensely and he was not the only one. He was just the most recent of generations of Cadets required to endure her for an entire year. She was one of the most senior instructors at the Academy, not only because of her expertise, but because she had been around longer than dirt.

Every instructor was identified by a number indicating his or her place in the pecking order of seniority. This was the way of Avalon. Cadets had numbers, instructors had numbers, citizens had numbers. There were only four instructors higher in rank than Instructor-5. Needless to say, one did not want to get entangled with this senior crank.

Tarro's wandering attention returned to the window. He could see in the distance a large complex adjacent to Avalon River and directly below the city that contained the primary generators. Yesterday's reading assignment described in great detail how they worked but he still didn't quite understand it, as evidenced by Instructor-5's disapproving scowl which had met his answer. He marveled at how an entire city was held up by the electromagnetic forces generated from this complex. He made a mental note to review his reading again.

Advanced Physics finally ended, and Tarro darted out of the classroom, breathing the fresh oxygen outside of the oppressive dungeon Instructor-5 called a classroom. He returned to his quarters at Lenon Hall, the dormitory for the Cadets, and threw his gear on his bed. It landed with a thud on the hard, stiff sleeping pad. He frowned at the gray wool blanket, tightly tucked with perfect hospital corners per Academy regulations. Most of the Cadets didn't seem to mind it, but his skin found its scratchiness near intolerable.

Everything was sterile, uniform, gray, and utterly drab at Avalon Academy, giving the school the look and feel of a military academy. The Cadets entered at the age of ten. From birth until that time, they were raised by Kreplin state officials in Avalon's Human Development Center, referred to as HDC. Their "parents" were simply stewards of the children and were referred to as such. The stewards possessed no parental rights under the State which maintained full authority over the children at every phase of their development.

Upon transfer from HDC to the Academy, children entered into a rigorous ten year program to prepare them for life in Avalon. Every stage of education and training was designed to mold the prospective citizen into the model Avalon patriot, completely devoted to the State and the State controlled way of life.

HDC and the Academy were located just north of Lake Vessi and were combined into one giant complex called Likbez. While the rigors of education and indoctrination were designed to craft the compliant citizen, the austere environment was fashioned to make the prospective citizen enthusiastically yearn to be assimilated into the opulent life of Avalon. Only those Cadets who passed the rigors of their training would do so.

The class groupings of the Academy were designated by letters, beginning with "J" for first-year Cadets and descending chronologically to "A" for tenth-year Cadets. Each class was divided into twenty regiments. Tarro was in his ninth year, with a solid class ranking of 358 amongst roughly two thousand classmates. As a ninth-year Cadet in Class B, or "Bravo," he identified as "Bravo 3–58." Tarro was quite pleased that he had managed to advance his ranking last year from 416 to his current standing. It had required tremendous drive and energy, but the nearing reality of graduation and citizenship made it all worthwhile.

He was determined to work even harder this year for a specific reason. By far, throughout his education, his favorite class had been *Collective Security and Happiness*, taken in his sixth year. The class was taught by Peace Officer 35. Officer 35 was impressive. He had a command presence that garnered instant respect. His white uniform was always impeccably pressed, matching his confident demeanor and meticulous habits. He was strict but had a sense of humor which was rare amongst instructors.

Tarro was awestruck by the man but also fell in love with the mission of the Peace Officer, which, as Officer 35 laid out in great detail, embodied the noble and prestigious role of preserving the security and happiness of the citizens of Avalon. From that time on, all Tarro could think about was becoming a Peace Officer.

In every graduating class, only the top three hundred Cadets would be considered for the Peace Officer Corps. With his ninth year having just begun, Tarro's singular goal was to break into this top-ranking group which he knew could only be achieved with near perfect behavior and academic performance.

"Hey, Tarro!" piped a voice behind him. Tarro instantly recognized the voice of his classmate, Sye. For as long as Tarro could remember, they had been friends. The problem was that over the last couple of years, Sye found himself getting into more trouble. He had become increasingly snarky, and the Academy didn't like snarky. His growing surliness didn't quite match Tarro's goal of becoming a Peace Officer which is why Tarro had been trying to put some distance between their friendship. But this was difficult, considering they were roommates in Regiment-12.

"Tarro, you gotta auditory problem or are you just stupid?" Sye was always needling him, and Tarro sighed, weary of the incessant poking.

He dryly acknowledged his friend without turning, "Sye, it's so great to see you."

"*See*? You're not even looking—" Sye was cut off by the announcement that blared throughout Regiment-12's wing of Lenon Hall. "Ten minutes until noon formation."

Grateful to have Sye interrupted, Tarro quickly wiped the smudges off his boots and jetted off to formation, arriving several minutes early to his assigned spot. Every regiment of the Academy formed ranks twice a day in their respective courtyards at precisely 7:30 am and noon. The accounting of Cadets was reported to the regimental leader, a high-ranking tenth-year Cadet, and then the regiments marched inside to their class dining halls.

Tarro always tried be the first to formation, and today he had pulled it off. Little things like this affected your performance grade which factored into one's ranking. Tarro waited at the prescribed posture of attention as the rest of Regiment-12 poured into the courtyard. The best part of being early was that *her* formation placement was directly in front of him, and when she took her place, he would get a momentary glimpse of her pretty face—Bravo 18–60, otherwise known as Nya. Nya possessed a simple beauty, and Tarro had taken notice of her last year. It wasn't just her beauty that struck him though, it was her whole persona.

Nya was different from the rest of the girls. Most of the other girls acted like the boys, but not Nya. She had a certain quality about her that made her stand out from the others, boy or girl. They were told from day one that gender distinctions did not exist and that gender had been an ancient construct best left to a by-gone, primitive, unenlightened age. Gender-specific pronouns were forbidden, and the Cadets were treated as non-binary human beings, referred to by the "they" pronoun. This was the new age of enlightenment.

Tarro wasn't sure what he thought about all this. Nya took her position in formation, glanced at Tarro, and smiled. She brushed a wisp of hair out of her face and tucked it behind her ear. He loved it when she did that. She blushed slightly as she noticed his playful wink and quickly turned away to stand at attention. Tarro admired her perfectly tailored uniform, and he couldn't help but notice that she had some curves that Sye standing next to her didn't seem to possess. Tarro chuckled to himself and thought, *We might be equal, but we certainly aren't equally packaged.*

Lunch was one of seven meals continuously rotated in the same order. As Tarro entered Class Bravo's dining hall, the smell made him cringe, reminding him that today was his least favorite of the rotation. After choking down the insufferable meal involving some unidentifiable meat, his spirits were lifted with an announcement given by the Chancellor of the Academy.

The Chancellor wore a deep royal blue uniform with gold trimmings. He was young for the position, but his ambition made up for his lack of experience. He confidently strode to the small stage in the center of the dining hall and made his announcement: "Class Bravo, welcome to the beginning of another year of learning and development. You are being molded into future citizens by the best Avalon has to offer."

Tarro thought of the Instructor-5 hag and wondered what the rest of Avalon was like if she was the best it had to offer.

"Through hard work and dedication to Supreme Confidant Talin and the Avalon spirit, you have arrived at this point in your training. Provided you continue to perform with excellence, you will prove to be worthy of Avalon and graduate as citizens in less than two short years."

The Chancellor, knowing the Cadets were genuinely excited about this prospect, raised his fist to permit the Academy's acceptable form of applause. The Cadets enthusiastically responded with two successive claps in perfect unison. Tarro glanced over to the adjacent table where Sye sat. He didn't look quite as enthused as everyone else.

The Chancellor lowered his fist. He placed his hands behind his back and forced his chest out, highlighting the numerous medals that adorned it. "As you know, one of the great hallmarks of your ninth year is the tour of Avalon and the Kreplin parade. In fifteen days, you will enter into our beloved city for the very first time since your birth. I expect that you will conduct yourselves admirably, representing this Academy with dignity, honor, and perfection. This afternoon is also the Visitation. As you are reacquainted with your stewards, remember, they will be watching your parade in Avalon. Make them proud!"

After Bravo Class was dismissed from the dining hall, Tarro hustled off to his next class, *Modern Warfare*. It had been his favorite class of the year thus far, but today he didn't hear much of the lecture. All he could think about was the upcoming visit to Avalon and the parade. Divided into their regiments, they were to march past the Kreplin where Supreme Confidant Talin and all the dignitaries would review them in their official capacity. The entire city would be out for it. This was the annual parade of ninth-year Avalon Academy Cadets and a proud moment for the city to be able to glimpse its future new citizens.

Tarro was jarred out of his pleasant daydream when he remembered the Visitation which was scheduled right after this class. He never really liked this annual visit at the beginning of every new school year. It's not that his stewards weren't nice. It just always proved to be awkward.

The Visitation took place at 2:00 pm in the Great Rotunda. The enormous circular hall was by far the largest room at the Academy. Ornate glass and silver paneling lined the walls; the ceiling slanted upward from the outer walls toward the center, culminating in a voluminous dome, its interior covered with intricate carvings of the city of Avalon. Residing at the peak of the dome was the upper torso of Mother Earth, jutting downward from the dome's center with her arms lovingly extended toward a white marble statue standing thirty feet high on the Rotunda floor. The statue was a perfect representation of Talin. His left hand reached out to Mother Earth above him, his right held a tablet on which was inscribed, "Hail Mother Earth!"

Tarro, along with his classmates, sat at their individually assigned tables and waited for their stewards to arrive. Within a few minutes, an announcement was made and the stewards entered from multiple doorways located at intervals around the Rotunda. A sea of colorful clothing, hair, and accessories filled the room, a stark and extravagant contrast to the gray uniforms of the two thousand Cadets.

Tarro watched the large group of stewards bustle in, talking excitedly to one another like exhilarated kids visiting their favorite haunt. To his left, a man with a long, braided pony-tail wearing a vest of pink flamingo feathers sat down with a woman who had the most intricate pattern of markings on her shaved head. To his right, a woman with hair down to her waist sat down with her droid companion who evidently thought much of the woman's hair as she kept fondling it.

Soon, Tarro's two stewards arrived and sat down.

"Hi, Tarro," said the first man. He smiled and gently shook Tarro's hand. Tarro returned the greeting. "Good afternoon Neen."

The second man, Lon, also shook Tarro's hand and sat next to Neen. Both men were meticulously groomed. Lon, sporting a light touch of lipstick with heavy eye-liner, held a small dog with long white hair. Tarro wondered how much Neen and Lon had spent on the dog's elaborate braids.

Neen had been previously married to a woman whom Tarro barely remembered. By Tarro's first year at the Academy, Neen was visiting with his new husband Lon. Tarro never knew what happened to Neen's previous wife as he hadn't heard from her since Lon started making this annual visit in her place.

"So, Tarro," Neen said, "how have things been?"

Tarro tried to think of something intelligent to say. Where do you begin in summarizing a year of life? Tarro considered the question for a moment and said, "Well . . . it's been good."

Lon looked at Tarro's chest and the class ranking displayed digitally on his uniform. "Looks like you're doing well." As Cadets, their class rankings were always displayed on the left breast sections of their uniforms, a constant reminder of how they were performing.

"Yes, I've been working hard. I—"

"Isn't Giggi something?" Neen said as he began fawning over the dog that had jumped into his lap and was now licking his face. The couple then commenced in petting and cooing as if it were some little child.

Tarro looked at his watch. Twenty more minutes of Visitation. After Neen and Lon exhausted their fawning gibberish with Giggi, the three engaged in small talk for the remainder of the time, said their farewells, and Tarro watched them leave. He got the sense that these visitations were an annual opportunity for stewards to come look at their trophies, brush off their dust, admire them for a few minutes, put them back on the shelf, and then pat themselves on the backs for their consummate stewardship.

Tarro didn't care though. They meant as little to him as he seemed to mean to them. In the end, he knew it wasn't really their fault. This is all the State would allow.

Tarro looked over at the figures of Talin and Mother Nature. As the Academy had drilled into his head, they were his true parents.

Chapter 2

Avalon Tour

T HE DAY FINALLY CAME and Tarro could hardly contain himself. Every previous class that returned from its first tour of Avalon had one common assessment: it was more glorious than they had ever imagined. Tarro checked himself in the mirror and adjusted his uniform for the fourth time, taking quite seriously the Chancellor's call for perfection.

Bravo Class assembled in the Rotunda for the briefing where they were given strict instructions regarding every phase of what would prove to be a meticulously scripted visit to the city. The number one rule was to never leave their regiment. The number two rule was to not embarrass the Academy. A litany of others rules followed. Tarro didn't mind the laborious briefing. Anything was worth being able see the wonders of Avalon.

After the briefing, the Cadets were dismissed by regiment to board their rides to the city, AT-7s, Avalon Transport aircraft. Tarro stood in formation along the perimeter of the large landing pad outside the Rotunda and watched the long line of AT-7s in the distance, flying slowly toward them from Avalon. His heart raced with excitement as he watched the first transport pass through the force field dome that protectively covered the entire Likbez compound, similar to the BioDome possessed by Avalon. While the dome was barely visible, its presence was perceptible from the shadowy line which snaked along the exterior of the transport as it passed through.

They had been told that the BioDomes encased Avalon and Likbez and served as barriers to protect the occupants from the variety of viruses and diseases that plagued the rest of the planet. The Cadets never ventured outside the Academy walls because to do so not only meant expulsion from the Academy, but more importantly, certain death from disease.

When Regiment-12 finally boarded its transport, Tarro found Nya and sat next to her. They were not supposed to talk during the trip, but while taking his seat, he managed to stick his elbow out enough to touch her arm. He looked at her and mouthed a feigned "sorry," happy to have made even the briefest of physical contact. She looked away with a faint smile and brushed that same strand of hair out of her face. Tarro exhaled a small sigh.

The tour was to involve multiple stops throughout the city. Each regiment had its own tailored schedule, but all were to meet at precisely 3:00 pm in COMCIRC for the parade. Instructor-42, serving as Regiment-12's supervisor, gave final directions to the group as the pilot of their AT-7 began a vertical descent onto one of Avalon's landing pads. Each sector of Avalon possessed its own landing pad located just outside the city walls. Upon landing, Regiment-12 exited the AT-7 in a single file line. Two large doors set within the wall facing the landing pad slid open, and they entered a chamber sandwiched between the inner and outer wall sections.

When they had all squeezed into the chamber, Instructor-42 bellowed, "All outsiders entering Avalon must first enter a decontamination chamber to ensure no viruses or diseases are being brought into the city." He took a position behind them and the outer doors closed, sealing them into the room. "Maybe this will purge some of the stupidity we can't seem to dislodge out of your dull skulls," he added sarcastically. Tarro chuckled and elbowed Sye standing next to him as if to suggest Sye was the instructor's intended audience.

A loud hiss sounded and the Cadets felt a brief cold blast of moist air. Tarro cringed at the sudden noise and saw Sye wryly grinning at his jumpiness. Within a matter of seconds, another set of doors opened and the Cadets filed out, entering the city. Greeting them was a small crowd of citizens who were cheering their arrival enthusiastically. Instructor-42 led them through the crowd to meet their host, a quite rotund woman whose girth nearly achieved her height.

"Welcome, my lovely Cadets," she said exuberantly. "I am Citizen FX-89–52, but you can call me Noona. Welcome to our beloved city of Avalon," she added as she turned and dramatically swept her hand across the cityscape behind her. Tarro was dazzled. He had seen the pictures, but they simply weren't able to capture a fraction of the city's beauty.

Its grandeur was offset only by Noona's comically squeaky voice. "Our first stop will be your birthplace. You may ask any question along the way. Come along now." She waddled forward and waved for them to follow.

They followed her down the Domon, the wide corridor separating the housing district from the business district. The Domon traveled circularly through the entire city, connecting its sectors as the primary passageway for foot traffic. Having the appearance of a continuous courtyard, the Domon was filled with lush trees, flowering vines, and an endless variety of meticulously manicured vegetation. Fountains and elaborate waterfalls were interspersed among statues and large artistic structures constructed with of all kinds of precious metals. Most of the businesses they passed possessed all-glass storefronts revealing their patrons. Tarro was struck by how many citizens he saw both inside and outside, leisurely sitting or reclining, talking casually, or simply staring straight ahead absent-mindedly.

Noona stopped in front of a large fountain filled with mermaid statues and turned to the group. "One of the wonderful things about Avalon is that most work is done by droid companions." She pointed at a male-looking companion who was passing them at that moment. He gave them a smile and a wave. "The latest generation of companions, such as the one who just passed us, are so advanced that it is sometimes difficult to decipher them from humans. Most citizens don't have to work because they are partnered with these droids who work for them."

One of the cadets piped up and asked, "What do you mean 'partnered'?"

"Droid companions do not belong to the citizens for they are not owned. They are *not* property. This partnership allows citizens to maintain a comfortable and high quality of life."

Sye had made his way toward the front of the group near Noona. "So what do the droids think of this partnership?"

She quickly dismissed the question and began pontificating on the history of companions gaining person status in Avalon. She must have repeated the fact that they were partners and not property no less than a dozen times.

Tarro wasn't really paying attention. After not-too-subtly working his way to stand by Nya, he had begun watching a large holographic advertisement occupying the corner outside a nearby business. The advertisement featured a man with green-spiked hair holding a small dog with blue-dyed hair. The colorful pair commended the Pet Spa Palace where one's pet could be pampered for a full day with the finest cuisine and spa treatments.

The advertisement from Pet Spa Palace was promptly followed by one from "Companion Industries" showcasing the varied companion droids they offered. A very muscular droid appeared, rotating slowly displaying all his features. A "1,390 credits" price tag hovered over his head.

Sye simultaneously saw the advertisement and muttered to Tarro, "Gee, that's a pretty expensive we-don't-own *partner*."

Tarro ignored him. He couldn't believe how realistic the droids appeared. They were never present, or at least seen, at the Academy. He looked around, wondering how many other people around him were actually companions.

"I need a volunteer," Noona said. Always eager to play the role of the exceptional Cadet, Tarro immediately raised his hand and stepped forward even though he had no idea what he was volunteering for.

"Name?" she asked.

"Bravo 3–58."

Nya, noting his clueless state, leaned over and whispered to him, "Congratulations, Tarro, you just signed up to get your hair dyed pink."

Tarro stared at her. She rarely talked to him, so he savored the moment.

Noona snapped him out of his daze. "My dear, are you just going to stand there?"

The regiment watched as she ushered him over to a cylindrical capsule large enough to hold four people. Containing plush seats arranged in a circle facing the center, the body of the capsule was made of a single piece of transparent glass, capped on the top and bottom with metallic plates.

"This," she said proudly, "is one of many PODs we use to travel around Avalon. Thousands of these transport PODs connect riders to all parts of the city which sits on a foundation of two electromagnetic plates. Once these PODs descend from above the city's surface, they enter the space between the two plates and travel in electromagnetic suspension at high speeds through automated routes. We call this underground transit system the FLUXX." She ushered Tarro into the POD and said to him, "Bravo 3–58, I have already commanded it take you to the other side of the city. Once you arrive there, simply say, 'return' and it will bring you back here." Tarro nodded his head.

He approached the POD and the glassy cylinder rose vertically, allowing him to climb in and take a seat. The cylinder smoothly lowered, sealing him in. In an instant, the POD dropped below the city's surface into the darkness of the FLUXX, trading bright sunlight for soft blue illumination which radiated around the POD. As the POD smoothly accelerated, Tarro saw nearby PODs entering the FLUXX from the city's surface, glowing with the same blue lighting. In a matter of seconds, he was surrounded by dozens of the streaking blue lights appearing like shooting stars moving in all directions. One flashed by so close he couldn't believe they hadn't collided.

Tarro's POD soon decelerated, then smoothly came to a quick stop at an underground docking station. It then transitioned rapidly to the city's surface. He looked around for a moment at his new surroundings and gave the return command. In a moment he was back under the surface of the city, enjoying the light show as he returned to his starting point.

When he emerged from the POD, Noona asked him, "You just traveled to the other side of the city and back. How long do you think that took?" Tarro tried to do a mental calculation, but before he could give an answer, she delightedly proclaimed to the regiment, "Two minutes!" The Cadets applauded in amazement.

After this introduction to the city's transportation system, they arrived at their much anticipated birthplace. They had been told at different times throughout their schooling how this process worked, but to most of them, it was still a mystery.

They entered a rather large building that looked very different from the surrounding architecture. Lacking any glass in the front, it was constructed of black and gray composite material with abundant crevices and fissures illuminated by a variety of brilliantly colored lights, creating dazzling light patterns on its exterior. Inside, five meticulously dressed companions manned a reception desk. Tarro noticed that one looked distinctly female, one distinctly male, and the other three he couldn't determine.

As they entered, an automated voice greeted them pleasantly, "Welcome to Advanced Genome Labs where we make your future dreams come to life."

Noona gathered the regiment in a large atrium adjacent to the reception area. "This is where you all began," she said proudly to the group.

She pointed to the various kiosks lining the perimeter of the circular room. "After approval from the Kreplin, prospective stewards are able to come here and create their child."

A girl from the regiment spoke up, "How many can they create?"

Noona looked surprised that the girl didn't know the answer. "One, of course."

"Why only one?"

Noona looked a little flustered. "Because . . . because one is enough responsibility to handle." Tarro suppressed a laugh as he thought about the rigors his stewards experience with their little annual visits.

Noona gathered them around one of the pedestal-like kiosks and demonstrated how the process worked. She said, "begin," and a vivid hologram of a child, who looked to be around six years old, appeared at the top of kiosk at eye level with Noona.

The child said, "Hello, prospective steward, I hope to be able to meet you soon. What color would you like my eyes to be?"

Noona responded, "Blue." A holographic color bar appeared and hovered in front of Noona, displaying a spectrum of shades of blue. Noona selected different shades, instantly changing the child's eye color.

When the final eye color had been selected, the child said, "Thank you. Please select my hair color."

Noona made a few more quick selections for her demonstration, including the preferred body type, athletic ability, and personality type.

"Of course I'm just showing a few of the options," she explained. "There are actually over one hundred decisions new stewards will make. Once finalized, they will return in about nine months to meet their new child."

Tarro wasn't really paying attention, distracted by a group of three next to them who were arguing over whether they wanted an artistic child or one gifted in mathematics. The group included a man who stood between a woman and a female companion.

The man leaned over to the woman and said, "See, Beeva agrees, the child should be artistic."

"I don't care what your companion thinks. I'm your wife and this is between us!" said the woman, visibly perturbed. Tarro, along with others in the regiment who were now noticing the spat, watched to see which side would prevail until they were interrupted by Noona, who could see she was beginning to lose her audience's attention.

With a raised voice she said, "Now *this* is where it gets really exciting! Once this process is completed, lab technicians genetically engineer the child according to the selections, creating the embryo through in vitro fertilization. These engineers have mastered the process such that this particular facility is able to design the child according to the submitted order with an average 98.7% accuracy rate."

Sye, never shy to ask a question, spoke up, "So when do you pick the gender?"

Instructor-42 instantly began moving threateningly toward Sye, and Noona's cheerful demeanor became abruptly serious. She looked at Sye sternly as if he had no right to ask the question. "Future citizen. There *is* no gender."

Sye was undeterred. "But who decides whether the child has a . . . a . . ."

"A what?" Noona asked, clearly annoyed.

Sye pointed below his waist line, causing many in the regiment to snicker.

"Quiet!" yelled Instructor-42. "This part of the tour is over." As they left, Tarro saw Instructor-42 pull Sye aside. It did not appear to be a pleasant conversation.

Happily, lunch at a nearby cafe was the next stop. Noona gave instructions on how to order food and they all sat down at round tables. Digital touch-screen menus appeared within the tables and the Cadets placed their orders, amazed at the variety of food available at their finger tips. When orders were placed, the center of each table dropped down through the supporting column, reappearing moments later with their selections. The potpourri of cuisine and potency of the flavors were almost overwhelming for Tarro and his classmates who had grown up on bland Academy cuisine.

Tarro was debating whether to order a third dessert when he heard a commotion behind him. He turned and saw two Peace Officers standing on either side of a seated older woman. He admired the perfect white uniforms and thought to himself, *Someday, that will be me!*

"I don't want to go," muttered the older woman.

The officer to her right placed his hand on his holstered phaser. "Citizen JT-94–42, we are under orders to escort you to the Center." The officer reached down and grabbed her arm. "Citizen JT-94–42, you must come now."

"I don't want to die!" she cried as she jerked her arm out of the officer's hand.

Shocked at her response, Tarro watched the officers struggle to make her stand up. When it was clear she was going to have none of it, the officer to her left pulled out a small device and pressed it to her arm, causing her to immediately go unconscious. The officers quickly carried her limp body out of the cafe.

Tarro found this scene rather curious. As Cadets, they had learned about the Center and its advanced medical practices. The Center was the abbreviated name for the Center of Health and Wellness, the medical facility that served the citizens of Avalon. They had been told that Avalon was not only able to detect conditions and problems requiring immediate medical attention, but could also anticipate future ones with a high degree of accuracy. How this was possible he didn't know.

As the incapacitated woman was being carried out to receive the finest medical attention the world had ever known, Noona stood up and announced, "Time for the parade, everybody!" She clapped her hands quickly to get everyone moving. "Bravo Class and future citizens of Avalon, it has been a pleasure being your tour guide today. Instructor-42 will take it from here. Peace and Love!"

Instructor-42, who was quite ready to be done with this dog and pony show, stood up and barked with a tone absent of peace and love, "Bravo Class, move with a purpose to the front door and line up single file. Hopefully all this rich food won't make you puke your little guts out during the parade in front of the Confidant."

Chapter 3

Contraband

D ARK, GRAY CLOUDS ENGULFED the morning sky over Likbez, smothering it with a continuous drizzly rain. Tarro woke up feeling as gloomy as the weather. Last night he was on cloud nine, having returned from the Avalon visit. The parade route had traveled around the Kreplin through COMCIRC, the perimeter of which had been lined with the Avalon citizens. The parade was performed to perfection and Tarro recalled the great pride he felt passing by the reviewing Supreme Confidant Talin sitting with all the Kreplin dignitaries.

But now, he just felt depressed. He stirred the slop in his bowl that was being passed as breakfast, lifting some of it with his spoon, wondering what it was actually made of. The squishy "plop" the blob made when it fell from his spoon to rejoin its distasteful constituents offered no clues other than to suggest he was playing with lumpy mud.

He thought of the delicious food he had eaten the day before and the taste bud awakening he had experienced. After returning last night, he was amazed at how life at the Academy starkly contrasted that of Avalon. Up until that visit, all he'd known was Academy life with some distant childhood memories of HDC. Now, having experienced the opulence of Avalon, he realized how utterly austere and oppressive his current life was. Everything was regimented, with little recreation or leisure.

He began to wonder why they worked and studied so hard when it appeared that most of the actual work in the city was performed by companion droids. If that was what life was like in Avalon, why was the

Academy so different? What were they training them for? Was this really just to prepare them to be good citizens? The questions raced through Tarro's mind unanswered.

He was startled out of his deep thought by a high-pitched chime signaling the end of breakfast and the ten minute warning before the beginning of the day's first class. Tarro stopped playing with his food and thought, *Two more years. Two more years and I'll be done with this place.* The thought cheered him up a little and he dashed off to class.

His first class was with Instructor-29 for *Ancient History*. Sye sat down in his assigned seat to Tarro's left.

"Hey, Officer Wonderful, why so disconsolate?" Sye knew of Tarro's ambition to be a Peace Officer but didn't possess an equal fondness for them. He also like to use big words whenever possible. Whether it was just a joke to him or a way to not-so-subtly flaunt mental superiority, Tarro didn't know but also didn't really care. He just scowled at Sye, not saying a word.

"Brrr! What icy lake did you fall into this morning?"

Tarro was about to tell him which lake it was and how to jump in it when Instructor-29 began the class. "Today, we are going to look at the history of civilizations and walls. We begin with the ancient Great Wall of China."

Instructor-29 lectured for the next half hour on the importance of walls to the integrity and preservation of cities and nations. Instructor-29 was all business. Her straight, raven-black hair was slicked back, cropped at the shoulders in a perfect horizontal line. Her bony cheekbones protruded from her face, giving her a stern look that matched her temperament.

"Which leads us to the wall of Avalon," she said as she finally got to the main topic at hand. "The wall surrounding the city of Avalon is approximately fifty feet high and serves as an impenetrable barrier." She pointed to the three-dimensional holographic image of Avalon which had appeared beside her, rotating slowly for the students to view. "For review, who can tell me why Avalon has this wall?" she asked.

Sye raised his hand.

"Speak, Bravo 18–78." Tarro noted that Sye's ranking had dropped another two places since yesterday.

Sye stood, his posture far more relaxed than expected for Cadets. "Because Avalon venerates East Berlin," he said and then sat down.

Instructor-29 glared at him for a moment and said, "No, that is both nonsensical and incorrect."

Sye stood up again. "I apologize. I shouldn't have suggested that the good citizens of Avalon need a wall to maintain fidelity to the Kreplin." With a smirk on his face, he sat down again as if his statement was plain as day. Tarro shot a quizzical glance at him.

Instructor-29 shook her head. "Bravo 18–78, see me after class. Would anyone else like to offer an intelligent answer?" Her glaring eyes, still fixed on Sye, narrowed to a condemning squint. After a few awkward moments, she recognized Tarro's raised hand. He stood and answered, "The wall protects against two primary threats. First, it houses the force-field generators which power the BioDome, providing a protective barrier against diseases and viruses." He smugly looked at Sye who rolled his eyes at him. "Secondly, the wall protects against any possible infiltration by the Barbs or Mutts."

Ever the disciplinarian and never one to praise, Instructor-29's simple "correct" elicited silent applause from Sye. Tarro smiled wryly, pointing to Sye's class ranking and then to his own.

From the beginning, the dangers resident outside Likbez had been drilled into them. Earth was a treacherous place, and were it not for the benevolent, ongoing protection of the Kreplin, Avalon and Likbez would simply be consumed and annihilated by earth's evils. If disease didn't get them, then the Barbs or Mutts would.

"Barb" was shorthand for barbarian. Avalon viewed the Barbs as a backward, primitive group of people. Mostly contained by the Kreplin in the expansive Hanni Valley, they were the remnant of the world's population that had been wiped out by Engels-23, the plague of the 23rd century that had ravaged the planet, killing over seventy five percent of the world's population. It obliterated nations and governments and plunged the world into chaos and anarchy. By the end of that century, over half of the surviving population had been killed through wars and genocide as regional powers fought for tribal supremacy.

This age of anarchy came to an end when the few remaining world elites, who controlled most of the world's wealth, consolidated their resources and power and formed a new nation. The nation of Avalon was thus born in the year 2305. Possessing tightly controlled borders, only the strong and disease-free were permitted to populate and reside in this nation. The rest were left to fend for themselves and became the people-group eventually dubbed the "Barbs" by Avalon.

By the end of the 24th century, Avalon had constructed its present-day elevated city, largely made possible by an army of high-tech construction droids and the resources provided by the Barbs. The Barbs lived as indentured slaves to Avalon who ruled them with an iron fist. They labored to provide the resources needed to sustain life in Avalon, and in return, Avalon gave them vaccinations and some protection from the Mutts.

The Mutants, more commonly referred to as "Mutts," were scattered all over the earth with a heavy concentration residing just north of the Zeenuk mountains. The Mutts were the result of uncontrolled human genetic engineering which took place in secret labs in the ancient countries of China and North Korea. Over time, North Korea, aided by China, attempted to create super humans in order to develop a superior army. Unbeknownst to the world at the time, North Korea began inserting various animal DNA into its genetic experiments.

Instead of producing superior physical traits, humans with severe deformities resulted. Most of them were killed off by the North Koreans but many were maintained in underground labs for research. When Engels-23 wiped out much of the planet, many of these research mutants escaped and continued to multiply, further exacerbating their genetic abnormalities. Present day Mutts were largely violent and routinely hunted Barbs for sport.

For Tarro, the day of classes dragged on, and by the time he and Sye got to their quarters that night, he felt like two days had transpired instead of one. But it certainly was an interesting day. Over the past year, Sye had become increasingly combative in their classes, but today was exceptional.

Tarro looked over at Sye seated at his desk having just begun his homework. Tarro wondered what made him tick. Though he had been distancing himself from Sye, he was actually beginning to worry for his old friend. The Academy required strict adherence to its rules and did not tolerate failure or disobedience. Fear of not graduating plagued the Cadets and kept them in line, particularly since no one knew what happened to those who failed the Academy. Fear seemed to sufficiently motivate all Cadets. All except for Sye.

"Sye, why are you always getting into trouble with the instructors?"

Sye smirked and said, "Because they're wrong . . . and delusional, stupid robots. They couldn't empty a bowl with the directions written on the bottom."

Tarro quickly shot a glance over his shoulder and, in a whisper, said, "Sye, be quiet. You know they're always listening."

"So what?" Sye said in an intentionally loud voice. "I know I'm probably not going to graduate anyway."

"What do you mean?" Tarro asked quizzically.

Sye suddenly looked a little sad and stared at Tarro. "I know too much," he said in a low voice.

Tarro thought about all the strange things he'd heard Sye talk about and wondered where he came up with the stuff.

Sye seemed to read his mind. He got up from his desk, sat down next to Tarro, and whispered into his ear, "Tomorrow after combat training, meet me at the Plaza. I have something I want to show you."

ରୋ

The next day, Tarro finished his last class and headed off to combat training. Combat training occurred three times a week and involved all sorts of instruction, from hand-to-hand combat to training in various weaponry—knives, clubs, spears, bows—every rudimentary weapon imaginable. Each class concluded with some type of competition or sparring between Cadets. As they were always being graded, the Cadets were naturally aggressive . . . at least most of them were.

The expansive u-shaped combat facility bracketed a large arena where the class demonstrations and sparring took place. Today's weapon was the wood cane and Tarro watched with the rest of the class as Nya was paired up with a much larger boy named Gront for a bout. The combatants faced each other, holding their long canes.

Instructor-15 paced militantly around the two combatants as he instructed the class. Contrary to most of the well-manicured instructors, Instructor-15 had a gruff look to him. He was the only one that Tarro had ever seen with stubble on his face. Tarro didn't know if that was to cover the large scar on the instructor's right cheek or if he just liked the tougher look.

"The trick is to engage your opponent without breaking your own cane," he barked. "It is thick enough to injure an opponent but thin enough to break with too hard of a strike to either the opponent's cane or body."

Tarro was inwardly fuming while looking at the match-up. Gront was a good foot and a half taller than Nya and at least a hundred pounds heavier, not to mention much uglier. Nya was not a fighter. She was one of the most gentle people Tarro had ever observed, and he was extremely nervous for her.

"Gront, wack them good!" yelled a boy referring to Nya. Tarro glared at the boy standing opposite him on the other side of the arena. Next to the boy stood the presiding instructor, looking on with a smirk on his face. The instructor knew what was about to happen, and Tarro hated him for it. Even though there weren't supposed to be differences between the sexes, everyone knew it wasn't going to be a fair fight.

"Combatants, face off!" Instructor-15 yelled.

Nya approached Gront in the center of the arena. Gront was laughing, and Nya looked scared.

"Fight!" commanded Instructor-15.

Gront circled Nya menacingly as she held her ground. "Come on little girl, hit me!"

"Cease fight!" screamed the instructor with veins popping out of his neck. Tarro assumed this sudden explosion was due to Gront's usage of the word "girl," a clear violation of Academy rules.

Looking at Gront, Instructor-15 growled, "Bravo 1–34, approach the center and turn your back to Bravo 18–60. Bravo 18–60, you will strike Bravo 1–34 once for their violation."

Nya reluctantly approached Gront. "Where, Instructor-15?" she asked.

"Anywhere!" he shouted.

Nya knew the command wasn't optional so she gingerly hit Gront on his backside with her cane. Several of the Cadets laughed, only to be immediately silenced by the instructor who seemed to be on the verge of exploding into uncontrolled rage. Clearly disgusted with the show of weakness, he immediately jumped in, grabbed Nya's cane, and violently swung it at Gront, breaking it over his back. Gront didn't budge, maintaining his smug look.

Instructor-15 gave Nya a new cane and resumed the fight. Nya took a few half-hearted swings at Gront who easily dodged them. He taunted her for a good minute as she did her best just to make contact with him. Suddenly, he lunged toward her, slamming the end of his cane into her stomach. She instantly doubled over, gasping for breath. With one smooth swing he brought his cane over his head and crashed it down onto her exposed back, causing his cane to splinter into a dozen pieces.

Nya crumbled to the ground in the fetal position, her gasps for air the only sign that she was still conscious.

It took Tarro every ounce of restraint not to rush over to Nya and help her. To do so was not permitted and would have resulted in a painful beating and an inevitable drop in class rank.

Instructor-15 barked to an adjacent instructor, "Instructor-52, attend to Bravo 18–60."

Unfazed by Nya's pain, Instructor-15 said, "*That* was a text-book maneuver." He had Gront demonstrate his maneuver to the group in slow motion as Tarro watched Instructor-52 help Nya to her feet to escort her, no doubt, to medical. He was sick to his stomach, wishing he could take a cane to Gront's repugnant, smug face.

After combat training, a still fuming Tarro had begun heading back to Lenon Hall when he remembered his scheduled meeting with Sye. Grateful to have something, anything, to take his mind off of Nya's plight, he headed over to the Plaza.

The Plaza was a large courtyard facing the mountains on the northern side of Likbez. Tarro loved this location. It was one of his favorite places to hang out during the brief periods of allotted free time they were given on most evenings. The Plaza contained multiple gazeboes and overlooked a small lake surrounded by a shallow forest. A lazy brook cut through the Plaza, terminating in a twenty foot waterfall that cascaded into the lake below.

"Hey, meathead!" Tarro turned to the familiar voice behind him. Without waiting for a response, Sye said, "Follow me."

Tarro followed Sye out of the Plaza and down to the edge of the lake. From there, they picked up one of the trails that meandered through the surrounding woods. They walked silently until they arrived at an area on the north side of the lake. Here, the trail entered a large rock formation that lined the path on both sides, forming a small gorge. Midway through the gorge, Sye took a sharp turn to the left and squeezed through a narrow gap between two boulders. Tarro followed and found himself in a small grassy patch surrounded by rock, as if he were in a cave with no ceiling.

Sye turned to Tarro and said, "I overheard an instructor talking about the surveillance of Likbez. Evidently, this area is one of a few places within the compound not covered by surveillance cameras."

"Are you sure?" asked Tarro.

"No," replied Sye. He smiled at Tarro's nervous look. "But, I'm pretty sure," he added.

"How do you know?"

"Because I've never been caught."

If he hadn't been so angry from watching Nya take a beating, Tarro might have left Sye at this point. He didn't need trouble. And he was certainly not about to be dragged down by his rebellious friend. But Sye had stoked enough of his curiosity for him to stay.

"You asked me where I come up with what some would call recalcitrant ideas." Sye saw Tarro's confused look and clarified for his less erudite friend. "My *crazy* ideas."

Sye stooped down and moved aside a rock the size of a man's head, revealing a small cleft at the base of one of the large boulders. He reached in and pulled out a wooden box.

"Here, open it," he said to Tarro, handing him the box.

It was intricately carved, with a single latch. Tarro released the latch and opened the lid. He looked at Sye, confused.

"Take it out," Sye said amused with his friend's reaction.

The object was engraved with the words "World Civilizations." Tarro pulled it out of the box, gingerly opened it, and began flipping through the pages observing the various printed words and pictures.

"It's called a book," Sye said. "Congratulations, you are probably one of only two people in Likbez who have ever seen one."

Tarro, marveling at what he was holding, said absent-mindedly, "Who's the other?"

Sye laughed. "As far as I've been able to tell, I don't think even the instructors know of books. But I've learned a lot from this thing. Pretty much everything it says is opposite of what we're taught."

"Like what?" asked Tarro.

"Well, I'll give you an example. Turn to the page numbered 173." Sye helped Tarro find the page, and Tarro saw that its corner was folded over. "Remember last year when we studied what they called Nazi Germany in . . . when was it?"

"The twentieth century," Tarro added.

"Yes, thank you, Captain Competent," Sye said sarcastically. "Anyway, do you remember what they taught us?"

Tarro thought about it for a moment. "I think I remember them comparing it to Avalon. That Nazi Germany was one of the great examples of a superior culture which was able to . . . to benefit the world in providing stability and peace."

"And that their empire flourished well into the 21st century alongside the Soviet Union," added Sye. "But that's not at all what this book says."

Tarro began reading aloud from the top of the earmarked page, "Under the dictatorial leadership of Adolph Hitler, the Third Reich was responsible for the Holocaust, the genocide of over six million Jews. These Jews were murdered via gas chambers and mass shootings in concentration camps which—"

At that moment, a loud and prolonged deep-throated siren interrupted Tarro. Startled, he dropped the book as Sye looked at him with alarm.

Chapter 4

Sirens

BIORN LOOKED AT HIS reflection in the window from inside his cafe in Avalon. The floor-to-ceiling windows automatically tinted in response to sunlight intensity and now, as the sun was setting and daylight began to give way to a darkening orange-red sky, he could see his reflection more clearly. He turned his head slightly, noticing the gray streaks in his hair. He was in his early sixties but he took pride in the fact that he was still fit—in better shape than most half his age, in fact. He wondered if he could still pump out fifty push-ups and resolved to try when he got home, preferably without pulling a muscle.

As the hard-working owner of the cafe, Biorn loathed the sedentary lifestyle most of Avalon lived. In his estimation, half of them were too plump, too lazy, and as a whole, lived only for the singular ignoble goal of leisure. And Avalon had much to offer in that department. The city was designed for relaxation and pleasure.

Biorn started the cafe ten years ago once he'd gotten approval from the Kreplin to do so. Every new business had to be approved by the Kreplin. Once approved, the business was assigned a Kreplin ambassador who reported directly to the respective sector's Minister. The ambassador monitored every aspect of the business, and every business decision had to go through him.

Biorn shook his head as he remembered his ambassador scrapping half of his proposed menu when he began the cafe. He wondered what it would be like to actually own a business and not just be a managerial puppet of the Kreplin which kept eighty percent of all profit. He didn't like the Kreplin's monopoly, but he understood why his menu was micromanaged as almost all of the food imported into the city was provided by the Barbs. He could only provide what Avalon was able to extract from them. And it wasn't just the food that was imported. Just about every material resource used by the city was acquired through this tightly controlled group of people.

Biorn checked the time, and with an hour remaining before closing, he began making the final rounds to check on his patrons. In most other cafes, companions usually did this, but Biorn enjoyed the work. It kept him active and his mind engaged. His ambassador initially balked at this. He didn't understand why Biorn wouldn't let droids serve the customers. Biorn finally convinced him that some people actually preferred human interaction, and more business meant more profit for the Kreplin, to include, most notably, the ambassador himself.

Biorn had hired a few others in the city who enjoyed working as he did. Most were older as it was hard to find any in the younger category who were willing to disengage for even a moment from their lives of recreation. He chuckled when he thought about the young applicant who walked out in a huff when he saw that a serving position would actually involve exerting energy. "Wait, you want me to . . . *work*?" was all he'd said before he stormed out of the interview. To this day, Biorn couldn't figure out what the young man thought he was actually applying for.

But to Biorn, the cafe, the meager business profit, even the work which he enjoyed—all this was not his mission in life. There was something much bigger. In fact, the business was only a front to a particular type of work which animated him and gave him purpose. If the Kreplin ever found out—well, that would be the end of him.

He sauntered over to one of the tables where four younger people were seated. As he approached, he overheard them still going on about their day at the spa and the exotic new skin moisturizer the spa had just rolled out today which involved rare snails from the Zeenuk Mountains. They had been blathering about this non-stop for the last hour, and he looked at them with pity. He genuinely cared about people and was saddened by the meager, self-absorbed lives almost all of them lived.

He was about to ask them if there was anything more he could do for them when the door to the cafe opened. That's when he heard it . . . at least he thought he did. It was ever so faint, so faint that he knew none of the other patrons heard it. And even if they did, they wouldn't have cared.

He moved quickly to the front door and stood outside. The sound was a little louder now, yet still only faintly perceptible. There was no doubt, though. That was it. His heart sank. Off in the distance in the direction of Likbez came the low howl of the compound's siren. Likbez issued two more long blasts, each of which seemed an eternity to Biorn. He marked the time. They would have thirty minutes tops to make it happen. He needed to alert the Ferret and do it quickly.

☙❧

After a few moments of staring at each other as the last blast of the siren sounded, Tarro and Sye began to move. Sye picked up the book that Tarro had dropped and quickly returned it to its hiding place. They then briskly set out for Lenon Hall with Sye in the lead. Neither spoke until Tarro broke the silence.

"Do you think it's true?" he asked Sye.

Sye stopped so quickly that Tarro nearly ran him over. He turned and looked at Tarro. Tarro could see genuine loathing in his eyes. "What do you mean, 'Do I think it's true?'" he demanded.

Tarro was so shocked by this sudden display of visible anger that he didn't answer. He felt Sye's eyes bore into his own as Sye stood there, waiting for him to answer.

After a few awkward moments, Tarro finally said, "Don't get so mad, Sye. I just asked the question."

"What do you think, Tarro?" he asked, still glaring at his friend.

"Well, we've always just heard about it, but I've never actually seen it happen." Tarro looked down in an attempt to escape the intense gaze of Sye.

"Of course it's true," Sye said in disgust. "Why wouldn't it be?"

"Have you ever seen it happen?"

"No. But I've talked to Cadets who have and they swear to me that it's true."

"I just can't believe the Academy would do such a thing. How could they just toss a Cadet over the wall to be hunted by Mutts?"

"Are you kidding me, Tarro? What world have you been living in?" Sye shook his head in disgust. "How do you think they keep us in line? How do you think they ensure perfect obedience in everything they demand?"

Tarro looked at him blankly, still processing his friend's venting. He knew Sye had somewhat of a chip on his shoulder, but he had never heard him go off on the Academy like this.

Sye sighed in frustration in light of his friend's naïveté. "Fear, Tarro, fear. They control us with fear. Fear of them. Fear of failure. Fear of not making it to Avalon. You think all of this goes away in Avalon? You think in Avalon *they* are any different?"

Tarro began to feel a little uncomfortable with the way this conversation was going. He had learned to assume that what was done and said were always being monitored by the authorities.

Sye could see Tarro's discomfort and read his mind. "What, Tarro? You afraid someone's listening to our conversation?" Sye continued to wag his head in disgust. "See? See what I mean?" Sye began walking away from Tarro as he barked over his shoulder, "Fear!"

Tarro sullenly followed, stewing over Sye's analysis. Fear of failure wasn't necessarily a bad thing, especially if it made one excel. But if the Academy was actually throwing Cadets over the wall and alerting the Mutts with a siren, well, that was a little extreme. Tarro had heard about this form of punishment for as long as he could remember. They all had. But he had also wondered if it really happened, as he had never been in a regiment where this occurred.

Over the years, he had occasionally heard the siren that evidently signaled the occurrence of this harsh disciplinary measure. To the best of his recollection, it happened about a couple of times a year. Whenever it occurred, the Cadets buzzed about who it was and why it happened. The instructors never talked about it, seemingly content to let the rumor mill churn its way through the collective psyche of the Cadets.

Tarro thought about how horrible it would be to be hunted by a Mutt, or even worse, a pack of Mutts. Years ago, during free time one evening, he had been at the compound's perimeter by the wall when he heard a noise on the other side. He stopped to listen and heard heavy, raspy breathing, the tell-tale sign of a Mutt. It spooked him so badly he had never since ventured that close to the wall. But Tarro was still not completely convinced that the Academy would take Cadets, no matter how bad they were, and simply chuck them over the wall to be victimized by Mutts, disease, starvation, or all of the above.

By the time they arrived back at Lenon Hall, the rumor mill was in full swing among the Cadets. Who was it? Which regiment? Where did it occur? What could he or she have possibly done? All the usual questions and speculation were already circulating like wildfire and would go on for at least a week.

Tarro heard so many competing stories he stopped counting after ten—it was a ninth-year Cadet who hit an instructor; no, it was actually a Cadet from Regiment-2 who was caught stealing food from the kitchen; no, a tenth-year did the unthinkable and snuck out of Likbez, but couldn't find her way back in and was found the next morning yelling for help outside the wall—the list went on and on.

Tarro shook his head, still not quite convinced of it all. It seemed just a little too extreme to believe. But even if it were true, the offending Cadet probably deserved it. If a Cadet was going to defy the Academy, he probably shouldn't be here. And he certainly didn't deserve to live in Avalon.

He glanced down at the class ranking displayed on his chest and forced his mind to stick to the main thing, and the main thing was keeping his nose to the grindstone to get his ranking down to three hundred or better. Every day, the prize of Avalon became a closer reality. The possibility of putting on that crisp, white Peace Officer uniform put a smile on his face, and he sat down to begin his homework with a renewed intensity.

Chapter 5

Rescue

AFTER THE SIRENS FINALLY ceased their horrid wail, Biorn approached his cafe manager and informed her that he wasn't feeling well and that she would need to close the store. She immediately began asking a lot questions which he knew was out of concern for him. She was a conscientious worker, and he never liked misleading her. So he kept his answers vague and short and quietly left the cafe.

After exiting, he made an immediate right, working his way toward the nearest POD station. He checked the time and saw that he needed to get to Sector-19. Each of the twenty sectors possessed a SC-5 Supply Cargo aircraft which served as part of the supply chain bringing resources from the Barbs into the city. Each sector's aircraft departed its respective landing pad once per day at staggered intervals on the hour. In this manner, there was always an aircraft departing Avalon between 1:00 am and 8:00 pm. Sector-1's SC-5 departed at 1:00 am, Sector-2's at 2:00 am, until the last flight for the day departed at 8:00 pm from Sector-20. It was now 6:48 pm and Biorn knew that Sector-19's departure in twelve minutes would be hard to make, but not impossible.

He needed to quickly but cautiously get word to the Ferret. Like every citizen, he possessed the Bionet, which communicated with the Kreplin who continuously monitored its citizens. The Bionet was an integrated network of five computer chips and sensors implanted within each citizen. Two tiny eye terminals were implanted in the eyes, providing an array of digital interfaces through projections which could be overlaid onto one's visual surroundings or viewed with the surroundings black-ened out.

This personal eye projection system was called Vizitar and worked in concert with the two audio sensors planted within the ears. Combined, these audio-visual sensors enabled the citizen to perform a myriad of tasks such as speaking remotely to a friend, viewing an announcement from the Kreplin, looking up information in the Avalon central library, or simply tuning out the world with the latest entertainment.

The fifth sensor of the Bionet constituted a medical chip implanted within the body. Citizens were told that the chip communicated only vital sign information in order to enable the best, continuous medical care Avalon could offer. But Biorn knew what many others suspected—that the Bionet relayed to the Kreplin far more than heart rates and blood pressure.

Years ago, he'd known a Kreplin official who, on his death bed, warned him through a hand-written note that the Kreplin monitored all citizen activity and that the Bionet was so sensitive it could pick up conversations within a fifty-foot radius. The only consolation, as Biorn discovered later, was that the monitoring was done almost exclusively by artificial intelligence that would alert Kreplin officials only when certain criteria were triggered. Biorn didn't know exactly what all these triggers were. He just knew he had to be incredibly cautious.

Biorn, along with the Ferret and a handful of other Avalon citizens, was part of a small network dedicated to rescuing those who found themselves on the receiving end of the Kreplin's totalitarian flashes of brutality. The Kreplin made sure its citizens had everything they wanted. A fat and happy populace made for a compliant citizenry. But there were always those who lacked the required gratitude, those compelled to push back against the Kreplin. For such inclined to this subversion, retribution was swift. This system of governance filtered down into Likbez, and so at the top of this group's rescue list were Cadets who got "fed" to the Mutts.

Over the years, this group had cautiously formed, calling itself the Libs, short for Liberators. Biorn was its defacto leader for he was the one who found and organized the members. The organizational side of operations was difficult but doable with this particular group who used its own system to communicate secretly outside the gaze of the Kreplin. The slow and arduous part was the recruitment. It took time and great care to get to know someone well enough to ensure that he or she was like-minded who would be faithful to the cause. One betraying word, one wrong person with greater allegiance to the Kreplin, or one who got wobbly under pressure, and the whole thing would implode.

Besides Biorn, the most integral member in their little rescue group was a man they called the Ferret. He had many strengths, but chief among them was the absence of a Bionet. He could not be monitored, and even better, the Kreplin didn't even know he existed. He was a Barb whom Biorn had managed to connect with and smuggle into the city fifteen years ago. With similar goals as the Libs, the Ferret took residence in Avalon and began to work with them in their rescue missions. He lived in the shadows underground and was rarely seen, even by Biorn.

Biorn continued walking briskly, arriving at the nearest POD station. "Sector-19 loading dock," he said, taking a seat. As the POD entered the FLUXX, his eyes toggled through the menus in his Vizitar display to call up Vera, a Lib member who resided in Sector-15. She was quirky but was also the most fiercely loyal person Biorn had ever met.

"Good evening, Vera," Biorn said as she appeared in the video call.

"Bonjour! What are you doing on this fine evening, Biorn?"

"Well, I'm on my way to check on my shipment. Some new spices for my cafe should have been delivered yesterday, but for whatever reason, I think they're still at the loading dock." Biorn didn't really have any such shipment, but he figured the chances of a Kreplin official actually hearing and checking this was slim, and it was always better to be as obvious and normal as possible when hiding the covert.

"Well, that sounds simply humdrum, Biorn. Surely you didn't call me up to bore me with your shipment woes," she said in an intentionally playfully manner.

"I actually wanted to see if I could persuade you to test a new dessert recipe of mine."

"New dessert recipe" was code, indicating a needed mission to rescue a Likbez Cadet. The Libs openly socialized as a foodie group who enjoyed sharing their favorite cuisines, recipes, and newly discovered menu items from their preferred eateries. While most of them truly loved good cuisine, the food topics simply provided the cover for them to meet and discuss mission-related subjects under the watchful eye of the Kreplin.

"Oooh, sounds wonderful," Vera said.

"I have a new dessert which requires nineteen of the finest ingredients you've ever tasted. You should come over to my cafe now and sample it. You'll love it." Biorn was the mastermind behind the coded language. "Nineteen" represented Sector-19 and "ingredient" was the Ferret's codename. Vera easily deciphered the message: Biorn needed to meet the Ferret at Sector-19's loading dock immediately.

"I'm sorry, I didn't quite pick all that up. Kinny jumped on my lap when you were talking . . . can you say that again?" Biorn hated cats, especially Kinny who had to be the most ornery creature he had ever met, but he appreciated Vera's dependability. Whenever mission instructions involving the Ferret were given, they were always to be repeated. Biorn repeated the dessert invitation to Vera.

"I'm sorry, Biorn. I won't be able to make it tonight, but perhaps tomorrow." The call to Vera was just the means to relay this latest mission request out to the Ferret who was always monitoring calls made between Lib members. Biorn knew the stealthy Ferret, wherever he was at the moment, was already springing into action.

Biorn said farewell to Vera just as his POD emerged near Sector-19's loading dock. He exited and scanned the area. Directly in front of him was the loading dock where large containers of various materials were stacked, having recently been offloaded from the SC-5 sitting on the landing pad.

The doors of the city wall separating the landing pad from the loading dock were open, and Biorn spotted the parked aircraft, its idle engines quietly humming. Multiple droids were busily pushing empty containers on flat carriers that hovered above the ground to be loaded onto the aircraft. They appeared to be almost complete, and Biorn knew he had to hurry.

Biorn checked the time again. Eight minutes until takeoff. He looked for any sign of the Ferret. Nothing. He was confident the Ferret would show, but now he needed to do his part and create a bit of a diversion. He looked for the dockmaster and saw him through the large window of the small office which overlooked the loading dock. His heart rate quickened—of all the nights and of all the dockmasters, it had to be him! He grunted in disgust. He had developed a good relationship with nearly all the dockmasters precisely for missions like this. But he never got along with this crotchety dockmaster. Worse, the curmudgeon's brother was a Minister so his allegiance was firmly entrenched with the Kreplin.

Biorn felt the building pressure of slipping time . . . seven minutes until takeoff. If they didn't make this flight, a rescue was unlikely. A 7:00 pm takeoff time would put them fifteen minutes past the initial siren at Likbez. Once the Mutts heard the siren, a hunting pack could reach Likbez from their region just north of the Zeenuk Mountains in about forty minutes. The rescue plan for any Cadet thrown over the wall was always the same: get to a sector's loading dock and distract the dockmaster, allowing the Ferret to slip onto the SC-5; the Ferret would then parachute off the aircraft as it passed near Likbez on its way to Hanni Valley and attempt to find the Cadet before the Mutts did. It all hinged on the Ferret.

Biorn scanned once more for the still unseen Ferret and then entered the dockmaster's office to create the diversion.

"What do you want?" the dockmaster asked gruffly, without looking up.

Biorn saw he was reviewing the inventory list of the recently arrived cargo displayed through the console behind which he stood. The dockmaster was facing the window overlooking the loading dock, and Biorn's mind raced on how to turn him so that his back would be to the window, giving the Ferret the best chance to slip onto the aircraft.

The insufferable dockmaster repeated himself, "I *said* . . . what do you want?"

Biorn quickly concluded that his usual nice and friendly approach would not do, so he adopted an angry look and tone and yelled back, "What I want is my shipment! What do you mean taking my shipment of spices?!"

"What are you talking about?!" The dockmaster yelled back, now even more perturbed.

"I was just down at my sector's dock to receive my shipment and they didn't have it. They said droids from your supply ship picked it up." Biorn moved to the side of the dockmaster and pointed at his shipping list.

"You're crazy!" shouted the dockmaster. "Get out of here!"

"Let me look at your flight manifest and inventory list and I'll see for myself."

"You're not looking at anything!"

Biorn now moved behind the dockmaster, forcing him to turn his back to the window and continued to accuse him of taking his shipment. Then Biorn saw him. Out of the corner of his eye he caught the Ferret slipping into the loading frenzy with the droids. Wearing a gray jumpsuit, the Ferret looked identical to them, perfectly mimicking the more fluid droid body movements. Biorn could see the slight bulge under his jumpsuit, evidence of the low-profile parachute he had strapped to his back.

Within seconds, the Ferret was through wall doors and out of sight. Relieved, Biorn ended his unpleasant conversation with the dockmaster, leaving in a feigned huff. As he left the office he heard the SC-5 take off. His part was over. Now it was up to the Ferret.

Biorn thought about what it would be like to ride attached to the bottom of the aircraft's fuselage, held there by an array of special magnets lining his jumpsuit. In about seven minutes, the Ferret would be at the closest point to Likbez along the aircraft's flightpath. He would detach and free fall for as long as possible, deploying his chute at the last second in order to minimize the total descent time. By angling his descent, he could usually land about a quarter of a mile from Likbez. If he was lucky, he'd have around fifteen minutes on the ground to search and find the Cadet before the Mutts did. Time was never on their side, but it was the best they could do.

⚬〤〇

Two days later, Biorn woke up to a chilly morning. He stepped outside, his clothes automatically warming to accommodate for the decreased temperature, and began walking to his favorite place, a grassy knoll in an oak grove overlooking Lake Caesar. Each sector possessed a lake located between the housing district and the Kreplin. Each was unique and Biorn enjoyed exploring all twenty of the lakes. But Lake Caesar was his favorite, especially when the city's rotation yielded a sunrise directly over the lake, which was the case this morning.

He approached the grassy knoll. While he usually enjoyed sitting and watching a good sunrise, on this particular morning, he was not here for the view. He continued on, following a lazy stream that trickled into the lake. A stone bridge crossed the stream near the lake's edge, and as he neared it, he looked for the Ferret's signal indicating the outcome of the mission. It usually took two or three days for the Ferret to get back into Avalon after a rescue attempt. It had been two days since the siren, so if the signal wasn't in place, he would have to come back and look tomorrow.

He thought about this unique man they called the Ferret. Biorn's interactions with him were usually brief as he generally liked to stay out of sight. He smiled, recalling the time their Barb friend surprised the Libs by unexpectedly joining them for lunch in his cafe. It was the first time Biorn was able to really study him and he was struck by the fierce intensity in his eyes, a stark contrast to his refined demeanor and articulate conversation.

Biorn was dying to know if their wiley Ferret had been successful. Of the twenty three attempts they had made over the years, they had been able to rescue thirteen, smuggling them into the Barb communities. He neared the bridge, looking intently for the Ferret's sign. At the foot of the bridge was a large, flat boulder. If the rescue was successful, the Ferret would place a rock on top of it; if unsuccessful, a small tree branch.

Biorn silently lamented his aging eyesight. It seemed like every year he had to get closer to the bridge before he was able to see clearly enough. At first, he thought he saw a stick-like object on the rock. But as he got closer, his momentary disappointment turned into a sigh of relief. The small stone perched on the boulder was like a beacon, radiating the light of a little goodness and decency in an otherwise dark and sinister world.

Chapter 6

Love

TARRO COULDN'T DECIDE IF the intense school year felt like a lingering, sweltering day or a brief, gorgeous sunset. On one hand, the intense studying made the year seem endlessly long. He had never applied himself to his studies so vigorously, and it was paying off. His class ranking had been incrementally increasing, getting closer and closer to that magic three hundred mark. The year had become an endless grind. On the other hand, it seemed like a blur, but that wasn't because of his work. It was Nya.

Tarro and Nya's friendship had grown and Tarro couldn't have been happier. Previously she had paid little attention to him as she usually liked to keep to herself and didn't care for many of the boys who were generally harsh and full of themselves. But she'd begun to take notice of Tarro when he talked to her the day after her beating at the hands of Gront. She was struck by his genuine concern for her and his confession that he had wanted to pummel the brute. When he said of Gront—"He should never have hit a girl like that"—that was when she'd begun to see him differently. It was rare that someone dared to utter any of the banned gender specific pronouns because of risk of punishment. Plus, most accepted the normalized idea that boys and girls were all the same anyway. That Tarro had called her a girl and thought she should be treated as such instantly endeared him to her.

Nya saw things a little differently than most of the other Cadets, primarily because of her early childhood. Unlike most of the Cadets who had been created through Avalon's labs, she was a Barb, taken from her parents at the age of six. She was one of a handful of such Cadets who were part of Avalon's immigration program. Like Nya, these Barbs were taken from their parents at a young age and entered into Likbez. They would receive the full scope of Likbez's training, as the Kreplin prided itself that it could take primitive barbarians and refine them into the Avalon mold.

The Kreplin maintained a steady stream of Barbs into this program. The ones who graduated became attendants in the Kreplin, serving the Confidant, the Ministers, and other officials as their personal servants. Many of the Kreplin officials viewed them as a sort of exotic novelty which made them all the more desirable. The program had been in operation for several decades and only a handful graduated, namely the most beautiful and gifted Barb Cadets from each class who demonstrated devout loyalty to the Avalon way. The rest simply disappeared. All this was kept from the Barb Cadets; instead, they were told that as long as they graduated they would all become full citizens of the great and magnanimous city of Avalon.

The Kreplin required equal treatment of the Barbs within Likbez in order to better identify the best and brightest. So even though the Barb Cadets were informed regarding their differing heritage, they were generally treated the same as all the rest by the instructors. Sure, there was the occasional snide remark or ostracizing from a Cadet, but such overt and blatant activity would get one in trouble. In the end, Nya and the hundred or so other Barbs at the Academy were like all the other Cadets just trying to get to graduation.

The school year went from January to December with classes held six days a week. Twice during the year, they received a week off from classes, April Week and October Week, during which most of the instructors disappeared to spend time in Avalon. The two weeks of reprieve were simply the best times of the year, but were also a little strange as Cadets would often go the entire time without seeing a solitary instructor. Even though it was never stated, the Cadets knew the time off was a test, a test to see their true colors—who would lead, who would be productive and make use of the time, who would be lazy, and who would disobey any of the numerous Academy rules while, supposedly, no one was watching.

They had just begun October Week, and Tarro was enjoying a leisurely stroll with Nya on the softest trail he had ever been on, a path carpeted with a lush moss that felt like velvet. Nya had taken her shoes off to walk barefoot, relishing its sumptuous feel. A gentle breeze played with her hair, causing it to dance around her pretty porcelain face. Tarro watched her feet, enamored by their delicateness, debating whether he should try to hold hands with her.

Suddenly, something very large came crashing through the forest to their left. Tarro jerked his head in the direction of the sound and saw an instructor burst through the trees riding a zebra, wielding something that looked like a flaming sword and screaming like a banshee. Ding . . . ding . . . ding. A soft chime caused the instructor to halt and look around for the source of the strange sound. The chime sounded again, this time more loudly. The instructor jumped off the zebra, and Tarro joined him to look for the misplaced sound. Ding . . . Tarro finally woke from his sleep, the sight of the dreary, gray ceiling above his bed replacing his pleasant dream turned bizarre.

For a moment, he tried to go back to sleep to resume his lovely walk with Nya. After laying there for several unsuccessful minutes, he decided to get up, figuring his luck would put him back with the crazy instructor on the zebra instead of with Nya. He looked at the time displayed next to his bed—5:35 am. While a ten mile run was first on his agenda, he made a mental note to take a walk with Nya in the afternoon. Though this was a week of no instructors and classes, Tarro knew they would be watching and resolved to be as productive as possible.

That afternoon proved to be the reason Tarro loved autumn. Many of the trees scattered throughout the compound had changed colors. All sorts of reds, yellows, and the brightest oranges canvased the Academy grounds, surrounding the drab assortment of depressing gray buildings. The beautiful scenery was further enhanced by the presence of Nya with whom Tarro now happily conversed as they walked by the lake. Over the last several months, these walks had become more frequent during their free time and were always the highlight of the day for him. He smiled, thinking about the extra time they would have today with no class or responsibilities.

"Nya, do you remember your parents?" he asked. On every walk, Tarro tried to learn something more about her, intrigued by her Barb roots.

"Tarro, does it bother you that I'm a Barb?" The non-answer and left-field question surprised Tarro. A few years ago, he would have thought yes, but Nya had changed everything he thought about Barbs.

He quickly recovered from his surprise and said emphatically, "No, no, of course not. You . . . you are"—he searched for the right words in order to be convincing, without blubbering too many of his feelings—"I . . . I really, uh . . . think highly of you, Nya."

She smiled faintly, and Tarro wasn't sure if she believed him as he chided himself for his idiotic word selection. *Think highly . . . think highly? That's the best you can do, Tarro?*

She returned to his question. "I remember my parents a little." A small wren landed on a branch next to her and she stopped to watch it. She didn't say anything for a few moments, and Tarro wasn't sure if she was just observing the bird or didn't want to talk about the distant memories of her parents.

She turned and looked at Tarro and he could see a little sadness in her face. "I don't remember my mother too much, but for some reason, I can see the face of Daddy quite clearly." She paused reflectively. "He had the most kind and gentle face. And I remember the song he always sang to me."

"Sang? A song? What is that?" Tarro was genuinely flummoxed by these foreign words which were not used at Likbez.

She resumed walking and began humming. Tarro followed, mesmerized, as if pulled along by an invisible rope. The humming soon became singing, something Tarro had never heard before in his life. No one ever talked about songs or singing and certainly, no one had done whatever it was she was doing with her voice. He wondered if this was authorized by the Academy, but the question quickly evaporated as he drank in the delicious sweetness of her voice.

She continued singing for several minutes and Tarro had never felt so peaceful. Everything seemed to become very clear and focused for him. He didn't know exactly what love was, but he was pretty sure he had it or it had him.

She stopped singing and blushed slightly when she saw that he was staring at her.

They stood awkwardly until Tarro broke the silence, flashes of last night's dream in his head. "Say, Nya, would you want to take your shoes off?"

Nya laughed at him. "You're funny." She turned and resumed walking down the path, leaving Tarro wondering if being funny was a good thing. Still laughing, she said playfully over her shoulder, "Why in the world would I take my shoes off?"

ⓧ

October Week ended far too quickly for Tarro. The beginning of another laborious week of classes and study put Tarro in a dreary mood. By the time he arrived at Monday afternoon combat training with Instructor-15, his mood had gone from glum to foul. Ever since Nya had taken the beating in this class, Instructor-15 seemed to have it out for her. He was constantly berating her and using her as the example of what not to do, and by now, Tarro truly detested the harsh man.

Instructor-15 gathered them in the familiar combat arena. "Today, we have a special training event for you," he said, pointing to one of the near doors of the combat training facility. "Today, you will demonstrate your acquired combat skills on a live adversary."

As Tarro and the other Cadets pondered what he meant by "live adversary," two Peace Officers emerged from the training facility dragging a very tall man by his arms. The man was wrapped in chains, limp and hooded, his bare feet trailing on the ground. He wore only ratty pants, and the Cadets stared at his bizarre physique, an inhuman mixture of lean muscle and thick hair covering his dark, leathery body.

As they gaped at the man or creature or whatever it was, the officers yanked him over to a large steel chair positioned in the middle of the combat arena. They shoved him into it, secured him with more chains, and then stepped to either side of the chair to face Instructor-15. Having assumed their guard positions, they removed the chivvies strapped to their backs. The man in the chair remained still, his head hanging lifelessly with his chin resting on his chest.

No Cadet moved or made a sound, transfixed and anxiously awaiting what was to come next.

Instructor-15 marched over to the chained man and placed his hand on the hood covering his head. "Cadets, today for the first time in your training, you get to meet a Mutt!" He then dramatically ripped the hood off, eliciting gasps from the Cadets.

Tarro wasn't sure if the Mutt was unconscious or dead, but his face was as strange as his body. His long, matted hair reached his shoulders, framing a hideous face that looked part man and part wolf. His face was just as leathery and grisly as the skin on his body. His ears were abnormally large, the tops of which came to points and protruded through his mangy hair. Tarro noticed the multiple bruise-like discolorations canvasing his body and face and wondered how long he had been in captivity.

Instructor-15 resumed his instruction, giving a detailed description of Mutts, their superhuman strength and speed, the bone-crushing power of their jaws, the incredible senses that made them incomparable hunters—he went on for a solid fifteen minutes.

Finally, he said, "You may wonder why it is here." He looked around, making eye contact with all the Cadets. "Today, each of you will take the baton and strike the Mutt, employing any of the striking techniques you have learned. You will be graded on the technical precision of your maneuvers."

One of the Cadets raised her hand. Instructor-15 recognized her and she asked what everyone else was thinking. "Is it dead?"

Instructor-15 laughed maniacally. He didn't answer but turned to the officer on the right and ordered, "Level two charge." The officer made an adjustment on his chivvy and then jabbed it into the side of the Mutt. The electric discharge jolted the Mutt out of his unconscious state. He immediately began yanking on the chains and screaming while snapping and snarling like an angry mongrel, as if he would devour the two officers in a moment were it not for his restraints.

Instructor-15 lined the Cadets up and the exercise began.

The first Cadet took the baton and cautiously approached the Mutt who froze and locked his eyes on the hesitant student, his flared nostrils pulsating, matching the rhythm of his raspy breathing.

Instructor-15 commanded, "Attack!" The Cadet hesitated. "Cadet 13–21, strike!"

The Cadet resumed his approach toward the Mutt whose tiger-like eyes were still locked on his nearing attacker. When the Cadet was at arm's length from his target, he swung the baton at the Mutt's head who quickly jerked it back just enough to cause the Cadet to completely miss. The Mutt snorted and continued his stare-down of the shaky student.

"Cadet, learn from your mistake and repeat," barked the instructor.

After having taken a couple steps backward in retreat, the Cadet approached again. This time he raised the baton over his head with two hands and then swung vertically downward, intentionally aiming for the left side of the Mutt's head. He anticipated the Mutt's head dodge to the right and quickly swung the baton around to meet it. It was a direct strike to the face, and dark crimson blood began to drip from the Mutt's nose and cheek. The Mutt recovered quickly and glared at the Cadet as he handed the baton off to the next one in line.

"Good!" bellowed Instructor-15. "Next!"

Now that the ice was broken, the next Cadet stepped up with more confidence and delivered two solid strikes to the Mutt. Tarro was twentieth in line, and not only did he not want to do this, he was starting to have pity for the creature who was being pummeled without having a fighting chance. This wasn't a test of skill. The Mutt couldn't even fight back. It was a just a merciless beating.

The fifth Cadet in line was Gront who had been salivating from the moment this exercise had begun. When it was his turn, Gront grabbed the baton and immediately rushed the Mutt.

The Mutt, seeing Gront's visible hubris, shouted, "Strike! Strike me! I'm defenseless! Show everyone what kind of fearless warrior you are!" Gront stopped a few feet from the Mutt, genuinely shocked, as were all the watching Cadets. Until now, the Mutt had not uttered a word, and they had all assumed he couldn't talk.

"Oh, they didn't tell you us Mutts could talk, huh?" He shot Instructor-15 a condescending glance and then glared at Gront, daring him to strike.

Instructor-15, perturbed at Gront's hesitation, yelled, "Cadet, you will immediately advance and strike!"

Gront quickly regained his composure and gave the Mutt a crushing blow to the head, knocking him out cold. Instructor-15 signaled for one of the officers to wake the Mutt up, which the officer promptly accomplished by shocking him again with his chivvy.

Tarro was getting increasingly queasy as his turn approached. But as much as he was dreading his turn, his bigger concern was Nya. She was next in line, and he feared greatly for her. This exercise was void of all compassion and she was tenderness personified.

"Bravo 18–60, you're next!" Instructor-15 smirked as he eyed the weak Cadet.

Nya took the baton and slowly approached the Mutt. The Mutt sat silently, having been beaten so badly he no longer had the energy to fight against the chains or taunt his attackers. Nya studied his blood-soaked face. His eyes were so swollen she could barely see them, his raspy breathing slow and deliberate. Life had been nearly clobbered out of him.

Nya dropped the baton and inched closer to him.

"Cadet, pick up the baton!" shouted Instructor-15.

Nya ignored him and slowly extended her hand toward the Mutt's face. He growled quietly and she reflexively pulled it away.

"Bravo 18–60, what are you doing?! You will strike the Mutt *now*!"

The Mutt sized her up and concluded that she wasn't there to beat him. Blood was dripping into his eyes from the gashes on his head. She reached out again, and this time, he let her wipe the blood off his rough forehead. She then placed her hand gently on his cheek, and he slowly closed his swollen eyes. A tear trickled down from his eye to her hand, mirroring the tears that streamed down her own face.

"Class is dismissed!" screamed the instructor whose veins were now popping out of his neck and forehead.

Tarro's heart jumped into his throat as he watched Instructor-15 rush over, grab Nya by the arm, and violently drag her toward the nearest wing of the combat training facility. Tarro stood there, paralyzed and utterly helpless.

Instructor-15 yelled over his shoulder, "I said, class is dismissed!"

Chapter 7

Loss

TARRO WOKE UP THE next day exhausted, although to call it "waking up" would be generous as he wasn't even sure if he ever really fell asleep. All through the night he had agonized over Nya with a million questions, all of them coming back to the most basic: Was she ok?

He arrived at morning formation, this time ten minutes early, still fretting over her well-being which could only be relieved by seeing her. After five long minutes of standing alone, other Cadets began streaming in, taking their places in Regiment-12's ranks. Tarro checked the time. Nya now had only four minutes left before being late. Three minutes . . . still no Nya. Two minutes . . . Tarro was now feeling positively sick to his stomach. He couldn't remember a time she had ever been late to a formation.

The regimental commander called the Cadets to attention, and after the usual reporting and announcements, they marched to the dining hall for breakfast. Tarro tried to think of every best-case scenario to explain Nya's absence, but it was no good. He knew she was in trouble. The only question was, how much?

All throughout the day, he looked for her. She wasn't in the two classes they had together, and he was able to confirm through several other Cadets that she had missed her other classes. No one had seen her since yesterday afternoon. That evening, when he arrived at the dining hall, he realized that he was not hungry and in no mood to eat, so he returned to his quarters. He tried to take his mind off of her by doing some homework, but it was no use. So he resorted to pacing back and forth, much to the annoyance of his other roommates who were trying to study.

At 9:00 pm that evening, the usual nightly announcements blurted out over the Academy's ubiquitous speaker system. "Attention Regiment-12. Tomorrow at precisely 4:00 pm, you will assemble in your parade ground." The announcer repeated the message, and Cadets everywhere began hypothesizing about the purpose of the looming assembly.

The next day provided more anxious frustration for Tarro as he searched everywhere for Nya. After classes, he sat on his bed staring at his stale, gray wall until Sye jolted him out of his stupor with a reminder about the afternoon's assembly.

The parade ground was a beautifully manicured lawn which served as the location for all their group exercising and marching drills. Overlooking the parade ground was a large and impressive platform constructed of white granite from which the Chancellor and other dignitaries would view any training or practice parades. Directly behind the platform ran the Likbez wall.

The Cadets of Regiment-12 efficiently took their places in the usual formation facing the platform and stood at attention with five minutes to spare. Tarro stared at Nya's empty position in front of him and tried to not lock his knees beginning to feel a little woozy after his sleepless night. To top it off, he hadn't eaten since the incident with Nya and the Mutt. Fatigue and hunger now tried to push him into unconsciousness, and he fought the faintness that threatened to overtake him.

At precisely 4:00 pm, he snapped out of his weak stupor as the Chancellor emerged from behind the platform and slowly and deliberately climbed the stairs of the stage like a king mounting his throne. He strode to its center and then faced the Cadets, pausing for several moments before placing his hands behind his back. He then simultaneously sucked in his gut and puffed out his chest in order to exude maximum command presence.

"Cadets of Regiment-12," he finally said, "you are a privileged group." He paused to allow his assertion to sink in. "You have received the finest training, care, and instruction this world has to offer. We at the Academy lovingly provide everything you need to succeed as future Avalon citizens."

Tarro once again began slipping into his weak stupor as the Chancellor droned on for several minutes, cataloguing all the benevolent provisions of the Academy. Amidst the physical weakness, Tarro had a growing, sinking feeling that this was all leading to a not-so-philanthrop-ic conclusion.

"Every staff member and instructor at the Academy has poured their lives into you so that you, dear friends, can enjoy your future citi-zenship with maximum success and happiness." The Chancellor turned to his right and gave a subtle head nod as if signaling someone unseen.

"But despite all the good that you receive—" *here it comes*, Tarro thought—"some Cadets choose to return this love with hate. We only give you a few rules"—some of the Cadets quietly snickered beside Tarro at the word "few"—"yet, some of you refuse to follow them. Instead of showing gratitude, you show thanklessness by your rebellion."

As if on cue, from behind the platform to the Chancellor's right, Instructor-15 appeared and marched briskly along the parade ground in front of the platform, assuming a position of attention facing the Cadets. Tarro bristled at the sight of him. Trailing him were two other instruc-tors whom Tarro didn't recognize, but the person walking between them caused his knees to buckle and he almost collapsed. Sandwiched between the two instructors, with her wrists cuffed in front of her as if she were some criminal, was Nya.

Nya and her guards joined Instructor-15, and the four of them now faced the Cadets with the Chancellor looming above and behind them on the platform. The Chancellor thundered with anger, "Before you is Bravo 18–60. Two days ago, Bravo 18–60 directly defied Instructor-15 who gave them clear orders which they summarily disregarded."

Tarro looked on in horror, desperately trying to keep himself sup-ported with his increasingly weak legs.

"In order to be an Avalon citizen, you must understand that alle-giance and loyalty to the Avalon way of life and its leader, our beloved Supreme Confidant Talin, are our highest ideals. To deny these values is to deny your privilege of becoming a citizen." Tarro had flashbacks of the Mutt being brutalized and wondered how this fit into the Avalon way of life. He stared at Nya who was now looking straight ahead with an impassive expression.

"Bravo 18–60 has clearly denied this great privilege with insolent disregard for our values. Consequently, there is no place for this Cadet in Avalon, and therefore, there is no place for this Cadet in the Academy."

The Chancellor motioned to the instructors below. They proceeded to escort Nya up the stairs to the top of the platform. As she climbed the stairs, Tarro was struck by the grace she exuded, her head held high while offering no resistance to her guards.

When they reached the top, a walkway telescopically extended from the back of the platform to the top of the Likbez wall behind it, bridging the fifty feet that separated the two structures. Nya turned and glanced in the direction of her normal place in formation and smiled faintly. Tarro, who assumed this was for him, was now shaking violently. His anger had been building and sweeping over him, engulfing him like a raging inferno. At that moment, in his blind rage he wanted to rush the stage, and it was only the thin shred of rationality he still possessed which kept him in place. He knew there was nothing he could do to save her.

The Chancellor motioned to Instructor-15 who grabbed Nya by the arm and walked her along the walkway toward the wall. The Chancellor then descended from the stage as if this was all beneath him. Nya and Instructor-15 reached the end of the walkway resting on top of the wall, and without hesitation, the instructor shoved her. She stumbled forward and passed through the BioDome, tumbling over the wall's edge.

In an instant, she was gone.

In response to the Cadet's demise, the Likbez siren disgorged the first of its three wails. No sooner than it began, Tarro felt himself falling to the ground. Then everything went black.

≔

Biorn muttered angrily to himself. The Likbez sirens had sounded just a few scant months ago, and here they were again. The Libs usually experienced a longer reprieve between rescue attempts, and he wondered what poor Cadet was now outside the wall. Over the years, they'd found that a majority of the Cadets who were thrown over the wall generally stayed in one place, not venturing far from where they landed, paralyzed with fear and too stunned to move, a natural reaction as nothing in their training would have given them the slightest idea of what to do in this frightening and deadly circumstance. A few, though, immediately started moving. Some very quickly. These were always the harder ones to find, as by the time the Ferret arrived, they were significantly farther away from Likbez.

Biorn had already made the usual call to Vera from his POD and was careening through the FLUXX to Sector-17's loading dock in order to execute his normal diversionary routine for the Ferret. He emerged from the POD with a good view of the loading dock. The loading was almost complete. He began searching for the dockmaster when he heard a familiar voice.

"Biorn! What are you doing here?" the voice said good-naturedly.

Before he had a chance to respond, the Peace Officer, who had appeared from around the corner of an adjacent building, approached Biorn and said, "It's been too long since I've seen you, my friend."

"Yes, you haven't come by my cafe in a while." Biorn forced a smile. "Surely you aren't two-timing on me, going to another cafe." Biorn's eyes were searching the loading dock, looking for any sign of the Ferret, when he saw the dockmaster exit her office. He scrambled to think how to disengage from the officer whom he had gotten to know over the years. The officer was friendly, but Biorn was convinced he loved to hear himself prattle even more than he loved to eat Biorn's food.

The officer had placed himself between Biorn and the loading dock, and Biorn watched the dockmaster as she began inspecting the recently arrived shipment scattered about in various containers. Every time Biorn tried to end the conversation, the officer had some other story to tell, and Biorn got increasingly nervous as he felt the precious minutes slip by.

Suddenly there was a commotion on the loading dock and they looked simultaneously to see several droids in a pile on the ground. They appeared to be wrestling someone or something underneath them.

"Peace Officer! We need assistance!" screeched the dockmaster. The Peace Officer immediately ran to the pile of droids who had managed to disentangle themselves from one another, revealing a rather large droid. The sizable droid had another pinned face down to the ground with a knee on his co-worker's neck.

Biorn remained frozen in place as the Peace Officer pulled out his phaser and pointed it at the droid pinned to the ground. "Get up! Put your hands on your head and get up. Now!"

The larger droid removed his knee from the one on the ground and stood aside as the smaller droid slowly stood and faced the Peace Officer. Biorn's heart virtually stopped as he saw what he had been dreading. Dressed as the smaller droid, the Ferret's luck had just run out. Biorn kicked himself for failing in his part of the mission, and now he awaited the inevitable outcome.

With his phaser still trained on the Ferret, the Peace Officer handed a pair of cuffs to the large droid. As Biorn expected, the Ferret quickly pulled something out of his breast pocket and shoved it into his mouth.

Within seconds, foam oozed from his mouth as he collapsed on the ground, dead from the poison pill he'd swallowed.

ϾϮϿ

That evening Biorn retreated to his grassy knoll and gazed at Lake Caesar stretched before him. The Libs had operated all these years without losing a single member. And now, not only had they failed to rescue a Cadet who'd just become another casualty, they'd lost the Ferret. He'd done what Biorn would have done if in his shoes. In fact, they were all prepared to pop the little pill if necessary, for capture would likely lead to torture. And everyone, no matter how tough, would eventually break under the Kreplin's ruthless torture. The names of everyone in their group would inevitably be squeezed out, and death would come to them all.

The evening presented a brilliant and beautiful sunset, but Biorn didn't notice as he numbly sat late into the night, barely moving as he considered it all. So much sorrow, so much injustice, so much pain, and so few of them to make any difference. His mind couldn't help but think about the Cadet who, earlier in the day, had no doubt been running for his life from the Mutts. Without the Libs' rescue, the Cadet was doomed. Biorn prayed that however long the harrowing chase, the end had been quick and painless for the Cadet.

And then there was the Ferret, a Barb who had given up whatever life he had in order to live unseen, unheard, and unnoticed in a dark city to accomplish some good. In the end, he'd given his life for them.

For Biorn, the good seemed to be completely overwhelmed by the evil. The Kreplin was a tidal wave of misery and malevolence which couldn't be stopped. He bowed his head and wept.

Chapter 8

Knowledge

I NSTRUCTOR-15 WAS ALWAYS ILL-TEMPERED, but today, he was espe-cially nasty. Pointing to the Cadets gathered in front of him for combat training class, he snarled, "It is apparent that I have been far too lenient on you slime-balls." The class didn't flinch, keeping their eyes locked on his. "Today, we will finish where we left off, and I expect you to follow my instructions to the letter . . . without exception!"

Tarro looked at the all-too familiar scene of a Mutt chained to the chair in the middle of the combat arena. Ever since the monstrous punishment of Nya the day before, Tarro had existed in a numbed state. All the Cadets of Regiment-12 were quite shocked, but it went far deeper for Tarro. After Nya had been pushed over the wall, he had stumbled back to his quarters. Anger began to rapidly percolate, boiling into a pent-up rage that kept him from even a moment of sleep. This morning, Sye hadn't said a word to him, Tarro's seething bloodshot eyes and stone-like face clearly communicating that he was in no mood to talk.

The morning had been a blur. Now, with the afternoon sun staring down on him, Tarro stood in line waiting for his turn to demonstrate his supposed combat skills on the chained Mutt. Throughout the day his thoughts had raced through every sweet memory of Nya, and every thought of her was like a knife stab to his heart, deepening his sadness. And his fury. He hadn't said a single word to anyone all day, and now he was an emotional bomb of rage about to detonate.

He slowly advanced in line toward the Mutt as each Cadet took their best wack at the hapless creature. Then it was his turn.

"Bravo-3–58, what are you waiting for?!" Instructor-15 yelled. Tarro looked down at the baton in his hand. "Bravo 3–58, commence!"

Tarro took a good look at the Mutt. For the first time, he noticed this Mutt was different from the last one, and he wondered what happened to the one Nya had refused to strike. The thought of Nya instantly caused his eyes to swell with tears. After flooding his bed all night with them, he had managed to dam the tears, but now the dam was breaking.

The wheezing Mutt snarled at Tarro, baring his jagged teeth. Tarro glanced at the baton and saw it shaking from the white-knuckled death grip he was squeezing it with. Then, in a flash, he rushed the Mutt—all his sorrow, all his rage, all his spite toward the Academy bursting forth like a violent thunderstorm. He unleashed it all on the bound Mutt, striking him again and again and again.

Before he knew what was happening, Instructor-15 was pulling him off the Mutt, yanking the baton out of his hand. When he finally got Tarro under control, he roared, "Excellent, Bravo 3–58! Your maneuvers lacked technical precision"—he turned to the rest of the class—"but that . . . that is how you assertively initiate an attack!"

Tarro stumbled away from the instructor, making his way to the back of the line. He glanced back at the Mutt and saw him bloody, slumped unconsciously in the chair. A wave of nausea swept over him, wrenching his stomach, and he leaned over to empty its contents.

The next morning began like the previous for Tarro, except that he had managed to get a couple of hours of sleep only because he was utterly exhausted. That night he had wept over his attack of the Mutt, haunted by the contrast of his violence and Nya's compassion, angered further by the thought that he was no better than Instructor-15. By the end of the day, he had managed to get a grip on himself, and by the end of the week, he had succeeded in forcing his volatile emotions into desensitized numbness.

He had no idea how to deal with the gaping hole in his soul so he crammed every free moment with activity and study. As the remainder of the school year trudged onward, he found himself increasingly drawn to Sye's secret book and would make frequent visits to read the ancient text, sometimes with Sye, but usually alone.

While he kept his visits brief in order to minimize the risk of being caught with the illegal contraband, he managed to finish reading the book by the end of the school year. He was fascinated by its account of history. Almost everything it described was different from what he had been taught at the Academy. Before, he would have been skeptical of the book, but his rage against the Academy now predisposed him to accept it over the teachings of his tyrannical institution. And while before he had tried to distance himself from Sye, he now found himself gravitating toward him, enjoying the times they met in their hidden rock cove to discuss the finer points of Sye's history book.

Today was the day before the end of their ninth school year. Tarro felt compelled to do some reading, so after dinner, he visited the cove. He opened the little box, pulled out the book, suppressed a sudden thought about Nya, and dove into his reading.

"Oh! Hey, Tarro. Didn't know you were here," Sye said, seeing Tarro as he entered the cove. "I'll come back another time if you'd like some quiet."

"No, please stay." Tarro was slightly amused at Sye's rare expression of thoughtfulness.

Sye plopped down on the ground next to Tarro. "Finish the book yet?"

"Yep. Interesting stuff. I was just re-reading the section on socialism." Tarro paused and then looked at Sye quizzically. "We've been taught that socialism creates equal success and prosperity."

"Ha! You mean equal poverty and misery," chided Sye.

"Well, the book certainly does have a different perspective."

Sye laughed. "That's the understatement of the year. So what did you learn?"

Tarro squinted trying to remember details from the fog of last year. "Well, you remember in *Ancient History* class, when Instructor-32—"

"You mean the Woodchuck Witch?" Sye had nicknames for all the instructors and the mental picture of this particularly mean one with her unusually large front teeth made Tarro do something he hadn't done since Nya's demise—laugh. It felt good as he felt a little bit of pressure release from his broken heart.

"Yes, the Woodchuck Witch," Tarro confirmed, still smiling. "Well remember when she was talking about the successful economies of past countries? Didn't she cite the ancient countries of Venezuela, Cuba, and the Soviet Union as socialistic countries that thrived economically?"

Sye nodded his head. "And even more recently, the countries of Tenecca and Romiden."

Tarro pointed to one of the pages of the open book. "But here it cites these countries as examples of states with high poverty rates and eventual failed economies." Tarro paused, staring at the book, deep in thought. "If this is true, why would the Academy lie about this? And why lie about all this other stuff?"

Sye grunted in disgust. "I don't know all the reasons, but I do know this: the Academy is run by the Kreplin, and the Kreplin lives by one principle."

"What's that?"

"Something I overhead an instructor whisper to another one time. I got the sense he was a little ticked off about something related to the Kreplin. He said the Kreplin lives by the motto: 'From each according to our benefit, to each according to our need.'"

Part 2

Avalon

Chapter 9

Graduation

B OOM! The walls of Lenon Hall shook and Tarro felt his bed vi-
brate with the thunderous explosion. Tarro turned over and the
faint glow of "2:00 am" met his tired gaze. In another hour, Likbez's ten
large cannons would ceremoniously fire again as they had been doing
since noon yesterday and would continue to do so every hour until their
graduation at noon today.

This was supposedly a tradition that stretched back to the incep-
tion of the Academy, designed to jubilantly announce the graduation
ceremony, but Tarro wondered if it wasn't just the final chance for the
Academy to inflict misery on the Cadets. Tarro was actually in the dis-
gruntled minority on this. Most of the other graduating Cadets stayed
awake all night, too excited to sleep and certainly not bothered by the
celebratory cannons.

Tarro stared at the ceiling and contemplated his life. Despite the
emotional roller-coaster, he had managed to finish his ninth year with
excellent grades. He had begun this year as a member of Alpha Class,
his final year of the Academy. He started the year with a class ranking of
331 and finished at 228 making him the first in the Academy's history to
advance over a hundred places in ranking in the span of one school year.

This wasn't accidental, for he had poured himself into his studies
with a feverish drive motivated by a simple desire to push out his pain
and any associated memory of Nya. In the end, he had stopped caring

about achieving a sub-three hundred class ranking and qualifying for the Peace Officer Corps, but had ironically succeeded in both.

After tossing and turning all night, Tarro finally forced himself out of bed, cursing the inventor who'd come up with the bright idea of a cannon. They were allowed to go to breakfast without the normal prerequisite formation, and Tarro enjoyed the freedom of moseying into the dining hall on his own time.

He saw Sye and sat down next to him, doing everything he could to avoid looking at Sye's class rank which had steadily decreased this past year, plunging him into the bottom one percent. To make matters worse, Sye's incessant cynicism and cocky questions to instructors had only increased, even as Tarro had tried to get him to tone it down. If there was ever a Cadet who qualified for the nebulous group the Academy warned wouldn't graduate and make it to Avalon, it was Sye. And this worried Tarro.

Sye sensed Tarro's anxiety and said to him, "So, Captain Academy, you ready to graduate with the other top class nerds?" He gave a playful elbow to his friend's side, and Tarro stole a glance at Sye's ranking.

"Don't worry about me, Tarro. They'll graduate me just to get me out of their hair."

A nagging feeling that Sye wouldn't graduate had plagued Tarro for the last couple of weeks. Sye always said he knew too much, and he was right. Tarro was keenly aware that he also knew too much, but unlike Sye, he'd had the sense to keep his mouth shut. His nagging feeling about Sye was only exacerbated by the unknown of what actually happened to the Cadets who failed to graduate. Tarro and Sye quietly finished breakfast, returned to their quarters, and got ready for graduation.

Great fanfare accompanied the ceremony which took place on the Academy's main field. The Kreplin's trumpeters and drummers of the H&D Brigade, the elite fifty-member Horn and Drum Brigade, provided the grand introduction. The entire Academy sat in neat rows, facing a platform constructed for this occasion. The H&D's trumpets blasted to the rhythm of a dramatic drum beat, and Supreme Confidant Talin strode onto the platform. He was followed by the twenty Ministers of Avalon, all of whom wore regal robes with sashes across their chests embroidered with their sector's respective numbers and symbols.

The dignitaries took their seats, making way for the Chancellor to provide the opening remarks after which Talin gave the main address. Tarro remembered hearing things like "you are the pride of Avalon" and "Avalon expects only the highest loyalty," but apart from that, he ignored the majority of the speech, quite repulsed by Talin's fake warmth which did little to mask his icy persona. The only thing Tarro cared about was the final number of graduates to be announced at the end of the ceremony. He looked for Sye as they all sat in their assigned seats, but he couldn't find his friend who, at least at breakfast, was ranked 2,021.

The H&D Bridgade played its final salute and then Talin concluded the ceremony. "Today we are graduating the smallest class to date but one of the most talented." Tarro's right leg reflexively began to nervously jitter up and down. "Today we are graduating two thousand and ten new citizens!" With the news that Sye had just missed the cutoff, Tarro's heart broke. He was accustomed to having his heart wrenched apart, but it never made it easier. "To you graduates who have achieved your citizenship, I congratulate you for eschewing mediocrity and individual interests to embrace collective excellence. Avalon awaits you and your future contribution to its common good!"

After the ceremony, Tarro looked all over for Sye but couldn't find him anywhere. He overheard several other Cadets talking about the thirty or so others that didn't make the cut-off who similarly could not be found. With deep sadness, Tarro sauntered over to the dining hall for the required graduation party with the stewards.

"Congrats, Tarro!" Lon called out exuberantly as Tarro entered the dining hall.

Tarro glumly greeted Lon and Neen who accompanied him. With Sye on his mind, Tarro was in no mood for a celebration, so he perfunctorily shook both their hands with a meager greeting.

Neen said, "Boy, Tarro, time sure has flown! But we are so happy to have been able to make your world-class education possible. You are a lucky Cadet!"

Lucky? I'm lucky? Yeah, the luckiest guy in the world, Tarro thought. He looked at the same dumb, white-haired dog Neen carried and had the sudden thought that the mangy canine probably had more sense than either of its owners.

Dripping with sarcasm, Tarro said to the dog, "Giggi, you're the luckiest dog in the world. I wish you the best of luck." He then turned and walked away from his very shocked stewards.

Chapter 10

Peace Officer

I T WAS CONVERSION DAY at the Academy and all the new graduates bustled with activity, getting ready to make the big transition from the Academy to Avalon where they would take their oaths as new citizens. Relishing the moment in his quarters precisely because it was his last moment, Tarro packed his paltry possessions. He thought about Sye's book and was briefly tempted to retrieve it and smuggle it into Avalon, but common sense prevailed. The risk was too great. Besides, he pretty much had it memorized anyway.

He began making his way to the Rotunda, joining a gaggle of other Cadets heading to the aircraft pad to board the AT-7 that would take them to Avalon. Tarro walked in silence, surrounded by the excited chatter of Cadets.

"The first thing I'm going to do is get rid of this drabby uniform and get some new clothes," said one girl.

Next to her, a boy said, "I can't wait to visit the Colonnades. I wonder how you get Colonnade credits?"

"I can't wait to see where I'm going to live!" gushed another.

Tarro splintered off from his fellow graduates and headed toward the Rotunda to join a different group, the elite three hundred graduating Cadets who qualified for the Peace Officer Corps. Tarro wondered if all of them actually wanted to be Peace Officers. If not, it wouldn't have mattered anyway because, at this point, none of them had a choice in the matter.

He arrived in the Rotunda and took a seat in the designated area with his fellow prospective Peace Officers, snorting in disgust when he saw Gront a few rows back. He quickly turned around and faced the front as the sight of Gront only induced painful memories of Nya.

When they were all seated, a Peace Officer walked crisply into the Rotunda to address them. Tarro instantly recognized him as his picture had been frequently shown at the Academy over the years. He was the Commandant of the Peace Officer Corps, the right hand man of the Supreme Confident and the highest ranking Peace Officer in Avalon.

"Welcome, prospective Peace Officers," said the well-polished officer. "You have proved to be the best of the Academy and that is why you are here. Only the finest join our corps of officers. The rest of your classmates will become simply common Avalon citizens." Tarro was a little surprised by the apparent disdain he had for these "common" citizens.

"You will be given the best of everything, provided you succeed in becoming Peace Officers. Half of you will make it through the officer program. The best half. Those of you who do not pass the program will become regular citizens." Tarro discreetly looked around to see if anyone else shared his surprise.

They had been told from the beginning that the top three hundred would qualify for the Peace Officer Corps, but no one had ever mentioned this little nugget of information. *Only half will make it?* Tarro cynically figured this would be the first of many little surprises they would encounter along the way in their transition to Avalon.

After this initial briefing from the Commandant, they boarded their designated transport. As the large transport lifted off from the pad with all three hundred of them on board, Tarro looked out the window to his left. The aircraft gained altitude, pushing the Academy further into the distance below and bringing more of the surrounding terrain into view. Spotting their parade ground and the wall section where Nya went over, he let out a deep sigh. Considering the height of the wall, he wondered if she had been able to walk after her fall, much less run from the Mutts who had surely pursued. Question after question flooded his mind. So many questions, so few answers . . .

"Attention graduates, we will be arriving in approximately ten minutes," announced an automated voice, snapping Tarro out of his trance.

The AT-7 landed effortlessly on one of Avalon's landing pads, and after an announcement to exit, they all made their way down the aircraft's ramp where they were led into the decontamination chamber in groups of fifty. Once sufficiently cleansed from any foreign contaminants, they began a long day of administrative processing which involved no less than a dozen different briefs on everything from how to utilize their new banking accounts to the laws of Avalon.

The wearying day culminated with an intensive psychological and medical evaluation. Tarro nervously reported to his assigned room at the prescribed time. During one of the administrative briefings, he had overheard someone say that some did not pass this particular evaluation and were instantly dropped out of the Peace Officer program. Tarro was quite confident in his physical shape, but he wasn't looking forward to the psych test. He had been an emotional mess as of late, and he knew it.

The medical evaluation was first, and the only thing that went wrong was accidentally kicking the doctor in the shin with the reflex test. "Ouch! Wow, you're quite sensitive" was all the doctor said. Besides this little incident, Tarro felt it went pretty smoothly.

After the doctor left, a very tall person in black pants and a matching tailored jacket entered. The person had soft features and blonde hair with green accents on its spiked tips, and Tarro couldn't decide if he was talking to a man or a woman.

"I am here to evaluate your mental health," said the examiner very clinically, taking a seat directly in front of Tarro. The examiner studied him intently, and Tarro felt as if he or she were trying to peer into his soul.

The examiner finally asked, "First, are you happy to be here?"

Tarro thought about it for a moment as the examiner cocked his or her head, still fixated on him. Whether intended or not, the examiner's use of "first" suggested that this was not friendly small talk, but an evaluation question. "Yes, I've wanted to be a Peace Officer for as long as I can remember."

"No, I mean are you happy to be *here*?"

"Well, if you mean here with you, I'm actually a little hungry and ready to eat." Tarro saw the examiner's lips purse slightly forming a subtle frown, and he quickly concluded that the examiner's threshold for humor was nil, and that it was best to stick to the answers Avalon wanted to hear. "But if you mean happy to be here in Avalon, the answer is absolutely."

"What makes *you* happy?" came the next question.

After Tarro dismissed the temptation to say "the thought of concluding this examination," he reflexively thought about Nya. And thinking about Nya only managed to deeply sadden him.

"You seem hesitant to answer?" asked the examiner. Tarro wasn't sure why the examiner felt compelled to put the supposed observation into the form of a question but concluded that it was what these examiners do—just ask a bunch of questions.

Tarro thought about the question for a few long moments. On one hand he was trying to think of the "right" kind of answer to give to his humorless examiner. On the other hand, he was genuinely wondering what, in fact, *did* make him happy.

"Perhaps you are unable to answer?"

The additional question flustered Tarro. He knew the longer he went without answering it, the more questions the examiner would have about him. It shouldn't be a hard question, but before Tarro knew what he was doing, he blurted out, "I don't know."

"You don't know what makes you happy?"

Tarro, you stupid idiot! he thought to himself. *Just answer the dumb question. Make up something . . . anything!* He looked intensely at the examiner and said with forced eagerness, "Actually, what makes me happy is the idea of becoming a Peace Officer and protecting the values of Avalon. Apart from that, I am eager to find happiness in Avalon."

The examiner remained expressionless and continued with a series of additional questions that Tarro thought were not only irrelevant to becoming a Peace Officer but were, at times, nonsensical. After the rough start, he quickly got into a rhythm providing all the canned answers that any new Academy graduate and prospective Peace Officer would no doubt give. The examiner finally dismissed him, and Tarro breathed a sigh of relief, sensing that he'd done well enough in the end.

He then proceeded down a very long hallway to his final station and checked in at the reception desk of very large lobby where many of the other officer candidates were already sitting. He noticed that they were all sitting quite motionless, wearing sleek, glass eye visors.

"Welcome, prospective officer," said the female companion at the reception desk. Tarro looked up and was floored. For a moment, he thought he was looking at Nya. Reality quickly set in, but it was uncanny how similar this companion's features were to hers. He studied the companion, marveling at the similarities. He had never really looked at a companion this closely before and was captivated at how real she looked. The skin, the hair, even the way the eyes blinked and moved. For a wonderful moment, Tarro imagined he was staring into the beautiful eyes of his Nya.

The companion blushed from Tarro's intense gaze and said sweetly, "I said welcome, prospective officer."

"Oh, yes—uh—yes, thank you," Tarro stammered.

"Please put this visor on and take a seat. The brief will last about twenty minutes. Peace and Love."

After bumbling a farewell to the companion receptionist, Tarro made his way over to an empty seat. He sat down and noticed a graduate handing her visor to another companion standing at one of several door-ways located behind the reception desk. The graduate wore a nervous expression as she then followed the companion through one of the doors.

As soon as Tarro sat down, the visor instantly blackened out his surroundings and a video screen appeared, revealing Supreme Confidant Talin seated behind a massive and ornate desk. He wore a deep royal blue robe providing a striking backdrop to his long, straight silver hair and very tanned skin.

"Welcome, new Avalon citizen," he said. "I congratulate you on your achievement. You have proved yourself worthy to join our beloved city, the crown jewel of the world, a beacon of light and hope in a dark and sinister world."

Tarro thought about the Mutts that had been beaten in the combat arena and wondered what they would say to this assertion of Avalon national virtue.

"As the leader of this glorious city, it is my privilege to watch over you and protect you. It is my cherished duty." Tarro's mind began to wander as Talin droned on, extolling his and the city's eminence with all his standard talking points.

The recorded brief then shifted away from Talin to an eagle's eye view of the city from above the Kreplin as the narrator began to detail the wonders of Avalon. As if he were in an aircraft, the video began zooming Tarro through COMCIRC in an expanding circular route, extending to the outer edge of Avalon, giving Tarro a sweeping aerial view of the city. In his first and only visit, he had seen pieces of Avalon, but now he was truly astonished at the diverse beauty of the city. For a moment, he swelled with a little pride as a new citizen. Once the entire city had been viewed, the video raced back to its center, coming to a hovering stop in front of the Kreplin. And then came the next little surprise.

The faceless voice resumed its narration. "Our beloved Supreme Confidant is our Father who provides benevolent leadership to all who have the privilege of giving allegiance to him and to the Kreplin. This collective personal care is largely made possible through the Bionet you will receive today." Tarro watched suspiciously as he was shown the wonderful features of the Bionet.

Finally, Talin concluded the briefing. "Know this, citizen. You and your fellow comrades are joining the most advanced society this world has ever known. It is now your privileged duty to maintain our great way of life through your faithful loyalty. Peace and love."

It had been a very long day and Tarro was happy to be finally sitting and especially glad to at last be in his new living quarters. He moved his hand across the arm of the chair as if petting it, marveling at the synthetic leather-like material, which not only perfectly contoured to his body but automatically adjusted its temperature based on his body temperature transmitted to the chair through his Bionet. The insertion of the chips into his eyes and body had only taken a few minutes, and while his eyes were still a little blurry from the insertion, it had been relatively painless.

He focused on the material of the chair and commanded his Bionet's Vizitar, nicknamed "V," into action. "V, evaluate this material," he said.

In a split-second, his eye transmitters provided a display of descriptions and images of the material through his Vizitar. He scrolled through the catalogue of information with movements from his eyes. He then exited this informational display and toggled through various menus and options amazed at the wealth of information and entertainment accessible with just a flick of the eyes.

After fiddling with the display for a few minutes, he turned his Vizitar off and looked around his new home. As a prospective Peace Officer, he and the other candidates were taken to a sprawling compound in Sector-1 which was simply referred to as the Pound. While the citizens of Avalon were divided between the other sectors, Sector-1 was dedicated entirely to both active and retired Peace Officers. Each retired Peace Officer was provided an opulent personal residence within this sector while the Pound served as housing for active Peace Officers and, at least for now, all the prospective officer candidates.

Tarro was quite surprised by the lavishness of his quarters located on the third floor of the Pound. Provided he passed the Peace Officer training, this would become his permanent home. It was a sprawling space with a wide wall of glass dividing the interior from a beautiful outside terrace that overlooked Sector-1's magnificent lake. In the middle of the terrace, a six-foot wide waterfall softly cascaded into a swimming pool.

As Tarro sat in his new chair, he pondered the accommodations and the salary he was told he would receive provided he passed the officer training. It was an astonishing amount. *Nothing like purchased loyalty*, Tarro thought with contempt.

A sweet female voice interrupted his thoughts. "Master, is there anything I can do for you?" She had been asking him all sorts of questions ever since he had arrived. She was the voice of the artificial intelligence built into his quarters which controlled everything from the lighting to the conjuring of meals that were served through the food generator.

"You've already asked me that," said Tarro.

"I'm sorry, I didn't mean to be impertinent," she said with a slightly pouty voice.

"Don't take it so personally. You didn't do anything wrong." Tarro chuckled at how, for a moment, he almost forgot that he was talking to a computer.

"What's so funny, Master?"

"Nothing. But call please me Tarro."

"As you wish, Tarro."

"And what should I call you?"

There was a pause as if she were thinking. "Whatever you would like to call me, Tarro."

A name instantly came to mind. He knew he shouldn't say it. He knew he would regret it. But he figured he could always change the name later, and before he knew it, he blurted out, "Nya."

"Nya. Nya is a very nice name."

Tarro leaned back in his chair, closed his eyes, let out a long sad sigh . . . and dreamt of Nya.

Chapter 11

Kindred Spirits

A SOFT CHIME SOUNDED IN Tarro's ears, indicating an announcement from the Kreplin through his Vizitar was forthcoming. Citizens received announcements at least once a day. He wondered if the primary purpose was to disseminate information or simply to remind them of the Kreplin's ubiquitous presence. A woman appeared in his view to deliver the announcement. She wore bright red clothing which glowed and glistened with her movements, producing a shimmer, like dancing light on rippling water.

"The Kreplin is pleased to announce that tomorrow is Colonnade Day," the woman said. "So be sure to stop by your local Colonnade where all your wishes come true. Peace and love, citizens of Avalon."

She disappeared when the announcement ended, and the cafe Tarro was about to walk into quickly came back into focus. He was still getting used to interfacing with these eye projections while still functioning in the real world. Yesterday's announcement aired just as he was about to walk out onto his terrace. He laughed to himself as he remembered being distracted by the video and walking into the glass doors. He made a mental note to take advantage of Colonnade Day when visits to the Colonnade cost half the normal credits, compliments of the Kreplin.

Standing in front of the cafe, he looked at his reflection. His new white uniform was perfectly assembled without a trace of even the slightest wrinkle or defect; a single navy-colored band on his right arm signified his junior rank. He looked down at his white boots gleaming in the sunlight and thought about how much work he had put into becoming a Peace Officer. The day before had been selection day when the best half of the officer candidates had been selected for the Peace Officer Corps. He was not only in the upper half, he'd finished in the top ten. He looked again at his reflection. Everything he had always wanted looked back at him. He let out a long sigh. Everything he'd always wanted. Yet, he felt so empty.

The doors to the cafe automatically opened as he moved forward to enter. His training was complete and it was time to celebrate a little at his favorite dining establishment. This cafe was the first one he had visited during his initial visit to Avalon as a Cadet. There were many other cafes with equally good food, but Tarro like the manager of this one. He had gotten to know the older man through his many visits during officer training, and there was something unique about this manager. He was refreshingly different.

"Hello, Tarro!" said Biorn to the new Peace Officer who had entered his cafe.

"Hey, Biorn," Tarro said. He stopped in front of Biorn and raised his arms a little so Biorn could get a full look at his uniform. "What do you think?"

"They made *you* an officer? The one who couldn't shoot and hit the Avalon wall even if you were standing right in front of it!"

"Very funny, Biorn. I only have one regret in life—sharing my shooting difficulties with you." During phaser training, Tarro had struggled with shooting accuracy. He had worked very hard and eventually honed his skills to an expert level, but not before making the mistake of divulging to Biorn his early struggles. Ever since then, Biorn took every opportunity to needle him on his former shooting deficiencies.

Laughing, Biorn said, "I just hope that if a Peace Officer ever shoots at me, it's you." With a giant grin on his face, he clasped Tarro's shoulder. "Now come, my friend. I have a new entree I think you'll like."

"You mean you need some poor sap to test it for you," chided Tarro.

The two laughed as Biorn sat him down at his usual table in the corner. He ordered the new entree for Tarro and then left to attend to his other patrons.

Biorn glanced back at Tarro. He usually avoided Peace Officers like the plague. A Peace Officer, especially one who seemingly didn't care for people, was always a threat to his covert line of work. But he had taken a liking to this young man who had begun dining in his cafe about a year ago.

At first, Tarro came across as very stoic, a loner who just seemed to want to keep to himself. But over time, Biorn interpreted his aloofness differently. Most patrons who came in by themselves just sat in his cafe, staring ahead and remaining generally placid except for occasionally eating or drinking whatever was in front of them. These simply zoned out, watching their entertainment of choice through Vizitar. But Biorn had noticed very quickly that Tarro never checked out mentally.

Even when off duty, the young man was aware of his surroundings and always seemed to be deep in thought. As he cautiously got to know the young officer, he was impressed by his thoughtfulness and intellect but even more intrigued by the antagonism toward the Kreplin he sensed. To what degree, he didn't yet know as Tarro was very guarded. But every once in a while Tarro would say something that hinted at this, and consequently, Biorn took every opportunity to explore the depths of this possible Kreplin disdain.

Biorn returned to check on Tarro to garner his assessment of the new cuisine.

Tarro had just taken a rather large bite and garbled to Biorn, "Your new menew idem is esse—esselent."

The attempted compliment was overshadowed by the food which flew out of Tarro's mouth and landed on his lap. Biorn roared with laughter as he watched the officer furiously work to remove the blot of food from his previously spotless uniform.

"I blame you for this," Tarro said without looking up.

"Ah, yes. It was my fault for creating ornery food which finds amusement in jumping out of my patrons' mouths."

Tarro laughed and took another bite. "Biorn, despite the bad attitude of your food, I gotta tell you, this is really good."

"It's the least I can do for a new Peace Officer of Avalon . . ." Biorn paused, choosing his next words intentionally, "who has dedicated his life to protecting our way of life."

Tarro immediately stopped chewing, put his fork down, and looked intensely at Biorn. "Protect Avalon from *what*?"

And there it was—another glimpse of animosity or something close to it. Biorn marveled at the sudden fierceness that glared in Tarro's eyes. A normal Peace Officer loyal to the Kreplin would never ask such a question. He decided to probe, choosing his words carefully.

"What do you mean, Tarro? The Kreplin always has enemies." Tarro looked down at his food and began playing with it with his fork. Biorn noticed his clenched jaw. "Tarro, I think there is another side of you. I think . . . I think you and I might be more similar than you realize."

Tarro looked up, and Biorn locked eyes with him. Tarro remained silent, at a loss for words. As Biorn continued to study him, he saw the fierceness replaced with a look of pain and deep sadness. Yes, there was more to this young man, much more.

Biorn decided enough had been said for now. He smiled at Tarro, gave him a wink, and left him to resume his usual isolated contemplation. As he walked away, he said over his shoulder, "I also have a new dessert for you to try . . . a new dessert for a new Peace Officer."

✆

That night, Tarro sat on his terrace and stared at the surrounding lights. It was almost midnight and he had been sitting there for several hours. He thought about Biorn and their conversations. While his own moods usually bounced between depressed and angry, Biorn always seemed happy. There was a genuine warmth to the man that was foreign to most others. Ever since he had been asked the "Are you happy?" question by that psych quack during his medical evaluation, he had been plagued with this question and a slew of related ones. What provides happiness? What does it even mean to be happy? Why does one even want to be happy? And why does it seem to be so elusive?

For some reason, Tarro enviously thought about Neen and Lon's dog, Giggi, concluding that she was not bothered by such questions, content with her daily ration of dog food.

He looked down to his right and saw Sector-1's Colonnade in the distance. Covered in an eye-stimulating array of blue and pink lights, it beckoned pleasure seekers. He considered his many visits and was continually amazed at what it offered. If you could dream it up, the Colonnade could create it, and any desire could be satisfied there. It was fun, but though he went in feeling empty, he always left with even greater emptiness. He wondered why the happy feeling in the Colonnade didn't continue after leaving. Did that mean that the feeling in the Colonnade wasn't actually happiness or was there something else he was missing?

Tarro shook his head as it began to ache with all the questions that swirled within, questions that seemed to have no answers. He stood up to go to bed. These questions would have to wait another day. He thought again about Biorn and resolved to ask him some of these questions the next time he visited his cafe. *He seems happy. Maybe he has some answers,* Tarro thought.

Chapter 12

Peace Keeping

T HE AVALON JUDGE ENTERED the courtroom with an air of self-importance. He slowly approached his judicial seat perched above the floor of the courtroom. His throne-like chair was surrounded on three sides by a half-wall of thick black marble that matched the color of both his robe and hair.

Standing below and to the right of the Judge on the courtroom floor, Tarro watched as the black-robed Kreplin official sat down and, with a deep voice, loudly called for the trial to begin. New Peace Officers were assigned the benign task of overseeing the security of Avalon's courts. Located on the second floor of the Kreplin, there were twenty court rooms, each corresponding to the city's twenty sectors.

Today he had been assigned to Sector-6's courtroom, and while this duty was usually quite boring, he had been looking forward to this case ever since this morning. Every day at 7:00 am, he received a daily briefing along with his assignment from SD-6. The brief description he received of today's trial promised to be quite entertaining. His suspicion was proving to be accurate as he surveyed all the dogs present in the courtroom.

"This court is now in session," bellowed the Judge. "The prosecution will state its case."

The prosecuting lawyer, another Kreplin official, stood up behind his table, then moved out from behind it to stand before the Judge. A large, shaggy dog sat in a chair adjacent to the one the prosecutor had just vacated. The dog, deciding that he wanted to follow, started to jump off the chair.

Having caught the dog's movement in the corner of his eye, the prosecutor wheeled around and commanded, "Stay!"

The dog obeyed but seemed a little startled and began to pant nervously.

"Your honor, representing the State and my client, Bufney"—the prosecutor pointed to the panting dog—"it has come to the Kreplin's attention that Citizen VT-72–85 illegally married Bufney, as Bufney never consented to this marriage."

Citizen VT-72–85, seated next to his lawyer behind another table facing the Judge, frowned and shook his head at the prosecution's assertion.

Several years ago, due to the advocacy of various groups of animal-loving Avalon citizens, pets were granted personhood by the State. And while citizens had long been able to marry their pets, the fact that these animal "persons" had never given consent to these unions had recently captured the attention and concern of these same advocacy groups. There was enough clamoring amongst the citizenry for the Kreplin to resolve the issue, and so the Kreplin, ever desirous to keep the populace placated, took up the case.

The prosecutor turned to address the courtroom which had filled with many eager spectators, most of whom were anxious citizens who had similarly married their pets and were therefore quite concerned about the outcome of this trial. "The State maintains that the marriage of Bufney to Citizen VT-72–85 was illegal and is therefore null and void due to the lack of consent to said marriage by Bufney."

The defense attorney, also a Kreplin official, immediately shot to his feet. "Your honor, can the prosecution *prove* that Bufney did not consent to this marriage?"

"Sit!" yelled the prosecutor to Bufney who, having noticed her owner sitting across the aisle, tried to again leave her seat.

After rebuking the dog, the prosecutor turned back to the Judge. "Yes, I can, in fact, prove that Bufney did not consent to marriage." He briskly approached the bench and placed a small device on the table located directly in front of the Judge. He tapped it and a holographic image as tall as a man appeared, displaying the marriage license in question.

"It really is quite simple," the attorney said. "The court will notice that this Kreplin-issued marriage license has the signature of Citizen VT-72–85, but there is no signature from Bufney."

A murmur immediately rippled through the gallery, and the defense attorney again jumped up from his seat. "Your honor, the lack of a signature does not—"

"I believe I have the floor!" interrupted the prosecutor. Tarro looked at Bufney who was still panting, her tongue hanging out of the right side of her mouth.

The Judge affirmed the prosecutor, and the defense attorney sat down. Tarro saw both lawyers smirk at each other. He was convinced that this was all just a game to these two Kreplin officials. The Kreplin provided all prosecution and defense attorneys, and by now, Tarro had observed enough trials to conclude that these State attorneys didn't really care about the citizens or their problems. They just entered each trial to try to best the other. And after the battle of wits, they would invariably head off together to attend the next Kreplin dinner party.

After the brief review of the marriage license lacking Bufney's signature, the prosecutor gave the floor to the defense attorney.

"May it please the court," began the defense attorney, "we concede that Bufney's signature is not on the marriage license. However, she is not capable of producing such a signature. Therefore, the lack of a signature is an unfair criteria by which to measure consent."

The Judge asked, "Are you suggesting that Bufney is incapable of providing consent?"

"No, no, of course not," said the defense attorney. "Bufney, as a member of the canine species, and whom—may I remind the court—is viewed as a person by the State and by the city of Avalon, is a person with the highest degree of intelligence and dignity. My client recognizes this and values Bufney's own desires and would never want to infringe upon her own free will."

As the attorney continued to wax eloquently on the esteemed qualities of Bufney and how much his client loved and respected his canine spouse, Tarro watched the shaggy dog. Bufney had noticed little light spots on the ceiling, reflections coming from the gaudy diamond bracelet worn by the prosecutor. Her head jerked back and forth as she followed the light spots dancing above her.

The defense attorney reached the climax of his argument just as Bufney finally decided that the mysterious light spots needed to be spoken to and let out a string of barks directed at the ceiling. This set off a chain reaction of barking from the other dogs in the courtroom, none of whom knew why they were barking other than it seemed the thing to do at the given moment.

"Order! Order in the court!" shouted the Judge. "Citizens, if you cannot control your dogs, spouses, or whatever they are to you, I will remove you from this courtroom!"

After the humans mostly got their dogs under control, the Judge conceded to the defense attorney's proposal to test consent. Bufney was to be placed on one side of the courtroom and Citizen VT-72-85 on the other. With the citizen remaining still and quiet, Bufney would be released. If she willingly went to VT-72-85, this would be regarded as consent. If not, then the marriage would be dissolved. After both parties agreed to the test, everyone took their places.

The prosecutor walked Bufney on a leash over to one side of the room. Her tail wagged vigorously, evidently happy to finally be free of the oppressive chair. Citizen VT-72-85 took his place on the other side of the room.

"Release Bufney," ordered the Judge to the prosecutor. The prosecutor let go of the leash, and for a moment Bufney just sat there. Citizen VT-72-85 desperately attempted to get her to look at him by moving his head around as much as he thought he could get away with. Tarro then noticed the citizen slowly tap his leg with his right hand which was balled up in a fist as if he was holding something. At that moment, Bufney darted over to her owner who quickly put the treat he was holding into her mouth.

"Objection, your honor!" yelled the prosecutor who had noticed the treat. "Citizen VT-72-85 unfairly used a—"

The Judge interrupted, having had enough of this trial. "Since it has clearly been established that Bufney came to Citizen VT-72-85 on her own free will, I declare this marriage to be valid. However, from here on out, this test will be used to determine consent in all such future marriages. Cased closed."

As the Judge left the courtroom, the chain-reaction of barking began again and Tarro shook his head, laughing to himself. This turned out to be far more entertaining than he had even anticipated. The prosecutor smiled broadly at his fellow defense attorney and gave a mocking salute. Citizen VT-72-85 put a leash on his spouse, and as they left the courtroom, Tarro noticed for the first time how similar the man's shaggy hair was to his dog's.

The next morning, Tarro reported as usual to SD-6's briefing room. He and his fellow Peace Officers were divided amongst twenty divisions and he had been assigned to Division-11. His Division Commander, Peace Officer-16, was a rather pudgy man who was as cold and hard as the winter ice of the Zeenuk Mountains. Tarro loathed these daily task briefings.

After all the officers of Division-11 took their seats, Officer-16 said, "You will receive today's specific tasking from your respective unit commanders. However, we have been tasked by the Kreplin to execute a special mission. We have a team already established but we need two additional volunteers to supplement the team."

Tarro's hand shot up. He didn't know what he was volunteering for, but anything would be better than guard duty in another courtroom, even if it proved to be another entertaining circus like the day before. Officer-16 acknowledged Tarro and another volunteer and dismissed them to report to Special Operations. Tarro smiled, happy to finally be able to do something different, and maybe, just maybe, something actually meaningful.

ೋ

It had been over two years since the loss of the Ferret. Biorn once again sat on his beloved grassy knoll and watched the sun disappear below the horizon. At that moment, the rotation of the city positioned him looking due west at a beautiful array of sunset colors which crept over the silhouetted city skyline and spilled over onto the lake stretched before him. It was if he were sitting in front of a giant fire, basking in its warmth.

Yet, as much as he usually enjoyed this satisfying moment of nature, he was deeply troubled. Ever since the Ferret died, the Libs had ceased operations. They really didn't have a choice since the missions had all hinged on their clandestine friend. But the need for rescues had not stopped. Since the loss of this key asset, the Likbez sirens had sounded no less than four times.

The glow of the sunset slowly faded, giving way to the increasingly bright lights of Avalon. The serenity of incoming nightfall caused Biorn to contemplate his life. He was not an ordinary citizen. Unbeknownst to all except for one other man in Avalon, Biorn was a Barb. The man who knew of Biorn's past was a Kreplin doctor whom Biorn had paid an inordinate sum for Bionet chips to be inserted into his body.

The doctor was loyal to the Kreplin, but fortunately for Biorn, his greater loyalty was to money. The doctor conducted the surgery and created an identity for him, inserting him into the Kreplin database, complete with a fake background and record from Likbez. This enabled Biorn to transition into Avalon as a registered citizen along with a graduating Academy class thirty-five years ago. Last year, Biorn had learned that the doctor had passed away, and so his secret finally died with him.

His previous life as a Barb had been both hard and happy. He didn't really know how grueling their lives had been as Barbs until he'd gotten to Avalon. As a Barb, he had worked in a metal fabrication factory for as long as he could remember. Whether it was mining for Avalon, or farming, or working in their factories, Barbs never moved out of their designated occupation, passing whatever knowledge and experience they possessed onto the next generation to work their trade under the oppressive control of the Kreplin.

As a boy, he worked alongside his father and continued to do so until his father died at the age of forty-three. The average lifespan of a Barb wasn't very long, but Avalon didn't care as long as the quota was met and the birth rate kept pace with the mortality rate. He married shortly after his father's death, and within a year, he and his new bride had a baby girl together. The days working the factory were long, hot, and exhausting, but coming home to his sweet wife and baby girl made every day at work fly by.

An image of his wife flashed in his mind and he thought about the last day he'd seen her. Over the years, he had trained his mind to avoid going there, but he suddenly had an overwhelming desire to see her again so he let his thoughts wander back into the memories.

One day he had returned home from the factory to find his entire village lined up, facing ten Peace Officers. A transport aircraft was parked off to the side with its rear ramp lowered. There were hundreds of Barb villages, but on that day, they were the unlucky ones. Twice a year, the Kreplin would randomly select a village and take from it a handful of Barbs. Some would be publicly executed on trumped up charges while others would be sent to the Center where they would be used to test various cutting-edge medical procedures or the latest vaccination. The Kreplin was determined to avoid a repeat of the Engels-23 virus. The ones executed were the sacrificial lambs to ensure continued compliance of the Barbs. It was cruel but effective.

When he arrived at his village, his worst fears were realized. He watched from a distance as twenty or so of his fellow villagers were pulled from the line and forced up the transport ramp. To his horror he saw his wife and daughter in the group. In blind rage he and several other men rushed the Peace Officers, only to wake up a few hours later from the phaser stun they'd received.

When the subsequent executions occurred, they were broadcasted like always to the villages, each of which possessed a large holographic generator, compliments of the Kreplin. When his wife was publicly executed under the false charge of attempted murder of a Peace Officer, Biorn never imagined he could feel so dead while still alive. His baby girl was only five years old, and he could only assume that she had been sent to the Center.

At first, he was driven by a focused rage with a singular purpose of trying to rescue his daughter. During the years that followed, he had managed to sneak into Avalon on board a transport, steal money from various dockmasters, and pay the doctor who gave him his Avalon identity. Eventually, he accrued enough Colonnade credits to bribe a Peace Officer assigned to the Center into allowing him to see the directory of its Barb occupants. The Peace Officer took his money and then showed him the directory, warning him that the average resident only lasted a few months. When the directory showed that no children were present, whatever part of him was still alive after the loss of his wife died that instant.

Biorn now watched the lake which was beginning to reflect the faint moonlight. Now, he was at peace. It had taken him many years to make peace with it all, but he finally did. He knew he would see his wife and daughter again someday in the afterlife. In the meantime, he would strive to live his life nobly. For him, to live nobly meant protecting the innocent.

His thoughts returned to the Ferret—a little eccentric, but highly effective. He knew the chances of finding another Ferret were slim to none. Ever since the Libs had formed, they had been planning their next phase of rescue operations—rescuing Barbs like his wife and daughter brought into Avalon from the routine raids of the villages. All this planning was put on hold when the Ferret died. They needed another insider, but who? Biorn's thoughts turned to Tarro. A Peace Officer on their side would be a tremendous asset. But was Tarro the one?

Biorn took one more look at the tranquil lake splashed with moonlight. It was time to find out. And if Tarro wasn't able to be turned to their side, it was just as well. If he could save some people while he still had life, great. But if not, he'd just as soon be reunited with his wife anyway.

Chapter 13

Village Raid

T HE PILOT'S VOICE PIERCED through the intercom into the peaceful cabin of the transport aircraft. "Ten minutes out," he said cooly as he put the aircraft into a slow descent.

Sitting comfortably in the forward cabin, Tarro and ten other Peace Officers in black jumpsuits began to casually check their gear and weapons. After a quick check of his phaser, Tarro noted the material of the combat uniform worn for all operations outside the city. He marveled at the rubbery texture, relatively thin and elastic, yet engineered to be as hard as steel, making it virtually impenetrable.

"First time outside the city, Cato?" asked the officer next to Tarro. Peace Officers gave each other nicknames, and it wasn't long before Tarro, always serious and contemplative, earned the name "Cato" after the ancient stoic philosopher.

"Yeah . . . first since the Academy," said Tarro. "What are we doing on this mission anyway?"

"What? Weren't you at the brief?"

"No." Tarro jerked a thumb to his right, pointing to the other Peace Officer from his division. "He and I volunteered because we were told you guys needed a couple more hands. They said we would be briefed airborne."

"Yeah, two of our guys got pulled to escort the Confidant around the city for some monument dedication." The officer smiled slyly. "Whatya bet it's another monument to himself?"

The SRO, or Senior Ranking Officer of the unit sitting in front of them, quickly turned around. After glaring at them for an intense moment, he faced forward again, satisfied that he had communicated a sufficient "shut up."

Getting the clear message that this part of the conversation was off-limits, Tarro returned to his original question. "So what's the mission?"

"A village raid," said the officer matter-of-factly.

Tarro's heart immediately sank. "How many are we arresting?"

"Eighteen."

Tarro was now kicking himself for volunteering. "Did they tell you in the briefing what we're arresting them for?"

"Nope . . . does it really matter, Cato?" He laughed and began checking his phaser.

Tarro turned away from the officer, disgusted by his flippant attitude. They might as well have packed a lunch for a picnic in the park.

The pilot interjected again, "One minute to touchdown."

Tarro put his helmet on and followed the other officers who stood and made their way to the rear of the transport. Upon landing, the rear ramp lowered, and the Peace Officers quickly exited, forming a shoulder-to-shoulder line with phasers drawn.

The SRO stood in front of their single rank as they faced the village before them. The village was larger than Tarro had expected. A network of dirt roads connected what appeared to be hundreds of simple concrete homes. It was an eerie sight, for not a single soul was visible. The only movement came from a strong breeze that captured a large cloud of dust and blew it through a section of homes to their right.

The silence was broken by the SRO who addressed the village. The transport aircraft rebroadcast his voice, blasting it to the village through its external speakers.

"Barbs of Village-58," he said gruffly, "you will assemble in front of me now. You have ten minutes. Anyone who is found hiding will be executed on the spot."

The broadcast was repeated twice, and before it finished echoing through the village, the villagers began spilling out of their homes—men, women, and children, all walking toward the Peace Officers quickly but quietly.

Tarro was stunned. All the Barbs he had seen executed at the Kreplin looked like savages with matted hair, covered in dirt and grime, wearing tattered rags. But these Barbs looked like normal, civilized people.

While they were dressed simply without the extravagant hair styles and clothes common in Avalon, they looked nothing like the savage Barbs he had seen. He watched one pregnant woman hold a baby with her right arm while struggling to pull along a frightened boy with her left hand, attempting to coax the little boy against his instinctive better judgment.

The villagers gathered in several long rows facing the Peace Officers, all wearing somber expressions, most staring at the ground. Watching the scene unfold, Tarro felt his right hand getting sweaty as he gripped his phaser tighter and tighter with growing dread. He noticed the men had positioned themselves in the front rows, many staring straight at the senior officer who stood as still as a statue with his hands clasped behind his back in confident control of his little operation.

"Ten minutes is up!" bellowed the SRO to the village who had formed into twelve long rows. At that moment, an old man appeared from behind a house, struggling to join his fellow villagers. Several of the villagers noticed him shuffling his feet and turned to watch, causing the rest of the village to take notice. As all eyes were now fixed on him, he stumbled and fell to one knee. A young woman broke from the formation of villagers and ran toward him to help, but before she could reach him, a laser pulse shot out from behind her and instantly disintegrated the old man.

"Get back in line villager!" screamed the SRO. The woman quickly returned to the group with a look of shock on her face, her hand over her mouth in an attempt to dam her suppressed sobs.

The SRO holstered his phaser with a chuckle. He turned to Tarro and the other officers and said, "I bet none of you milksops could have made that shot." Several of the officers laughed with him. Tarro wasn't listening. He was preoccupied with the young woman who was now standing at the very end of the back row. As he studied her from a distance, he couldn't help but think of Nya and how trying to help the old man was something she would have done.

"Officers," snapped the SRO, "you already have your tasking. Now execute!" The officers immediately fanned out toward the village. The SRO looked at Tarro and the officer next to him. "You two from Division-11—stand fast and prepare to cuff the prisoners."

Two of the officers made their way over to the Barbs while the others entered the village to check with their scanners for any concealed evaders. Tarro watched as the two officers moved amongst the assembled Barbs, clearly assessing them. After they had inspected the group, they began pulling individuals from their ranks. Every selection elicited a helpless cry or muffled sob from either the one who was yanked out or a loved one left behind.

Within a matter of minutes, a gaggle of eighteen villagers were huddled together between the remaining villagers and the SRO. By now the officers in the village had completed their scan and had taken positions at intervals around the rows of villagers. With weapons drawn, any objection to the Kreplin's operation would be a wasted show of bravado achieving only a swift death.

The two officers who had made the selections bracketed the group of chosen Barbs. They led them toward the landing craft, stopping in front of the SRO. There were three men and fifteen women, most of whom were pregnant. The SRO surveyed the group. "Pretty and preggie—just what the Kreplin likes." He then barked to Tarro and his fellow officer, "Cuffs!"

Tarro begrudgingly approached the group of Barbs who had formed a single column with two of the men in the front and one taking a position in the rear. He wondered if Avalon men would show such chivalry if the tables were turned. Per the SRO's orders, he and the other officer began placing cuffs on their new prisoners. Tarro started in the back of the line and began moving forward. He avoided looking at their faces, afraid of what he might see in their eyes and ashamed to look. But what choice did he have?

As he cuffed each one in turn, he was amazed at their compliance, holding out their hands to be cuffed without resistance. By the time he reached the last one, Tarro's hands were shaking so badly he dropped the cuffs on the ground. He quickly looked around, relieved that none of the other Peace Officers saw it. Then it happened. Before he could catch himself, he looked into the prisoner's face.

She had deep blue eyes, puffy from crying, her face wet from the tears which had been streaming down her face. And that's when it hit him—the full force of what he was participating in—and he froze, her sad blue eyes looking into his visored face. She might as well have thrust a knife into his heart. Still unable to discharge his duties, he looked down at the cuffs in his hands which were now shaking even more violently. Seeing his pending breakdown, she reached out and touched his arm. She then gently took the cuffs from him and locked them onto her own wrists.

"Move them into the transport!" ordered the SRO.

Tarro continued staring at the ground, still too shaken to move. "Officer 43–65, move it!" barked the SRO. He numbly followed the officers and prisoners into the transport. Being the last one up the ramp, he turned to look at the villagers, still standing in their ranks. The ramp began to close, and he found the young woman who had tried to help the old man. The exhaust from the aircraft engines caused her long hair to blow in her face, and just before she disappeared behind the closing ramp, Tarro saw her tuck a loose strand of hair behind her ear.

෧෮

Vera watched from a distance pretending to be on a routine walk with her cat on what was proving to be a beautiful day. The temperature was cool but not cold, and there wasn't a cloud in the sky to obscure the perfectly balanced warmth of the sun. If the circumstances were different, Vera would have enjoyed this walk. But not today.

She watched out of the corner of her eye as a group of Barbs led by several Peace Officers emerged from a building near the landing pad of Sector-1. Although this was the Peace Officer sector, citizens were permitted to move in and out of this district just like all the other sectors of Avalon. Vera intentionally walked her cat here often so that her appearance wouldn't be viewed as abnormal for occasions such as this.

"Hello, Hoth," Vera said to the man she had just called up through her Vizitar.

"Greetings, Vera," replied the man on the other end. Vera had always been fond of Hoth. He was both refined and kind and had the sharpest wit she had ever encountered. Her only beef with him was that she had never been able to get him to notice her beyond being a fellow member of the Libs.

"I'm thinking about going to a new bakery I found here in Sector-1. Just need to finish walking Kinny. Would you care to join me?"

Hoth gave a hearty laugh. "Ahh, your feline felon. The only cat in Avalon who will tolerate being chained like a criminal to a leash. How ever did you get her to comply?"

Vera didn't immediately reply as she took inventory of the group of Barbs. Biorn had asked Hoth and her to conduct reconnaissance on the arrival of this new wave of captives. They needed more information on how the prisoners were transferred into the Kreplin and into the Center. If they were ever to attempt a rescue of these hapless Barbs, they needed to figure out the how and when.

Vera casually looked around, wondering where Hoth was located as he too was supposed to be surveilling the area. She said to her unseen co-worker, "As I was saying, I'd like to go to this bakery this afternoon if you'd care to join me. I had these chocolates which were divine. I just might eat eighteen they're so good."

Today the code name for Barb was chocolate. While "chocolate" was nondescript, "eighteen" was not, and Vera kicked herself for being careless. She hadn't really needed to call Hoth, but she wanted to know that he was there, and more so, for him to know she was there.

"Uhhh, yes, that sounds lovely," said Hoth, also recognizing the carelessness. "I will try to join you later today. I'm busy right now though. Don't eat too much without me." Hoth ended the call.

Vera shook her head at herself, sensing Hoth's shortness with her. She continued to watch as the Barbs and Peace Officers neared Sector-1's transportation center where they would be transported through the FLUXX to either the Kreplin or the Center. The sight of all the pregnant women almost brought her to tears, and it took every ounce of restraint to keep the tears dammed.

⟳

Tarro walked alongside the Barbs as they funneled into a large POD located in Sector-1's transportation facility. This particular Kreplin station was part of the transportation network only accessible by State officials and Peace Officers, serving as the only means of accessing the Kreplin via the FLUXX. The POD was capable of seating fifty-plus people, plenty of space for their eighteen prisoners.

As the prisoners were herded into the POD, the SRO stopped having received a message from the Kreplin. He turned to Tarro and another officer and said gruffly, "You two will be receiving new tasking from SD-6. Exit the building now."

Tarro and the other officer immediately complied and headed back to the entrance. Tarro just wanted to go home and be done with this miserable day. He was relieved to be away from the prisoners who only served to plague his conscience with the crushing weight of the injustice he hated, but in which he was now complicit.

"Officers 592 and 43–65," said the perky voice of SD-6 through Tarro's Vizitar, "you will proceed to the following location." Tarro and the other officer glanced at each other as they simultaneously acknowledged SD-6's mutual tasking. An aerial view of a nearby section of the city appeared through their Vizitars, displaying their position along with the assigned location.

"Mother-6, location received. Proceeding," said Officer 592.

"Copy," replied SD-6. "You will acquire Citizen GB-54–28 and bring the citizen in for questioning." A live video of a tall, slender woman casually walking a cat on a leash appeared in both officers' view.

"Target received," said Officer 592.

Tarro found the word selection of "target" a little curious as the aerial map reappeared.

The woman's location was about half a mile away, and the two officers proceeded rapidly toward the location indicated by the flashing red marker displayed on their moving maps. As they neared the location, Tarro saw the woman approach a nearby POD station located just outside the corner of a large gated private residence belonging to a retired Peace Officer.

"Halt, Citizen GB-54–28!" yelled Officer 592, who began running full speed toward the woman. Tarro followed in trail.

When the woman heard the Peace Officer's order and saw the two officers rushing toward her, she immediately scooped up her cat and turned to enter the POD. The door slid open for her.

"Mother-6, shut down POD-68 now!" shouted Officer 592. The half-opened POD door instantly reversed direction and closed, leaving the woman standing outside holding the cat.

Surprised at the speed of Officer 592, Tarro finally caught up to him, and they both stood in front of the woman.

Officer 592 barked, "Citizen, you will put the animal down and follow us."

The woman slowly stooped down and put the cat on the ground. It purred and nuzzled its furry face into its master's extended hand. The woman stroked the cat's head a few times with her right hand while her left hand extracted the small pill from her pocket.

"Be a good girl, Kinny," she said to the cat. She looked up at the officers, forced a smile, and then popped the pill into her mouth.

Chapter 14

Village Return

T HE CAT SAT SPHINX-LIKE on Tarro's couch and stared at him with an inscrutable expression. She was a rather striking cat with bright green eyes and long, fine, jet-black hair. Tarro sat on the couch opposite her and stared back. They had been studying each other like this for the last hour while Tarro had been wracking his brain for an explanation of the woman's sudden suicide. It had all happened so fast—the collapse on the ground, the discovery of self-induced poisoning, the call into SD-6, and the prompt body disposal by a Kreplin official.

Tarro disliked the official from the moment he showed up. Dressed in a black uniform, he arrived without even the slightest acknowledgement of them, inspected the body, and then incinerated it on the spot. After leaving without saying a word, Tarro surmised that if the Grim Reaper were real, he had just met him.

When Officer 592 left the scene, Tarro was left standing with the woman's cat, sitting on the empty spot where her master previously lay. He didn't particularly care for cats, but after the heart-wrenching events of the day, rescuing an abandoned life seemed like the right thing to do, even if that life left hair all over his couch.

Tarro was still reeling from the events of the day. He'd already been an emotional mess from their raid, but the strange suicide of the woman had thrust him into even deeper inner turmoil. He tried to shut out recollections of the day's events which had been flashing hauntingly in his mind. The cat, who seemed to think she was already queen of the place,

seemed rather unfazed by the loss of her owner and began gingerly licking her royal paws.

For a moment, Tarro wished he could trade places with her. Relief.
He needed relief. His sadness, his anger, his confusion, his questions. It
was as if he were pinned down under an invisible, suffocating boulder
crushing his chest, causing him to gasp for air.

He took another drink of Xcape, a powerful mix of alcohol and
elixirs, a favorite Avalon brew, especially of those craving elusive sleep.
He again checked the time which was getting increasingly blurry—two
or three minutes more before the drink would take its full effect. Soon
the room began to groggily fade, leaving two bright green eyes still staring at him, the last visible things to be swallowed by the darkness of
unconsciousness.

Tarro woke up the next day around 1:00 pm. As far as he could remember, he had never slept in past eight o'clock. Ever. Today was his day
off, but that didn't explain the late wake-up. Rather, it was the two bottles
of Xcape Tarro had drained last night. The most he had ever consumed
was half a bottle, and that was over the course of a whole evening. Last
night he had guzzled the bottles as fast as he could, and now he was paying the price with a piercing, pounding headache that felt like he had an
army of miners pounding the inside of his skull with pickaxes.

He sat up on his living room couch which had been his bed for the
night, groaning with every movement that added a new throbbing to his
head.

"What are you looking at?" he said to the cat who was sitting in the
same place he'd left her last night. The cat jumped off her perch, moseyed
over to Tarro, and rubbed up against his right leg, purring.

"Oh, so you have a heart after all?" Tarro said as he stroked her back.

Nya, his artificial intelligence home manager, spoke up, "Tarro, I see
you have a new friend. Would you like some food and water for it?"

"Yes," said Tarro abruptly.

"Would *you* like anything? I sense you could use some happiness,"
she said sweetly.

"No!" Tarro caught himself. It was just a computer, no need to get
angry. "But you can turn my shower on."

"Usual temperature?"

"No. Make it as cold as you can."

After showering, he fed his new feline roommate and headed to Biorn's cafe. Today was his day off and he was desperate to get out of his quiet home and his own despairing thoughts. Plus, he was hungry.

He arrived at the cafe, sauntered over to his normal table in the corner, and began to brood over the menu, squinting from the table's digital display which seemed abnormally bright. He cradled his throbbing forehead with his hand and swore to himself to never again drink that much Xcape in one sitting.

"You look like jak." Tarro didn't even look up at Biorn who had appeared at his table, but was surprised at his uncharacteristically biting tone.

"I look how I feel," said Tarro.

"Well, that makes two of us."

Tarro looked at Bjorn and, with some difficulty, focused on his face. Biorn just stared at him, and Tarro was taken aback by the look. He had never seen Biorn with such an expression and couldn't decide whether it was a look of sadness or anger.

"What would you like to eat today, Tarro?" Biorn asked blandly.

Tarro looked down and stared at the menu. After a few moments, he said, "I was a part of a Barb raid yesterday." He felt Biorn continue to stare, and it made him uncomfortable. Tarro used his finger to absently flick through the various pages of the menu. "And then to top it all off, I was sent to arrest a woman who then killed herself right in front of me."

The moment he finished his sentence, Biorn turned and abruptly left him without saying a word. A wave of emptiness flooded Tarro, and for a moment, he thought about ordering a glass of Xcape.

☙❧

Biorn headed to his office to compose himself. Hoth had given him the news about Vera last night. Hoth had watched the whole thing go down, and both he and Biorn thought Vera had taken the pill prematurely. Their covert activity of late had simply been the surveillance of captured Barbs from periodic village raids as they were transported into the city. They were discrete, their communication limited and coded. The Kreplin may have had some suspicions of Vera, but Biorn and Hoth thought that she would have likely been released after any questioning. But Vera knew the risk. If the Kreplin decided to use their more extreme forms of interrogation, including the use of various drugs, she was likely to spill secrets, putting every Lib in grave danger.

Biorn respected her sacrificial decision, but that didn't make it any more tolerable. He thought his own mood was pretty foul until Tarro entered. The officer's despondency seemed to eclipse his own. He quickly sized up Tarro and his revelation of both the raid and Vera. Tarro's aversion to it all was obvious and now was the time to take their relationship to another level. It was time to refocus on the real work of rescuing the innocent. Vera's precious life would not be wasted.

Biorn reappeared next to Tarro. "Decide on anything yet?"

"No," Tarro said glumly.

"Why don't you take a look at the 'New Entree' section." Biorn quickly typed something into the pad he held which was connected to Tarro's digital menu. "I would recommend the Justice Scramble. I think you will like it."

Tarro searched for the item on the menu. As soon as he found it, he saw the words *Do you think the raid was wrong?* appear below the listed entree. He shot a surprised glance at Biorn whose face was expressionless. He looked back down at the menu. The question had disappeared. Biorn typed again, and the following appeared: *Tap finger once for yes, twice for no.*

As soon as Tarro read it, the cryptic communication disappeared again. He thought for a moment, wondering where this was going. Without looking up, he tapped his finger once on the table.

Do you want to do something about it?

Biorn had hoped for a positive response to this second question and was pleased by the quick single finger tap which Tarro gave without hesitation. "Tarro, I'm closing the cafe a little early today. Why don't you come over to my place for dinner?"

Chapter 15

Barbarians

Tarro glanced over at the small joystick located between himself and the pilot of their two-man patrol aircraft, the PX-35, affectionately referred to as "the Hummer," due to its fast and nimble flight characteristics shared by the hummingbird. The pilot, who deftly operated the joystick controlling their sprightly aircraft, was Peace Officer 25–73, otherwise known as "Snakejak." He was one of the best PX-35 pilots but was also a real jerk with a proclivity for seeking advancement by running over fellow Peace Officers.

For weeks after his visit to Biorn's home, Tarro had begged his unit commander to put him on patrol duty. The Peace Officer Corps possessed two squadrons of PX-35's which they flew routinely on patrol sorties in the Barb territory.

The expansive collection of Barb villages were assembled into twenty regions, its cumulative size equating to a small country. Each region was separated by a highly secure wall. The wall and routine patrols ensured that the Barbs stayed in their villages and kept their noses to the grind. The Barbs complied, gathering their daily required quotas of various harvested and mined natural resources and manufactured products to be picked up by the SC-5 aircraft sent daily to their respective regions.

These cargo ships continuously arrived at staggered intervals in the Barb regions, and it was the patrolling Peace Officers' duty to ensure the whole operation ran smoothly. Avalon was to be kept fat and happy. But

Tarro didn't care about any of this. He had other reasons for getting on patrol duty.

Trees lining the Avalon River flashed by the Hummer's windscreen in a green blur as Snakejak flew their Hummer just above the water of the river, racing it south through the Hanni Valley toward Lake Vessi. Tarro didn't like flying at this unnecessarily low altitude, but he knew that voicing any objection would only make his spiteful pilot fly even lower.

The only thing Tarro cared about was getting back to Village-58, the location of the raid, and that's precisely where they were heading. He would have preferred different circumstances due to the nature of their assigned task for today's sortie, but it was the price of patrol duty. Not only did he want to learn more about the Barbs, but he wanted to see her again—the young woman who reminded him of Nya.

"Watch this, Cato," said Snakejak as he jammed the throttle forward, pushing Tarro back into his seat with the acceleration. "Think I can make that turn at 400 knots?" Tarro didn't respond. He knew the crazy pilot was going to attempt it no matter what he said. Up ahead, the river entered a canyon and then took a sharp turn to the right, disappearing from view behind the canyon walls lining the river.

They continued to careen along river's surface. The bend rapidly approached, the canyon walls quickly growing in height on either side of them. Tarro suddenly felt quite trapped and claustrophobic as the canyon walls and shadows engulfed them. Just before the bend, Snakejak banked hard right, putting the Hummer into a level, violent right hand turn in an attempt to follow the river through the canyon. The sudden onset of g-forces slammed Tarro further into his seat, and he felt himself growing faint as the blood rushed from his head toward his feet.

Midway through the turn, Snakejak realized he had too much speed to make it. He quickly leveled the aircraft and pulled back on the joystick putting the aircraft into a steep climb. The left canyon wall instantly filled the windscreen as they rocketed upward, barely clearing the wall's ledge. Once clear, he pulled the aircraft into a tight loop, gaining speed on the backside of the loop as they zoomed inverted back toward the river below them. With the ground quickly approaching, he snap-rolled the aircraft upright and, moments before hitting the water, pulled up, bringing the aircraft level a few feet above the river's surface, just on the other side of very canyon section which almost killed them.

He turned to Tarro and, referring back to his original *Think I can I make it?* question, said with a smirk, "I guess not."

Tarro silently cursed the stupidity of his pilot as the blood slowly returned to his fuzzy head.

They continued their more benign flight along the river toward Village-58, and Tarro reflected on his recent visit to Biorn's home. Throughout the evening they had engaged in casual conversation until Biorn did something extraordinary. While they were conversing, he wrote a small hand-written note on a digital tablet for Tarro to read. It was risky due to their Bionets and the Kreplin's ability to monitor what a citizen saw and heard at any moment, but it was a necessary explanation for what Biorn did next. With Tarro's approval, Biorn took a syringe and inserted a tiny chip into Tarro's right eye.

The tiny chip was an invention of Biorn's which all the Libs possessed. While it functioned independently of the Bionet, it hacked into the individual's personal Vizitar, allowing fellow chip wearers to communicate silently with typed text. Within minutes of the insertion, Tarro and Biorn were messaging one other through their Vizitars, undetectable to the Kreplin. Biorn called it the Lib Net, and it was a brilliant invention. The only limitation was its relatively short range, requiring Libs to be within close proximity to each other in order to use the covert network.

With Biorn now freely able to communicate with Tarro, it was a stunning night of enlightenment for the young officer. He learned more about the Barbs and how they were far from the savage barbarians depicted by Avalon. Biorn explained why the Kreplin raided the villages, but Tarro already knew it was to keep them from revolting by reminding them of who was in control.

What he couldn't figure out was why so many pregnant women were selected, and he was shocked by Biorn's explanation. In part, the capture of pregnant mothers inflicted the most pain on their communities. But the more astonishing reason involved their placentas. The placentas were valued for their supposed benefits to healthy vigor, and Avalon citizens would pay the Kreplin obscene amounts to get their hands on them. These purchased placentas would usually be used as nourishment centerpieces for debauched dinner parties celebrating Mother Earth.

The night with Biorn had certainly been illuminating. He knew Biorn was being careful in what he told him and he suspected the man knew far more. Tarro was, after all, a Peace Officer of the Kreplin, so he decided not to push it and let Biorn inform him at his own pace.

By now the pilot had climbed to a higher altitude, and various villages began to appear below them. The moving map projected on the

Hummer's front windscreen indicated that they were one mile from Village-58. The close proximity of the village made Tarro painfully aware of what they were about to do, and he loathed it.

When Village-58 came into view, the Hummer descended and decreased its approach speed, arriving on the north edge of the village. Snakejak placed the aircraft into a hover about twenty feet off the ground. There was little activity since most villagers were working in their assigned food packaging factory.

"Release the package," said Snakejak.

Tarro reluctantly pushed the button on the panel to his right. The Hummer jerked slightly from the release of the small container which fell to the ground.

"Let's see what happens," said the pilot as he slowly reversed the hovering Hummer to a position about a hundred yards from the drop zone.

The package was a gift from the Kreplin. The pregnant women taken to Avalon in the last raid experienced the immediate fate of all other such captives—forced abortions. The remains of the aborted babies were then bundled into containers which were always returned to the home villages of the women via similar container deliveries. Yet another reminder of who was in charge.

Tarro and the pilot watched and waited. At first, nothing happened. But after a few minutes, about a dozen villagers emerged, mostly older men and women with a handful of younger children. The assembled group encircled the container and looked down on it in silence, ignoring the hovering aircraft in the distance. The last person to join them was a very frail old lady who hobbled over to them and then collapsed on the ground, her upper body and arms draped over the container.

Tarro wondered if she had fainted until he saw her rise to her knees, fold her hands in front of her chest, and look high up into the sky. The movement of her mouth suggested she was vocalizing something, and he wished he could hear what she was saying. When she finished speaking toward the sky, the rest of the group joined hands, forming an unbroken circle around the container with the old lady still kneeling on the ground, now with her head bowed.

When the group appeared to start talking in unison, Snakejak said, "Let's see what they're saying." He flipped a switch on the cockpit dashboard and aimed the Hummer's directional microphones toward the group.

"What is *that*?" Snakejak asked incredulously as the sound of sing-ing filled their cockpit.

"Singing," said Tarro.

"What?"

Tarro, mesmerized by what he was watching, didn't answer. He hadn't heard what Nya had called "singing" since her captivating performance at the Academy and hadn't considered the absence of singing in Avalon until Snakejak's reaction. Heart-broken over what he was watching and sickened by his own contribution as a Peace Officer to this travesty, he wondered if all Barbs sang like this. These Barbs clearly knew what was in the container. Eighteen of their own had been unjustly arrested, most of whom were pregnant women. The Kreplin then dropped into their laps what was left of their dead babies as a final gesture of tyrannical control . . . and they sing.

"What a bunch of freaks," muttered Snakejak. He flipped the switch, turning off the microphone, and banked the Hummer to the right to re-turn to Avalon.

The flight back was significantly less eventful as they maintained a higher cruising altitude. Tarro was grateful that his pilot didn't feel an-other urge to test the flight capabilities of their little Hummer. Yet the quiet and peace in the cockpit violently clashed with the clamorous noise and unrest in Tarro's heart.

These Barbs mystified him. The singing actually sounded somewhat happy given the circumstances, and if not happy, at least content. But how could they sound so peaceful in light of the hand they had been dealt? Some of their future children lay dead in a box at their feet. Why in the world would they sing? He could have sworn he saw two of them even smile at each other while singing. *Impossible*, he thought. *There was absolutely nothing to smile about.*

When they arrived at Avalon, Snakejak landed the Hummer on Sector-1's pad. As the engines spooled down, the pilot exited the aircraft, leaving Tarro sitting in his seat. He stared out the windscreen observing Hanni Valley and the northern edge of Lake Vessi in the distance, the rest of which disappeared into the hazy horizon. The knowledge of the Barbs beyond the lake now caused anguishing questions to swirl like a brewing storm in his heart. One thing was now clear though. These "barbarians" were anything but.

Chapter 16

Rescue Recruit

A GENTLE BREEZE WHISPERED THROUGH the brilliantly colored leaves, stirring them just enough to bring a pleasant rustle to the ears of Biorn. Sitting on his customary grassy knoll with his back to an elm tree, he soaked in the sight—vibrant red, orange, and yellow leaves everywhere, in the trees, on the ground, and an armada of them floating on the lake's edge.

He closed he eyes and ran his hands over the soft grass, savoring the cool breeze and this exquisite gift of creation. He sighed longingly. Someday, in eternity, he would enjoy an even better version of this. He opened his eyes and saw the spires of the Kreplin looming above the tree line in the distance. But not today. Today there was work to do, and this delicious taste of the afterlife would have to remain an appetizer.

His mind raced over recent events. The death of Vera had been a depressing loss to the Libs. It was so unnecessary. If only she had been more careful with her words, she would still be alive walking that silly cat. Biorn shoved the thoughts from his mind. It was done, and nothing could reverse it. If there was any good that came out of her death, it was the reminder that the game they were playing was a dangerous one. They were all up for the risks, but they needed to avoid the unnecessary ones.

The bright spot in all this was the recent acquisition of a powerful ally. Well, not quite a full-blown ally yet, but Biorn was sure that he soon would be. Biorn considered the progress he was making with Tarro. Tarro had been over to his home three times now, and each time, Biorn divulged more on the Kreplin and its evils. Happily, Tarro was always in full agreement.

Hoth had cautioned him to take it slow. After all, Tarro was a Peace Officer and a potential spy for the Kreplin who was always on the prowl for rebels to the State. Biorn embraced the wisdom of Hoth's counsel, but he knew Tarro was on their side. He could see it when they communicated secretly in his home, an intense hatred for the Kreplin that visibly burned in the officer's eyes.

Biorn had been considering how to crack the nut of rescuing captured Barbs brought into the city. After years of surveillance, the Libs still weren't exactly sure where they were taken after entering Sector-1's transportation facility. Now that Tarro was on board, he'd been able to fill in the knowledge gaps.

From the transportation facility, the Barbs were taken to a secure wing of the Center. After initial screening, the most healthy and attractive Barbs were separated and sent to the Kreplin for further processing to be converted into personal attendants for various officials. Some were later sent to be executed, and the rest remained at the Center as the Kreplin's lab rats. These eventually died through the testing process or were simply killed off when their usefulness was expended.

Once at the Kreplin, a rescue was virtually impossible as the Kreplin was impregnable. And once they were admitted to the Center's secure wing for testing, no one knew of its operations other than the select few medical officials who had access to this sinister and very secure section of the Center.

Tarro confirmed that access was virtually impossible and a rescue from this secure wing was out of the question. The best and only opportunity for a rescue was during the captives' initial screening. This took place for several days in a holding area adjacent to the secure testing wing. While there, the Barbs were held in various cells, and security was relatively light with only two Peace Officers guarding its entrance located in the lobby of the Center.

While this small window provided an opportunity for a rescue, there were several massive hurdles. Biorn gazed again at the Kreplin in the distance and found himself cursing its existence. The primary problem they had was that every member of the Libs was a citizen of Avalon which meant they all had a Bionet. Every movement was tracked, and any unauthorized entry into the Center or out of the city would trigger Kreplin alarms. Even with Tarro on board, they needed another Ferret.

Biorn was confident that if he were able to get outside the city, he would be able to find several young Barb men more than willing and eager to fill the Ferret's shoes. But he had no way of getting outside the city undetected. The other big hurdle was the rescue itself. Even if they were able to find a way to break the Barbs out of their cells at the Center, they then had to figure out how to get them out of the city and to do it very quickly with the Kreplin likely in hot pursuit.

That's why Biorn desperately needed Tarro. He was the key, the perfect solution to recruiting a Barb to be the next Ferret. Plus, he could maneuver unimpeded in the Center as a Peace Officer. Biorn considered the recently captured Barbs and his heart sank. There was no hope for them. But maybe, just maybe, they would be ready for the next group of captives.

ᘉᕥ

Once again Tarro found himself clenching his seat with a death grip as he watched the tops of trees race past just below the PX-35. He looked over at Snakejak who had the throttles full forward at max power. If there was ever the face of a madman, his pilot had it.

Tarro had worked hard to get on the patrol rotation. That was the good news. The bad news was that he had been partnered once again with this psychopath. He had now spent almost three weeks on daily patrols with him, and Tarro was convinced that he was not only a safety-averse flyboy, he was also the biggest scoundrel who made his old nemesis Gront look like a saint.

"Have you peed your pants yet?" Snakejak asked after hearing the top of a tall tree brush the bottom of their patrol aircraft. Tarro ignored the jerk.

They landed in Region-9 just outside of Village-43, one of ten villages responsible for producing and packaging beef. These villages surrounded a giant complex that housed both the packaging facility and the laboratories which produced the lab-grown meat. Each region of Barb villages was overseen by a governor, himself a Barb. These governors were richly paid by the Kreplin, and between the twenty governors, they operated like a corrupt mafia. Region-9's governor, identified as G-9 by the Kreplin, claimed that the meat production plants were experiencing sporadic genetic abnormalities in their labs which was forcing them to discard too many batches to keep up with the Kreplin quota.

Snakejak and Tarro were tasked with validating the problem and ascertaining whether the Barbs were being inefficient and lazy or if G-9's assertion was valid. While the Kreplin controlled the Barbs directly through these regional governors, it had learned early on to temper its tyranny over the Barbs. The Kreplin controlled them with an iron fist but knew that squeezing too hard would yield an unhealthy level of despair. Too much despair and one might be tempted to give up on life. But too much freedom and one might feel inclined to revolt against the tyranny. It was a fragile house of cards which the Kreplin aggressively micro-managed. The prosperity of Avalon depended on it.

Snakejak and Tarro put their helmets on and exited the aircraft. Tarro didn't particularly care for these helmets which were required to be worn at all times outside Avalon. As standard Peace Officer gear, they provided protection from disease along with a slew of tactical functionalities. Tarro was convinced, however, that the main reason for their existence was simply to intimidate the Barbs. A Peace Officer wearing a helmet with a dark visor was simply more ominous.

When Snakejak and Tarro exited the patrol craft, they were greeted by G-9.

"Snakejak, my friend, it's been too long," said G-9 as he gripped the pilot's hand.

"Yes, G-9 it has been—"

"How many times do I have to tell you to call me Kivv."

Snakejak grunted with a smirk and said, "G-9, you know why we're here. Let's get on with it."

"Come. Come to my place first. We'll have a drink before we get down to business."

Tarro instantly disliked G-9. He was well-dressed compared to the simply clothed Barbs of the village. He exuded sliminess and corruption and Tarro wondered how a fellow Barb could betray his brethren by serving as a puppet of the Kreplin and an arm of their oppression. Tarro watched as the two headed for G-9's residence where the governor would no doubt pull out all the stops to cull favor with the Peace Officer whose report could effect his quality of life. Governors were expendable and replaceable, and they knew it. Consequently, each worked vigorously to stay in the Kreplin's good favor, even if it meant sucking up to a visiting Peace Officer.

Tarro's task was to meet with the lab officials to receive their report and evaluate the supposed genetic abnormalities experienced by the meat factory. Glad to be rid of these two representatives of human degeneracy, Tarro made his way to the factory. By now, he had visited several villages, but he had never been inside a Barb manufacturing facility.

He began heading to the facility, walking down the main road that cut through the village. Both sides of the dirt road were lined with similar-looking, simple concrete block homes. He stopped in front of one and studied it for a moment. It was very plain with one door and two open windows in the front. Two chairs surrounded by a variety of potted plants sat on its petite front porch. To the right of the porch was a tidy little garden of vegetables and flowers surrounded by a small rustic fence. Tarro wondered how an Avalon citizen would react to living in what would no doubt be considered a squalid prison.

He was about to continue down the road when the door to the house swung open. A young boy burst through the doorway and launched himself off the edge of the porch, tumbling onto the ground a few feet in front of Tarro. After the boy sprang to his feet, he saw the officer and froze. He was smeared with dirt from head to toe, and his bright blue eyes gleamed through the grime at the Peace Officer unexpectedly standing outside his home. Tarro didn't move, curious to see what this dirty bundle of energy would do. After a brief moment, the boy bounded over to Tarro.

"Mister officer, what's your name?" he asked as he began jumping around him. Tarro didn't say anything, amused by the child. Children were rarely, if ever, seen in Avalon as they were raised at HDC. Avalon's Human Development Center and the Academy were kept separated, and the only times Tarro could recall seeing young children at the Academy were the occasional HDC groups that passed through the school on their field trips.

The boy stopped momentarily in front of Tarro. "I saaaaaid, what's your name?"

"My name is—"

"Hey, can you stand on your head? Watch this!" Not waiting for Tarro's answer, the boy put his head and hands on the ground and flipped his legs up, promptly causing him to tumble over onto his back. His backside had barely touched the ground before he had bounced up to begin another attempt.

Tarro chuckled. "I now see why you attract so much dirt, little man."

Tarro was watching the boy repeatedly fall onto his back while trying to stand on his head when an older woman appeared at the door and called out, "Gonny, get over here now!"

The boy froze as if standing still would make him invisible.

"Gonny, I said get over here!"

"Mister Officer," whispered the boy. "Do you have any food? I'm hungry."

The question caught Tarro off guard. If his helmet was designed to intimidate Barbs, it certainly was not having its intended effect on this boy.

The older lady made her way over to Gonny as it was clear the boy was going to require a more hands-on approach to facilitate compliance. She grabbed Gonny's hand, keeping her eyes averted from the Peace Officer.

"Why is he hungry?" asked Tarro. The lady paused, keeping her eyes on the ground as if her hopes to avoid engagement with the Peace Officer had been dashed. She wore a simple tan tunic tied at the waist with a rope-like belt. Her curly gray hair framed a gentle face lined with the wrinkles of age.

Finally, she looked up at Tarro. "Because he hasn't eaten since yesterday," she said as she turned to head back to the house.

"Wait!" She dutifully stopped and turned again to face the Peace Officer. "I'm sorry, I didn't mean to shout at you," said Tarro. The lady looked quizzically at him, surprised by the apology. He then asked with as much disarming kindness as he could muster, "Why hasn't he eaten since yesterday?"

The old lady smiled faintly and looked down at Gonny with pity. "Because that's the life of a barbarian."

The remark cut Tarro to his core. He could feel his anger swelling as he considered all the false Barb characterizations he had been indoctrinated with over the years.

"Where are the boys parents?" Tarro asked.

"The boy's father is no more. Now, if you would permit, I would like to take young Gonny in to take a bath." Tarro sensed her nervousness at the direction the conversation was going.

"What about his mother?" asked Tarro.

She hesitated and then finally said, "She works in the plant."

"What's her name?"

The old lady looked straight at him. "Peace Officer, I've lived a long life. I do not fear the Kreplin. But please—please—for the sake of this boy, we do not want any trouble."

"I'm not here to give you trouble," Tarro said as convincingly as he could. "I only asked for her name."

She looked down at the ground again. "Her name is Kat . . . Kat or B9–43-29–51."

Tarro knew it was a lie. While they had been talking, he had run the old lady's face through the Kreplin's facial recognition database. While not every Barb was registered in this database, many were. The old lady popped up in the system, and he saw that she was the grandmother of this boy and the mother of a woman actually named Meena, or B9–43-82–34.

Tarro looked down at the boy and said, "Little boy—"

"My name is Gonny!"

"Yes, Gonny . . . keep working on that headstand." Tarro left them and headed for plant. He didn't blame her for lying. She was just trying to protect her daughter from trouble and unnecessary interaction with a Peace Officer.

The database informed him that Meena worked in the packaging department of the plant. The plant was a massive and highly automated complex which, like all the other Barb production facilities, was constructed by Avalon. After entering through the decontamination chamber required for all entrants, Tarro headed straight for the packaging department. The laboratory inspection would have to wait.

The facility was spotless. Everywhere robots busily cleaned, keeping the floors sparkling white. All the Barb workers wore white full-body suits with hoods to ensure all possible contaminates were kept from the packaged meat so as to protect the Avalon citizens from any pollutants.

Tarro found the floor supervisor. "Where is B9–43-82–34?"

The Barb supervisor looked nervous. A Peace Officer in the plant looking for one of his workers did not bode well for anyone.

"Uh . . . let me . . . let me check the schedule, sir," mumbled the supervisor. Tarro could see his hand shaking as he fumbled with the electronic pad he held, and he cursed the helmet he was required to wear which seemed to intimidate everyone except little boys. After perusing the schedule, the floor supervisor scanned the packaging floor and pointed out Meena.

Tarro slowly made his way toward her. She was working a control box that operated a conveyor belt. Wrapped pieces of meat on the conveyer passed in front of her on their way into another machine that efficiently packaged them into neat individual boxes.

Her back was to him as he approached her, and he could see through her clear hood her auburn hair neatly pulled back into a pony-tail. He cleared his throat, not quite sure why he felt a twinge of nervousness. "Excuse me, Meena."

She turned and instantly went wide-eyed upon seeing the Peace Officer standing behind her. "Yes? Sir?" she replied.

Tarro wasn't sure if she was more shocked to see a Peace Officer behind her or to hear an officer use her actual name.

Considering her boy he'd just met, he was surprised at how young she looked, certain that she could not have been any older than twenty. She had large, almond-shaped brown eyes. They could have been rather beautiful, but instead, they looked dull, sad, and just plain tired.

At that moment, Tarro realized he hadn't planned what he was going to say to her. He looked around as if inspecting her work. "How long have you been working here?"

She quickly glanced to her right and left, wondering why she had been singled out. Was this an inspection? Was she not meeting the quota? Her mind raced to explain the Peace Officer's presence. "I—I have been working here since I was fifteen."

"How long ago was that?"

She fidgeted nervously. "I guess . . . about five years."

"How often do you work during the week?"

"Six days."

"You've been working six days a week since you were fifteen?" Tarro asked incredulously.

"Yes. Yes, I have."

Tarro knew he shouldn't have been surprised, but he was. What a meager existence. He felt the familiar anger rising up in him. "I'm sorry."

Meena was caught off guard but was instantly intrigued by this Peace Officer's apology. "Sorry for what?"

"For everything." Tarro fished a small package from his pocket. The package contained emergency rations, enough compressed calories to sustain a man for a week. He held it out for Meena. "Give this to Gonny. He's hungry."

Chapter 17

Justice Day

T HE SUN BEAT DOWN on COMCIRC with unusual intensity. It was
July 10th, and so far in the year 2498, this was the hottest day on record. Tarro felt his temperature-controlled uniform working overtime to
keep him cool. The misery of the abnormally scorching heat matched the
wretchedness of the day, at least from Tarro's perspective. It was Justice
Day, but unlike the dread experienced by Tarro, the city was vibrating
with excitement.

Earlier in the morning, Tarro had received a brief report on the accused. The report was concise: "Business owner, age 23, failed to pay lawful taxes to the Kreplin for the last two years. Citizen has defied the sound
laws of Avalon and stolen from its law-abiding citizens and is therefore
guilty of sedition against the Kreplin." Tarro dreaded what was about to
happen. This business owner would be made into an example through
swift Kreplin brutality. It would be the main event, but he was dreading
the prelude even more so.

Tarro's morning report also included the following: "The trial of this
Avalon citizen will be preceded by a trial of five Barbs." Tarro was still
seething from the use of the sterilized word "trial" used to describe what
would simply be an execution.

Tarro took a position in the middle of his assigned Sector-11 amid the
crowd which was getting antsy for the trials to begin. All the citizens were
present in their respective sectors of COMCIRC, a sea of people encircling

the Kreplin. Finally, the great double doors leading out to the Kreplin's expansive balcony opened, eliciting a raucous ovation from the crowd.

Tarro was tasked along with other Peace Officers to mill about the crowd for the purpose of providing security and maintaining order. As security was rarely a problem, he knew they were there, more than anything else, to provide a visual reminder to the citizens of the power and ubiquitous presence of the Kreplin.

Through the ornate double doors emerged three Peace Officers in helmets. Normally, the helmets were only worn outside Avalon. Trials were the exception. The three Peace Officers fanned out, taking positions on the left, right, and center of the circular-shaped balcony. Upon reaching the edge of the balcony, they pivoted smartly in unison to face the double-doors. The crowd anticipated this customary beginning to Justice Day trials and began shouting "Barb" repeatedly and in unison. The spectacle had begun.

The beckoning chant finally had its intended result as five Barbs were led out onto the balcony by ten more Peace Officers, each carrying a chivvy. Tarro inwardly scoffed at the excessive show of force—as if ten Peace Officers were necessary to ensure these "savages" were contained. Tarro's irritation quickly turned to sadness as he observed the Barbs, no doubt captured from the recent raid he had participated in.

The prisoners truly did look like savages, covered in grime, their hair mangled and matted. They wore garments that were as dirty as they were tattered. They stood shoulder-to-shoulder with their hands and feet bound, the restraints on their feet providing just enough slack to allow them to shuffle across the balcony. These were the savage, wild animals known as Barbs. The Kreplin's costume and make-up department had once again outdone themselves in transforming these peaceful, civilized Barbs to visually match the Barb caricature the Kreplin perpetuated.

Tarro's heart broke as he watched. Four of the five were women, and he wondered if the Barb who hand-cuffed herself during his raid was in their midst. He remembered her gentle face and compassionate eyes.

He turned away from the scene and began walking with his back to the balcony. He couldn't watch, and it took every ounce of his effort to control his boiling anger. The crowd continued to chant, calling for their deaths, and it dawned on Tarro that there were, in fact, savages present, but they weren't on the balcony. Still with his back to the Kreplin, Tarro looked with disgust at the elated faces of the citizens, pampered prima donnas who neither knew what kind of people these Barbs really were, nor would likely care even if they did.

He meandered through the crowd which erupted into cheers at various moments. He knew each eruption corresponded to an execution, each of which was being staggered at long enough intervals to draw out the spectacle, but short enough to avoid testing the patience of the crowd, hungry for so-called justice. He stewed over the ignominious designation of "Justice Day," for there was nothing just about this.

After the fifth explosion of applause and cheering, Tarro glanced back at the balcony to see the five dead bodies being dragged back into the Kreplin through the double doors. The Supreme Confidant Talin had not yet appeared. This part of Justice Day was beneath him. The real pageantry was about to begin. Tarro looked for Biorn, knowing that, as a citizen of Sector-11, he was somewhere in the vicinity and Tarro craved some sanity.

SD-6 chirped in his ear, "Officer 43–65, status report."

Masking disdain, he replied in a professional tone, "Sector-11 secure."

"Mother-6 copies, 43–65. Peace and love."

Tarro was still looking for Biorn when Talin emerged onto the balcony, draped in a crimson robe trimmed with elegant patterns of inset silver cord. An orb hovered near his face, broadcasting large holographic images of him to locations all throughout COMCIRC. He took a long look into the orb, allowing it to project his beaming face to the people. The gold cord that weaved through his hair produced the appearance of a crown, a symbol of the singular power by which he ruled over Avalon.

With choreographed precision, Talin raised his hands to the crowd and said, pausing after each word for effect, "Welcome . . . citizens . . . of . . . Avalon!" A new wave of excited cheers rose from the crowd. Various instruments trumpeted Avalon's anthem while brilliantly colored flashes peppered the sky. The cheering crescendoed to a fevered pitch as thousands of gold and royal blue silk streamers began to descend from the sky above COMCIRC. The citizens scrambled over each other, attempting to capture the valuable streamers, each of which could be exchanged to the Kreplin for a month of Collonade credits.

Once the streamers had landed and been collected, the music stopped and the Supreme Confidant greeted the crowd, "Welcome, my friends." He slowly scanned the crowd, pausing for effect. "Today it saddens me to have to tell you that we have discovered a traitor to Avalon."

The crowd let out a collective groan of disapproval. "I love this city. I love you all. I love our way of life. But this city, this life, you yourselves, dear friends, must be protected. This is my duty. But this is my privilege."

Tarro could hardly stomach the pompous speech. He tried to tune it out and continued to look for Biorn. He was relieved to finally locate his friend who was unsurprisingly dressed in black, a stark contrast to the sea of festive, bright colors displayed in the extravagant clothing, make-up, and accessories adorning the assembled citizens.

When the rebel was finally revealed, the crowd burst into another ovation. And that's when the wave of nausea hit Tarro, for the young man was his Academy classmate and fellow Peace Officer, Klon. Feelings of nausea were quickly replaced by rage as the rest of the trial unfolded in a dizzying blur—the accusation against Klon of sedition against the Krep-lin; the charges brought against his wife; the ridiculous performance of her companion droid to save her own skin; and of course, the merciless executions. The final punch in the gut was the wretched promotion he received from SD-6 due to the elimination of Klon. He was now Peace Officer 43–64. Never had his hatred for the Kreplin been greater.

After the executions, the citizens began to dissipate and the world came into focus for Tarro. He glared angrily at the opulent Kreplin, a symbol of power that, like a giant leech, sucked the life out of countless individuals to keep its slimy, fat existence alive. In that moment, a wave of calm swept over Tarro as the rage gave way to a settled new clarity, a new purpose in life. *I will work my way into the belly of the beast*, he thought. *And then I will end it. I will end it all.*

❧

Tarro stood outside the operations department of SD-6. The sun had just disappeared behind the Zeenuk Mountains but was still manifest-ing its presence by making the bottom of the clouds above it burn like smoldering fires, producing a vibrant panoply of orange, red, and purple hues. Tarro didn't notice this beauty. In ten minutes his shift would end and he would go home, leaving behind this utterly dark and miserable Justice Day.

The moment of calm he experienced in COMCIRC with his newly affirmed purpose hadn't lasted long, and soon the familiar emotional storm clouds of his heart had re-formed. They were heavier and darker than they had ever been, and he was both weary and scared of them. He felt as if unseen forces were carrying him to edge of a great precipice, a ledge which overlooked an abyss of darkness, a great void of ruin and terrifying unknowns. He felt the precipice nearing, and having no power to stop its encroachment, panic began to rise.

"Cato!" Tarro turned to the familiar voice, frankly the last voice he wanted to hear at the moment, though he was glad for the distraction.

Snakejak walked over to him. "Just got word from OPS that we launch at 0600 tomorrow with two other patrol units. A pack of Mutts has apparently been harassing one of our production facilities."

"Great," Tarro muttered. He was considering the possibility of calling in sick later that night when SD-6 broke into his contemplation.

"Officer 43–64, Mother-6."

"Go ahead, Mother-6."

"We have a situation at Nexus-56 in Sector-5. Depart immediately and join Officer 10–32 outside the building. You will be briefed with more specifics en route. Peace and love."

Tarro replied numbly, "Copy, Mother-6. En route now." Tarro fumed at the new tasking so close to the end of his shift.

Within minutes he arrived outside Nexus-56, one of the many housing complexes in Sector-5. Officer 10–32 was already there waiting for him. They didn't say anything. They didn't need to. Both had received the brief from SD-6 including the location of citizen TY-15–85 and the order to arrest him and bring him to SD-6's detention center. They were not given an explanation for the arrest. They never were. They were given their orders, and nothing else was needed.

The two Peace Officers quickly entered Nexus-56, a cylindrically shaped building possessing fifty floors. They entered the expansive lobby and headed to the elevator hub located in its center. The circular lobby stretched upward past all fifty floors, creating a voluminous space. Its large elevator column containing twelve individual shafts passed through the lobby's center, rising to the fiftieth floor. The elevator shafts were constructed almost entirely of translucent glass through which brilliant white light coursed, radiating from light sources on the ground floor. The light beamed upward through the glass elevator column and refracted through its many bevels and edges, splashing a spectacular pattern onto the cylindrical wall of the fifty-story lobby.

The floors possessed circular balconies overlooking the lobby providing access to the front doors of the residences. Every balcony was connected to the central elevator column by twelve glass walkways configured like spokes on a wheel. Each floor's set of spoked walkways sat slightly offset from the one above it, creating an architectural helical pattern, causing the fifty floors of walkways to look like a DNA strand.

Normally, as an appreciator of Avalon's countless architectural wonders, Tarro would have taken notice of the stunning design of Nexus-56. But not tonight. They entered one of the elevators and Tarro glumly commanded it to the thirty-seventh floor. The glass elevator shot smoothly upward as Tarro studied the current data provided by SD-6.

"Officers 10–23 and 43–64, confirm receipt of schematic," said the voice of SD-6.

Through his Vizitar, Tarro took a quick look at the schematic which depicted the floor plan of the residence of the citizen to be arrested. The diagram showed two red dots representing human beings real time. Both were present in the living room and relatively stationary. The flashing dot represented the citizen to be arrested. Tarro focused first on the static dot and an information graphic appeared describing citizen MP-83–90 as a married woman, age 38. He shook his head at the fact that they pretended to be in a genderless society, but when it came down to it, gender was still needed, if only to allow for the arrest of the right person.

The flashing dot provided an info graphic detailing the following: "CITIZEN TY-15–85, MALE, SECTOR-16 JUDGE, MARRIED TO MP-83–90." Tarro shot a nervous glance to the other officer who returned the look, having just read the same description through his own Vizitar.

Being higher in rank, Officer 10–32 said to Tarro, "When we go in, I'll make the arrest. You cover me." Tarro gave a head nod, wondering what this Kreplin Judge had done to warrant this treatment.

When the elevator reached the thirty-seventh floor, the two officers exited and crossed the walkway to the balcony. Following the moving map provided by SD-6, they turned left upon reaching the balcony and arrived at the door of the citizen in question.

"Mother-6, we're in position," said Officer 10–32 quietly.

"Copy, Officer 10–32. Opening door in five seconds. Stand by."

Tarro never liked the fact that the Kreplin monitored every aspect of their lives, and he certainly didn't care for its ability to unlock and open any door to a not-so-private residence. Tarro took one more look at the schematic. The two dots were still in the living room. When they received the "go" alert from SD-6, the door of the residence slid open, compliments of the Kreplin.

The two of them entered the residence, Tarro with his GP-9 drawn and Officer 10–32 with cuffs ready to be slapped on the wrists of the Kreplin Judge. They quietly moved down the main hallway to the living room and could hear the voices of the couple talking. Tarro entered the living room first and was greeted by surprised looks from the man and woman. A young girl sitting on a couch to their left let out a short scream, a look of horror gripping her face. Shocked to see the girl and still processing why she was present, Tarro kept his phaser trained on the Judge. He then moved to his right, allowing Officer 10–32 to advance from behind and make the arrest.

"Citizen TY-15–85," barked the officer, "by orders of the Kreplin, you are under arrest. Get on your knees now!"

Instead of getting on his knees, the Judge remained standing and demanded, "What am I being arrested for?"

"Citizen 15–82, Get on your knees now!"

"No! You first tell me what I'm getting arrested for!" shouted back the Judge.

"I will only tell you once more—"

"I'm a judge of Avalon"—the man began approaching Officer 10–32—"I deserve an answer!"

Officer 10–32 held his position and began drawing his GP-9. When the Judge saw this, he rushed the officer. Instantly, a laser pulse shot out from Officer 10–32's right side hitting the Judge in the chest and vaporizing him instantly. Without thinking, Tarro had reflexively taken the shot, an instinctive reaction and the result of years of Peace Officer training.

"No!" shouted the woman who rushed over to the spot where her husband had just disappeared. Officer 10–32, who by now had his phaser drawn, shot and vaporized the woman.

"Mooooommy!" screamed the girl.

"What did you do?!" yelled Tarro who was still shaking from his own shooting. "Why did you shoot her?!"

Avoiding Tarro's unauthorized pronoun, the officer said, "They rushed me and was therefore a threat!"

Tarro was furious, not only with himself for shooting the Judge but with Officer 10–32's unnecessary use of force. "No, she wasn't! She was just going over to where her husband died!"

Officer 10–32, now angry at the more junior officer's challenge to his judgment, yelled back, "Officer 43–64, stand down!"

SD-6 broke in, "Officer 10–32, what is the problem? Status report."

Tarro heard Officer 10–32 relay the sequence of events to SD-6, but he didn't care what the other officer had to say. Two people had just been killed. He cursed the training that caused him to instinctively shoot the man. It was a text-book shooting. The Judge was acting in a hostile manner by aggressively approaching a Peace Officer. Tarro did exactly what he was trained to do. Still, he hated it. And then there was the second shooting. So unnecessary. He fumed inwardly.

Tarro looked over at the young girl who was still on the couch and appeared to be around the age of ten. Her large brown eyes conveyed a look of shock and sadness. Tears cascaded down her face as her lower lip quivered. Tarro wanted to go over to console her but knew the only emotion he would invoke in her would be more fear. He wondered what she was doing out of HDC, but the related questions were drowned out by his overwhelming sorrow for her.

Officer 10–32 arranged for a neighbor to watch the girl until she could be picked up by the Kreplin, and they left as quickly as they had arrived. As they descended to the lobby floor, Tarro noticed his hands were shaking. The girl's look of shock and grief was emblazoned in his mind. Yet another innocent face to add to his growing pool of victims.

The totality of the day had run him emotionally dry to such a degree that he now just felt utterly numb. By the time the elevator came to a stop on the lobby floor, he was certain he had reached rock-bottom and that he could not go any further into the dark abyss of despair.

He was wrong.

Chapter 18

Darkness

"TARRO . . . TARRO, YOU ALL right?" asked Biorn sympathetically. Tarro stared past him, deep in his own thoughts. He was back in Nexus-56, reliving the scene and his killing of the man, and not just any man, a husband and apparent steward of a young girl. For the last three months, the scene had hung over him like a dark, sinister storm cloud. It cut off every ray of happiness from his life, a brewing tempest which refused to depart from him, threatening at any moment to burst forth and drown him with a deluge of cold, black rain.

Tarro had decided to finally visit Biorn's cafe. Ever since the fatal shooting, he had gone downhill, reverting back to drinking Xscape. Every night had become an attempt to run away from his problems through the elixir which had now taken over his life, but he didn't really care anymore. It was this, though, that compelled him to avoid Biorn. He was miserable and apathetic, but he was also ashamed at what he had become—a drunken, killing, depressed man.

He had selected a table outside on the cafe's rear patio. It was a pleasant day and he was joined by other customers who were taking advantage of the pleasant weather. Tarro had decided to bypass his usual indoor corner table, but it wasn't because of the inviting weather. He just desired something different.

Biorn, who had sat down to join him, tried again. "Hey, Tarro, what's going on?" He had observed his young friend in emotional turmoil before. But this was a frightening level of despair he had never seen.

Tarro pulled out his phaser and laid it on the table. "You ever wonder what exactly a phaser pulse really is?" Biorn eyed Tarro warily, caught off guard by the random question. "I mean, is it light? Energy? A ball of fire?" Tarro stared at the phaser laying on its side and slowly turned it with his index finger until the muzzle was pointing at his own chest. "How . . . how does something so small . . . just disintegrate a man . . . How does it—"

Commotion at a table behind Tarro caused him to break away from his dark musings. He jerked his body around and saw two people, one standing and shouting at the other sitting.

The face of the standing woman was beet red with fury. "I told you that if you took my companion to the Colonnades one more time we would be moving out!"

The sitting man shot back, "That is *not* your companion! I purchased Maxa myself! If you want to go down that road again, fine. You have no right—"

"Excuse me, what seems to be the problem?" Tarro said, now standing by their table, cursing the fact that he was still on duty and, therefore, obligated to keep the greater peace of Avalon.

Upon seeing the Peace Officer, who had until then gone unnoticed by the woman, she quickly sat down. Her voice was suddenly pleasant. "Oh, nothing's wrong officer. My husband and I were just having a conversation." She smiled sweetly at the man, gently rubbing his hand as it rested on the table as if they were two lovebirds just having a nice lunch together.

Tarro glared at the both of them. "Keep it down or shut up. None of us care about your stupid companion." He abruptly left the couple who were sufficiently shell-shocked into civil silence.

After sitting back down at his own table, Biorn said to him, "You want to talk or not?"

"No."

Biorn stood up. "Ok, friend. But be careful how deep you try to stuff the pain. It has an uncanny way of exploding when you least expect it."

"Don't look so concerned." Tarro coerced a smile which looked as forced as it was. "You make too many assumptions. I'm fine."

Biorn grunted, unconvinced. "Tarro, you can tell me anything." He smiled kindly at the young officer and left to attend to his customers.

☙❧

Later that evening, Tarro checked out with SD-6 and decided to walk the city. He wandered aimlessly for a couple of hours, not wanting to return to the solitude of his quarters. Finally, fatigue set in, and he begrudgingly headed home.

He entered his residence, and the lonely emptiness greeted him with familiar gloom.

"Good evening, Tarro," said his computerized Nya in a sultry voice, a not-so-subtle attempt to help change the foul mood she detected.

"Shut up," growled Tarro.

"Have it your way," said Nya with a pouty tone.

Tarro stood in the middle of the living room and stared at the glass doors leading to the terrace. Nya had dimmed the lights, either in an attempt to accommodate his sullenness or out of spite at being scorned. Tarro neither noticed nor cared. He remained frozen with an acute numbness, a cold indifference that penetrated his very soul. Time stopped.

Then he saw it. The reflection of his face in the glass doors stared back at him. It mocked him with a vacuous stare, and it struck him that he didn't really know who he was looking at. It was as if he were looking at an apparition that at any moment would disappear into the netherworld. But the face wouldn't go away. It just peered at him with hollow, accusing eyes. The eyes blinked intentionally, as if attempting to ensure that they were seeing everything correctly, attempting to make sense of it all. Yet there was no sense. Nothing made sense. Nothing seemed real.

"Curse you! Who are you anyway?!" Tarro pleaded out loud.

As if on cue, the reflected face in the glass changed. The image had such a clarity, as if she were standing in the same room. It was all happening again. The Judge killed by Tarro's own phaser. Instant disintegration. The scream of the wife who rushed to her husband, now dead. Then her death. Another life snuffed out instantly. Two instant killings—no, *murders*. Then the little girl, her image now staring at him from the glass door. Her big brown eyes half covered by the mountain of curly blonde hair that cascaded over her head. Eyes which didn't blink. Staring. Tears streaming down her face. Her whole world having just vanished like a vapor in front of her. She stared back at him with haunting eyes, beacons of innocence that pierced his own heart like a violently-thrust knife.

Rage suddenly flooded him. He grabbed a metal sculpture from the nearest end table and chucked it at the terrace door. It mockingly bounced off the glass, successfully knocking the image of the girl away but replacing it once again with his own.

He ripped the door open and stormed out onto the terrace. The silhouette of the city was fading fast with the setting sun, and for a few minutes he stood with hunched shoulders, watching the last sliver of sun disappear below the horizon. As the pink hues in the sky gave way to gray and black, every shade of darkness began to overwhelm him. Despair. Guilt. Emptiness. Rage. A crushing weight descended upon him. He began physically shaking and breathing irregularly as he gasped for air which seemed increasingly elusive. But there was no relief, no solution, no escape . . . or was there?

With tears streaming down his face, he mechanically walked back inside. It was on on the table right where he'd left it. He went over and slowly pulled his issued GP-9 Gamma Phaser out of its holster. He sat down and studied it. It dawned on him that he had never really looked at it very closely. He turned it over in his hand, struck by the power contained in such a small block of laser-cut titanium. Small lettering impressed into the metal on the underside of the barrel caught his eye. He had never noticed it before. The inscription read "Peace and love." The empty words of the State mocked him.

Tarro walked back outside and sat down in one of the deck chairs. Without hesitation, he put the phaser to his head. He closed his eyes and paused for a moment with the thought, *Peace and love . . No . . . There is none.* He gently squeezed the trigger.

☯

A steady tone emitted from the gun. Tarro pulled the trigger again. Nothing. He looked at the GP-9, bewildered. A red light flashed above the hand grip, indicating that there was no charge. Tarro slammed the phaser on the table. These highly advanced weapons never malfunctioned. He started furiously taking it apart, and then he saw it. The Thorium fuel crystals were missing. His mind raced. *How? How was this even possible?* He never let it out of his sight. He was trained to treat it like his own appendage.

There was only one known officer who had ever lost his phaser and the Kreplin had made an example of him through a very public and brutal execution. Then he remembered . . . Biorn. He had left his phaser on the table earlier that day to attend to the arguing couple. *But how would he have removed the crystals? I couldn't have been gone more than a minute. Only a few people even know how to remove the crystals . . . how could he have done it so quickly?* Tarro became fixated on this mystery, forgetting why he was even holding the phaser in the first place.

The horrifying scream of a woman from somewhere below his terrace shattered the solemn silence. Through his Vizitar, Tarro heard the voice of a Peace Officer report to all officers over SD-6's open communication channel. Referred to as the "PO Channel," normally, Tarro would turn this channel off while off-duty, but he had forgotten to do so tonight.

The officer at the scream's location reported, "Mother-6, target eliminated. Returning to base."

"Copy, Officer 689," the pleasant voice replied matter-of-factly. "Peace and love."

Tarro felt a hot wave of violent rage quickly consume his placid numbness. His rage against the Kreplin and his original mission came into sharp focus once again with a renewed intensity. He looked again at his phaser. He would die. Yes, that was the only way. But not here. Not tonight. Not this way.

He picked up the weapon and squeezed the grip with a cold resolve. He pictured the smug faces of the Supreme Confidant and the Ministers. And then he pictured his Nya. *Yes, I will die. But not before I kill them . . . every blasted one of them.*

Chapter 19

Sighting

B IORN HATED HAVING TO go to the Emporium. Each sector possessed one of these massive markets where its citizens shopped for food and anything else they needed or wanted. While most of Biorn's cafe supplies came directly from Barb shipments into Avalon, occasionally, he ran out of various food items prior to the next shipment which necessitated a visit to this horrid venue.

He stood in front of the very reason he despised these places. Before him rose a twenty-foot white marble statue of the goddess Venus. Her arms extended from grossly accentuated physical features to welcome her Emporium patrons. It was considered good luck to kiss her feet, and Biorn watched as several shoppers came in and paid homage, wondering if they really believed that good fortune had been transferred to them through the kiss of hardened limestone.

But it wasn't the statue or ritual that really bothered Biorn. What rankled him to the core sat at the goddess's feet. On a small pedestal lay a petite package covered with intricate gold trimming. It sat alone on the pedestal which kept the package cool and preserved. Biorn drew closer and studied the encased item visible through the package's clear cover. He stared at it, and his anger rose.

The placenta which sat in the package represented the loss of life, the child of a pregnant Barb. Now, siting on Venus's altar of brutality, the remnants of two lives were available to the highest bidder looking for a supposed source of consumable vitality. The bidding for this desirable item would continue until the Kreplin was sufficiently satisfied with the final price. The current price displayed below the package glowed mockingly at Biorn. It was already an obscene amount, and he knew it would probably double before its final sale.

The familiar feeling of sadness drenched him as he stood deep in thought. Life was meaningless to the Kreplin, and it was no wonder. They taught their Likbez children evolutionary theory from day one. Man was simply a highly evolved machine, the product of random mutations brought about by an impersonal and arbitrary cosmos, a universe with no purpose. In the end, it was survival of the fittest and man was just an animal at the top of the food chain. It was the natural order of things for the strongest to live as the strongest. The weak were simply an impediment to the evolution of mankind, and their removal, by whatever means, served to advance the human race. No, there was no value to life. Except for the lives of those in power.

Biorn sadly shook his head as he considered the Kreplin, full of self-appointed, powerful bureaucrats who exploited and tyrannized the weak, imagining themselves as the custodians of natural selection. In reality, the citizens they feigned to love simply existed to prop up their own power and cruel egos.

A bump into Biorn's lower back startled him out of his stewing stupor. He turned to see a small, meticulously groomed dog sitting on a hover carrier. Apparently not liking the situation, the canine immediately began yapping at him.

"Excuse me," said an approaching and rather eccentric looking woman to Biorn, "you don't need to get mad at him." The hovering dog carrier, elevated by the city's electromagnetic grid, had rebounded off Biorn's back and had begun to slowly drift back to its vexed owner.

Biorn was more amused at the odd pair than perturbed at the false accusation. He gave a courteous apology before she left him in a huff with the dog carrier in trail, its occupant still yapping, spooked by everything that moved. He watched the woman bark at anyone who even remotely got in her way, and he wondered if the dog had learned its yappy behavior from its owner or if fate had simply joined these two irascible creatures together.

The diversion was welcomed though, and Biorn left the statue of Venus and the sickening offering that lay at her feet. His thoughts shifted to recent, more positive developments. It had been a month since Tarro's attempted suicide. As Tarro had suspected, Biorn had removed the crystals from his phaser in fear of the very thing Tarro had tried. Biorn had returned the phaser crystals to Tarro only after the officer had clearly snapped out of his depressed stupor with a self-proclaimed mission to bring down Talin and as many Kreplin officials possible.

There was no doubt now that Tarro was on their side, and Biorn had brought him into the full confidence of the Libs. Biorn's main concern now was that Tarro would operate with too much reckless abandon. But he was one of the missing links they needed. Soon, if they were lucky, they just might be in a position to actually begin rescue operations within the city. A smile creased Biorn's face as he thought about Tarro, wondering how the young Peace Officer was faring in his current mission.

ᘒᕐᘓ

Tarro walked alongside a group of Barb villagers with his head down, careful to avoid eye contact, not wanting to risk engaging in conversation. The more he talked, the more he risked exposing his cover. For the last two weeks, he had intensely studied their dialect, but with many phrases and words unique to Barb culture, he doubted two weeks of study was sufficient to blend in perfectly.

The group he'd joined had just left the quarry. They were the workers of Village-58 and, due to their recently experienced raid, the best village to recruit from. Dressed in Barb clothing, he posed as a fellow villager. Before slipping into the group, he had observed them working in the quarry, mining the marble and limestone to be sent to Avalon. It was grueling work, and most were now walking in silence, too tired from their twelve-hour shift to talk. Tarro had initially been surprised at how many women and teenagers were working in the quarry, but after considering the Kreplin, he concluded he should be more surprised that young children hadn't been thrown into the mix.

The thought of the Kreplin focused his mind. He had three days to accomplish his mission which was to find another Ferret, a Barb free of the Bionet who could operate in Avalon undetected and slip in and out at will. Biorn assured him it would not be difficult and that many men would jump at the opportunity. Tarro wasn't quite as convinced, especially since it was he, a Peace Officer, who was to do the recruiting.

Per Biorn's plan, Tarro had convinced SD-6 that on one of his recent patrols, he had observed certain hints of activity in the village that made him concerned that some of the Barbs were planning revenge against the Kreplin. He kept the reasons for his suspicions vague and general enough so that SD-6, should they go back and review his Bionet recordings, wouldn't be able to easily dismiss his concerns or detect his lies.

While SD-6 could at any time monitor what a Peace Officer was seeing and hearing through his Bionet, Tarro had heard from reliable sources that due to the high number of Peace Officers, they were not usually monitored in real-time unless they were engaged in something significant. Everything they saw and heard, however, was recorded. SD-6 could go back and review anything that transpired with a Peace Officer, hence the need to keep his concerns convincing but vague.

Fortunately for Tarro and his new team of Libs, the Kreplin was the embodiment of paranoia. They readily approved Tarro's proposal to go undercover as a Barb to acquire information on any hostile plans these villagers might be cooking up. This gave Tarro the opportunity to do what he was really here for, to find another Ferret. He had asked for a week. SD-6 gave him three days.

Biorn's plan was relatively simple: blend into the village and look for a single, younger man with no family. Physically, he needed to be strong and athletic. Finding those qualities was the easy part. The harder part was finding one who was fearless but not reckless, one who could think on his feet and work well autonomously, not to mention one who could be persuaded by a Peace Officer to join some unseen ragtag band of Avalon citizens. Tarro chuckled to himself and thought, *This is going to be easy, huh, Biorn?*

The first day yielded nothing promising. All able-bodied villagers were broken up into day and night shifts. After he returned with the day shift, most of them went immediately to their homes to eat dinner and no doubt collapse in exhaustion.

He had wandered around the village for about hour when he found a group of younger men playing a game in a dirt field just outside the village. He had never seen such a game. They ran up and down the field kicking a ball back and forth. Pairs of vertical wood posts bracketed the ends of the field, and it appeared the objective was to kick the ball between these post.

Tarro was intrigued. Games like this weren't played in Avalon. Best of all, these were men who had the stamina and energy to play after a long day of work. Unfortunately, they were just finishing when Tarro arrived, but he was relieved to discover he would be able to observe them the next evening as they played just about every night.

When night set in, Tarro slipped out of the village to a location about a mile east of the quarry. Snakejak had dropped him off here earlier in the morning with the food and supplies he would need for the next few days. His little camp was set in a clearing along a large creek. Surrounded by trees and the peaceful stream, Tarro relished the first night of his life spent outside the controlled spaces of Likbez and Avalon. He grabbed a container from the ground and pressed a button on its small control panel. Within seconds, his one-man shelter emerged from the container, automatically erecting into a hemisphere-shaped structure made of honey-combed composite panels.

After eating a quick meal, he climbed in and lay down, listening to the sounds of nature. From across the creek, an owl hooted, briefly interrupting the continuous sound of the creek and the breeze that rustled through the trees. For the first time in years, Tarro felt peaceful. He savored the rare moment as he drifted off to sleep.

He awoke before sunrise in order to get into position unseen near the quarry. The night shift workers soon departed to return to the village, and he once again slipped into the group. It was a chilly morning and as they ambled toward the village, Tarro couldn't figure out why he was so stiff and cold until he remembered that he wasn't wearing his temperature controlled uniform. The temperature in both Likbez and Avalon never dropped below sixty degrees, their climates regulated by their BioDomes. He exhaled and watched with fascination the smoke-like breath billow out of his mouth.

His visible breath made him think about his helmet, or lack of one. While they were always required as officers to wear their helmets outside of Avalon, Tarro had always assumed that this was, in part, to protect from them from contagions and viruses. While SD-6 had given him permission to keep it removed for this undercover operation, he was a little concerned about the risk—that is, until his conversation with Snakejak during the flight out.

When he expressed his concern to Snakejak, the more senior officer just laughed and told him not to worry. Yes, there had been a deadly virus ages ago, but Avalon kept the Barbs well vaccinated. A sick Barb was no use to the Kreplin. Plus, fear of deadly viruses made for an even more effective wall than the physical wall of Avalon. A fearful populace was a contained and compliant populace. Such was the analysis of Snakejak which all seemed to make sense, but only served to fuel Tarro's disdain for Kreplin tyranny, especially when the pilot added that everything he'd just shared was classified information.

Tarro began making his rounds in the village, trying his best to look inconspicuous to the Barbs while also trying to look convincing to anyone watching his movements at SD-6. He couldn't have them thinking he was wasting time on some wild goose chase. The day yielded no leads for him until the evening came when the same group of men resumed their kicking game. Tarro took a position near the middle of the playing field to watch. This time he wanted to be seen, because he wanted to see who in the group would notice.

Within a few minutes, he observed one of the young men repeatedly glancing in his direction. He had jet-black hair which topped a very muscular body. He was the fastest on the field and, judging from the repeated looks at Tarro, the most observant. Finally, during a break in play, he jogged over to where Tarro was standing.

"Hey, you've been standing there for a while," he said to Tarro. "Do you want to play?"

Tarro purposefully didn't say anything. The man had already proved to be the most observant, now it was time to test him.

The man asked again, "You look like you can play. Do you want to join us or not?"

"Sure, as long as I'm not on your team. I've seen children play better than you," Tarro said.

The man laughed. "That's big talk for someone standing on the sideline in his work clothes. You're more than welcome to join the other team. They keep losing, and evidently, you have the skills to help them break their losing streak." Tarro returned the man's big grin with a smile. Athletic. Observant. Good temperament. Now for the real test.

Playing the part of both insurrectionist hunter and Lib recruiter, Tarro lowered his voice to almost a whisper, "I'm actually looking for some men who want to get back at the Kreplin." Tarro had planned this part with Biorn. If he immediately jumped at the opportunity, he was probably reckless. An overly cautious and fearful man would not take the bait. But someone both cautious and fearless would navigate the proposal wisely.

The young man drew closer to Tarro, glancing to his right and left. "That is dangerous talk, friend."

"Yes, but these are dangerous times."

"True, but why are you asking me this? You don't even know me . . . as a matter of fact, I don't even recognize you. Where exactly do you live anyway?"

Tarro smiled. "It's a big village." So far the man was navigating the conversation wisely. Shifting the conversation away from the unanswerable questions, Tarro said, "I'm asking you because I can tell you're the type who would be intrigued by the prospect."

The man looked around briefly and then studied Tarro. "And how do you propose we go about something like that?"

"Meet me here tomorrow."

"Give me one reason why I should trust you."

Tarro locked eyes with him. "Because I watched the Kreplin take eighteen of our people, most of whom were pregnant women. The Kreplin needs to feel some pain."

The man stared at the ground for a few moments then said, "Ok. I'll think about it."

The next day, Tarro continued to play the part of his Peace Officer mission. He was scheduled to be picked up by Snakejak later that night, so he had some time to kill. The meeting with the young man wouldn't happen though. Tarro would go back to the rendezvous point in order to maintain the appearance of his Peace Officer mission. The man wouldn't show up, and Tarro would report back to SD-6 that he was not able to confirm any plans against the Kreplin even though he actively tried to recruit one of the savages.

The real reason the man wouldn't show up was because of the mastermind, Biorn. Since everything was potentially seen by SD-6, they needed a way to lay out their situation and the proposal in a convincing way while circumventing Tarro's Bionet. Biorn's solution was to send a Holopuck with Tarro. These small devices were common in Avalon and were used to project holographic images and videos. They were used in a variety of ways, everything from sending a message to a loved one to displaying the latest building design proposal to the Kreplin construction department. Every Holopuck operated on the city's network and was assumed to be monitored by the Kreplin. With fortuitous foresight, one of the members of the Libs had spent a year quietly learning the technology in order to assemble a Holopuck that could be used by the Libs outside of the Kreplin's watching eyes.

Before the exchange with the young man the night before, Tarro had written a message in the dirt without looking at it in order to keep it out of his Bionet's purview. The message simply said, "Take it and don't ask questions." During the conversation with the man, when it was clear he had seen the message in the dirt, Tarro looked away and handed him the Holopuck while continuing his recruitment conversation. Whether or not the man could be convinced to join the Libs was now dependent on how convincing Biorn had been in the recorded message contained in the Holopuck. The message was lengthy as Biorn laid out his own history as a former Barb and the activity of the Libs, including their need for a new Ferret.

No doubt the man had watched the Holopuck by now, and Tarro wondered what the Barb would do. He gave him about a fifty-fifty chance of saying yes to the proposal. If he agreed to take the role of the new Ferret, he was to hit one of two buttons underneath the Holopuck. Either button would send an encrypted signal to a transponder in the possession of Biorn. A green light would indicate that he was on board. A red light or no light would mean they would have to try this all again with someone else.

"Excuse me, would you like to join us for our meeting?" asked a woman who was standing with a young girl.

Tarro had been walking down one of the village's numerous dirt roads, deep in thought. The question startled him. "I'm sorry, what did you say?"

The woman, who appeared to be around forty, smiled sweetly at Tarro. "I just asked if you would like to join us." She pointed to a nearby small building into which several people were entering.

Tarro had a moment of panic as he considered the possibility that he might have stumbled upon an actual meeting to plot against the Kreplin. "What is the meeting about?"

"I think Plin is speaking on redemption today."

Tarro, now more curious than concerned, accepted the invitation and entered the building. As soon as he passed through the front door, he heard singing coming up from a stairwell to his right. Upon seeing a new visitor enter, an older man standing by the stairwell kindly welcomed Tarro and ushered him down the stairs.

The singing got louder as he descended into a basement room. The room was surprisingly much larger than the small building above it, and Tarro figured that there were over a hundred men, women, and children, all of whom were standing and singing, led by a man up front. It was a bizarre scene, the likes of which Tarro had never seen.

He grabbed on open seat in the back row and a singing man to his left greeted him with a nod and a smile. His face was still dirty from his recent shift in the quarry. Tarro wondered what he could be so happy about, having just come off an arduous twelve-hour shift. As a matter of fact, they all looked, if not happy, at least content. They sang for a few more minutes and then sat down. Another man, whom Tarro assumed was Plin, replaced the one who had been leading the singing and began speaking to the group.

Tarro didn't really pay attention to what the man was actually saying. Instead, he was transfixed on a young woman sitting several rows in front of him. She was desperately trying to keep a little boy next to her seated and quiet, but the boy wanted none of it and only seemed interested in escaping the clutches of this stifling meeting. Tarro suppressed a laugh, mesmerized by the interaction between the boy and the one who was no doubt his mother, another scene foreign to Avalon who raised their children from a distance at HDC.

The young woman was losing the battle with the indefatigable boy. She turned to give him a motherly evil eye, and Tarro's heart jumped so far into his throat he thought he was going to choke. Nya! Impossible! He had watched her be pushed over the Academy wall. He had heard the howls of the approaching Mutts. No, it simply was not possible. Tarro shook his head. No, it had to be someone who looked like her.

He continued to stare, watching her every move. Every one of her mannerisms conjured memories of his sweet Nya. It was too uncanny and too similar. He could hardly stand it. Every fiber of his being wanted to get up at that moment and see if it could possibly be her.

The man's speech lasted longer than either the young boy or Tarro would have preferred. Finally, he concluded and dismissed the group. Tarro sat frozen in his seat as the group stood up and began filing out of the basement. His eyes tracked the young woman as she walked by him, holding the hand of the little boy dragging her down the aisle. Then she saw Tarro. She stopped for a moment, wide-eyed, trying to process the same reaction Tarro had just experienced. She blinked forcibly, as if to convince herself that what she was seeing was equally impossible.

"Hi," she finally sputtered sheepishly while tucking a loose strand of hair behind her right ear.

Tarro was speechless. There was no doubt now that he was looking at Nya. Every muscle in his face had petrified to rock and he awkwardly gaped at her, unable to move his lips.

The boy tugged at her, jolting her forward. She smiled and resumed her attempt to keep up with the lad.

Tarro finally managed to force his body and mouth into motion. He stood up and cried out to the woman whose back was now to him, "Nya!"

Hearing her name, she spun around to the voice. "Tarro?"

"Yes, Nya, it's me!"

Tarro watched her instantly get wobbly. He rushed to her, catching her in his arms just as she fainted.

Chapter 20

Discovery

TARRO LOOKED DOWN IN utter disbelief at the young woman he was holding. It had been about seven years since he had last seen her and she was exactly as he remembered, only more beautiful. Her shorter Academy haircut had been traded for long, flowing locks which cascaded down around her porcelain face. Having just fainted, she lay limp in his arms. Her eyes were closed, a slight smile frozen on her delicate lips. For a moment, the insane world made sense as he stared at this angel, a girl he had loved—a flood of warm emotions hit him—no, still loved.

"Mommy!" The voice of the concerned little boy broke him out of his trance.

The sound of the child's distress also jolted his mother back into consciousness. She opened her large, brown eyes and looked up at Tarro still holding her. She smiled widely and said softly, "Tarro, you're standing on my foot."

Tarro awkwardly shuffled his feet backward and helped her stand. "Nya, it's nice to see you, too."

"Who's dat?" the boy asked Nya.

"This is Mommy's old friend."

"Whatz his name?"

"Tarro."

"Hey, that's *my* name!" cried the boy. Nya blushed slightly and gave a sheepish smile to the bigger Tarro, who smiled back, pleased at her name selection.

Reality then slammed into Tarro with the realization that the boy, no doubt, had a father. He mentally pushed down the dull pain that seized his heart.

Reality also began setting in with Nya as she began to process why an Academy graduate and likely Avalon citizen was walking around looking like a Barb. Unless he too had been thrown over the wall. She thought that was unlikely and glanced at her boy. Caution was needed.

She looked around at some of the concerned villagers who had gathered around them and assured them she was fine. She then thought about inviting Tarro to her home to talk, but prudence won out. "Tarro, let's sit down here for a moment."

The boy was about to crawl out of his skin with pent up energy, and one of the ladies kindly took the boy upstairs for Nya.

Tarro and Nya pulled a couple of chairs together and sat down. For a moment, they just looked at each other, not knowing where to start.

"You—" They both started speaking at the same time, then stopped.

"You go first," Tarro said as a flood of questions filled his mind. "Tell me how you got here. How did you survive being thrown over the wall? Who's the boy's father? Where—"

"Whoa, slow down!" Nya said with a laugh. She had a lot of questions herself, but she found herself quickly warming up to her old friend. The return of old feelings caught her off guard, and she paused, slightly ashamed as the thumping sound from a jumping boy above them reminded her of her husband.

"Well?" Tarro said quizzically.

Nya regained her composure. "So, where to begin . . . I remember . . . I remember standing on the parade ground as the Chancellor laid out the accusations. I knew what was about to happen. I was so scared . . . You know, I was watching you."

"Yes, I know."

"I remember walking down the walkway to the edge of the wall, wondering what it was going to be like to be mauled by Mutts. I knew I wasn't going to be able to outrun them, but I was determined to try. When I got pushed off the wall, though, I landed hard and sprained my ankle. It was so bad I could hardly walk. But I moved away from the wall as fast as I could. After some time, I heard howls in the distance. I knew I was done for and my foot hurt so bad, I just stopped and sat down."

Tarro sat, spellbound, and Nya was a little uncomfortable at the intent way he was looking at her.

"So I sat down and I just cried . . . You know, I thought about you. I thought about how you stood there in formation as the Chancellor gave my sentence. I could see how angry you looked. I was afraid you were going to break rank and come after one of the Peace Officers."

Tarro looked down slightly, ashamed that he hadn't.

Nya noticed this and grabbed his hand. "I'm glad you didn't—you would have died a useless death." The touch of his hand and the spike of feelings caused her to quickly let go and resume her story.

"So what happened next?"

"I was sitting there when, all of a sudden, I heard heavy breathing behind me. I knew it was a Mutt, and I simply froze. I think I closed my eyes as I braced for the worst to happen. I was just hoping that the Mutt would make it quick . . ." She paused, deep in thought. It had been a while since she had recounted that day to someone. The experience had given her nightmares for years after, and the terror of that moment now returned with an uncomfortable realness.

She refocused, seeing the wide-eyed Tarro eagerly waiting for her to continue. "So I sat there cringing, and then he spoke to me. 'Young lady,' he said. 'I'm not going to hurt you.' I turned, and to my surprise, there stood a Mutt. He repeated that he wasn't going to hurt me, and I thought it might be a ruse. But then it hit me. I had seen him before. At that moment, I was pretty sure he was the Mutt at the Academy who I refused to beat. He slowly approached me and sat down right in front of me."

"You must have been scared out of your mind," Tarro said.

"Oh yeah—I was scared, but I also figured that if he was going to hurt me he wouldn't have sat down as if he wanted to chat. He then said to me, 'I will never forget how you treated me in the arena.' Tarro, you can't imagine how surreal this all was. One moment I'm looking down over the edge of the wall wondering what it's going to be like to be hunted by Mutts, and the next moment a Mutt is sitting cross-legged in front of me, thanking me. I was speechless . . . and I just sat there looking at him. Then I heard the howls of Mutts again, and this time they were much closer. As soon as he heard them he quickly stood up and told me he was going to take me to a nearby village. I told him I couldn't even walk because of my ankle. Before I knew it, he picked me up and started running."

"He carried you?" Tarro asked incredulously.

"Yes, and I won't lie—when he picked me up I had a moment of panic, but as soon as he started running with me, I could see he was running away from the direction of the howls. He was incredibly strong and fast. I've never seen anything like it. I don't know how long he ran, but it must have been several hours. He never stopped, never slowed down for a second. The howls followed us, and he told me that they were following my scent. But he then told me that he was not going to let anything happen to me."

Nya stopped deep in thought. When she had wiped the blood off the Mutt's face in the combat arena, she could see in his eyes that he was not an animal. He was a person. Ugly and deformed, yes. Maybe the others acted like animals, but there was at least one Mutt who had a kind heart.

"So that's how you got here to this village?" asked Tarro.

"Yes. We arrived just outside the village, and he stopped at the surrounding wall, placed me on the ground, and collapsed in exhaustion. I didn't know how I was going to get over the wall, but soon he got up, pulled a huge log out of the woods, and propped it on the wall for me to climb. By the time I got to the top of the wall, he had collapsed again. The howls had become fainter, and I knew that he had pushed himself hard. He finally got up, pulled the tree off the wall, and told me that he was fine, just a little tired, and that the people in the village would help me. I thanked him, and I'll never forget his craggy smile. Before I could say anything else, he disappeared into the woods. I've never seen him since . . ." Nya's voice trailed off as she fondly remembered her unlikely rescuer.

"That . . . that has got to be the most incredible story I've ever heard," Tarro said. "So then you had a child?"

The sudden query confirmed to Nya what she suspected was the main question on Tarro's mind: what man was in her life? "So yes, that bouncing bundle of energy up there is mine. His father"—she paused for a moment—"my husband, is working in the quarry right now." She thought she detected a subtle but noticeable disappointed look on Tarro's face.

"What's his name?"

"Tarro."

"Tarro? Your husband's name is Tarro?"

"No—I—I mean, Hon—Hon is his name," she said suddenly flustered.

"So your boy's name is Tarro?" Tarro was relishing the moment and her visible blushing.

Nya smiled sheepishly.

Tarro laughed. "Well, I'm flattered."

Nya quickly changed the subject. "So enough about me . . . how in the world did you get here?"

It was at that moment that Tarro realized the gravity of the situation and the potential danger he had just put Nya in. In his excitement, he'd been so caught up in the unexpected moment with Nya that he hadn't thought through this interaction with his friend. He kicked himself for his lack of discretion and the potential danger he had just placed her in. He had gotten quite comfortable playing the part of a Barb and for a brief moment, had almost forgotten he was a Peace Officer.

His mind raced, reviewing the last few minutes of their conversation. Yes, he had certainly put her in danger. The Academy, an arm of the Kreplin, had basically executed her, or so they thought. If the Kreplin was monitoring their conversation right now—unlikely, but possible—they wouldn't just let this little mistake go. No, they would certainly come after her and correct the act of justice which had miraculously been subverted.

Tarro bolted to his feet. "I must go."

"Why?" Nya asked, utterly confused by his abruptness and sudden change in demeanor.

"Because . . . because I must. I can't explain." He turned away from her, simultaneously squeezing her hand. The ominous feeling of terror forced him to start walking toward the basement stairs while the feeling of love compelled him to look back at his bewildered Nya.

"When—when can we talk again?" she asked.

"I don't know."

"You don't *know*?"

"Soon." Her dejected and hurt look seized his heart. He tore his eyes away from her and left. Tarro had no idea how he would ever talk to her again. He just knew he needed to get the eyes of the Kreplin away from her.

He bounded up the stairs and burst through the building's front door. He stood outside for a moment, the sun now at its peak above him. He closed his eyes as if to try to absorb its warmth. But the sun's bright rays could not calm his body now shaking with fear. Nor could the sunshine fill the gaping hole in his heart. She had a husband . . . it could never be. And now, he may have put her in grave danger.

ⵔ

Tarro was not the only one who was shook up that day. It was almost 2:00 am, and Biorn sat staring at his living room wall opposite him. It had been an emotional day for the older man. All throughout the day he could hardly focus on his cafe as he waited for the small transponder to indicate a response from a possible Ferret replacement. It was Tarro's last day of the mission and, to Biorn's great delight, the little light on the transponder had illuminated green earlier in the evening. A Barb had been found and Biorn had immediately begun to formulate the next phase of their recruitment plan with this new volunteer.

But then a very shaken Tarro returned. He and Tarro had just spent the last three hours together, casually talking about the usual meaningless stuff while carrying on their covert messaging conversation through the Lib Net. It was the latter conversation that rocked Biorn's world as Tarro recounted the discovery of Nya. In disbelief, Biorn had asked a myriad of questions until Tarro was pretty sure that Nya's whole life as Tarro knew it had been shared with his inquisitive friend. Tarro was deeply worried that he had put her in danger, and Biorn had attempted to console him, trying to convince him that the chances of the Kreplin actively monitoring him in the few minutes he was with Nya were slim.

Tarro left feeling a little better, but Biorn did not. He had misled Tarro. He actually thought the chances of the Kreplin monitoring their Peace Officer on a mission to uncover a supposed plot against the Kreplin were, in reality, very high. And that's why Biorn now stared at the wall. The elation of discovering that his daughter, Nya, was alive was quickly tempered by the sickening reality that Tarro had likely put her in grave danger. It wasn't his fault though. Biorn's heart broke for his Peace Officer friend and the absolute angst he was in. Both men loved this girl—each with a different kind of love, but with deep love. And both now feared for her life.

Biorn sat numbly. He was always thinking of the next step, always planning, always pushing forward with a hope that he could do something good, something worthwhile, something to counter the upside-down world he lived in. But now he felt lost. The faces of those he cared about flooded his mind—the Ferret, Vera, Tarro, and now . . . now his baby girl.

He knew she had been integrated into HDC. After she had been brought captive into Avalon and his search at the Center had come up empty, he later discovered she had been transferred to HDC. Since that time, he had been able to keep tabs on her through occasional updates from the Ferret. Then the Ferret had been captured, and it wasn't until a year later that he learned that their failed rescue attempt involved none other than Nya. And that's when his world collapsed. His wife had been killed by the Kreplin which had ripped out his heart. But there was still a little piece of it left that went by the name Nya. The Kreplin had decided that she was to be a member of their Barb integration experiment, and for years, that little joy of Biorn's heart remained intact. That is, until it was ripped out again by the Kreplin.

He calmed himself, focusing on the positive. She was alive. And there was still hope. There was always hope. The Kreplin didn't have her yet, and he would do everything in his power to protect her. His mind kicked back into its normal mode of operation as he began to consider all the options while wondering if he should divulge to Tarro his own relationship to Nya.

Chapter 21

Dark Clouds

Z AUN WAS SUSPICIOUS OF the man from the moment he had shown up at their little dirt field. There was something about the way he carried himself, an air about him which put Zaun on alert. The man had intently watched them play, but Zaun had also been watching him. After the man showed up the second time, Zaun knew he needed to investigate.

It didn't take long for his suspicions to be proved true when the man wrote the cryptic message in the dirt and handed him the Holopuck. At first he didn't know if he should take it or throw it back at the dubious man. The Kreplin was both ruthless and deceptive, and he smelled a possible trap. But his hatred for the Kreplin exceeded his fear, so after considering it for a moment, he took the Holopuck.

Zaun couldn't have been more surprised by the Holopuck's message. The recorded transmission lasted about an hour as an Avalon citizen named Biorn laid out in detail the Libs, their mission, and the need for an insider without a Bionet. This insider was crucial to their two-fold mission to rescue Cadets thrown over the wall and to smuggle captured Barbs out of Avalon. After viewing the Holopuck, Zaun knew it could still be a trap, but there was something quite genuine and convincing about the older man in the message who claimed to be a former Barb himself.

Zaun's parents had died at an early age, and he really didn't have anyone close in his life. This fact, combined with his hatred of the Kreplin, made the decision easy. He gladly pushed the acceptance button on the Holopuck and began to make preparations for his new life. He was to receive further instructions from the deliverer of the Holopuck within a week.

The old man called his role the "Ferret," and his excitement began to rapidly build with the prospect of being able to save some Barbs from the insidious clutches of the Kreplin. He was going to plunge into the belly of the beast and operate as an unseen virus to the Kreplin, a virus which probably wouldn't kill this evil animal, but could hopefully make it at least choke on its own vomit.

☯

It had been five days since they had received the acceptance signal from their new recruit. Tarro had been able to persuade SD-6 that while he had come up empty in his last undercover operation in Village-58, he was still convinced that there was potential seditious activity amongst the villagers and that another such operation was needed. SD-6 consented, but Tarro knew this would be his last authorization and thus, his best opportunity to deliver the package to the new Ferret who was waiting for further instructions in the village.

The petite package contained a magnetic suit and was tucked away in his container of gear packed into the back of their patrol craft. The plan was to get the suit to the new Ferret who would then attach himself to the SC-5 cargo ship that departed Village-58's sector every night at 3:00 am to bring its shipment into Avalon. In the package were detailed instructions on how he was to pose as a droid dock loader before meeting Biorn at a specified location in Avalon. There were many things that could go wrong, but such was the nature of the operations of the Libs.

Snakejak landed outside of Village-58 near the creek where Tarro had set up camp the previous time. As usual he flew hot and fast into the landing with an unnecessarily steep and high-speed descent. With the Hummer's nose pointed at the ground, he pulled up at the last possible second, flaring into a brief hover ten feet off the ground before gently touching down.

Snakejak looked at him from the left seat with a giant, wry grin plastered on his face.

"You're ridiculous," Tarro muttered to him.

"Yeah, ridiculously good!" exclaimed Snakejak.

"Give me a minute to unload, then I'll be gone and you can do all the joyriding you want."

"Without you? That won't be nearly as much fun!"

Eager to set foot on ground that didn't violently move, Tarro shoved his container of gear out the back of the patrol craft and jumped out. After briefly adjusting his Barb clothing, he checked the knife strapped to his right thigh, a utility tool many Barb men carried in their primitive lives. His phaser would be left behind.

He surveyed the area and located his previous encampment spot along the creek. A gentle breeze wafted through the thick tree line that formed a line-of-sight barrier between their position and the village. The tree line merged with the creek's left bank ahead of them, and he relished the idea of being able to spend a few more nights in this exquisite slice of nature. He breathed in deeply, soaking in the invigorating fresh air which seemed to infuse new, hopeful life into him outside the stifling confines of Avalon. The city was a prison, and out here he felt free. At least, he could imagine he was free.

Tarro glanced back at Snakejak sitting in the cockpit and gave a slight head nod, once again happy to be alive after another flight with the maniac. He began walking toward the creek with his container in tow and then stopped. In the distance, a couple hundred yards away, he saw a woman emerge from the woods and stand at the creek's edge. For a moment, he didn't know what to do. If she saw them, his undercover mission would likely be compromised, making it all that much harder to get the package to the Ferret. He remained motionless, hoping she would just turn around and leave.

"She looks kind of pretty," said Snakejak in a low voice. The unexpected presence behind Tarro startled him, and he slowly turned and glared at the pilot who hadn't had the sense to stay put in his aircraft.

Tarro whispered angrily, "If she sees us, my mission is over."

Snakejak grunted in disgust with little interest in his fellow officer's precious mission.

"I'm going to check her out. You can stay here picking your nose if you want."

Snakejak darted into the tree line, and a fuming Tarro followed, now more concerned about the intent of his insufferable pilot. Using the woods for cover, Snakejak quietly picked his way through the trees, moving steadily closer to the woman. Tarro followed, his mind racing with ways to stop the pilot. They arrived at a patch of bushes jutting out from the tree line and peered over its tops, now no more than fifty yards from the woman.

The woman had her back to them and was standing in about a foot of water with a plain white dress hiked above her knees. She was stooped over, washing a clothing article in the water. As a citizen of a highly advanced city, Tarro was intrigued, having never seen this done by hand, and certainly not in a natural body of water. She turned to retrieve another piece of clothing from the bank, and the sight of her profile seized Tarro with instant panic. Nya! It couldn't be! Tarro blinked hard and twitched his head as if his eyes were deceiving him and momentarily shutting out the world would make this evolving bad dream go away.

"She really is a beauty," Snakejak said with a sneering smile. "I think I'll go introduce myself." Tarro glared at him, fearing the hunger he sensed in the pilot's voice.

Snakejak left Tarro and continued making his way through the trees toward Nya who was washing another garment in the creek, completely unaware of the snake slithering its way toward her with intentions to strike with its venomous fangs. Tarro's initial wave of panic quickly shifted to a focused and calculated anger as he rapidly sifted through his options. One thing was certain, though. Under no circumstances was he going to let this viper lay a single, scaly finger on Nya.

He was watching Snakejak pop in and out of view through the thick forest when he landed on a plan. It wasn't perfect, but it would have to do. Without looking at his knife, he slowly and quietly pulled it out. For his plan to work, he had to maintain sight discipline. With his Bionet recording everything he saw, he had to carefully manage where he was looking, and his timing would have to be perfect.

He gripped his knife tightly. He only needed to give him a wound. While his conscience would have allowed for a mortal wound in the defense of an innocent person, covering up the killing of a Peace Officer would be a lot more difficult than a simple injury that Avalon medical care could easily patch up.

He moved quickly to catch up to the pilot, grateful to have the noisy, gurgling creek mask the sound of his movement. Snakejak stopped behind a large oak tree and removed his helmet. His back was to Tarro who was approaching as slowly and quietly as possible. Tarro stopped about ten feet from him with the knife still in his right hand. He glanced at a rock by his foot and Snakejak's exposed head and saw a new opportunity, and no doubt a less risky one.

Tarro looked at the creek to his right as he simultaneously picked up the rock. He stealthily moved to within a couple of feet behind Snakejak who was still eyeing Nya. For his potential Bionet audience, he looked around jerkily as if he heard a noise and then shouted, "Snakejak! Barb!" Tarro simultaneously looked into the woods to his left as if searching for the attacking Barb, then struck the pilot's head as hard as he could with the rock. Snakejak immediately crumpled to the ground, knocked out stone cold.

Continuing his performance, Tarro grabbed Snakejak's phaser and quickly scanned the woods, looking for the phantom Barb, then made his report. "Mother-6, Officer 43–64 reporting from outside Village-58."

After a moment, the cheery voice of SD-6 responded, "Go ahead, Officer 43–64."

"I have an officer down at my location. Officer 25–73 was just attacked by a Barb and has sustained a head wound. Officer is stable. Request an immediate medical evacuation."

"Copy, Officer 43–64. Dispatching Medvac to your location. ETA sixteen minutes. Please advise if further assistance is needed."

"None required at the moment. Standing by for Medvac."

SD-6 signed out, leaving Tarro standing there with the pilot. His head was a little bloody and he would certainly have a headache, but he would be fine.

He wondered if Nya had heard the commotion. He peered out from behind the trees. She was gone. Good. Crisis averted, but now he had the problem of getting the package to the Ferret as he would soon be recalled back to Avalon in light of the attack. He retrieved his container and placed it just inside the tree line.

As promised, a transport aircraft arrived, carrying a robust array of medical equipment and supplies to treat any physical problem experienced outside Avalon. Two Kreplin medics disembarked the Medvac, then carried the now conscious but groggy pilot back into the aircraft. A spare pilot jumped into their patrol craft to fly it back to Avalon as Tarro boarded the Medvac. As anticipated, SD-6 recalled him.

As the Medvac lifted off, Tarro looked out the side window in the direction of the container. They would have to send a message to their new Ferret via the Holopuck to alert him to its location. Not the preferred method as any signal could be intercepted, but it would have to do. Now, he needed to think through and rehearse his story for his debrief with SD-6.

Chapter 22

Interrogation

T ARRO SUBTLY BRUSHED HIS palms on his uniform. He glanced down at his right hand and wondered why the hands, of all the body parts, were the quickest to perspire when nervous. He breathed in and out methodically in an effort to control his heart rate and focus his thoughts. He was about to enter into a situation where one mental error and one wrong answer could jeopardize not only his life, but the lives of the handful of people he loved.

After his return yesterday on the Medvac with the pilot whose head had been bashed in by a "mysterious Barb," Tarro fully expected a comprehensive debrief at SD-6 but was surprised to be told to come back the next day. Now he knew why. He was not to give the usual debrief at SD-6. No, today he had the privilege of debriefing with Supreme Confidant Talin himself.

He walked alone down a long hallway lined with white marble leading to the Confidant's chambers. He had never been to this exclusive section of the Kreplin. As a matter of fact, he couldn't think of anyone he knew who had. He reached the end of the hallway, arriving at a set of double doors. He felt claustrophobic, like a mouse inside a cage—no, more like a rat in a sewer pipe reeking with the stench of power and corruption.

The double doors opened automatically for him, and he entered into a large hall. The transition from the white hallway was stark as he entered the voluminous room filled with black marble and dark gray granite.

Giant ornate pillars lined both sides of the hall, reaching a ceiling of silver paneling which gleamed from light beams shining from the floor. In front of each pillar stood individual statues of men and women, all of whom were holding mallets and chisels and carving themselves out of the rocks from which they emerged.

The enormous hall led to another set of doors. Two officers dressed in red uniforms bracketed the giant doors which appeared to be made entirely of silver. The doors contained an intricate carving of the goddess of Mother Earth, under which was the inscription: "Queen of the Universe—The Universe is Queen." Tarro had never seen these red uniforms and assumed that they were the regalia of the Confidant's personal security detail.

Tarro's other assumption that this entrance led to the Confidant's suite was confirmed when he heard the officer on the right report, "Supreme Confidant, Officer 43–64 is here." He then held out his hand and said, "Phaser." Tarro dutifully handed over his weapon.

Nothing else was said and the two guards remained motionless as Tarro stood, waiting for something to happen. He fought the urge to wipe his hands again, knowing that the Confidant was no doubt watching him from the other side. Yet, despite the fragile nerves, this was the moment he had waited for and dreamed of.

He considered how years ago he had resolved to work his way into the heart of the Kreplin lair, and here he was. It was not under the circumstances he had imagined, but he also never anticipated being able to get this close to the Confidant. He thought about the Barb knife he had strapped to his right ankle under his uniform. He had agonized all night as to whether he should attempt it. If it weren't for Nya, there would be no hesitation to do it, but every action he took against the Kreplin potentially put her in more danger. This morning, at the last moment, he had decided to bring it, concluding that whether or not he used it would be determined by opportunity and how the debrief went.

Finally, after what seemed like a little dose of eternity, the same officer who spoke previously said, "You may enter." The double doors slowly swung open and Tarro entered, knowing he was not receiving permission but a command.

Tarro entered and was immediately greeted by an opulent room that appeared to be the living quarters of the Confidant who was seated behind a green glass desk on the far side of the room. Two young ladies quickly disappeared through a door to his right. The likelihood of their Barb ethnicity steeled his nerves.

The Confidant stood and motioned Tarro over to him. "Good morning, Comrade. Please have a seat." He pointed to the lone metal chair in front of his desk.

Tarro took a seat in the chair, its hard austerity clashing with the plush surroundings of the leader's chambers. Talin remained standing, placed his hands on the desk, and leaned forward. He studied Tarro for a few moments and then said, "So Officer 43–64, you had a little trouble yesterday."

Tarro wasn't quite sure if this was a statement or a question. "Yes, Supreme Confidant, we did."

Talin still stared at Tarro who tried to read the dictator's eyes. Tarro noticed how distinctly older he looked. Up until this point, he had only seen him from a distance or from various images and holograms. The now visible, flesh-colored make-up plastering his face in an obvious attempt to hide the deep wrinkles only marginally succeeded in doing so.

Finally, Talin sat down in a gold-carved chair that looked more like a throne. He continued to study Tarro with his jet black eyes, stark contrasts to his tanned face and silver hair. He reeked of an arrogant vileness, and Tarro felt cold inside as if he were in the presence of an evil incarnate that had managed to suck away all his warmth and well-being.

"How did you feel when Nya went over the wall?" Talin asked clinically.

Tarro was thrown for a loop with the question, and his mind went numb. He thought he had rehearsed every conceivable question related to the incident with Snakejak. But not this one. Tarro sensed doom. This was not boding well. It was apparent Talin knew much. But how much? Tarro pushed the rising panic down as his mind raced to his reunion with Nya in Village-58. *Did he know about that, too? Why else would he ask that question?*

Talin squinted at Tarro, and Tarro noticed a faint but perceptible smile. A sneer rather. Tarro focused on Talin's face and allowed his percolating anger to focus his mind. He had to toe the line carefully, and he needed to concentrate.

"You seem hesitant to answer my question."

"It was a while ago, Supreme Confidant. I was trying to remember the details."

"Hmm." Talin pursed his lips slightly.

"I do remember it though, and I will be honest, a part of me was a little sad. We were friends at the academy. But . . . but, I understand now what the Academy did. I understand now that it was right and necessary to maintain order and discipline."

"So you think the little piece of Barb trash deserved to get mauled to death by Mutts?"

Tarro clenched his jaw, desperately trying to keep his anger in check. Talin's eyes darted quickly to his left and right, and Tarro wondered if he was viewing his own Vizitar, that is, if he even had a Bionet. Tarro knew he had waited too long to answer as he mentally scrambled to formulate something coherent.

Referring to Nya he said, "They—yes, they ultimately deserved it. They had proved to be . . . to not be subservient to the Kreplin."

"Ah . . . . subservient. That is an interesting word choice."

Tarro looked down. This was not going well. And worse, Nya was undoubtedly in danger because of their rendezvous in the village. He slowed his breathing down as he felt his heart rate increasing. If Talin did have a Bionet, he would be monitoring Tarro's vitals. Lies were often betrayed by abnormal blood pressure levels and heart rates.

Talin leaned back in his chair. "I would have chosen the word loving. Nya was not *loving* to Avalon. I gave that wretched Barb a new opportunity at life, a chance to join our ranks in our beloved city. And what did they do? They spat in Avalon's face. My face. That is not how you return my love."

Tarro desperately tried to shut out thoughts of the Kreplin's senseless executions and Talin's ludicrous idea of love.

Talin leaned forward in his chair. "Do you believe in equality?"

Tarro looked up at Talin whose oily black eyes projected only malevolence. Every question felt like a trap. He scrambled for an answer. "Well . . . Avalon is built on the idea that everyone is equal."

"Ha! Most in Avalon are fools!" Talin bellowed. Tarro was surprised by the leader's candidness. "Sure, all are equal. But not all are equally equal."

Talin tapped a digital control pad imbedded in the green glass of his desk and a holographic video appeared above the desk's surface. Tarro's heart jumped when he saw that the video was a recording from his Bionet. As the video played, they began to relive the incident in question through his own eyes.

"Here you are," said Talin slowly, "approaching Officer 25–73. I believe you call them Snakejak. This is moments before Snakejak was attacked by a Barb, yes?"

"Yes." Tarro loathed the fact that he was asking a question to which he knew the answer. He watched himself approaching the pilot, and then Talin paused the video.

"This is interesting, Tarro." Tarro hid his surprise at the use of his name and not his officer designation. "For one joining up with their pilot, you are moving rather slowly."

Tarro had anticipated this question. "There was a Barb in the area. I was trying to be quiet so as to not alert the villager to our presence."

"I see." Talin unpaused the video, and Tarro watched the familiar scene unfold—the quick look into the woods as if he heard something, the simultaneous shout of warning to Snakejak, the quick grab of his phaser and search of the surrounding woods. Tarro had done as well as could be expected.

Talin paused the video again with the frozen image of Snakejak crumpled on the ground. "I also find it interesting that at no point do you actually see this mysterious Barb attacker."

Tarro had rehearsed this one too. "I'm pretty sure there were at least two Barbs in the woods. I heard a noise to my left, and as I looked in that direction, the other Barb attacked from my right. I saw it peripherally, but the one shoved me as they struck Officer 25–73 and by the time I spun around they were gone."

"Ah," grunted Talin. Tarro sensed the skepticism. Tarro considered his knife, and his mind raced. They were alone in the room. With one quick lunge over the desk he could possibly end it. Talin was old. He would be an easy target. But he knew about Nya. And he probably knew she was still alive. Why else would he ask about her demise over the Academy wall? It dawned on Tarro at that moment that he would never really be able to protect her. Maybe the elimination of her chief threat was her best chance at life.

The Avalon despot leaned forward slightly and said, "But here's what I find most interesting. As you approached your pilot simply to join up with them, your heart rate was racing—"

"I was afraid we were going to be detected, Supreme Confidant," interrupted Tarro.

"Ah, yes, but then after the attack, while you are searching for your Barb attacker and making the call to SD-6, your heart rate is decreasing rapidly. Curious. I would think your heart rate would be at its peak at this point."

Tarro was speechless. He thought he had anticipated every possible question, even the one regarding his quickening heart rate prior to his assault of Snakejak. But the decreasing heart rate at a time when for most, it would be increasing—well, he hadn't thought of that one. He now remembered the calm and relief he had experienced after striking Snakejak knowing that Nya, at least for the moment, was safe. But his calm had produced a vital sign abnormality.

The metal chair suddenly felt quite hard. "Well . . . I . . . I can't really explain that."

"You know, Officer 43–64, you seem to have unhealthy blood pressure levels. Even now, it is really quite high. Tomorrow, I want you to check into medical and get an evaluation. We care about our people, especially our officers."

The floodgates of rage burst open within Tarro. Care?! The Kreplin's lies, corruption, arrogance, and utter disdain for the lives of people who didn't serve its purposes made the assertion of caring galling.

"Officer 43–64, I think I have a clear picture," said Talin. "You are dismissed."

For a moment, Tarro didn't move. He knew the game was up. Talin knew everything, and this fact alone tossed fuel on the fire of his rage. Rationality quickly gave way to overwhelming anger, and Tarro began reaching down for the knife.

Talin simultaneously stood with an air of self-importance and said, "And one more thing. The only authorized weapon a Peace Officer is permitted to carry is their issued phaser. For your own welfare, I suggest you follow regulations."

೦X೦

Tarro studied the phaser he held in his hand as the AT-7 lifted off, filled with a dozen other Peace Officers. Yesterday, he had come close to grabbing his knife, but before he could get to it, Talin had stood and the two door guards had entered the room. At that point, any attempt on the Confidant's life would have been futile and suicidal.

At first, he wondered why Talin would let him leave if he knew Tarro was carrying an additional weapon against regulations with potential ill intent. But that question, along with the others Tarro left with yesterday, was answered when he was assigned to the raid detail tasked with retrieving twenty Barb captives.

The pilot's voice came over the intercom, "Recommend strapping in. We will be going through some rough weather soon. Approximately seventeen minutes to Village-58."

Tarro cringed at the village reference. It was no accident Nya's village was chosen as the location of this raid. And it was no coincidence that Tarro had been assigned to this Peace Officer detail. It didn't take a genius to see why they were going to Village-58. Talin was going to make him suffer.

Tarro looked at his phaser again. If he was quick enough, he could take down every officer. He quickly dismissed the thought. If Nya was truly in jeopardy, that wouldn't save her. Plus, he couldn't bring himself to kill his fellow officers. Yes, they were the agents of horrific injustice, but he knew some of them did not support what they were doing and were begrudgingly just doing their duty.

He holstered his phaser and closed his eyes as he leaned back into his seat. This morning he had stopped by Biorn's quarters to give him a recap of the last twenty-four hours. Initially, Biorn was visibly optimistic as he informed Tarro that their new Ferret had successfully stowed away on a supply ship and was now safely inside Avalon. But his cheery disposition soured instantly when Tarro recounted his meeting with Talin and today's assignment to Village-58.

Tarro sighed deeply. He looked out the window to his right and saw the sky darkening as the aircraft began to bounce in the growing turbulence. The familiar feeling of despair began to rush in like a wave. Biorn had advised him to keep his head down and fulfill his Peace Officer duties in the raid. Once the Barbs were in the city, they would attempt a rescue if they could get the pieces in place quickly enough. With the Ferret having just arrived, Tarro figured the chances of this were slim.

The transport vibrated violently in the turbulence as they began their descent. Tarro glanced again out the window only to see water streaming across the glass against the backdrop of a dark gray bank of storm clouds.

"Five minutes to touchdown," reported the pilot.

The operational commander for the detail stood up in front of the cabin and faced the seated Peace Officers. "After the village forms up, I want you to move quickly. The weather is rapidly deteriorating. You all have your assignments." It dawned on Tarro that he had not been given an assignment, but before he was able to ask, the commander looked at him and barked, "Officer 43–64, you will accompany Officer 10–51, who has your tasking."

The feeling in the pit of Tarro's stomach couldn't have been more monstrously dreadful. He was the only one on-board who hadn't received tasking. And there could only be one possible reason.

Chapter 23

Glimmer

B IORN WALKED SLOWLY NEAR the Kreplin's transport facility located
near Sector-1's landing pad. Tarro's transport had just landed. Biorn
nervously waited for the brief glimpse he would get of the Barb prisoners
as they traversed the relatively short distance between the decontamination chamber and the transport facility. From there they would then be
whisked away to the Center.

The walkway leading to the transport facility stretched a couple
hundred yards and was lined on either side with Avalon Firefly trees. For
a moment, Biorn forgot his crushing anxiety as he soaked in the exquisite flowering trees whose blossoms were designed by Avalon's botanical
engineers to naturally glow. It was dusk and the white and pink blooms
were already beginning to glimmer.

The brief anxiety hiatus ended when the first Peace Officer emerged
from the decontamination chamber. Behind him followed the Barb prisoners. Biorn quickly counted a total of twenty, and as usual, most of
them were young, pregnant women. Biorn cursed the Kreplin under his
breath as he scanned their faces, desperately hoping his baby girl wasn't
among them.

It was hard to see the faces, though, as they popped in and out of
visibility between the Firefly trees. At the back of the entourage he spotted Tarro whose bowed head was perched on slumped shoulders. Biorn
didn't like the looks of his body language. Biorn was walking in the

opposite direction of the group, so he reversed direction to walk parallel with them.

He discretely scanned the Barb faces again and that's when he saw her. A gentle breeze had kicked in, causing many of the blossoms to detach from their branches. Hundreds of glowing blossoms gently rained down, creating something like a slow-motion meteor shower, a scene fit for a wedding procession, not a death march.

By now, Biorn had lost track of himself, and all discretion went out the window as he stared at his Nya. In contrast to the dejected Tarro, her head was held high on her graceful neck. Surrounded by the glowing blossoms, she carried herself like a queen, her natural regality betrayed only by her bound hands. Then, to Biorn's horror he saw the small, unmistakable bulge of her stomach. He did a double-take as she disappeared behind another tree.

The sight of her pregnancy served as the final twist of the knife in Biorn's heart, and the floodgates of sorrow burst open. He desperately tried to contain his weeping as his chest began to heave. He knew he needed to leave. There was nothing more he could do at this point. He picked up his pace and headed for the nearest POD, leaving behind the love of his life and a trail of tears.

☙❧

Tarro sat in his usual corner of Biorn's cafe in a familiar foul mood. So obvious was the foulness of his mood that Biorn initially avoided him. But this avoidance wasn't just because of the stewing Peace Officer. Unbeknownst to Tarro, Biorn had a ghastly mood to match.

Biorn had debated all morning whether or not to tell Tarro that Nya was his daughter. From the corner of the cafe, he studied the dejected young man. He knew what it was like to be in love. He also knew the pain of lost love. At that moment he made a conscious decision to compartmentalize his anguish. She wasn't dead yet, and as long as he had his wits and strength, he would do everything possible to free her.

He stuffed his sorrow into the recesses of his heart and focused on the task at hand, the first of which was to help Tarro pull his head out of the mire of his own grief. Time was not on their side. To complicate matters, Talin was clearly now aware of Tarro and Nya's past in addition to Tarro's assault on the pilot. No doubt, Tarro was now being monitored continuously by the Kreplin, and all interactions with him needed to be extremely discreet and infrequent. But like the Ferret, Tarro was needed.

Biorn went over to Tarro who was slumped over the table on which his elbows rested, his head propped up by his hands cradling his depressed face. His eyes were closed and Biorn decided that the young man had enough burdens. He would keep his fatherly secret for now. He felt a pain of sadness for the young man, but if they were to have any chance at success, they needed to get their heads into the game. And fast.

"Officer, have you decided what you want?" asked Biorn.

"Yeah, how about a big bowl of jak," Tarro said with disgust.

"Would you like that fried?" Biorn's retort got the intended smirk out of Tarro. "Well, when you figure it out, let me know."

Biorn left Tarro and began a covert conversation on the Lib Net with him. "NEED YOU TO FIND OUT WHEN TRIAL IS."

Tarro messaged back, "THEY HAVE NYA."

"I KNOW."

"THINK SHE'S PREGNANT."

Biorn didn't respond, desperately trying to keep his own emotions in check.

Tarro messaged, "MY FAULT. SHOULD NEVER HAVE TALKED TO HER."

"STAY FOCUSED."

"THEY HAVE HER HUSBAND, KAINO."

Biorn's heart sank at this new piece of information. Yet another variable to an increasingly desperate situation. He replied, "NEED TO LET IT GO."

"EASY FOR YOU TO SAY."

Biorn was helping other customers and shot a glance at Tarro who was staring at him from across the cafe. If he only knew.

The time when Biorn first saw Nya at the Academy flashed in his mind. He had managed to get on one of the occasional tours the Kreplin gives to Avalon citizens. She was only seven at the time, and it had been two years since the death of her mother.

He and the tour group had been watching a group of children being led in intense calisthenics outside. Almost immediately after beginning exercising, little Nya stopped when a butterfly landed on her arm. She stood there watching it gently flutter its wings, her face full of wonder at the little creature. She watched it with joy on her face until the instructor's rebuke snapped her out of distraction. She had such a sweet, innocent face, a light in her eyes that was so different from many of the dull, hardened children around her. Biorn smiled with the memory.

A customer's loud laugh jolted him out of his happy daydream.

He refocused and transmitted to Tarro, "CAN YOU GET INTO THE CENTER TONIGHT?"

"YES. ON DUTY. WILL REPORT TONIGHT."

Biorn felt a glimmer of hope, but he knew their chances of successfully rescuing Nya, let alone any of the other Barbs, were quite small. Everything depended on how much time they had before the trial. Biorn considered the odds and all the possible outcomes. Most were not favorable. And then it hit him—a back-up plan. He mulled it over for a moment. It was a long shot, but it just might work. He would need to call in a big favor from his friend at the factory, but with a little luck, his friend just might be able to pull it off. And if so, it could be brilliant.

Chapter 24

Reconnaissance

Tarro exited Biorn's cafe with two hours to kill before checking in for duty. He stood outside and looked in the direction of the Kreplin. A gap between two buildings on the opposite side of the Domon provided a view of the top of its spires. Before the sight of the Kreplin was able to plunge him deeper into his anguish, he shifted his focus to the Zeenuk Mountains. In the city's rotation, the highest peak in the mountain range now sat directly behind the Kreplin. Its snow-covered peak, glowing a faint orange from the setting sun, almost touched the full moon becoming increasingly visible in the darkening sky.

The majesty of the scene gripped Tarro. He looked around at his fellow citizens meandering up and down the Domon, wondering if anyone else noticed the beauty. Two young men passed in front of him, holding hands and walking briskly, talking about a new attraction at the Collonade. Near a pool fed by a ten foot waterfall sat a woman on a bench staring straight ahead, enjoying the newest entertainment through Vizitar. Another man or woman walked with a companion. The companion was talking excitedly while the man or woman looked down at the ground, obviously uninterested in what the droid was saying and seemingly apathetic to life itself.

Tarro's gaze returned to the mountains, and the beauty that awed him suddenly seized him with terror. Instantly, he felt very small and insignificant. Questions flooded his mind. What was the point of life? Even if he were able to rescue Nya, it would be just a matter of time before they died anyway . . . Why even try? What happens when one dies? Why did he feel so deeply? The pain, the sorrow, the yearning for relief and happiness . . . Why did he love Nya so much? Where did those mountains even come from in the first place? Why were they there? Why was *he* here?

Tarro shook his aching head and started walking as if he could evade his own thoughts. There were no answers, at least no good answers. He shook his head again and sighed deeply. That fact alone added to his inner turmoil. He quickly threw up a mental dam to the flood of questions that threatened to drown him. There was only one thing to do. Try to live. Try to squeeze some meaning out of life. Try to survive. He would save Nya or die trying. The only question that mattered right now was "how?"

He checked in early to SD-6, partly because he needed duty to help take his mind off his unrelenting thoughts, but mostly because he was eager to get into the Center. After receiving his usual patrol assignment, he headed for the ominous medical facility. The first step of the Libs' operation was reconnaissance. They needed information, and Tarro was the only one who could get it. Over the past year, Biorn had encouraged Tarro to incorporate routine visits to the Center into his patrols so that such reconnaissance trips could be accomplished without raised eyebrows. He marveled at how Biorn was always thinking ahead.

He arrived at the Center and after passing through the main entrance, was greeted by the companion receptionist who sported short, spiked blue hair.

The female-looking droid spoke with a man's voice. "Welcome, Peace Officer 43–64."

Tarro nodded his head in acknowledgement.

"Can I help you with anything?" she asked.

"No, just making the usual rounds. Anything I should be aware of?"

"No, not particularly. Our new Barb guests are quite compliant. You would think those uncivilized barbarians would be more trouble." She laughed mechanically.

Tarro bit his tongue. "Thank you. I'll make a general check and be out of your hair in a few."

"Ok, officer. Peace and love."

Tarro nodded and walked past her into the large lobby. In its center, a large hologram of a caricature of Mother Nature greeted him with the same automated greeting she gave every patron who entered. "Welcome, citizen." She then stretched out her arms in a welcoming gesture. "The

Kreplin sends its love. May you find health and wellness here during your visit. Peace and love."

Tarro thought of all the older citizens and those who had been told they had some terminal disease that had been brought here against their will, citizens whose lives had been deemed unworthy to continue, who otherwise would be burdens on society. How many had entered into this very lobby to be embraced by this cold expression of love from the State only to be "lovingly" euthanized?

Behind Mother Nature were two entryways. The larger one to the right led to the main wing of the Center which accommodated the citizens who came voluntarily for routine medical attention or plastic surgery operations. The smaller entryway on the left led to the secure wing of the Center, the section where the involuntarily visitors went. The Peace Officers had given this section the nickname "the Rosa," short for Dolorosa.

Tarro approached the door leading to the Rosa which was bracketed by two other Peace Officers standing guard. "So, what did you two do to tick off the Kreplin to pull *this* guard duty?" he asked them. He consciously interacted with them as he normally would, although this particular patrol was anything but normal.

The two guards laughed, and the one on the right said, "You'll get your turn soon enough. And it will probably be tomorrow since you just impugned our boss."

Tarro forced a laugh, thinking they were probably more right than wrong. The officer on the left touched a control panel on the wall, and the door whisked open for Tarro. Tarro passed through and said over his shoulder good-naturedly, "Suckers!"

He continued down the long, sterile corridor of the Rosa and wondered what Nya would say or do if she saw him. After he had abruptly left her in the village during his undercover operation, he knew he had left her utterly confused. Certainly, she would have been wondering why he had been there looking like a Barb and how he had even gotten there in the first place.

The most recent raid tragically threw them together again only adding to her confusion. On-board the transport, after he had removed his helmet, her shocked and bewildered look upon seeing his face still haunted him. Not once during the trip back into Avalon had he dared to make eye contact with her. Her despondent brown eyes would have only made him more miserable. He was torn apart inside, and there was no way to communicate the real story to her.

He reached the end of the corridor where another set of doors opened automatically to reveal a room that served as the processing center for incoming patients. In this wing, the only out-going patients were the ones sent to Justice Day. Two men in white jumpsuits stood behind the processing counter along with the chief administrator.

Tarro approached the counter and greeted the administrator, a stern looking woman whom Tarro had met several times while making his rounds in the Center. The only thing Tarro had ever received from her was a scowl, and he was just fine not conversing with her. She was the embodiment of the savagery of the Kreplin, and he loathed every ounce of her. She left the two men and entered into a room behind them. Just before she disappeared through the door, Tarro noticed a large, red splotch on the sleeve of her white jumpsuit.

Tarro said to the men working busily, "Just here to check on the recently processed Barbs." One of the benefits of being a Kreplin Peace Officer was that no one ever questioned what you were doing.

The nearest man glanced up at Tarro, gave him a quick head nod, and went back to work. Tarro passed by the counter and entered a much wider corridor, the sides of which were lined with individual cells. Once new Barbs arrived after a raid, they were kept in these cells until Justice Day, typically occurring about a week later. Just before Justice Day, they would be divided into two groups: those who would be publicly executed and those who would be designated for medical testing and experimentation.

Tarro looked at the vault-like door located at the end of the corridor of cells. Behind this impenetrable access point occurred all manner of atrocities. Tarro shuddered at the thought. Only Kreplin officials with top level clearance could access this area. Any rescue would have to occur before they were sent through this access point into the bowels of the Rosa. Once on the other side of this impervious gateway, it would be impossible to get to them.

Tarro arrived at the first cell and peered in to see three women. The entire front wall of the cell was constructed of a single piece of clear kevlar, an indestructible barrier through which even sound couldn't pass. The other three walls of the cell were made of steel, each of which supported thin slabs of steel appearing like floating shelves which served as beds. A latrine sat in the corner.

The women sat huddled together on a steel bench in the middle of the cell and stopped talking when they saw the Peace Officer standing in front of them. They looked at him with sad faces and swollen eyes presumably from crying. They glared at him, unmoving. He sensed their anger and figured that, were it not for the wall that separated them, they might just come after him. Never had Tarro felt so unnerved and appalled.

He moved on to the next cell which similarly held three women. Two were lying on their backs on their steel beds, and the other was pacing back and forth. Only the one pacing saw him. She stopped and turned to face him. Like the previous women, she glared at Tarro with swollen eyes and an angry ferocity that surprised him. He had expected sadness and fear but not such anger from these prisoners. If looks could kill, he would have been dead already.

With increasing dismay, he proceeded to the next cell, desperate to see if Nya was alive but equally dreading the encounter. Inside the third cell, a woman sat on her bed while one of the male Barbs did push-ups. When the woman saw Tarro, she said something to the man who bolted to his feet. He took one look at Tarro and then rushed the translucent wall that separated them, slamming into it with the full force of his body. He bounced off and then rushed it again, this time repeatedly hitting it with both palms of his hands.

Tarro instinctively took a step back, recognizing the man as Nya's husband. Kaino screamed at Tarro, but because of the sound proof barrier, all Tarro could see was the spit flying from his shouting mouth. It was all so surreal as he stood in this corridor of despair which was utterly and eerily silent, insulated from the shouting of a furious victim of injustice.

Kaino continued to yell at Tarro as he moved to the woman on the bed now visibly crying. He pointed at her as he vented his verbal wrath at the Peace Officer. Tarro wanted to open up the intercom and see what he was saying but was afraid the man's yelling would draw unwanted attention from personnel down the hallway.

Tarro was about to move to the next cell when it hit him. Kaino was still yelling and pointing at the woman, but Tarro now noticed that he was pointing at her stomach. Tarro looked at her face again and remembered that she was one of the women who had been in the later stage of pregnancy, seemingly due to deliver at any moment. He looked at her flat stomach, slammed by the realization.

He wheeled around and returned to the previous two cells in order to verify his newfound comprehension. As feared, none of the women were now pregnant. His tormented mind raced to Nya, and he nearly ran back down the corridor to continue looking for her. Each empty cell he passed induced more panic. He arrived near the end of the corridor. No Nya . . . and there was only one cell left.

He hesitantly approached the last cell, not wanting to face the horrific possibility of her absence. Taking a deep breath, he inched closer until he could peer into the cell, exhaling with relief when he saw her. Lying on her back, she appeared to be asleep. Her right hand lay on her stomach which, like the others, was flat. Tarro was overwhelmed by the sight of her. She looked so peaceful in her state of rest. Tarro thought that if there were such a thing as a sleeping angel, he'd just seen it.

He hastily left the Center to continue his patrol duty. His heart miserably ached for Nya. For some reason, he wondered if she had picked out a name for the baby that was no more. He kicked himself for not being more mentally prepared for his visit. He knew what the Kreplin did to pregnant women. He knew the hopelessness of their situation as they awaited their fate in those cells. Yet, he hadn't been prepared to see it all first hand, especially with Nya involved.

But now was not the time for tears and trepidation. Now was the time for bold action. If he was going to rescue Nya, he needed to stay focused on the task at hand. He would emote later. He looked at the time—six more hours of duty. Then, he would pass his intel to Biorn. He knew Biorn and the Libs would then hash out the rescue plan and he was anxious to hear the details.

☯

Biorn had always admired Hoth. Of the Libs, he was by far the most capable. He was one of the most famous and well-known architects of Avalon. His handiwork could be seen all over the city, but his magnum opus was the Kreplin. He had been part of a team of a dozen or so architects who designed the centerpiece of Avalon, but as the chief architect, it was really his design and everyone recognized it as such. As an architect, he was very detailed and thought of every conceivable contingency to their operations. Biorn smiled as he thought about the reactions Avalon citizens would have if they knew what their prized architect did as a side hobby.

Biorn checked on a table of customers as he communicated with Hoth on their covert network.

"T CONFIRMED ALL PRESENT," messaged Biorn to Hoth referring to Tarro.

Hoth was sitting on the patio eating breakfast, close enough to be in range for their secret conversation but far enough to maintain a healthy distance from his co-conspirator. "HOW MANY ARE WE GOING TO RESCUE?"

Biorn noticed he didn't say "try to rescue." That was another reason he liked Hoth—confident, never one to question success. Biorn balked at the question, though. He had been agonizing about this one. This would be their first attempt at a Barb rescue within the city. The Ferret had just arrived and was still getting familiar with the underground network the previous Ferret had mapped. Additionally, a large-scale rescue jeopardized the success of getting Nya and her husband out. He had labored over the question all night, but in the morning it was clear. It was the only decision he would be able to live with whether they succeeded or failed.

Biorn replied, "ALL OF THEM." It was going to be all or nothing. He would not rescue his daughter and leave the others to die or be tortured in the Center.

He waited for Hoth's response and was concerned about the pause. He knew he had just decreased their chances of success with this more comprehensive objective.

"AGREE," responded Hoth. "OFFLOAD THEM OUT VIA CRATES?"

Biorn considered the challenge of sneaking them into empty crates on departing supply cargo aircraft, but if there was anyone who could orchestrate it, it was Hoth. "YES. I'LL GET THEM TO YOU. YOU GET THEM ONBOARD."

"HOW DO WE SPRING THEM FROM THE CENTER?"

"THE FERRET DRESSED AS PEACE OFFICER WILL FOLLOW T INTO CENTER. WE WILL CREATE THE DIVERSION."

"CODES TO OPEN CELLS?"

"GOT THEM FROM T."

"HOW DOES FERRET GET THEM OUT OF CENTER?"

"WE NEED THAT DIVERSION."

"IDEAS?"

"MEET AT MY PLACE THIS AFTERNOON. 1500."

Biorn had a plan for the diversion. It was big, maybe too big. He thought about the precedent being set for future operations. If they needed a diversion this big now, how would they repeat future missions? Biorn pushed aside questions about the future. He needed to focus on the here and now, and he needed to do whatever it took to save his baby girl.

Chapter 25

Jail Break

T HE BRISK NIGHT INVIGORATED Zaun, and he forced himself to slow his quickening pace. As the new Ferret, if he was to blend in like any other shiftless Avalon citizen, he needed to meander, not walk with purpose. He glanced at the two young women who passed by him holding hands. One carried a little dog in a purse covered with pink sequins. The other wore an extravagant sequined pink outfit to match. He despised these people. They were the elite of the world, the chosen glitterati oblivious to the plight of the rest of humanity. The thought of his fellow Barbs waiting for their inevitable demise like rats to be exterminated only fueled his disgust. The real rats were out here.

They were two days away from the announced Justice Day. Biorn and the Libs had decided that the rescue would be initiated at midnight. Under his clothes, the Ferret felt the small package that would begin the operation. He marveled at the resourcefulness of Biorn who was somehow able to acquire or construct—he wasn't sure which—the incendiary device. He had asked Biorn how it worked, but Biorn lost him when he started talking about ion pulses and gamma-rays. All he knew was that it would put a big hole in the Kreplin wall and create the diversion they would need.

Having lost his parents at a young age, he had become quite resourceful himself. Friends of the family had taken him in, but their care was pretty much limited to food and shelter, at least when food was available. He had known nothing other than the simple Barb life until he overheard a group of men in the village cafe talking about Avalon. He sat in the dark corner for almost two hours, listening to them rail against the Kreplin and its oppressive corruption. Since that day, he had determined he would do something about it, and now he was. Feeling invincible with a new-found purpose in life, he forced himself to slow down again.

He reached the outer perimeter of COMCIRC and scanned the circular plaza. His indomitable feelings waned a bit as he surveyed the expansive open area surrounding the Kreplin. He observed a couple of shadowy figures walking in the distance, but apart from them, the plaza was void of life. He reminded himself of what Biorn had told him, that citizens freely walked in this plaza all the time and that he wouldn't be doing anything unusual.

He suppressed the thought that the Kreplin might be actively monitoring the area and casually sauntered into COMCIRC, setting out on a straight path that would intercept a point along the outer wall of the Kreplin. As he neared the wall, its looming height rose along with his quickening heartbeat. He selected one of the numerous statues surrounding the Kreplin and placed his package behind it. He then stepped back and studied the statue as if he were interested in its artistic qualities, just in case anyone was watching.

The statue was white marble, a smug-looking man whose hands gripped his coat lapels. He stood on a base with an inscription that read, "Comrade Pheti Marxim, Avalon City Founder, 2418—2483."

Zaun glanced to his left and right and, after seeing no one, spat on Comrade Marxim. He resumed his walk across COMCIRC, wishing he could see his little gift to the Kreplin go off, but he had more important matters to attend to. Biorn's bomb was programmed to detonate at precisely midnight. He glanced at the time. He had two hours to change and get into position with Tarro. Then the real challenge of the mission would begin. This had been the easy part.

๑๐

Tarro fidgeted with his holstered phaser as he made his way to the Center on his supposed routine patrol. In fifteen minutes, he would rendezvous with Zaun who would be posing as a Peace Officer. Fortunately, they were about the same size, so Tarro had been able to give him one of his own uniforms through Biorn. Tarro hadn't actually seen Zaun since his recruiting trip to Village-58, and he wondered if he would be anywhere as good as the original Ferret. Zaun was the key in all of this. Tarro didn't like that this all hinged on one man, but there was no other way. He was the only one without a Bionet.

Tarro mentally rehearsed the plan that Biorn had communicated to the Libs earlier that morning. At 11:57 pm, Zaun would rendezvous with Tarro outside the Center and fall in behind Tarro. At no time was Zaun to communicate with Tarro who was simply there to get him into the Center. Additionally, he was to try to stay out of Tarro's field of view as much as possible in order to keep him from the watching eyes of the Kreplin, protecting Tarro from being associated with Zaun's criminal activity.

They were to be in position inside the Center by 11:58 pm. After the diversionary explosion, it would be up to Zaun to get to the Barbs, release them from their cells, and lead them out of the Center. From there, they would make a bee-line to the closest water processing plant, about a quarter of a mile away, where they would enter the catacombs. The "catacombs" was the name the Libs gave to the largely unused service tunnel that paralleled the water piping network located below the city. Hoth has inserted this tunnel into his design, knowing the water piping would rarely, if ever, need to be serviced. Its real purpose was about to be utilized tonight.

Once safe in the catacombs, the next phase would begin. Over the next several nights, Zaun would escort the Barbs in pairs to the surface of the city. They would get the Barbs out of the city by dressing them like loading dock droids. Zaun would get them to the pre-determined loading dock, a designated Lib would provide the diversion to the dockmaster, and the Barb pair would steal away in one of the empty containers being loaded onto the supply aircraft.

Tarro thought the plan was pretty sound. It was as simple as they could make it, but he couldn't help but be nervous. So many things could go wrong.

"Officer 43–64, check-in, please." Tarro hated these random check-ins from SD-6. There was rarely anything to report, and if there were, any Peace Officer would certainly take the initiative to report it.

"Officer 43–64," said SD-6 a little more vigorously, "check-in, please."

"All secure . . . as always." Tarro relished his little add-on, knowing that, if all went according to plan, the Kreplin was about to get a swift and embarrassing kick to the face.

"Copy, 43–64. Peace and love."

Tarro approached the front entrance of the Center and noted the time. 11:57 pm. He placed his hand on his holstered phaser, the gesture that would indicate his identity to Zaun. He glanced to his right and saw a Peace Officer walking toward him with his head down. The Peace Officer quickly scratched his face, signaling that he was the Ferret.

Without stopping, Tarro entered the Center.

"Good evening, Peace Officer," welcomed the receptionist.

Tarro nodded in acknowledgment and continued past. He heard another "Good evening, officer" behind him, confirming Zaun was in trail, exactly as planned.

Tarro entered the lobby. The next step was to engage the two Peace Officers outside the entrance of the Rosa and keep them engaged until the explosion, at which point Zaun would slip into the secure wing. The team was banking on the ensuing chaos to squelch any questions the guards would have for Zaun, a Peace Officer who would be unfamiliar to them and who would not show up on their PO grid if checked. The PO grid was the map accessible by every Peace Officer through their Vizitars, displaying all Peace Officers and their current locations.

Tarro ignored the hologram of Mother Nature as she greeted him with her customary, duplicitous well-wishes from the Kreplin. 11:58 pm. Tarro had passed the hologram and turned left toward the two guards when his heart sank.

Behind him, he heard the receptist say to Zaun, "Excuse me, Peace Officer, your credentials did not show up when you entered. Please follow me to the front."

Tarro stopped in his tracks, unsure what to do. He didn't realize that he was being scanned and verified by the receptionists every time he had entered the building, but he wasn't surprised.

"I'm sorry," said Zaun. "That's the second time that's happened to me today. Let me do a systems check of my Bionet."

Tarro checked the time. 11:59 pm. Zaun was proving to be able to think on his feet, so Tarro decided to engage the guards and let Zaun fend for himself.

He approached the guards and breathed a sigh of relief. He was familiar with both of them, and they were both junior in rank to him. While Tarro was not in their direct chain-of-command, they would be less prone to question Zaun who they would assume was his patrolling partner for the night.

"So, nothing like an exciting night of guard duty at the Center, huh?" Tarro said to the guards.

"Oh, you'd be surprised," said the guard on the left with a smirk. "That receptionist who's talking to your friend right now just asked Mr. Fabulous over here on a date."

"You're just jealous," said the other guard laughing.

Tarro forced a laugh as he waited for the 11:59 displayed in his Vizitar to change to midnight. "I didn't know they did that sort of thing."

"I think it's just new programming from the—"

BOOM! The floor and walls of the Center shuddered as a thunderous clap rifled through the building.

The two guards looked at each other and exclaimed simultaneously, "What was that?!"

SD-6 provided the answer as she urgently broke in with a broadcast on the open PO channel, "All Peace Officers within Sector-1 and COM-CIRC, converge on the Kreplin now. The Kreplin is under attack. This is not a drill. I repeat . . ."

SD-6 repeated the message, and Tarro relished hearing the incessant cheery voice traded for a rare, alarmed one. With his back still to Zaun, he gave him a quick wave forward.

"I'm checking the Rosa," said Zaun matter-of-factly as he quickly passed the guards and slipped through the doors.

"Copy," Tarro said without looking. He had been prepared to convince the two guards that they should accompany him to assist the Kreplin, but he didn't have to as SD-6 had just ordered all officers in their sector to do so.

Turning away from the guards, Tarro ordered, "Follow me!" The two officers complied with SD-6 still barking out instructions to all Peace Officers.

Outside the Center, Tarro said to the guards, "Continue to the Kreplin. I'll be right behind you."

He pretended to do a sweep of the area in front of the Center, keeping its entrance in his peripheral view while waiting for Zaun to exit with the prisoners. He was supposed to be heading to the Kreplin, but he had to see mission success with his own eyes. He inhaled deeply, allowing the refreshing coolness of the outside air to invigorate his body.

For the first time in a while, he felt hopeful. They had executed this phase of the mission flawlessly, and minus the little hiccup with the receptionist, it had gone according to plan. Getting them out of the Center was the hardest part, and as long as Zaun didn't meet much resistance in the Rosa, it would not be long before they would be out of that evil place and on their way to freedom.

He checked the PO Grid. He was relieved to see that, at least for the moment, there were no other Peace Officers in the vicinity of the Rosa. If Zaun met resistance from any Kreplin personnel, he had a knife strapped to his ankle. The knife was primarily to disable the receptionist droid on the way out, but Tarro knew he would have no compunction using it in the Rosa if needed.

He again checked the time which crept by ridiculously slowly. Zaun had been in there for about five minutes. Biorn had figured it would take him about seven minutes total to get in, release all the prisoners, give brief instructions to them, and get out.

Tarro breathed in deeply again, tasting the cool air. He smiled as he thought about Nya. She would soon be free from the clutches of the Kreplin, and its failure to hold onto its own prisoners would serve as a giant punch in the gut. *But what kind of retribution would come?* The abrupt thought pierced Tarro's mind, and he immediately squashed it. Now was not the time for "what if."

He was about a hundred yards from the front of the Center. He maintained a normal patrolling pace and demeanor while keeping the entrance in his peripheral view. Finally, to his great relief, Zaun appeared in the entrance. The Ferret paused for a moment and then casually exited, took an immediate right, and disappeared into the dark shadows.

Tarro waited breathlessly for the Barbs to appear in trail. Nothing. He stared intensely at the entrance as if his gaze could cajole them out. Still nothing. Time, which had been crawling, now froze in a state of horror. He could see the receptionist through the doors still sitting at her desk working. Impossible! Without thinking, he raced toward the direction of Zaun. He arrived at the spot where he'd lost sight of him, and as expected, he was nowhere to be seen.

Tarro tried to snap out of his panicked stupor. The mission had failed. But how? Zaun was long gone, and even if he had been able to catch up with him, doing so would only compromise him. For a moment, he considered going into the Center himself, but he already knew why Zaun had come out empty-handed. If it had been a trap, Zaun wouldn't have made it out. The only possible explanation was that the prisoners weren't there. He forced his numb legs to move toward the Kreplin. They would be questioning his delay to the scene of the attack if he dallied any longer.

Every footstep toward the Kreplin became more laborious, each step turning his legs and heart into hulking lead. With great effort, he arrived at the outer perimeter of COMCIRC already bustling with activity with Peace Officers everywhere. Tarro estimated about a hundred had formed a large circular perimeter around the explosion site. SD-6 was still spouting off on the PO Channel.

The fire from the explosion had been extinguished, its smoke from the smoldering hole in the Kreplin wall the remaining evidence of their failed mission. Tarro numbly gazed at the smoke, following its upward, meandering rise into the sky. The dome and spires of the Kreplin were engulfed in a smoky haze, giving it an even more sinister appearance. That's when it hit Tarro. There was no defeating this monster. Victory was not possible. The Kreplin had a vice grip of control, and no one was going to pry its iron fingers from the chokehold. The realization slammed into him with an acute pain of finality, and he crumpled to his knees in tears.

ତ୨ଡ

The next day, Biorn entered his cafe and immediately saw Tarro sitting stone-faced in his usual spot. He made his way toward the back kitchen, intentionally avoiding eye contact with the sullen officer. Whatever he was personally feeling, he knew it was ten times worse for Tarro who perpetually flirted with the cliff edge of an all-consuming anger that threatened to plunge him into an ever-present abyss of despair.

He knew Tarro would be looking for answers and wasn't surprised when the immediate question from Tarro came through the Lib Net. "WHAT HAPPENED?"

Biorn continued to work in the kitchen out of sight of Tarro. "FERRET FOUND THE CELLS EMPTY."

"HOW IS THAT POSSIBLE?"

Biorn didn't know how to answer. Anything was possible with the Kreplin, and they were only operating off the intel they had received which told them the prisoners would be held in the cells of the Rosa up until Justice Day. Whether or not it was bad intel or the Kreplin knew what they were up to, he didn't know.

Tarro didn't wait for an answer before asking, "WHERE ARE THEY?"

"WE DON'T KNOW."

"NEXT STEP?"

Biorn paused. He knew the answer he was about to give would only push Tarro closer to that cliff edge. "NOTHING. THERE'S NOTHING WE CAN DO."

For a few moments Tarro didn't respond. Biorn could feel his anguish through the walls of the kitchen.

Biorn added, "THERE IS ALWAYS HOPE."

"HOW? YOU JUST SAID THERE'S NOTHING WE CAN DO."

"TRUE. TOMORROW IS JUSTICE DAY. WE CAN'T STOP IT."

"WHAT ABOUT NYA?"

"TARRO. LISTEN TO ME." They always avoided using names in case their transmissions were ever intercepted, but Biorn needed to get through to his devastated friend. He paused, searching for the right words which were critically important at the moment. "HONOR HER MEMORY. DON'T THROW YOUR LIFE AWAY. LIVE TO FIGHT ANOTHER DAY. WE NEED YOU STAY IN THE GAME."

Biorn sighed heavily. He had given this speech to Tarro before, and it now seemed hollow. He suddenly felt very old, old and really worn out, like he just wanted to lay down and take a very long nap.

Tarro replied, "YEAH, IT IS A GAME ISN'T IT? ONE BIG JAKY RIGGED GAME."

Biorn inwardly feared Tarro was more right than wrong. But he had figured out a long time ago that they weren't in control of much. But neither was the Kreplin. There was something much bigger in play. A grand master plan. And no man, certainly not the Supreme Confidant, was in control of this plan.

He left the kitchen to try to console Tarro as best he could with his presence, but Tarro was gone. He looked at the empty seat wondering what would become of him. *If he can just make it through Justice Day*, he thought.

Chapter 26

Day of Infamy

I T WAS A DINGY and murky day with heavy gray clouds threatening to disgorge their watery innards at any moment. As usual for Justice Day, the Kreplin plaza was filled with the citizens of Avalon, except today, the dreary weather seemed to temper their usual festive mood. Supreme Confidant Talin was introduced with the customary pageantry, but there was at least one citizen who stood in COMCIRC unimpressed.

Tarro was off-duty and stood rigidly in a black jumpsuit draped with a hooded cloak. He had taken a position as close as possible to the Kreplin's balcony. Last night, as he sat in his living room with his adopted cat staring at him from the opposite couch, he had come to some conclusions. Biorn had implored him to stay in the game, and sitting in his living room, he had reviewed his life in this game.

Everything seemed like a distant memory. Even Nya seemed distant, like the faint wisp of a remembered dream which vanishes upon awakening.

He had almost decided to feign sickness and avoid the citizen requirement to attend Justice Day, but one of the conclusions he had made last night was that he needed closure. As painful as it would be to see Nya's last moments, he needed to see it. He needed to see her. And he needed finality. The other conclusion he made was that he was done playing the game.

The crowd cheered as four Barb prisoners were brought out onto the balcony. They had been transformed into the customary appearance of wild and uncivilized barbarians and Tarro searched frantically for the face of Nya. Until now, he had suppressed his worst fear, that she would not be brought out for execution but would instead be relegated to the tortuous testing inside the bowels of the Center. For her sake, he had desperately hoped for her appearance today on the balcony.

The whole scene which unfolded before his eyes became a slow-motion haze. None of the prisoners had the face of Nya and he winced as each collapsed in death with a jab from a Peace Officer's chivvy.

The cheering of the crowd was mere white noise that rang hollow in Tarro's ears. He watched as they dragged the four Barbs off the balcony while Talin began another self-adoring speech. Tears began to well up in Tarro's eyes, and he bowed his cloaked head. He remained motion-less, unable to look at the vile leader of Avalon as he pontificated to his manipulated audience.

The crowd suddenly burst into another round of cheers, forcing Tarro's eyes back to the balcony. Five more ragged-looking Barbs had been escorted out. To his mild relief, he saw Nya next to Kaino who was standing as close as possible to her. He breathed a sad sigh. At least their deaths would be swift. They would not suffer in the Center.

All five Barbs stood in a row facing the crowd with Nya on the far right end. Talin laid out the usual accusations, and Tarro wondered why they even bothered with trumped-up charges as neither State official nor citizen cared. To produce some drama, the Peace Officer with the chivvy started on the left and began killing the Barbs one at a time, allowing the crowd to cheer between each execution.

When the Barb next to Kaino collapsed from the deadly charge, Kaino quickly grabbed Nya's hand and kissed her on the cheek. In re-sponse, a Peace Officer crashed the blunt end of the chivvy down upon his head for his insolence, and Kaino crumpled to his knees. Anticipat-ing Nya's reaction, the second officer yanked her away from Kaino and held her as she screamed in anguish. The officer with the chivvy then jammed it into Kaino's back. The blue charge briefly enveloped him as he collapsed dead at Nya's feet. The crowd cheered, and Tarro spun around to look at their pompous faces, his eyes filled with an inferno of hatred.

He turned back to the balcony and saw Nya go limp in the Peace Officer's arms. Tears streamed down her face, matching Tarro's own. His protective instincts kicked in, and without thinking, he began to grab his phaser hidden underneath his cloak. Then he froze as she looked down from the balcony directly at him. He locked eyes with her, and her brown eyes beamed at him from a dirty face muddied by her own tears. A wave of warmth overtook him as if the sun had burst forth with full brilliance.

Still gazing at him, she pushed away from the Peace Officer and stood, holding her head high on her graceful neck. As Talin laid out the accusations, a breeze wafted over the balcony, blowing strands of tangled hair into her face. She took her two bound hands and brushed the strands out of her face, tucking what she could grasp behind her right ear. She smiled at Tarro who stood enraptured. The officer behind her raised his chivvy, and sensing it, she closed her eyes before the blue charge of death devoured her life and Tarro's heart.

The next few moments slowed as Tarro's senses quickened to a heightened state. He had prepared for this moment. He choked down his tears and smoothly reached for his phaser. A couple laughed behind him. Peace Officers began dragging the bodies off the balcony. He grasped the phaser and mechanically drew it out of its holster. Talin waved exaggeratedly to the crowd, and Tarro watched his lips move without hearing his voice. He brushed his index finger over the engraving underneath the barrel, feeling the "Peace and Love" inscription. He would get one shot. He eyed the pompous leader with intense hatred and aimed his phaser from underneath his cloak. It was a long shot but doable. Tarro exhaled slowly, placed the sight on Talin's forehead, and began to slowly pull the trigger.

At that moment, a Peace Officer moved in front of Talin directly into Tarro's line of sight, and he instantly released the trigger. He would shoot any Kreplin official, but not a fellow officer. The animated officer said something to Talin who immediately halted the other officers from dragging the Barbs off the balcony. As the Confidant hastily proceeded to Nya, one of the officers said something to him while pointing at her body. Talin stooped down over Nya and then rose with a look of fury in his face as he yelled something at the officer. He gave an "away" motion with his hand and stormed off the balcony through the double doors.

Tarro was stunned, not only because he had lost his opportunity to take out Talin, but also because of the bizarre scene on the balcony.

"Mother-6, calling all Peace Officers." The familiar voice crackled over the PO Channel. "We have an escaped Barb on the loose inside the city. Current location unknown at the moment. Sending image and last known position now. All officers stand by for specific tasking."

A digitized voice spoke through Tarro's Vizitar, announcing, "Incoming alert." An alert icon flashed in the upper right hand corner of his visual display, and he quickly opened the notification. "Escaped Barb was last seen at the following location," continued the computerized voice. A map display popped up to show a flashing marker at a location a mile from the Center. "Barb was last seen approximately four hours ago at 7:10 am this morning with eight other prisoners being escorted to the Kreplin for Justice Day."

Tarro's mind raced as he did a quick mental count. *Nine prisoners were just executed. If one of the nine escaped, how were there nine on the balcony? Maybe they substituted the missing one with one of the other remaining Barbs. No, the Kreplin obviously just found out about the escape. Did they miscount? How in the world could a Barb have escaped unnoticed until now?*

SD-6 broke into his thoughts with another broadcast, "Attention, officers. Barb is thought to have had outside assistance. Use all means to capture Barb, to include lethal force. Stand by to receive image of escaped Barb."

Tarro received specific tasking to patrol and search Sector-8. Then, in his visual display, a picture of Nya appeared.

ଡ଼ଚ

Biorn felt weak and a little woozy, and he steadied himself as he tried to walk as normally and nonchalantly as possible. Physically, he felt miserable. Mentally, he felt amazingly free. He was now off the Bionet network, or at least, he was pretty sure he was. After their failed rescue attempt of the Barbs, Biorn had employed his back-up plan which had two key components. The first required him to get off the Kreplin network.

To kill his Bionet, he drank a cocktail of acidic chemicals that he had been developing over the last several years for such a time as this. It was a near lethal mixture but contained the necessary ingredients to destroy the functionality of the digital hardware in his body. He had vomited all through the night, and early this morning, while he could barely move his body, his Vizitar was completely inoperative, suggesting his little concoction accomplished its intended results.

The second part of his back-up plan was initiated the moment he found out Nya was a prisoner of the Kreplin. One of the members of the Libs managed a companion production facility. Biorn coordinated with him to have an exact replica of Nya constructed, placing the order through a fake citizen identity in order to provide cover to the manager who would undoubtedly be investigated later by the Kreplin. The facility manager had pulled through brilliantly. The companion not only looked like Nya, but in accordance with the details provided by Biorn, mimicked her mannerisms.

Biorn glanced to his right and looked at the priceless treasure walking beside him. She looked ridiculous. He'd had Zaun shave her head, replacing her pretty hair with temporary tattoos on her head and arms. She wore brightly colored clothing with an array of gaudy jewelry. She thought she looked hideous, but more importantly, she looked like an Avalon citizen.

She glanced at him and said, "At least you guys were able to work a butterfly into these hideous body markings."

He smiled faintly. "Don't talk. And let me know if you see any Peace Officers."

The danger at this point was crossing paths with a Peace Officer, all of whom were now everywhere looking for her. Though she was unrecognizable, they would both be dead giveaways to the officers who would be checking all citizens through the Kreplin database. Without a Bionet, neither of them would register in the database and the game would be up.

Biorn's heart was heavy at losing the other Barbs, but he smiled inwardly at Zaun's successful rescue of Nya. So far, Zaun had made all the right decisions, proving to be highly capable. This morning, he had deployed Biorn's squadron of drones, swarming the Peace Officers and the group of nine Barb prisoners in transit to the Kreplin for Justice Day. Just before entering COMCIRC, Zaun exploded the drones in staggered intervals like large fireworks, providing the diversion for him to swap the companion droid for Nya. His main regret was that he couldn't rescue Kaino. Zaun reported that Kaino had seen the swap and immediately latched on to the companion as if it were Nya. He was valiant and manly to the end.

Biorn scanned the Domon ahead, looking for Peace Officers. He checked the time. He had twenty minutes to get to Sector-12's loading dock and get Nya onboard before its SC-5 departed. He would have preferred to have dressed her as a loading dock droid, but those droids didn't normally stroll around Avalon, so her current disguise was going to have to do.

At that moment, two Peace Officers emerged from a building on their right and entered the Domon. The officers began heading in their direction, briefly disappearing from view behind a large statue located in the middle of the Domon. Biorn grabbed Nya's arm and pulled her into the nearby Emporium.

He walked in and proceeded toward the right side of the market-place, far enough from the front door to remain out of sight but close enough to be able to watch for the Peace Officers to pass by. He was pre-tending to shop, keeping one eye on the front door when he realized Nya wasn't with him. In a moment of panic, he quickly scanned the store and spotted her near the entrance, standing in front of the packaged placenta display.

He tried to gain eye contact with her as she stood perilously close to the front doors. He cleared his throat, but she remained fixated on the display, a look of horror having gripped her face. He cleared his throat again, this time more loudly, but she didn't budge. He was about to go over and physically drag her away when one of the two Peace Officers ap-peared at the front doors. The doors whisked opened, and Biorn held his breath. As the officer stood at the entrance, scanning the store, the other Peace Officer emerged behind him and said, "SD-6 is pushing us to get to our assigned sector. We need to hustle."

Biorn breathed a sigh of relief as the two officers left and continued down the Domon. He darted over to Nya. "We need to go now!"

"What *is* this?" She looked at him with tears welling in her eyes.

"Come," said Biorn compassionately. Nya wiped her eyes and then quickly grabbed the packaged placenta and stuffed it under her cloak.

"What are you doing?" Biorn whispered. He grabbed her by the arm and led her out of the Emporium. He bit his tongue and held back the rebuke he wanted to give her for the unnecessary risk. In truth, though, this is why he loved her so much. She was his daughter, yes, but she was so much more. She was a loving and compassionate human being with an innocence foreign to Avalon.

They passed a nearby POD station, and Biorn checked the time. The diversion had cost them several precious minutes. They were still good on time but were now cutting it a lot closer than he would have preferred. Currently in Sector-11, they just needed to get one sector over, and the safest way was by foot. Hopping blindly into a POD was too risky as one never knew who was going to be on the receiving end.

"Citizens, halt!" called out a voice from behind them. Biorn turned and looked in the direction of the voice. As he feared, the order had come from a Peace Officer about fifty feet behind them.

"Quick, follow me!" Biorn barked to Nya. He dashed back to the POD station they had just passed.

"Citizens, halt!" The Peace Officer began running toward them with his phaser drawn.

Followed closely by Nya, Biorn jumped into the POD and commanded, "Sector-3, Station-21." He kept his back to the officer in order to hide his face from the officer's view. The officer arrived just as the door closed, and he slammed his fist into the POD's glassy exterior. As if in response, the POD swiftly dropped below the city's surface into the FLUXX. It smoothly accelerated toward Sector-3, and Biorn frantically considered his next moves, first of which was to simply shake their new pursuer.

ᐇ

SD-6 had directed all officers to make relevant situational reports on the PO Channel in order to keep all officers abreast of the situation as it unfolded in real time. Tarro had disregarded his tasking and had just arrived at Nya's last seen location in Sector-1 when a Peace Officer reported over the PO Channel, "Mother-6, Officer 23–71. I just made contact with likely Barb."

SD-6 responded, "Officer 23–71, confirm suspect matches sent image."

"I believe they match image."

"They? Is there more than one matching the description?"

"No, only one, and they just entered POD . . . standby . . . POD number 175."

"Officer 23–71, who entered POD-175?"

"They entered the POD. The suspect in question."

SD-6 asked, "How many entered POD-175?"

"Two."

"And they match the description of the Barb?"

"Affirmative, Mother-6. Facial recognition says it's a match."

"Officer 23–71, confirm you have two individuals who match the description of the Barb."

The officer sounded exasperated and spoke methodically. "Mother-6, there are two individuals who entered the POD. One male, one female. The female matches the description."

"Copy, Officer 23–71. Tracing POD now."

There was a brief pause before SD-6 broadcasted, "POD-175 with suspects is about to arrive at Sector-3, Station-21. Officer 15–88, you are closest to this station. What is your ETA to Station-21?"

"Forty five seconds," responded the Peace Officer.

"Copy, Officer 15–88, proceed to POD station immediately. Attention, all officers, you have three minutes to get to your assigned sectors before the FLUXX is shut down. All Officers in Sector-3, proceed to Station-21."

Tarro pulled up the FLUXX on his Vizitar. POD-175 had just arrived at its destination in Sector-3. He checked the time. Sector-3's cargo aircraft had taken off earlier in the morning. The next SC-5 to take off would be from Sector-12 in ten minutes. No doubt, Nya would be heading there. Tarro now feared that there wouldn't be an aircraft to catch. If SD-6 was shutting down the FLUXX, it would surely halt all departing flights.

Tarro sprinted to the nearest station and entered the POD. "Sector-12, loading dock." As his POD descended, he went back to watching the POD movements through his Vizitar. Another POD a block from where POD-175 had terminated began moving. Tarro checked its destination. Sector-12, loading dock. Bingo.

Tarro's POD raced toward Sector-12 as fast as his own adrenaline coursed through his body. Nya's escape remained a mystery, and he assumed that Zaun was the person with her. He still couldn't believe it was really her. It was just all too inconceivable. In the last few minutes, he had gone from suicidal rage to intense hope. All the helpless feelings he'd had at her supposed execution had transformed into a focused ferocity.

Standing in his POD, he felt like a caged lion ready to devour the enemy. He touched his phaser as if to reassure himself it was still there. If needed, he would torch anything and anybody that stood in the way of Nya's freedom. He was not going to lose her again.

The faint blue glow of another POD appeared just ahead and to his left, heading in the same direction. He quickly checked the FLUXX display, and as suspected, it was the POD that had just departed Sector-3. If his hunch was right, Zaun and Nya were on board. The POD's blue glow grew steadily brighter as their paths converged. Soon Tarro was able to confirm there were two figures inside.

Both PODs arrived in Sector-12 at the same POD station. Tarro's POD slid in behind the other as they simultaneously slowed down to dock. As the gap between the PODs closed, Tarro's heart sank when he saw the back of an Avalon woman with a shaved head standing with a man who was not Zaun.

He checked their citizen data through his Vizitar, and surprisingly, neither one of them registered with any information. As far as the Kreplin was concerned, they didn't exist. Perplexed, he toggled back to the FLUXX to see if any other PODs were inbound to their location when the man next to the woman turned around. Biorn! Tarro stared, dumbfounded, shocked at seeing Biorn with the unfamiliar woman. Biorn, however, seemed unsurprised to see him and gave him a "go away" wave of his hand.

Biorn's POD rose to the surface to empty its riders, and Tarro waited for his turn, finally comprehending Nya's disguise. Then it dawned on him. He had just implicated Biorn by seeing him through his Bionet. If the Kreplin wasn't currently watching, they'd review Tarro's video later.

Biorn and Nya's empty POD lowered and moved to the side to allow Tarro's POD to take its place above ground. His POD flooded with sunlight as it rose to the surface. He concluded that, in relation to his Bionet and Biorn, what was done was done. There was no turning back now. The POD door opened, releasing him from his cage.

The POD station was located around the corner from Sector-12's landing pad, and Biorn and Nya were already out of sight. Tarro quickly surveyed the area for other officers. Seeing just a handful of citizens wandering around, he checked the PO grid. To his horror, it showed an officer located in the dockmaster's office.

Tarro began running to the loading dock when SD-6 cut in, "Attention, all officers, FLUXX is now shut down. Suspects likely in Sector-3 near Station-21. Sending target search radius now."

As Tarro neared the dockmaster's office, he slowed to a walk. Inside he saw Biorn yelling animatedly at the dockmaster who stood next to a young Peace Officer. There was no sign of Nya. Tarro set his phaser to stun, relieved that he didn't know the officer should he have to take action against him. He entered the office and Biorn glanced in his direction without pausing from his rant.

"What do you mean my delivery is going to be delayed?!" he yelled at the dockmaster.

The dockmaster, a gruff, large man not accustomed to being bullied by a sniveling cafe manager yelled back, "I already told you the Kreplin shut down outgoing flights!"

"I don't care what the Kreplin did!"

"Well, maybe you should care! Without them, you get squat!"

"I can't run a cafe without food, and you're supposed to bring in my food!"

By now, the dockmaster was thoroughly enraged, and the young Peace Officer decided it was time to step in. "Excuse me," he said to Biorn, "this flight is not departing. You need to leave now."

Tarro figured it was youthful inexperience that explained the officer's failure to check Biorn through the citizen database and knew this lucky oversight was going to be short-lived. Biorn glanced again at Tarro, and for the first time, Tarro saw uncertainty in his eyes. Biorn was a brilliant planner, but even he was mortal. There were some contingencies which simply couldn't be planned for or foreseen.

At that moment, Nya entered the office and Biorn and Tarro looked at her alarmed, both scrambling to think of a solution out of a situation rapidly deteriorating.

Their whirling thoughts were interrupted by the young officer. "No one move!" He had his phaser drawn and pointed at Biorn. "Mother-6, Officer 49–68 reporting. I have two unregistered citizens at—"

Biorn lunged at the officer who reflexively stepped back and fired his phaser. Biorn crumpled to the ground from the blast.

"Daddy, no!" screamed Nya as she rushed over to Biorn.

In an instant, Tarro pulled out his phaser and shot both the officer and the dockmaster. Their stunned bodies fell to join Biorn on the office floor.

Nya dropped to her knees and draped her body over Biorn, wailing loudly. Tarro stood in shock. Biorn shot . . . the revelation of his relationship to Nya . . . an office with three bodies on the floor . . . an SC-5 going nowhere. Time would have frozen were it not for the aching sound of Nya's agony.

"Officer 49–68, report!" demanded SD-6. Lacking a response, SD-6 shifted to Tarro. "Officer 43–64, I see you're on location with Officer 49–68. Report."

Tarro didn't answer.

"Officer 43–64, come in. Confirm you are with Officer 49–68. 49–68 is not responding, and his vitals are abnormal."

Tarro stood there lost, his mind and body having turned to stone. He tried desperately to get either one to move, to do or think of something, but it was if he were stuck in a moment which had petrified.

The door to the office swung open and in strode Zaun. He stood for a moment, assessing the situation. He went over to Biorn and checked his pulse. Without saying a word, he grabbed the downed officer's phaser, checked the setting, pointed it at Tarro, and fired.

Chapter 27

Revelation

THE MAKE-SHIFT TENT SAT outside Village-58 alongside the creek. It was crudely assembled but was enough to shelter from the elements. Outside, Nya stood ankle-deep in the creek, scrubbing the body markings off her head and arms. She looked at her reflection in the water and nearly cried at the sight of her bare scalp but tried to squeeze a little solace from the removal of the tattoos.

"Tarro, get off that rock! You're going to hurt yourself" she cried out to her son. Little Tarro looked at her with a frown and then jumped as high as he could off the rock into the water.

Nya shook her head and muttered to herself, "That boy is going to be the death of me . . . if he doesn't kill himself first."

Inside the tent, Tarro awoke to see fluttering white canvas above his head, caressed by the gentle breeze of the afternoon. The sun pierced through, warming his face and body. An image of Zaun pointing a phaser at him flashed in his mind. He wondered if he was dead for a moment until a wave of nausea swept over him. He willed his aching body to move and managed with great effort to sit up on the edge of the cot he'd been lying on. For how long, he didn't know. He struggled to his feet and shuffled to the tent's opening.

Drawing back the flap, he saw Nya near the edge of the creek digging a hole in the ground with a fat stick. He slowly approached her in a daze, and as he neared, she stopped digging and said to him with a faint smile, "You look terrible."

Tarro looked at her bald head with puffy eyes and a red nose but decided not to return the compliment.

He suddenly looked worried, and Nya knew what he was thinking. "Don't worry, you no longer have . . . what do you call it . . . a Bionet? They don't know we're here." She returned to her digging. "I suppose you're wondering what I'm doing."

Tarro remained silent as he was wondering about a lot of things.

She picked up a small package and gently placed it in the freshly dug hole. Contemplatively, she slowly covered it with dirt and patted it down. "I got it from Avalon." She wiped the fresh tears off her face. "They took my baby from me. I know burying this is probably silly, but it's good to remember him . . . or her . . . and all the babies that were taken from us."

Tarro was struggling to comprehend, but he tried to comfort her. "I don't think it's silly at all." He sat down next to her and looked out over the creek. Her boy was playing in the water on the other side, oblivious to his presence. He wished he could be a care-free little boy, if only for a moment.

After a few minutes of silence, Nya said, "I guess you're wondering what happened."

"Yes, the question had crossed my mind," he said. He desperately wanted to ask about Biorn but was afraid of the answer.

"Zaun is pretty amazing," she said.

"Zaun? Last I remember he shot me."

Nya laughed. "He saved you. He saved us all."

"And Biorn?"

"Fortunately, that Peace Officer had his phaser on stun. It knocked Biorn out for a few hours, but he's no worse for wear." Tarro breathed a sigh of relief. "Of course, you know what that's like," she added.

"So Zaun stunned me. Why?"

"It's all a giant blur to me, so I'm repeating what Daddy told me when we got here."

"So how did we get here? And that's another thing . . . *Daddy*?" Tarro asked incredulously.

"Whoa, slow down. Let me try to give you the story. I don't quite understand it all, but Daddy told me you would. After Daddy was shot, Zaun knew he was still alive, but you were the most immediate problem as the Kreplin was no doubt monitoring us through your Bionet. He also wanted to make it look like you were a victim in all this—that's why he shot you. He then injected you with some stuff that killed your Bionet. That's why you feel so bad."

"That and getting phased," said Tarro chuckling.

"Daddy said it had been his plan to give you the injection later and get you out of Avalon, but Zaun saw the necessity and the opportunity to give it to you after he shot you. Fortunately, Daddy was carrying it, and Zaun was able to give it to you."

"Biorn never told me about this injection."

"He said there were some things he kept from you. Recently, he suspected that the Kreplin had broken into your secret communication network. That's why he didn't even tell you about his back-up plan to rescue me. He had a friend who was able to produce an exact replica of me, and Zaun was able to make the switch."

Tarro thought about the companion on Justice Day who mimicked Nya's mannerisms so well, and the remembrance of the droid brought the execution scene to mind. "I'm sorry about your husband."

Nya lowered her head. "Yes, he was a good man." She looked wistfully at her son still playing on the other side of the creek. "You know, Zaun told me that when he pulled me out of the group of prisoners—oh, it happened so fast—and replaced me with my look-alike, that Kaino immediately latched onto the droid as if it were me."

"You loved him a lot, didn't you?" Tarro said, immediately kicking himself for the stupid question.

"Yes, of course. Very much so." Tarro looked down, feeling suddenly awkward and out of place. Nya sensed his discomfort and touched him arm, sending a bolt of warmth through him. "So Zaun basically took out every droid on the pad, got us onto the aircraft, and forced the pilot to fly us out of Avalon."

"Where's the aircraft now?"

"I don't know, but it's a big pile of burned debris wherever it is. When Daddy finally came to, he and Zaun got a few bodies from the Quarry morgue and put them in the aircraft and then destroyed it to make it look like we all died in a crash."

Tarro resisted asking about the pilot and said, "Brilliant." Biorn never failed to amaze. And Zaun proved to be worth his weight in gold. "So where's your Father now?"

"He wanted me to tell you that he always wanted to be a Ferret. He said you'd know what that meant."

Tarro sat there for a while, taking it all in. It was all quite surreal. He felt a sense a relief, but it wasn't long before he felt all his demons returning as the darkness began to creep back in.

"What's wrong, Tarro?"

He thought for a while on how to answer her question. Finally, he said, "For so long, I have been consumed with anger . . . and bitterness. Ever since I lost you at the Academy,—I . . ." His voice trailed off. Nya let him gather his composure.

After a few moments of silence, he said, "You know, I almost ended my life. The only thing that gave me purpose in life was revenge. I have only known hate . . ."

Nya studied his tortured face. "Only hate? Did you ever love?"

"Yes—no . . . I mean, yes, I loved, but . . . but it was always consumed with rage. I hated the Kreplin. I still hate them. Now"—he turned to face Nya—"Now, you're alone. I couldn't save Kaino. I couldn't save your baby. There are things I've done that are terrible. I've killed people. I've done things I'm not proud of. I feel empty . . . I feel like . . ."

"You feel like what?" she asked gently.

"I feel like . . . like I have a black soul."

"Hmph," grunted Nya. "You probably do."

"What?" Tarro was surprised by her response.

"Black soul. You said it yourself. You have a black soul." She stood up. "Stay here, I'll be right back."

Tarro didn't know how to take this and decided there was nothing to do other than sit there.

After a few moments, she returned holding a small book with a well-worn leather cover.

"Ever see one of these?" she asked with a twinkle in her eyes.

"Actually, yes I've seen a book."

"Daddy gave this to me when we arrived here. He told me he always carried this with him. When I was a child, I remember him once telling me that there was always hope," she said. Tarro listened intently. "He was right, and it had nothing to do with what he could accomplish."

"Yes, he is the most confident and capable man I have ever known," Tarro said.

"Yes, but I don't think his confidence was in himself." She opened the book to a particular page and pointed. "Read that," she said.

Tarro looked at the words next to her finger and read them aloud, "There is therefore now no condemnation—" He stopped as a robin landed next to him. It cocked his head at him and then flitted off. He looked at Nya, and she gently took his hand. She then continued reading for him, and he put his head on her shoulder as he listened.

And for the first time in his life, he heard the words of hope.

Epilogue

True Hope

THE NOVEL YOU JUST read takes the average person 3.3 hours to read. Of course, that's with no coffee or snack breaks! On a more somber note, in that same amount of time, over 21,000 people in the world will die.

Someday, you and I will be in that number. Death comes to us all.

In the meantime, around the world, roughly 40 percent of us will be diagnosed with cancer at some point in our lives, including thousands of children. On any given year, over 800 million of us will experience significant undernourishment, and more than 400,000 of us will be murdered. Of course, death is not new. Glancing back into the recent history of the 20th century, we observe over a hundred million people killed as a result of war alone.

In short, the world is overwhelmed with endless genocide, famine, disease, murder, racism, rape, abuse, sex trafficking, tyranny, oppression, disasters of every kind . . . the list of woes is endless.

On a more personal level, as human beings we experience failure, guilt, depression, loneliness, sadness, addictions, sickness, and illness. Like our fictional Tarro, we encounter despair—sometimes deep and dark despair. Sure, most of us will have moments of happiness. But like an angry hornet, life keeps stinging us. The truth is, we live in a world that is deeply troubled and broken. So we live a life of suffering until we die. Until then, we try to squeeze out a little meaning and happiness.

Is there any hope to this bleak human condition?

Happily, the answer is a resounding yes. But before we explore the nature of this hope, consider some questions:

- Where did this unfathomably massive universe of some 100+ billion galaxies with 1,000,000,000,000,000,000,000+ stars come from?

- How does all the genetic code for human life get squeezed into just one self-replicating little strand of DNA?

- How does an atom, with a nucleus of neutrons and protons, hold together?

- Where does the force of gravity come from that holds us on this earth and keeps it at a precise distance from the sun?

- How does the Bar-tailed Godwit bird leave Alaska, migrate non-stop over the Pacific Ocean, and find New Zealand over 6,800 miles away?

The universe is an amazing catalogue of impossible precision and wonder. Her complexity is simply astounding. As much as we might enjoy her intricate beauty, she asks a piercing question: Where did it all come from? Regarding this question, there are really only two possible answers. Either it all originated on its own spontaneously out of nothing, or God created it.

If Darwinism is correct, a point of infinite mass birthed the universe through the Big Bang. Man did not evolve from an ape. No, his evolution goes back much further. According to the prevailing theory, man evolved from this point of infinite, impersonal mass. Through an immense burst of energy, random atoms somehow came into being and then decided to organize together for unknown reasons through unknown mechanisms to spontaneously produce the stars, planets, and life itself.

This point of infinite mass with unknown origin burst forth to produce the Milky Way galaxy which produced our solar system, which produced our earth, which produced the primordial soup, which produced living organisms, which produced personal man. Life miraculously emerges from impersonal matter, and amoeba evolves into man. Man who suffers and dies.

Yet curiously, man yearns to be something more than a cosmic accident and by-product of random genetic mutations. He yearns to have meaning and purpose in life. He lives with a sense of virtue and decency transcending the survival-of-the-fittest rulebook of the universe. He instinctively sacrifices his life for another when he should seek to advance his evolution at the expense of the weak and inferior. He wants to love and be loved. He sees evil and suffering in the world and seeks justice. Strangely, he lives in such a way that suggests he doesn't really believe that he is just an impersonal machine of arbitrary chemicals.

Yet, it is not strange. For the only other alternative is that the universe was created by a personal God. Psalm 19:1 points to the universe's own statement on the matter:

"The heavens are telling of the glory of God;
And their expanse is declaring the work of His hands."

Scripture is God's communication to man. God supernaturally guided men to write the books of the Bible such that the Word of God is the authoritative communication from the Creator to his creation (2 Tim 3:16–17; 2 Pet 1:19–21).

Here in Psalm 19:1, God makes a key assertion through the psalmist: his creation declares himself and his works. Thus, creation serves as the giant flashing sign that points to the fact that God is there.

At this point, let me be clear on my premise:

1. There is a God.

2. He is a personal God who created personal man.

3. He desires to be known.

4. He has communicated clearly and authoritatively through his Word, the Scriptures.

5. His Word gives man hope.

Herein lies the greatest news man can ever hear. There is hope! A hope for man outside himself. Human history is riddled with the futile efforts of man trying to pluck himself out of his own misery and despair. Every time he tries, he fails, while suffering and death remain inescapable.

The good news is that man is not left alone in his struggle. He is not left grasping in the darkness for a hope that can only be imagined. God has given us hope—real hope, lasting hope, eternal hope.

What follows is the book of John from the Bible with brief commentary. The Gospel of John is God's presentation of the only hope man has. So I offer a simple invitation. I invite you to read and consider carefully the words of John, who walked and lived with the Savior of the world, the God of hope.

Introduction to the Gospel of John

B.C. and A.D.—"Before Christ" and "in the Year of our Lord." The world's historical calendar revolves around the life of one man, Jesus Christ. The question is: Who was this man? Who was this man who did miracles and claimed to be God? As many have concluded, there are only three possibilities. He was a rotten liar, he was delusional and crazy, or he was who he said he was.

John, as a disciple of Christ, refers to himself in this gospel as one "whom Jesus loved" out of humility and deep gratitude for the undeserved love Christ personally extended to him. John's gospel features eight "signs" which show that Jesus is truly the prophesied Messiah and Savior of the world. Thus, John gives his simple purpose for this book:

> "Therefore many other signs Jesus also performed in the presence of the disciples, which are not written in this book; but these have been written so that you may believe that Jesus is the Christ, the Son of God; and that believing you may have life in His name. (John 20:30–31)."

The Gospel of John

Chapter 1

John 1:1–18

¹ In the beginning was the Word, and the Word was with God, and the Word was God. ² He was in the beginning with God. ³ All things came into being through Him, and apart from Him nothing came into being that has come into being. ⁴ In Him was life, and the life was the Light of men. ⁵ The Light shines in the darkness, and the darkness did not comprehend it.

⁶ There came a man sent from God, whose name was John. ⁷ He came as a witness, to testify about the Light, so that all might believe through him. ⁸ He was not the Light, but *he came* to testify about the Light.

⁹ There was the true Light which, coming into the world, enlightens every man. ¹⁰ He was in the world, and the world was made through Him, and the world did not know Him. ¹¹ He came to His own, and those who were His own did not receive Him. ¹² But as many as received Him, to them He gave the right to become children of God, *even* to those who believe in His name, ¹³ who were born, not of blood nor of the will of the flesh nor of the will of man, but of God.

¹⁴ And the Word became flesh, and dwelt among us, and we saw His glory, glory as of the only begotten from the Father, full of grace and truth. ¹⁵ John testified about Him and cried out, saying, "This was He of whom I said, 'He who comes after me has a higher rank than I, for He existed before me.'" ¹⁶ For of His fullness we have all received, and grace upon grace. ¹⁷ For the Law was given through Moses; grace and truth were realized

through Jesus Christ. [18] No one has seen God at any time; the only begotten God who is in the bosom of the Father, He has explained *Him*.

Consider . . .

Jesus is introduced as "the Word." As the Word, he is the revealed embodiment of truth and knowledge. John begins with an emphatic statement: Jesus is not just any man. He is God, who was at the beginning as the Creator. As the light of the world, he is the one who offers hope and eternal life. While "his own" (fellow Jews) largely rejected him, to those who believe and receive him, he gives the "the right to become children of God" (v. 12). These are the ones to whom eternal life is granted.

John details the magnificent reality that the Son of God, as the second person of the triune God, took on humanity and lived on this earth. God has now been made uniquely visible and known through Jesus who was fully God and fully man. As the God-man, Jesus possessed the complete fullness of God (Col 2:9; Phil 2:5–8).

Why would God stoop to his creation in such a way? Amazingly, he came to extend "grace upon grace" (v. 16), an abundance of undeserved favor to mankind.

This introductory section is the summary statement for the rest of the gospel, which details, in no uncertain terms, that there is hope outside of man. And this hope of eternal life rests exclusively in the person and work of Jesus Christ.

John 1:19–51

[19] This is the testimony of John, when the Jews sent to him priests and Levites from Jerusalem to ask him, "Who are you?" [20] And he confessed and did not deny, but confessed, "I am not the Christ." [21] They asked him, "What then? Are you Elijah?" And he said, "I am not." "Are you the Prophet?" And he answered, "No." [22] Then they said to him, "Who are you, so that we may give an answer to those who sent us? What do you say about yourself?" [23] He said, "I am A VOICE OF ONE CRYING IN THE WILDERNESS, 'MAKE STRAIGHT THE WAY OF THE LORD,' as Isaiah the prophet said."

24 Now they had been sent from the Pharisees. **25** They asked him, and said to him, "Why then are you baptizing, if you are not the Christ, nor Elijah, nor the Prophet?" **26** John answered them saying, "I baptize in water, *but* among you stands One whom you do not know. **27** *"It is* He who comes after me, the thong of whose sandal I am not worthy to untie." **28** These things took place in Bethany beyond the Jordan, where John was baptizing.

29 The next day he saw Jesus coming to him and said, "Behold, the Lamb of God who takes away the sin of the world! **30** "This is He on behalf of whom I said, 'After me comes a Man who has a higher rank than I, for He existed before me.' **31** "I did not recognize Him, but so that He might be manifested to Israel, I came baptizing in water." **32** John testified saying, "I have seen the Spirit descending as a dove out of heaven, and He remained upon Him. **33** "I did not recognize Him, but He who sent me to baptize in water said to me, 'He upon whom you see the Spirit descending and remaining upon Him, this is the One who baptizes in the Holy Spirit.' **34** "I myself have seen, and have testified that this is the Son of God."

35 Again the next day John was standing with two of his disciples, **36** and he looked at Jesus as He walked, and said, "Behold, the Lamb of God!" **37** The two disciples heard him speak, and they followed Jesus. **38** And Jesus turned and saw them following, and said to them, "What do you seek?" They said to Him, "Rabbi (which translated means Teacher), where are You staying?" **39** He said to them, "Come, and you will see." So they came and saw where He was staying; and they stayed with Him that day, for it was about the tenth hour. **40** One of the two who heard John *speak* and followed Him, was Andrew, Simon Peter's brother. **41** He found first his own brother Simon and said to him, "We have found the Messiah" (which translated means Christ). **42** He brought him to Jesus. Jesus looked at him and said, "You are Simon the son of John; you shall be called Cephas" (which is translated Peter).

43 The next day He purposed to go into Galilee, and He found Philip. And Jesus said to him, "Follow Me." **44** Now Philip was from Bethsaida, of the city of Andrew and Peter. **45** Philip found Nathanael and said to him, "We have found Him of whom Moses in the Law and *also* the Prophets wrote—Jesus of Nazareth, the son of Joseph." **46** Nathanael said to him, "Can any good thing come out of Nazareth?" Philip said to him, "Come and see." **47** Jesus saw Nathanael coming to Him, and said of him, "Behold, an Israelite indeed, in whom there is no deceit!"

48 Nathanael said to Him, "How do You know me?" Jesus answered and said to him, "Before Philip called you, when you were under the fig tree, I saw you." **49** Nathanael answered Him, "Rabbi, You are the Son of God; You are the King of Israel." **50** Jesus answered and said to him, "Because I said to you that I saw you under the fig tree, do you believe? You will see greater things than these." **51** And He said to him, "Truly, truly, I say to you, you will see the heavens opened and the angels of God ascending and descending on the Son of Man."

Consider . . .

John refers to Jesus as the "Lamb of God." Lambs were historically significant in Israel's worship practices. They were used during the Passover (Exod 12:1–36) and were part of the routine daily sacrifices. The sacrifice was a visible reminder that death is the penalty for sin (Rom 6:23). The shed blood of the lamb in the Old Testament sacrificial system was a temporary covering for sin which pointed to the perfect and complete sacrifice to come, Jesus, the divine Lamb who would shed his own blood for the sins of mankind.

Chapter 2

The First Sign: Jesus Turns Water Into Wine
John 2:1–25

1 On the third day there was a wedding in Cana of Galilee, and the mother of Jesus was there; **2** and both Jesus and His disciples were invited to the wedding. **3** When the wine ran out, the mother of Jesus said to Him, "They have no wine." **4** And Jesus said to her, "Woman, what does that have to do with us? My hour has not yet come." **5** His mother said to the servants, "Whatever He says to you, do it." **6** Now there were six stone waterpots set there for the Jewish custom of purification, containing twenty or thirty gallons each. **7** Jesus said to them, "Fill the waterpots with water." So they filled them up to the brim. **8** And He said to them, "Draw *some* out now and take it to the headwaiter." So they took it *to him.* **9** When the headwaiter tasted the water which had become wine, and did not know where it came from (but the servants who had drawn the water knew), the headwaiter called the bridegroom, 10 and said to him, "Every man serves the good wine first, and when *the people* have drunk freely, *then he serves* the poorer *wine; but* you have kept the good wine until now." 11 This beginning of *His* signs Jesus did in Cana of Galilee, and manifested His glory, and His disciples believed in Him.

12 After this He went down to Capernaum, He and His mother and *His* brothers and His disciples; and they stayed there a few days.

13 The Passover of the Jews was near, and Jesus went up to Jerusalem. 14 And He found in the temple those who were selling oxen and sheep and doves, and the money changers seated *at their tables.* 15 And He made a scourge of cords, and drove *them* all out of the temple, with the sheep and the oxen; and He poured out the coins of the money changers and overturned their tables; 16 and to those who were selling the doves He said, "Take these things away; stop making My Father's house a place of business." 17 His disciples remembered that it was written, "ZEAL FOR YOUR HOUSE WILL CONSUME ME." 18 The Jews then said to Him, "What sign do You show us as your authority for doing these things?" 19 Jesus answered them, "Destroy this temple, and in three days I will raise it up." 20 The Jews then said, "It took forty-six years to build this temple, and will You raise it up in three days?" 21 But He was speaking of the temple of His body. 22 So when He was raised from the dead, His disciples remembered that He said this; and they believed the Scripture and the word which Jesus had spoken.

23 Now when He was in Jerusalem at the Passover, during the feast, many believed in His name, observing His signs which He was doing. 24 But Jesus, on His part, was not entrusting Himself to them, for He knew all men, 25 and because He did not need anyone to testify concerning man, for He Himself knew what was in man.

Consider . . .

Many believed in his name, but Jesus did not entrust himself to them (v. 24). In other words, they *believed* Jesus but he did not *believe* them. The reason is simple. He knew their hearts and that their belief was a superficial head knowledge. Jesus performed miracles, like turning water into wine, which only God could do. These people believed what they were seeing, but their faith was not a saving faith.

It is clear from this passage that it is possible to believe facts about Jesus but not have the type of faith which forgives sins, granting eternal life. As James points out, even the demons believe and tremble before God (Jas 2:19). But the demons remain condemned because they refuse to follow Christ in true faith and obedience.

In the remainder of the gospel, Jesus teaches what it means to truly follow him with a genuine faith that results in eternal salvation.

Chapter 3

John 3:1–16

> **1** Now there was a man of the Pharisees, named Nicodemus, a ruler of the Jews; **2** this man came to Jesus by night and said to Him, "Rabbi, we know that You have come from God *as* a teacher; for no one can do these signs that You do unless God is with him." **3** Jesus answered and said to him, "Truly, truly, I say to you, unless one is born again he cannot see the kingdom of God."
> **4** Nicodemus said to Him, "How can a man be born when he is old? He cannot enter a second time into his mother's womb and be born, can he?" **5** Jesus answered, "Truly, truly, I say to you, unless one is born of water and the Spirit he cannot enter into the kingdom of God. **6** "That which is born of the flesh is flesh, and that which is born of the Spirit is spirit. **7** "Do not be amazed that I said to you, 'You must be born again.' **8** "The wind blows where it wishes and you hear the sound of it, but do not know where it comes from and where it is going; so is everyone who is born of the Spirit."
> **9** Nicodemus said to Him, "How can these things be?" **10** Jesus answered and said to him, "Are you the teacher of Israel and do not understand these things? **11** "Truly, truly, I say to you, we speak of what we know and testify of what we have seen, and you do not accept our testimony. **12** "If I told you earthly things and you do not believe, how will you believe if I tell you heavenly things? **13** "No one has ascended into heaven, but He who descended from heaven: the Son of Man. **14** "As Moses lifted up the serpent in the wilderness, even so must the Son of Man be lifted up; **15** so that whoever believes will in Him have eternal life.

16 "For God so loved the world, that He gave His only be-gotten Son, that whoever believes in Him shall not perish, but have eternal life."

Consider . . .

Nicodemus comes to Jesus with an important question on his mind. It's a most critical question: How does one gain entrance into heaven? Jesus knows his question and answers it before Nicodemus even asks. The answer is simple but immediately befuddling to Nicodemus. In order to enter into the kingdom of God, one must be "born again" (v. 7).

Jesus makes it clear that this necessary "rebirth" is a spiritual birth. Ephesians 2:1 says that man is spiritually dead in sin. He needs spiritual life. He needs to be cleansed from the filth of his own sin, and only God can bring about this spiritual cleansing that results in spiritual life.

To be "born of water and the Spirit" (v. 5) is a description of this very cleansing, a washing of a man's soul which only the Spirit of God can accomplish. The work of the Holy Spirit is necessary to produce eternal life. Jesus teaches that the effects of the life-producing Spirit can be seen, but like the wind, the Spirit cannot be seen nor controlled.

So if man cannot *do* anything to produce the new life he so desperately needs, then what recourse does he have? In this conversation with Nicodemus, Jesus gives the implied answer. No, man cannot do anything to save himself, but he can cry out for mercy and humbly ask God for the very thing he can't produce on his own—spiritual life and salvation. Spiritual rebirth.

John 3:17–36

17 "For God did not send the Son into the world to judge the world, but that the world might be saved through Him. **18** "He who believes in Him is not judged; he who does not believe has been judged already, because he has not believed in the name of the only begotten Son of God. **19** "This is the judgment, that the Light has come into the world, and men loved the darkness rather than the Light, for their deeds were evil. **20** "For everyone who does evil hates the Light, and does not come to the Light for fear that his deeds will be exposed. **21** "But he who practices the truth comes to the Light, so that his deeds may be manifested as having been wrought in God."

22 After these things Jesus and His disciples came into the land of Judea, and there He was spending time with them and baptizing. **23** John also was baptizing in Aenon near Salim, because there was much water there; and *people* were coming and were being baptized—**24** for John had not yet been thrown into prison.

25 Therefore there arose a discussion on the part of John's disciples with a Jew about purification. **26** And they came to John and said to him, "Rabbi, He who was with you beyond the Jordan, to whom you have testified, behold, He is baptizing and all are coming to Him." **27** John answered and said, "A man can receive nothing unless it has been given him from heaven. **28** "You yourselves are my witnesses that I said, 'I am not the Christ,' but, 'I have been sent ahead of Him.' **29** "He who has the bride is the bridegroom; but the friend of the bridegroom, who stands and hears him, rejoices greatly because of the bridegroom's voice. So this joy of mine has been made full. **30** "He must increase, but I must decrease.

31 "He who comes from above is above all, he who is of the earth is from the earth and speaks of the earth. He who comes from heaven is above all. **32** "What He has seen and heard, of that He testifies; and no one receives His testimony. **33** "He who has received His testimony has set his seal to *this,* that God is true. **34** "For He whom God has sent speaks the words of God; for He gives the Spirit without measure. **35** "The Father loves the Son and has given all things into His hand. **36** "He who believes in the Son has eternal life; but he who does not obey the Son will not see life, but the wrath of God abides on him."

Consider . . .

Man's sin produces a lethal problem. If not rescued, he perishes. Without salvation, the wrath of God remains on him. Because of man's sin and rebellion against the rule of his Creator, this wrath from a holy God is both just and eternal.

Yet while God must punish sin, he is also infinitely merciful. In love, God the Father gave his Son, Jesus Christ, to the world as its Savior. There is one clear path to eternal life, and it comes through Christ. Thus, there are only two possible courses and outcomes for every man: either he believes and obeys the Son or he rejects the Son in disbelief and disobedience. One path yields eternal life. The other eternal damnation.

Chapter 4

John 4:1–42

1 Therefore when the Lord knew that the Pharisees had heard that Jesus was making and baptizing more disciples than John **2** (although Jesus Himself was not baptizing, but His disciples were), **3** He left Judea and went away again into Galilee. **4** And He had to pass through Samaria. **5** So He came to a city of Samaria called Sychar, near the parcel of ground that Jacob gave to his son Joseph; **6** and Jacob's well was there. So Jesus, being wearied from His journey, was sitting thus by the well. It was about the sixth hour.
      7 There came a woman of Samaria to draw water. Jesus said to her, "Give Me a drink." **8** For His disciples had gone away into the city to buy food. **9** Therefore the Samaritan woman said to Him, "How is it that You, being a Jew, ask me for a drink since I am a Samaritan woman?" (For Jews have no dealings with Samaritans.) **10** Jesus answered and said to her, "If you knew the gift of God, and who it is who says to you, 'Give Me a drink,' you would have asked Him, and He would have given you living water." **11** She said to Him, "Sir, You have nothing to draw with and the well is deep; where then do You get that living water? **12** "You are not greater than our father Jacob, are You, who gave us the well, and drank of it himself and his sons and his cattle?" **13** Jesus answered and said to her, "Everyone who drinks of this water will thirst again; **14** but whoever drinks of the water that I will give him shall never thirst; but the water that I will give him will become in him a well of water springing up to eternal life."
      15 The woman said to Him, "Sir, give me this water, so I will not be thirsty nor come all the way here to draw." **16** He said to her, "Go, call your husband and come here." **17** The woman answered and said, "I have no husband." Jesus said to her, "You have correctly said, 'I have no husband'; **18** for you have had five husbands, and the one whom you now have is not your husband; this you have said truly." **19** The woman said to Him, "Sir, I perceive that You are a prophet. **20** "Our fathers worshiped in this mountain, and you *people* say that in Jerusalem is the place where men ought to worship." **21** Jesus said to her, "Woman,

believe Me, an hour is coming when neither in this mountain nor in Jerusalem will you worship the Father. **22** "You worship what you do not know; we worship what we know, for salvation is from the Jews. **23** "But an hour is coming, and now is, when the true worshipers will worship the Father in spirit and truth; for such people the Father seeks to be His worshipers. **24** "God is spirit, and those who worship Him must worship in spirit and truth." **25** The woman said to Him, "I know that Messiah is coming (He who is called Christ); when that One comes, He will declare all things to us." **26** Jesus said to her, "I who speak to you am *He*."

27 At this point His disciples came, and they were amazed that He had been speaking with a woman, yet no one said, "What do You seek?" or, "Why do You speak with her?" **28** So the woman left her waterpot, and went into the city and said to the men, **29** "Come, see a man who told me all the things that I *have* done; this is not the Christ, is it?" **30** They went out of the city, and were coming to Him.

31 Meanwhile the disciples were urging Him, saying, "Rabbi, eat." **32** But He said to them, "I have food to eat that you do not know about." **33** So the disciples were saying to one another, "No one brought Him *anything* to eat, did he?" **34** Jesus said to them, "My food is to do the will of Him who sent Me and to accomplish His work. **35** "Do you not say, 'There are yet four months, and *then* comes the harvest'? Behold, I say to you, lift up your eyes and look on the fields, that they are white for harvest. **36** "Already he who reaps is receiving wages and is gathering fruit for life eternal; so that he who sows and he who reaps may rejoice together. **37** "For in this *case* the saying is true, 'One sows and another reaps.' **38** "I sent you to reap that for which you have not labored; others have labored and you have entered into their labor."

39 From that city many of the Samaritans believed in Him because of the word of the woman who testified, "He told me all the things that I *have* done." **40** So when the Samaritans came to Jesus, they were asking Him to stay with them; and He stayed there two days. **41** Many more believed because of His word; **42** and they were saying to the woman, "It is no longer because of what you said that we believe, for we have heard for ourselves and know that this One is indeed the Savior of the world."

Consider ...

The Jews generally despised the Samaritans, viewing them as half-breeds, a racial mix of Jew and Gentile. Jesus, who was himself a Jew, not only converses with a Samaritan but with a woman, which for a man in public was a breach of strict social customs in this culture.

Jesus uses an object lesson to identify the woman's greatest need. She thinks she needs physical water, but Jesus points to her need for the "water" he offers. This "living water" is eternal life which is not only her greatest need, but something which only Jesus can provide.

Her sins are great and he knows them all. Spiritual renewal is her most desperate need, and Jesus not only shows her the only solution but freely offers it, even to the least of society, an immoral Samaritan woman.

The Second Sign: Healing of the Official's Son
John 4:43–54

> **43** After the two days He went forth from there into Galilee. **44** For Jesus Himself testified that a prophet has no honor in his own country. **45** So when He came to Galilee, the Galileans received Him, having seen all the things that He did in Jerusalem at the feast; for they themselves also went to the feast.
>
> **46** Therefore He came again to Cana of Galilee where He had made the water wine. And there was a royal official whose son was sick at Capernaum. **47** When he heard that Jesus had come out of Judea into Galilee, he went to Him and was imploring *Him* to come down and heal his son; for he was at the point of death. **48** So Jesus said to him, "Unless you *people* see signs and wonders, you *simply* will not believe." **49** The royal official said to Him, "Sir, come down before my child dies." **50** Jesus said to him, "Go; your son lives." The man believed the word that Jesus spoke to him and started off. **51** As he was now going down, *his* slaves met him, saying that his son was living. **52** So he inquired of them the hour when he began to get better. Then they said to him, "Yesterday at the seventh hour the fever left him." **53** So the father knew that *it was* at that hour in which Jesus said to him, "Your son lives"; and he himself believed and his whole household. **54** This is again a second sign that Jesus performed when He had come out of Judea into Galilee.

Chapter 5

The Third Sign: Healing of the Paralytic Man
John 5:1–47

1 After these things there was a feast of the Jews, and Jesus went up to Jerusalem.

2 Now there is in Jerusalem by the sheep *gate* a pool, which is called in Hebrew Bethesda, having five porticoes. **3** In these lay a multitude of those who were sick, blind, lame, and withered, [waiting for the moving of the waters; **4** for an angel of the Lord went down at certain seasons into the pool and stirred up the water; whoever then first, after the stirring up of the water, stepped in was made well from whatever disease with which he was afflicted.]

5 A man was there who had been ill for thirty-eight years. **6** When Jesus saw him lying *there*, and knew that he had already been a long time *in that condition*, He said to him, "Do you wish to get well?" **7** The sick man answered Him, "Sir, I have no man to put me into the pool when the water is stirred up, but while I am coming, another steps down before me." **8** Jesus said to him, "Get up, pick up your pallet and walk." **9** Immediately the man became well, and picked up his pallet and *began* to walk.

Now it was the Sabbath on that day. **10** So the Jews were saying to the man who was cured, "It is the Sabbath, and it is not permissible for you to carry your pallet." **11** But he answered them, "He who made me well was the one who said to me, 'Pick up your pallet and walk.'" **12** They asked him, "Who is the man who said to you, 'Pick up *your pallet* and walk'?" **13** But the man who was healed did not know who it was, for Jesus had slipped away while there was a crowd in *that* place. **14** Afterward Jesus found him in the temple and said to him, "Behold, you have become well; do not sin anymore, so that nothing worse happens to you." **15** The man went away, and told the Jews that it was Jesus who had made him well. **16** For this reason the Jews were persecuting Jesus, because He was doing these things on the Sabbath. **17** But He answered them, "My Father is working until now, and I Myself am working." **18** For this reason therefore the Jews were seeking all the more to kill Him, because He not only was breaking the Sabbath, but also was calling God His own Father, making Himself equal with God.

19 Therefore Jesus answered and was saying to them, "Truly, truly, I say to you, the Son can do nothing of Himself, unless *it* *is* something He sees the Father doing; for whatever the Father does, these things the Son also does in like manner. **20** "For the Father loves the Son, and shows Him all things that He Himself is doing; and *the Father* will show Him greater works than these, so that you will marvel. **21** "For just as the Father raises the dead and gives them life, even so the Son also gives life to whom He wishes. **22** "For not even the Father judges anyone, but He has given all judgment to the Son, **23** so that all will honor the Son even as they honor the Father. He who does not honor the Son does not honor the Father who sent Him.

24 "Truly, truly, I say to you, he who hears My word, and believes Him who sent Me, has eternal life, and does not come into judgment, but has passed out of death into life. **25** "Truly, truly, I say to you, an hour is coming and now is, when the dead will hear the voice of the Son of God, and those who hear will live. **26** "For just as the Father has life in Himself, even so He gave to the Son also to have life in Himself; **27** and He gave Him authority to execute judgment, because He is *the* Son of Man. **28** "Do not marvel at this; for an hour is coming, in which all who are in the tombs will hear His voice, **29** and will come forth; those who did the good *deeds* to a resurrection of life, those who committed the evil *deeds* to a resurrection of judgment.

30 "I can do nothing on My own initiative. As I hear, I judge; and My judgment is just, because I do not seek My own will, but the will of Him who sent Me.

31 "If I *alone* testify about Myself, My testimony is not true. **32** "There is another who testifies of Me, and I know that the testimony which He gives about Me is true. **33** "You have sent to John, and he has testified to the truth. **34** "But the testimony which I receive is not from man, but I say these things so that you may be saved. **35** "He was the lamp that was burning and was shining and you were willing to rejoice for a while in his light. **36** "But the testimony which I have is greater than *the testimony of* John; for the works which the Father has given Me to accomplish—the very works that I do—testify about Me, that the Father has sent Me. **37** "And the Father who sent Me, He has testified of Me. You have neither heard His voice at any time nor seen His form. **38** "You do not have His word abiding in you, for you do not believe Him whom He sent. **39** "You search the Scriptures because you think that in them you have eternal life; it is these that testify about Me; **40** and you are unwilling to come to Me so that you may have life. **41** "I do not receive glory from men; **42** but I know you, that you do not have the love of God in yourselves. **43** "I have come in My Father's name, and you do not receive Me; if another comes in his own name, you will receive him. **44** "How can you believe, when you receive glory from one another and you do not seek the glory that is from the *one and only God*? **45** "Do not think that I will accuse you before the Father; the one who accuses you is Moses, in whom you have set your hope. **46** "For if you believed Moses, you would believe Me, for he wrote about Me. **47** "But if you do not believe his writings, how will you believe My words?"

Consider . . .

The Jews were fixated on their extra rules and regulations they had created related to the biblical command to rest on the Sabbath. Jesus breaks their man-made rules by healing a man on the Sabbath. Through this verifiable healing, he demonstrates his divine power and compassion toward the lowliest of society while exposing the pettiness and misplaced priorities of the Jews. They hated him for breaking their rules, but their main objection was that he made himself to be equal to God.

Jesus drives an emphatic theological stake into the ground by asserting that he is equal to God in power and authority. He and the Father are one. Therefore he is not *like* God, he *is* God. The question for man today is the same question Jesus presented to the Jews: *Will you believe my words?*

Chapter 6

The Fourth Sign: Feeding of the Five Thousand
John 6:1–15

1 After these things Jesus went away to the other side of the Sea of Galilee (or Tiberias). **2** A large crowd followed Him, because they saw the signs which He was performing on those who were sick. **3** Then Jesus went up on the mountain, and there He sat down with His disciples. **4** Now the Passover, the feast of the Jews, was near. **5** Therefore Jesus, lifting up His eyes and seeing that a large crowd was coming to Him, said to Philip, "Where are we to buy bread, so that these may eat?" **6** This He was saying to test him, for He Himself knew what He was intending to do. **7** Philip answered Him, "Two hundred denarii worth of bread is not sufficient for them, for everyone to receive a little." ^8 One of His disciples, Andrew, Simon Peter's brother, said to Him, ^9 "There is a lad here who has five barley loaves and two fish, but what are these for so many people?" ^10 Jesus said, "Have the people sit down." Now there was much grass in the place. So the men sat down, in number about five thousand. ^11 Jesus then took the loaves, and having given thanks, He distributed to those who were seated; likewise also of the fish as much as they wanted. ^12 When they were filled, He said to His disciples, "Gather up the leftover fragments so that nothing will be lost." ^13 So they gathered them up, and filled twelve baskets with fragments from the five barley loaves which were left over by those who had eaten. ^14 Therefore when the people saw the sign which He had performed, they said, "This is truly the Prophet who is to come into the world."

^15 So Jesus, perceiving that they were intending to come and take Him by force to make Him king, withdrew again to the mountain by Himself alone.

The Fifth Sign: Walking on Water
John 6:16–34

^16 Now when evening came, His disciples went down to the sea, ^17 and after getting into a boat, they *started to* cross the sea to Capernaum. It had already become dark, and Jesus had not yet come to them. ^18 The sea *began* to be stirred up because a strong wind was blowing. ^19 Then, when they had rowed about three or four miles, they saw Jesus walking on the sea and drawing near to the boat; and they were frightened. ^20 But He said to them, "It is I; do not be afraid." ^21 So they were willing to receive Him into the boat, and immediately the boat was at the land to which they were going.

^22 The next day the crowd that stood on the other side of the sea saw that there was no other small boat there, except one, and that Jesus had not entered with His disciples into the boat, but *that* His disciples had gone away alone. ^23 There came other small boats from Tiberias near to the place where they ate the bread after the Lord had given thanks. ^24 So when the crowd saw that Jesus was not there, nor His disciples, they themselves got into the small boats, and came to Capernaum seeking Jesus.

25 When they found Him on the other side of the sea, they said to Him, "Rabbi, when did You get here?"

26 Jesus answered them and said, "Truly, truly, I say to you, you seek Me, not because you saw signs, but because you ate of the loaves and were filled. **27** "Do not work for the food which perishes, but for the food which endures to eternal life, which the Son of Man will give to you, for on Him the Father, God, has set His seal." **28** Therefore they said to Him, "What shall we do, so that we may work the works of God?" **29** Jesus answered and said to them, "This is the work of God, that you believe in Him whom He has sent." **30** So they said to Him, "What then do You do for a sign, so that we may see, and believe You? What work do You perform? **31** "Our fathers ate the manna in the wilderness; as it is written, 'HE GAVE THEM BREAD OUT OF HEAVEN TO EAT.'" **32** Jesus then said to them, "Truly, truly, I say to you, it is not Moses who has given you the bread out of heaven, but it is My Father who gives you the true bread out of heaven. **33** "For the bread of God is that which comes down out of heaven, and gives life to the world." **34** Then they said to Him, "Lord, always give us this bread."

Consider . . .

John records two more miracles which unequivocally demonstrate Jesus' deity. Yet, it is increasingly evident that many came to Jesus looking to be wowed or to gain something from him. Some wanted to see more signs and miracles. Others simply wanted to be fed.

Today, many approach Jesus as if he is a divine vending machine able to give them what they want—good health, a blessed life, prosperity, or whatever it is that their hearts desire at the moment. Jesus shows that these desires miss the very thing he came to provide, namely, eternal life. Regarding this, the crowd asks a question which has been echoed throughout human history: *What must we do to gain eternal life?*

Man is a doer. He designs and builds things. He sends men to the moon. He conquers nations. So when it comes to eternal life, this is his natural question—what can I do to get in? Every religion in the world answers this question with a call to do something, requiring man to work in some capacity for its version of heaven. The Catholic must do things like attend confession and mass. The Muslim must do enough good deeds. The Hindu must overcome ignorance and desires.

Every religion calls man to *do something* to achieve the eternal state—except for Christianity. Jesus makes it exceedingly clear that there is only one work that can save a man, the work of God (v. 29). Man can do absolutely nothing to save himself.

Jesus asserts that he is the only one who can save and that this salvation comes by faith and faith alone in him and his work on behalf of man. Only Jesus can bring about spiritual life. Man can no more give himself this spiritual life than he can physically raise himself from the dead!

John 6:35–71

35 Jesus said to them, "I am the bread of life; he who comes to Me will not hunger, and he who believes in Me will never thirst. 36 "But I said to you that you have seen Me, and yet do not believe. 37 "All that the Father gives Me will come to Me, and the one who comes to Me I will certainly not cast out. 38 "For I have come down from heaven, not to do My own will, but the will of Him who sent Me. 39 "This is the will of Him who sent Me, that of all that He has given Me I lose nothing, but raise it up on the last day. 40 "For this is the will of My Father, that everyone who beholds the Son and believes in Him will have eternal life, and I Myself will raise him up on the last day."

41 Therefore the Jews were grumbling about Him, because He said, "I am the bread that came down out of heaven." 42 They were saying, "Is not this Jesus, the son of Joseph, whose father and mother we know? How does He now say, 'I have come down out of heaven'?" 43 Jesus answered and said to them, "Do not grumble among yourselves. 44 "No one can come to Me unless the Father who sent Me draws him; and I will raise him up on the last day. 45 "It is written in the prophets, 'AND THEY SHALL ALL BE TAUGHT OF GOD.' Everyone who has heard and learned from the Father, comes to Me. 46 "Not that anyone has seen the Father, except the One who is from God; He has seen the Father. 47 "Truly, truly, I say to you, he who believes has eternal life. 48 "I am the bread of life. 49 "Your fathers ate the manna in the wilderness, and they died. 50 "This is the bread which comes down out of heaven, so that one may eat of it and not die. 51 "I am the living bread that came down out of heaven; if anyone eats of this bread, he will live forever; and the bread also which I will give for the life of the world is My flesh."

52 Then the Jews *began* to argue with one another, saying, "How can this man give us *His* flesh to eat?" 53 So Jesus said to them, "Truly, truly, I say to you, unless you eat the flesh of the Son of Man and drink His blood, you have no life in yourselves. 54 "He who eats My flesh and drinks My blood has eternal life, and I will raise him up on the last day. 55 "For My flesh is true food, and My blood is true drink. 56 "He who eats My flesh and drinks My blood abides in Me, and I in him. 57 "As the living Father sent Me, and I live because of the Father, so he who eats Me, he also will live because of Me. 58 "This is the bread which came down out of heaven; not as the fathers ate and died; he who eats this bread will live forever." 59 These things He said in the synagogue as He taught in Capernaum.

60 Therefore many of His disciples, when they heard *this* said, "This is a difficult statement; who can listen to it?" 61 But Jesus, conscious that His disciples grumbled at this, said to them, "Does this cause you to stumble? 62 "*What* then if you see the Son of Man ascending to where He was before? 63 "It is the Spirit who gives life; the flesh profits nothing; the words that I have spoken to you are spirit and are life. 64 "But there are some of you who do not believe." For Jesus knew from the beginning who they were who did not believe, and who it was that would betray Him. 65 And He was saying, "For this reason I have said to you, that no one can come to Me unless it has been granted him from the Father."

66 As a result of this many of His disciples withdrew and were not walking with Him anymore. 67 So Jesus said to the twelve, "You do not want to go away also, do you?" 68 Simon Peter answered Him, "Lord, to whom shall we go? You have words of eternal life. 69 "We have believed and have come to know that You are the Holy One of God." 70 Jesus answered them, "Did I Myself not choose you, the twelve, and *yet* one of you is a devil?" 71 Now He meant Judas *the son* of Simon Iscariot, for he, one of the twelve, was going to betray Him.

Consider . . .

To "eat" of the flesh of Christ is to "abide" in him (v. 56) through faith in the Bread of Life. (Later in Chapter 15, Jesus will further describe what it means to live in him.) Again, Jesus underscores the fact that man cannot save himself. Only the Spirit of God can give new life, and he does this through the very words of hope that Jesus gives (v. 63).

The words of Jesus are always divisive. Some receive them. Some reject them. Even some of his disciples found his words too difficult to continue to believe and abandoned him. Peter represents the only alternative when he says, "Lord, to whom shall we go? You have words of eternal life. We have believed and have come to know that You are the Holy One of God" (vv. 68–69).

Chapter 7

John 7:1–24

> 1 After these things Jesus was walking in Galilee, for He was unwilling to walk in Judea because the Jews were seeking to kill Him. 2 Now the feast of the Jews, the Feast of Booths, was near. 3 Therefore His brothers said to Him, "Leave here and go into Judea, so that Your disciples also may see Your works which You are doing. 4 "For no one does anything in secret when he himself seeks to be *known* publicly. If You do these things, show Yourself to the world." 5 For not even His brothers were believing in Him. 6 So Jesus said to them, "My time is not yet here, but your time is always opportune. 7 "The world cannot hate you, but it hates Me because I testify of it, that its deeds are evil. 8 "Go up to the feast yourselves; I do not go up to this feast because My time has not yet fully come." 9 Having said these things to them, He stayed in Galilee.
>
> 10 But when His brothers had gone up to the feast, then He Himself also went up, not publicly, but as if, in secret. 11 So the Jews were seeking Him at the feast and were saying, "Where is He?" 12 There was much grumbling among the crowds concerning Him; some were saying, "He is a good man"; others were saying, "No, on the contrary, He leads the people astray." 13 Yet no one was speaking openly of Him for fear of the Jews.
>
> 14 But when it was now the midst of the feast Jesus went up into the temple, and *began to* teach. 15 The Jews then were astonished, saying, "How has this man become learned, having never been educated?" 16 So Jesus answered them and said, "My teaching is not Mine, but His who sent Me. 17 "If anyone is willing to do His will, he will know of the teaching, whether it is of God or *whether* I speak from Myself. 18 "He who speaks from

himself seeks his own glory; but He who is seeking the glory of the One who sent Him, He is true, and there is no unrighteousness in Him. **19** "Did not Moses give you the Law, and *yet* none of you carries out the Law? Why do you seek to kill Me?" **20** The crowd answered, "You have a demon! Who seeks to kill You?" **21** Jesus answered them, "I did one deed, and you all marvel. **22** "For this reason Moses has given you circumcision (not because it is from Moses, but from the fathers), and on *the* Sabbath you circumcise a man. **23** "If a man receives circumcision on *the* Sabbath so that the Law of Moses will not be broken, are you angry with Me because I made an entire man well on *the* Sabbath? **24** "Do not judge according to appearance, but judge with righteous judgment."

Consider . . .

Is Jesus really a "good man" or is he, in fact, leading the people astray (v. 12)? The Jews crystallize the issue into this key question, the majority of whom accuse him of being possessed by a demon. Jesus, however, exposes their hypocrisy. They willingly circumcise a man on the Sabbath but are angry with him for healing on the Sabbath.

In light of this glaring disparity, Jesus calls them to judge rightly (v. 24). In other words, man is to judge right and wrong by God's righteous standards expressed in Scripture. Man is not to judge by his own criteria, nor judge the unseen hearts and motives of men. Man's continual problem is that he judges reality by what he thinks and feels instead of viewing reality as God defines it through divine revelation, the Word of God, the very words of Jesus.

John 7:25–53

25 So some of the people of Jerusalem were saying, "Is this not the man whom they are seeking to kill? **26** "Look, He is speaking publicly, and they are saying nothing to Him. The rulers do not really know that this is the Christ, do they? **27** "However, we know where this man is from; but whenever the Christ may come, no one knows where He is from." **28** Then Jesus cried out in the temple, teaching and saying, "You both know Me and know where I am from; and I have not come of Myself, but He who sent Me is true, whom you do not know. **29** "I know Him, because I am from Him, and He sent Me." **30** So they were seeking to seize Him; and no man laid his hand on Him, because His hour had not yet come. **31** But many of the crowd believed in Him; and they were saying, "When the Christ comes, He will not perform more signs than those which this man has, will He?"

32 The Pharisees heard the crowd muttering these things about Him, and the chief priests and the Pharisees sent officers to seize Him. **33** Therefore Jesus said, "For a little while longer I am with you, then I go to Him who sent Me. **34** "You will seek Me, and will not find Me; and where I am, you cannot come." **35** The Jews then said to one another, "Where does this man intend to go that we will not find Him? He is not intending to go to the Dispersion among the Greeks, and teach the Greeks, is He? **36** "What is this statement that He said, 'You will seek Me, and will not find Me; and where I am, you cannot come'?"

37 Now on the last day, the great *day* of the feast, Jesus stood and cried out, saying, "If anyone is thirsty, let him come to Me and drink. **38** "He who believes in Me, as the Scripture said, 'From his innermost being will flow rivers of living water.'" **39** But this He spoke of the Spirit, whom those who believed in Him were to receive; for the Spirit was not yet *given,* because Jesus was not yet glorified.

40 *Some* of the people therefore, when they heard these words, were saying, "This certainly is the Prophet." **41** Others were saying, "This is the Christ." Still others were saying, "Surely the Christ is not going to come from Galilee, is He? **42** "Has not the Scripture said that the Christ comes from the descendants of David, and from Bethlehem, the village where David was?" **43** So a division occurred in the crowd because of Him. **44** Some of them wanted to seize Him, but no one laid hands on Him.

45 The officers then came to the chief priests and Pharisees, and they said to them, "Why did you not bring Him?" **46** The officers answered, "Never has a man spoken the way this man speaks." **47** The Pharisees then answered them, "You have not also been led astray, have you? **48** "No one of the rulers or Pharisees has believed in Him, has he? **49** "But this crowd which does not know the Law is accursed." **50** Nicodemus (he who came to Him before, being one of them) said to them, **51** "Our Law does not judge a man unless it first hears from him and knows what he is doing, does it?" **52** They answered him, "You are not also from Galilee, are you? Search, and see that no prophet arises out of Galilee." **53** [Everyone went to his home.

Consider . . .

Jesus continually points to the fact that he is not operating on his own (v. 28). No, he is on a mission from God the Father. He teaches the Pharisees that some day he would not be found, for he would soon return to the Father (v. 34). In response, the Pharisees send officers to arrest Jesus, but they fail to do so. Instead, the officers recognize that Jesus has a power and authority like none other (v. 46).

Jesus again offers the living waters of eternal life while the people continue to divide over his teaching. The Chief Priests and Pharisees rightly point to Old Testament prophecy which spoke of the Messiah to come. The problem did not lie in the appeal to prophecy, but in their ignorance of the Scriptures. They claim that no prophet has arisen out of Galilee (v. 52). Yet, the prophets Jonah and Hosea both originated from Galilee.

John shows that rejection of Jesus is born out of rebellion and ignorance.

Chapter 8

John 8:1–47

> 1 But Jesus went to the Mount of Olives. 2 Early in the morning He came again into the temple, and all the people were coming to Him; and He sat down and *began* to teach them. 3 The scribes and the Pharisees brought a woman caught in adultery, and having set her in the center *of the court,* 4 they said to Him, "Teacher, this woman has been caught in adultery, in the very act. 5 "Now in the Law Moses commanded us to stone such women; what then do You say?" 6 They were saying this, testing Him, so that they might have grounds for accusing Him. But Jesus stooped down and with His finger wrote on the ground. 7 But when they persisted in asking Him, He straightened up, and said to them, "He who is without sin among you, let him *be the* first to throw a stone at her." 8 Again He stooped down and wrote on the ground. 9 When they heard it, they *began* to go out one by one, beginning with the older ones, and He was left alone, and the woman, where she was, in the center *of the court.* 10 Straightening up, Jesus said to her, "Woman, where are they? Did no one condemn you?" 11 She said, "No one, Lord."

And Jesus said, "I do not condemn you, either. Go. From now on sin no more."]

12 Then Jesus again spoke to them, saying, "I am the Light of the world; he who follows Me will not walk in the darkness, but will have the Light of life." 13 So the Pharisees said to Him, "You are testifying about Yourself; Your testimony is not true." 14 Jesus answered and said to them, "Even if I testify about Myself, My testimony is true, for I know where I came from and where I am going; but you do not know where I come from or where I am going. 15 "You judge according to the flesh; I am not judging anyone. 16 "But even if I do judge, My judgment is true; for I am not alone *in it,* but I and the Father who sent Me. 17 "Even in your law it has been written that the testimony of two men is true. 18 "I am He who testifies about Myself, and the Father who sent Me testifies about Me." 19 So they were saying to Him, "Where is Your Father?" Jesus answered, "You know neither Me nor My Father; if you knew Me, you would know My Father also." 20 These words He spoke in the treasury, as He taught in the temple; and no one seized Him, because His hour had not yet come.

21 Then He said again to them, "I go away, and you will seek Me, and will die in your sin; where I am going, you cannot come." 22 So the Jews were saying, "Surely He will not kill Himself, will He, since He says, 'Where I am going, you cannot come'?" 23 And He was saying to them, "You are from below, I am from above; you are of this world, I am not of this world. 24 "Therefore I said to you that you will die in your sins; for unless you believe that I am *He,* you will die in your sins." 25 So they were saying to Him, "Who are You?" Jesus said to them, "What have I been saying to you *from* the beginning? 26 "I have many things to speak and to judge concerning you, but He who sent Me is true; and the things which I heard from Him, these I speak to the world." 27 They did not realize that He had been speaking to them about the Father. 28 So Jesus said, "When you lift up the Son of Man, then you will know that I am *He,* and I do nothing on My own initiative, but I speak these things as the Father taught Me. 29 "And He who sent Me is with Me; He has not left Me alone, for I always do the things that are pleasing to Him." 30 As He spoke these things, many came to believe in Him.

31 So Jesus was saying to those Jews who had believed Him, "If you continue in My word, *then* you are truly disciples of Mine; 32 and you will know the truth, and the truth will make you free." 33 They answered Him, "We are Abraham's descendants

and have never yet been enslaved to anyone; how is it that You say, 'You will become free'?"

34 Jesus answered them, "Truly, truly, I say to you, everyone who commits sin is the slave of sin. **35** "The slave does not remain in the house forever; the son does remain forever. **36** "So if the Son makes you free, you will be free indeed. **37** "I know that you are Abraham's descendants; yet you seek to kill Me, because My word has no place in you. **38** "I speak the things which I have seen with *My* Father; therefore you also do the things which you heard from *your* father."

39 They answered and said to Him, "Abraham is our father." Jesus said to them, "If you are Abraham's children, do the deeds of Abraham. **40** "But as it is, you are seeking to kill Me, a man who has told you the truth, which I heard from God; this Abraham did not do. **41** "You are doing the deeds of your father." They said to Him, "We were not born of fornication; we have one Father: God." **42** Jesus said to them, "If God were your Father, you would love Me, for I proceeded forth and have come from God, for I have not even come on My own initiative, but He sent Me. **43** "Why do you not understand what I am saying? *It is* because you cannot hear My word. **44** "You are of *your* father the devil, and you want to do the desires of your father. He was a murderer from the beginning, and does not stand in the truth because there is no truth in him. Whenever he speaks a lie, he speaks from his own *nature,* for he is a liar and the father of lies. **45** "But because I speak the truth, you do not believe Me. **46** "Which one of you convicts Me of sin? If I speak truth, why do you not believe Me? **47** "He who is of God hears the words of God; for this reason you do not hear *them,* because you are not of God."

Consider . . .

There are many catastrophes in life that can occur, but nothing compares to the tragedy of dying in one's unforgiven sins. Jesus repeats the truth that unless one believes, he will experience this very outcome with eternal consequences. Until then, he is inextricably trapped in his sins, a slave to the very thing that cements his death sentence.

Jesus, however, speaks hope to this bleak picture: "If you continue in My word, *then* you are truly disciples of Mine; and you will know the truth, and the truth will make you free" (vv. 31b-32). The answer of hope is simple. Only genuine belief in the truth of the gospel of Christ can break the bondage of sin. Man cannot engage in any level of moral reform or self-improvement to free himself from this enslavement, and any attempt to do so will be an exercise of utter futility. He needs someone to rescue him, and only Christ has the power to free a man from the bondage to sin.

John 8:48–59

48 The Jews answered and said to Him, "Do we not say rightly that You are a Samaritan and have a demon?" **49** Jesus answered, "I do not have a demon; but I honor My Father, and you dishonor Me. **50** "But I do not seek My glory; there is One who seeks and judges. **51** "Truly, truly, I say to you, if anyone keeps My word he will never see death." **52** The Jews said to Him, "Now we know that You have a demon. Abraham died, and the prophets *also*; and You say, 'If anyone keeps My word, he will never taste of death.' **53** "Surely You are not greater than our father Abraham, who died? The prophets died too; whom do You make Yourself out *to be?*" **54** Jesus answered, "If I glorify Myself, My glory is nothing; it is My Father who glorifies Me, of whom you say, 'He is our God'; **55** and you have not come to know Him, but I know Him; and if I say that I do not know Him, I will be a liar like you, but I do know Him and keep His word. **56** "Your father Abraham rejoiced to see My day, and he saw *it* and was glad." **57** So the Jews said to Him, "You are not yet fifty years old, and have You seen Abraham?" **58** Jesus said to them, "Truly, truly, I say to you, before Abraham was born, I am." **59** Therefore they picked up stones to throw at Him, but Jesus hid Himself and went out of the temple.

Consider . . .

The Jews pick up stones to kill Jesus because of his shocking statement "before Abraham was born, I am" (v. 58). When Jesus said "I am," the Jews would have immediately associated this with God's ancient declaration to Moses, a man God sent to rescue his people from slavery in Egypt. At that time Moses asked, "Now they may say to me, 'What is His name?'

What shall I say to them?" God responded, "I AM WHO I AM. Thus you shall say to the sons of Israel, 'I AM has sent me to you.'" (Exod 3:13–14).

When God identifies himself as "I am," he is asserting that as God, he simply *is*. He exists eternally, separate from and independent of his creation. Thus, when Jesus told the Jews, "I am," they immediately understood his claim: *I am God who always was, who is, and who always will be.* Their unbelief consequently drove them to stone Jesus for his supposed blasphemy.

Chapter 9

The Sixth Sign: Healing of the Blind Man
John 9:1–41

1 As He passed by, He saw a man blind from birth. 2 And His disciples asked Him, "Rabbi, who sinned, this man or his parents, that he would be born blind?" 3 Jesus answered, "*It was* neither *that* this man sinned, nor his parents; but *it was* so that the works of God might be displayed in him. 4 "We must work the works of Him who sent Me as long as it is day; night is coming when no one can work. 5 "While I am in the world, I am the Light of the world." 6 When He had said this, He spat on the ground, and made clay of the spittle, and applied the clay to his eyes, 7 and said to him, "Go, wash in the pool of Siloam" (which is translated, Sent). So he went away and washed, and came *back* seeing. 8 Therefore the neighbors, and those who previously saw him as a beggar, were saying, "Is not this the one who used to sit and beg?" 9 Others were saying, "This is he," *still* others were saying, "No, but he is like him." He kept saying, "I am the one." 10 So they were saying to him, "How then were your eyes opened?" 11 He answered, "The man who is called Jesus made clay, and anointed my eyes, and said to me, 'Go to Siloam and wash'; so I went away and washed, and I received sight." 12 They said to him, "Where is He?" He said, "I do not know."

13 They brought to the Pharisees the man who was formerly blind. 14 Now it was a Sabbath on the day when Jesus made the clay and opened his eyes. 15 Then the Pharisees also were asking him again how he received his sight. And he said to them, "He applied clay to my eyes, and I washed, and I see." 16 Therefore some of the Pharisees were saying, "This man is not from God, because He does not keep the Sabbath." But others were saying,

"How can a man who is a sinner perform such signs?" And there was a division among them. ¹⁷ So they said to the blind man again, "What do you say about Him, since He opened your eyes?" And he said, "He is a prophet."

¹⁸ The Jews then did not believe *it* of him, that he had been blind and had received sight, until they called the parents of the very one who had received his sight, ¹⁹ and questioned them, saying, "Is this your son, who you say was born blind? Then how does he now see?" ²⁰ His parents answered them and said, "We know that this is our son, and that he was born blind; ²¹ but how he now sees, we do not know; or who opened his eyes, we do not know. Ask him; he is of age, he will speak for himself." ²² His parents said this because they were afraid of the Jews; for the Jews had already agreed that if anyone confessed Him to be Christ, he was to be put out of the synagogue. ²³ For this reason his parents said, "He is of age; ask him."

²⁴ So a second time they called the man who had been blind, and said to him, "Give glory to God; we know that this man is a sinner." ²⁵ He then answered, "Whether He is a sinner, I do not know; one thing I do know, that though I was blind, now I see." ²⁶ So they said to him, "What did He do to you? How did He open your eyes?" ²⁷ He answered them, "I told you already and you did not listen; why do you want to hear *it* again? You do not want to become His disciples too, do you?" ²⁸ They reviled him and said, "You are His disciple, but we are disciples of Moses. ²⁹ "We know that God has spoken to Moses, but as for this man, we do not know where He is from." ³⁰ The man answered and said to them, "Well, here is an amazing thing, that you do not know where He is from, and *yet* He opened my eyes. ³¹ "We know that God does not hear sinners; but if anyone is God-fearing and does His will, He hears him. ³² "Since the beginning of time it has never been heard that anyone opened the eyes of a person born blind. ³³ "If this man were not from God, He could do nothing." ³⁴ They answered him, "You were born entirely in sins, and are you teaching us?" So they put him out.

³⁵ Jesus heard that they had put him out, and finding him, He said, "Do you believe in the Son of Man?" ³⁶ He answered, "Who is He, Lord, that I may believe in Him?" ³⁷ Jesus said to him, "You have both seen Him, and He is the one who is talking with you." ³⁸ And he said, "Lord, I believe." And he worshiped Him. ³⁹ And Jesus said, "For judgment I came into this world, so that those who do not see may see, and that those who see may become blind." ⁴⁰ Those of the Pharisees who were with Him heard these things and said to Him, "We are not blind too,

are we?" **41** Jesus said to them, "If you were blind, you would have no sin; but since you say, 'We see,' your sin remains.

Consider . . .

Ironically, this simple blind man had more sense than the religious elite who refused to believe the miracle of Jesus performed in plain sight.

John indicates that the man's blindness existed in the plan of God to demonstrate the power of God. His physical blindness was removed by Jesus, but more importantly, the "Light of the world" (v. 5) removed his spiritual blindness. In contrast, the religious elite refused to believe and thus, remained in their stubborn spiritual blindness. They remained in darkness because, ultimately, they loved the darkness (John 3:19).

Jesus concludes with a great irony. Like the Pharisees, those who claim to "see" are actually spiritually blind. However, those who are "blind" are the ones who recognize their blindness and come to the Light, the Savior of the world who gives spiritual sight. The salvation of this common blind man, in contrast to the religious elite, serves as an example of how God uses the "foolish" things of the world to confound the "wise" in order to ultimately bring glory to himself (1 Cor 1:26–31).

Chapter 10

John 10:1–42

1 "Truly, truly, I say to you, he who does not enter by the door into the fold of the sheep, but climbs up some other way, he is a thief and a robber. **2** "But he who enters by the door is a shepherd of the sheep. **3** "To him the doorkeeper opens, and the sheep hear his voice, and he calls his own sheep by name and leads them out. **4** "When he puts forth all his own, he goes ahead of them, and the sheep follow him because they know his voice. **5** "A stranger they simply will not follow, but will flee from him, because they do not know the voice of strangers." **6** This figure of speech Jesus spoke to them, but they did not understand what those things were which He had been saying to them.

7 So Jesus said to them again, "Truly, truly, I say to you, I am the door of the sheep. **8** "All who came before Me are thieves and robbers, but the sheep did not hear them. **9** "I am the door;

if anyone enters through Me, he will be saved, and will go in and out and find pasture. ¹⁰ "The thief comes only to steal and kill and destroy; I came that they may have life, and have *it* abundantly.

¹¹ "I am the good shepherd; the good shepherd lays down His life for the sheep. ¹² "He who is a hired hand, and not a shepherd, who is not the owner of the sheep, sees the wolf coming, and leaves the sheep and flees, and the wolf snatches them and scatters *them*. ¹³ "*He flees* because he is a hired hand and is not concerned about the sheep. ¹⁴ "I am the good shepherd, and I know My own and My own know Me, ¹⁵ even as the Father knows Me and I know the Father; and I lay down My life for the sheep. ¹⁶ "I have other sheep, which are not of this fold; I must bring them also, and they will hear My voice; and they will become one flock *with* one shepherd. ¹⁷ "For this reason the Father loves Me, because I lay down My life so that I may take it again. ¹⁸ "No one has taken it away from Me, but I lay it down on My own initiative. I have authority to lay it down, and I have authority to take it up again. This commandment I received from My Father."

¹⁹ A division occurred again among the Jews because of these words. ²⁰ Many of them were saying, "He has a demon and is insane. Why do you listen to Him?" ²¹ Others were saying, "These are not the sayings of one demon-possessed. A demon cannot open the eyes of the blind, can he?"

²² At that time the Feast of the Dedication took place at Jerusalem; ²³ it was winter, and Jesus was walking in the temple in the portico of Solomon. ²⁴ The Jews then gathered around Him, and were saying to Him, "How long will You keep us in suspense? If You are the Christ, tell us plainly." ²⁵ Jesus answered them, "I told you, and you do not believe; the works that I do in My Father's name, these testify of Me. ²⁶ "But you do not believe because you are not of My sheep. ²⁷ "My sheep hear My voice, and I know them, and they follow Me; ²⁸ and I give eternal life to them, and they will never perish; and no one will snatch them out of My hand. ²⁹ "My Father, who has given *them* to Me, is greater than all; and no one is able to snatch *them* out of the Father's hand. ³⁰ "I and the Father are one."

³¹ The Jews picked up stones again to stone Him. ³² Jesus answered them, "I showed you many good works from the Father; for which of them are you stoning Me?" ³³ The Jews answered Him, "For a good work we do not stone You, but for blasphemy; and because You, being a man, make Yourself out *to be* God." ³⁴ Jesus answered them, "Has it not been written in your Law, 'I SAID, YOU ARE GODS'? ³⁵ "If he called them

gods, to whom the word of God came (and the Scripture cannot be broken), **36** do you say of Him, whom the Father sanctified and sent into the world, 'You are blaspheming,' because I said, 'I am the Son of God'? **37** "If I do not do the works of My Father, do not believe Me; **38** but if I do them, though you do not believe Me, believe the works, so that you may know and understand that the Father is in Me, and I in the Father." **39** Therefore they were seeking again to seize Him, and He eluded their grasp.

40 And He went away again beyond the Jordan to the place where John was first baptizing, and He was staying there. **41** Many came to Him and were saying, "While John performed no sign, yet everything John said about this man was true." **42** Many believed in Him there.

Consider . . .

In light of the suffering and misery in the world, many dismiss God as either uncaring or aloof. Jesus is neither, as evidenced by his identification as the "good shepherd." A good shepherd loves and cares for his sheep; he protects and defends; he guides and feeds. As the Good Shepherd of his sheep (those who believe in him), Jesus points toward his pending death with the statement, "the good shepherd lays down His life for the sheep" (v. 11).

Once again, to the great chagrin of the Jews, he claims "oneness" with the Father, thereby asserting his own deity. With a play on words, Jesus cites Psalm 82:6 which identifies evil human rulers as "gods" (v. 34). His point is that if men with authority can be called "gods" by the world, why would they oppose his assertion of being the Son of God?

Yet it is this divine assertion and reality which provides great comfort to the believer. God saves his sheep and no one can take them out of his hand. Their eternal life is secure and can never be lost precisely because it was given by a God whose saving love is permanent and eternal.

Jesus shows that he is no ordinary shepherd. He is the Divine Shepherd who loves his sheep to such a degree that he would willingly and freely give his life for them and secure their eternal life with infinite love.

Chapter 11

The Seventh Sign: Resurrection of Lazarus
John 11:1–57

1 Now a certain man was sick, Lazarus of Bethany, the village of Mary and her sister Martha. **2** It was the Mary who anointed the Lord with ointment, and wiped His feet with her hair, whose brother Lazarus was sick. **3** So the sisters sent *word* to Him, saying, "Lord, behold, he whom You love is sick." **4** But when Jesus heard *this,* He said, "This sickness is not to end in death, but for the glory of God, so that the Son of God may be glorified by it." **5** Now Jesus loved Martha and her sister and Lazarus. **6** So when He heard that he was sick, He then stayed two days *longer* in the place where He was. **7** Then after this He said to the disciples, "Let us go to Judea again." **8** The disciples said to Him, "Rabbi, the Jews were just now seeking to stone You, and are You going there again?" **9** Jesus answered, "Are there not twelve hours in the day? If anyone walks in the day, he does not stumble, because he sees the light of this world. **10** "But if anyone walks in the night, he stumbles, because the light is not in him." **11** This He said, and after that He said to them, "Our friend Lazarus has fallen asleep; but I go, so that I may awaken him out of sleep." **12** The disciples then said to Him, "Lord, if he has fallen asleep, he will recover." **13** Now Jesus had spoken of his death, but they thought that He was speaking of literal sleep. **14** So Jesus then said to them plainly, "Lazarus is dead, **15** and I am glad for your sakes that I was not there, so that you may believe; but let us go to him." **16** Therefore Thomas, who is called Didymus, said to *his* fellow disciples, "Let us also go, so that we may die with Him."

17 So when Jesus came, He found that he had already been in the tomb four days. **18** Now Bethany was near Jerusalem, about two miles off; **19** and many of the Jews had come to Martha and Mary, to console them concerning *their* brother. **20** Martha therefore, when she heard that Jesus was coming, went to meet Him, but Mary stayed at the house. **21** Martha then said to Jesus, "Lord, if You had been here, my brother would not have died. **22** "Even now I know that whatever You ask of God, God will give You." **23** Jesus said to her, "Your brother will rise again." **24** Martha said to Him, "I know that he will rise again in the resurrection on the last day." **25** Jesus said to her, "I am the resurrection and the life; he who believes in Me will live even if he dies, **26** and everyone who lives and believes in Me will never die. Do you believe this?" **27** She said to Him, "Yes, Lord; I have believed that You are the Christ, the Son of God, *even* He who comes into the world."

28 When she had said this, she went away and called Mary her sister, saying secretly, "The Teacher is here and is calling for you." **29** And when she heard it, she got up quickly and was coming to Him.

30 Now Jesus had not yet come into the village, but was still in the place where Martha met Him. **31** Then the Jews who were with her in the house, and consoling her, when they saw that Mary got up quickly and went out, they followed her, supposing that she was going to the tomb to weep there. **32** Therefore, when Mary came where Jesus was, she saw Him, and fell at His feet, saying to Him, "Lord, if You had been here, my brother would not have died." **33** When Jesus therefore saw her weeping, and the Jews who came with her *also* weeping, He was deeply moved in spirit and was troubled, **34** and said, "Where have you laid him?" They said to Him, "Lord, come and see." **35** Jesus wept. **36** So the Jews were saying, "See how He loved him!" **37** But some of them said, "Could not this man, who opened the eyes of the blind man, have kept this man also from dying?"

38 So Jesus, again being deeply moved within, came to the tomb. Now it was a cave, and a stone was lying against it. **39** Jesus said, "Remove the stone." Martha, the sister of the deceased, said to Him, "Lord, by this time there will be a stench, for he has been *dead* four days." **40** Jesus said to her, "Did I not say to you that if you believe, you will see the glory of God?" **41** So they removed the stone. Then Jesus raised His eyes, and said, "Father, I thank You that You have heard Me. **42** "I knew that You always hear Me; but because of the people standing around I said it, so that they may believe that You sent Me." **43** When He had said these things, He cried out with a loud voice, "Lazarus, come forth." **44** The man who had died came forth, bound hand and foot with wrappings, and his face was wrapped around with a cloth. Jesus said to them, "Unbind him, and let him go."

45 Therefore many of the Jews who came to Mary, and saw what He had done, believed in Him. **46** But some of them went to the Pharisees and told them the things which Jesus had done.

47 Therefore the chief priests and the Pharisees convened a council, and were saying, "What are we doing? For this man is performing many signs. **48** "If we let Him *go on* like this, all men will believe in Him, and the Romans will come and take away both our place and our nation." **49** But one of them, Caiaphas, who was high priest that year, said to them, "You know nothing at all, [50] nor do you take into account that it is expedient for you that one man die for the people, and that the whole nation not perish." [51] Now he did not say this on his own initiative, but being high priest that year, he prophesied that Jesus was going to die for the nation, [52] and not for the nation only, but in order that He might also gather together into one the children of God who are scattered abroad. [53] So from that day on they planned together to kill Him.

[54] Therefore Jesus no longer continued to walk publicly among the Jews, but went away from there to the country near the wilderness, into a city called Ephraim; and there He stayed with the disciples.

[55] Now the Passover of the Jews was near, and many went up to Jerusalem out of the country before the Passover to purify themselves. [56] So they were seeking for Jesus, and were saying to one another as they stood in the temple, "What do you think; that He will not come to the feast at all?" [57] Now the chief priests and the Pharisees had given orders that if anyone knew where He was, he was to report it, so that they might seize Him.

Consider . . .

The chief priests and the Pharisees ask a great question. In light of the miracles Jesus has performed they ask, *what are we to do?* (v. 47). Great question. Sadly their response was terribly deficient.

In a stunning turn of events, Mary and Martha go from mourning to rejoicing with the resurrection of Lazarus. Having been dead for four days, for Lazarus to walk out of his own tomb was a human impossibility. Certainly, no other man could enable him to do so. But Jesus proves to be no ordinary man. He is the "resurrection and the life" (v. 25). And to demonstrate his power to give eternal life, he commands human life back into Lazarus.

Indeed, *what are we to do?* Martha says: "Yes, Lord; I have believed that You are the Christ, the Son of God, *even* He who comes into the world." (v. 27). The Jews effectively say, *kill him.*

Jesus is either the Son of God or he is not. There is no middle ground. Neither is there middle ground for man's response. John's narrative once again illustrates only two possible responses: accept him or reject him. Accept and receive life or reject and remain dead.

Chapter 12

John 12:1–50

1 Jesus, therefore, six days before the Passover, came to Bethany where Lazarus was, whom Jesus had raised from the dead. 2 So they made Him a supper there, and Martha was serving; but Lazarus was one of those reclining *at the table* with Him. 3 Mary then took a pound of very costly perfume of pure nard, and anointed the feet of Jesus and wiped His feet with her hair; and the house was filled with the fragrance of the perfume. 4 But Judas Iscariot, one of His disciples, who was intending to betray Him, said, 5 "Why was this perfume not sold for three hundred denarii and given to poor *people?*" 6 Now he said this, not because he was concerned about the poor, but because he was a thief, and as he had the money box, he used to pilfer what was put into it. 7 Therefore Jesus said, "Let her alone, so that she may keep it for the day of My burial. 8 "For you always have the poor with you, but you do not always have Me."

9 The large crowd of the Jews then learned that He was there; and they came, not for Jesus' sake only, but that they might also see Lazarus, whom He raised from the dead. 10 But the chief priests planned to put Lazarus to death also; 11 because on account of him many of the Jews were going away and were believing in Jesus.

12 On the next day the large crowd who had come to the feast, when they heard that Jesus was coming to Jerusalem, 13 took the branches of the palm trees and went out to meet Him, and *began* to shout, "Hosanna! BLESSED IS HE WHO COMES IN THE NAME OF THE LORD, even the King of Israel." 14 Jesus, finding a young donkey, sat on it; as it is written, 15 "FEAR NOT, DAUGHTER OF ZION; BEHOLD, YOUR KING IS COMING, SEATED ON A DONKEY'S COLT." 16 These things His disciples did not understand at the first; but when Jesus was glorified, then they remembered that these things were written of Him, and that they had done these things to Him. 17 So the people, who were with Him when He called Lazarus out of the tomb and raised him from the dead, continued to testify *about Him.* 18 For this reason also the people went and met Him, because they heard that He had performed this sign. 19 So the Pharisees said to one another, "You see that you are not doing any good; look, the world has gone after Him."

20 Now there were some Greeks among those who were going up to worship at the feast; **21** these then came to Philip, who was from Bethsaida of Galilee, and *began to* ask him, saying, "Sir, we wish to see Jesus." **22** Philip came and told Andrew; Andrew and Philip came and told Jesus. **23** And Jesus answered them, saying, "The hour has come for the Son of Man to be glorified. **24** "Truly, truly, I say to you, unless a grain of wheat falls into the earth and dies, it remains alone; but if it dies, it bears much fruit. **25** "He who loves his life loses it, and he who hates his life in this world will keep it to life eternal. **26** "If anyone serves Me, he must follow Me; and where I am, there My servant will be also; if anyone serves Me, the Father will honor him.

27 "Now My soul has become troubled; and what shall I say, 'Father, save Me from this hour'? But for this purpose I came to this hour. **28** "Father, glorify Your name." Then a voice came out of heaven: "I have both glorified it, and will glorify it again." **29** So the crowd *of people* who stood by and heard it were saying that it had thundered; others were saying, "An angel has spoken to Him." **30** Jesus answered and said, "This voice has not come for My sake, but for your sakes. **31** "Now judgment is upon this world; now the ruler of this world will be cast out. **32** "And I, if I am lifted up from the earth, will draw all men to Myself." **33** But He was saying this to indicate the kind of death by which He was to die. **34** The crowd then answered Him, "We have heard out of the Law that the Christ is to remain forever; and how can You say, 'The Son of Man must be lifted up'? Who is this Son of Man?" **35** So Jesus said to them, "For a little while longer the Light is among you. Walk while you have the Light, so that darkness will not overtake you; he who walks in the darkness does not know where he goes. **36** "While you have the Light, believe in the Light, so that you may become sons of Light."

These things Jesus spoke, and He went away and hid Himself from them. **37** But though He had performed so many signs before them, *yet* they were not believing in Him. **38** *This was* to fulfill the word of Isaiah the prophet which he spoke: "LORD, WHO HAS BELIEVED OUR REPORT? AND TO WHOM HAS THE ARM OF THE LORD BEEN REVEALED?" **39** For this reason they could not believe, for Isaiah said again, **40** "HE HAS BLINDED THEIR EYES AND HE HARDENED THEIR HEART, SO THAT THEY WOULD NOT SEE WITH THEIR EYES AND PERCEIVE WITH THEIR HEART, AND BE CONVERTED AND I HEAL THEM." **41** These things Isaiah said because he saw His glory, and he spoke of Him. **42** Nevertheless many even of the rulers believed in Him, but because of the Pharisees they were not confessing *Him,* for fear that they would be put out of the synagogue; **43** for they loved the approval of men rather than the approval of God.

44 And Jesus cried out and said, "He who believes in Me, does not believe in Me but in Him who sent Me. **45** "He who sees Me sees the One who sent Me. **46** "I have come *as* Light into the world, so that everyone who believes in Me will not remain in darkness. **47** "If anyone hears My sayings and does not keep them, I do not judge him; for I did not come to judge the world, but to save the world. **48** "He who rejects Me and does not receive My sayings, has one who judges him; the word I spoke is what will judge him at the last day. **49** "For I did not speak on My own initiative, but the Father Himself who sent Me has given Me a commandment *as to* what to say and what to speak. **50** "I know that His commandment is eternal life; therefore the things I speak, I speak just as the Father has told Me."

Consider . . .

Jesus enters Jerusalem and the crowds greet him as the king of Israel, hopeful that he is the conquering Messiah who will liberate them from political oppression and injustice. Jesus instead comes to Jerusalem to die.

He will be the conquering king in his future second coming, but his mission in his first coming was singular—to suffer and die as the savior of the world.

As the only Savior of men, Jesus calls all to believe in him. While he indicates he did not come to judge men at this time (v. 47), he points to the reality that his spoken words will judge men in the final day of judgment (v. 48). As John details Christ's path to the cross, he shows us the first coming of Jesus as the Suffering Servant. Yet, Christ will come as the Conquering King in his second coming (Rev 19:11—20:15). Then the judgment spoken of in Hebrews 9:27 will be realized: "it is appointed for men to die once and after this comes judgment."

Chapter 13

John 13:1–38

1 Now before the Feast of the Passover, Jesus knowing that His hour had come that He would depart out of this world to the Father, having loved His own who were in the world, He loved them to the end. **2** During supper, the devil having already put into the heart of Judas Iscariot, *the son* of Simon, to betray Him, **3** *Jesus,* knowing that the Father had given all things into His hands, and that He had come forth from God and was going back to God, **4** got up from supper, and laid aside His garments; and taking a towel, He girded Himself. **5** Then He poured water into the basin, and began to wash the disciples' feet and to wipe them with the towel with which He was girded. **6** So He came to Simon Peter. He said to Him, "Lord, do You wash my feet?" **7** Jesus answered and said to him, "What I do you do not realize now, but you will understand hereafter." **8** Peter said to Him, "Never shall You wash my feet!" Jesus answered him, "If I do not wash you, you have no part with Me." **9** Simon Peter said to Him, "Lord, *then wash* not only my feet, but also my hands and my head." **10** Jesus said to him, "He who has bathed needs only to wash his feet, but is completely clean; and you are clean, but not all *of you.*" **11** For He knew the one who was betraying Him; for this reason He said, "Not all of you are clean."

12 So when He had washed their feet, and taken His garments and reclined *at the table* again, He said to them, "Do you know what I have done to you? **13** "You call Me Teacher and Lord; and you are right, for *so* I am. **14** "If I then, the Lord and the Teacher, washed your feet, you also ought to wash one another's feet. **15** "For I gave you an example that you also should do as I did to you. **16** "Truly, truly, I say to you, a slave is not greater than his master, nor *is* one who is sent greater than the one who sent him. **17** "If you know these things, you are blessed if you do them. **18** "I do not speak of all of you. I know the ones I have chosen; but *it is* that the Scripture may be fulfilled, 'HE WHO EATS MY BREAD HAS LIFTED UP HIS HEEL AGAINST ME.' **19** "From now on I am telling you before *it* comes to pass, so that when it does occur, you may believe that I am *He.* **20** "Truly, truly, I say to you, he who receives whomever I send receives Me; and he who receives Me receives Him who sent Me."

21 When Jesus had said this, He became troubled in spirit, and testified and said, "Truly, truly, I say to you, that one of you will betray Me." **22** The disciples *began* looking at one another, at a loss *to know* of which one He was speaking. **23** There was reclining on Jesus' bosom one of His disciples, whom Jesus loved. **24** So Simon Peter gestured to him, and said to him, "Tell *us* who it is of whom He is speaking." **25** He, leaning back thus on Jesus' bosom, said to Him, "Lord, who is it?" **26** Jesus then answered, "That is the one for whom I shall dip the morsel and give it to him." So when He had dipped the morsel, He took and gave it to Judas, *the son* of Simon Iscariot. **27** After the morsel, Satan then entered into him. Therefore Jesus said to him, "What you do, do quickly." **28** Now no one of those reclining *at the table* knew for what purpose He had said this to him. **29** For some were supposing, because Judas had the money box, that Jesus was saying to him, "Buy the things we have need of for the feast"; or else, that he should give something to the poor. **30** So after receiving the morsel he went out immediately; and it was night.

31 Therefore when he had gone out, Jesus said, "Now is the Son of Man glorified, and God is glorified in Him; **32** if God is glorified in Him, God will also glorify Him in Himself, and will glorify Him immediately. **33** "Little children, I am with you a little while longer. You will seek Me; and as I said to the Jews, now I also say to you, 'Where I am going, you cannot come.' **34** "A new commandment I give to you, that you love one another, even as I have loved you, that you also love one another. **35** "By this all men will know that you are My disciples, if you have love for one another."

36 Simon Peter said to Him, "Lord, where are You going?" Jesus answered, "Where I go, you cannot follow Me now; but you will follow later." **37** Peter said to Him, "Lord, why can I not follow You right now? I will lay down my life for You." **38** Jesus answered, "Will you lay down your life for Me? Truly, truly, I say to you, a rooster will not crow until you deny Me three times.

Consider . . .

On the night before his crucifixion, Jesus gathers his disciples to celebrate the Passover and instructs them one last time. His teaching begins with a stunning display of humility. The one who spoke the intricate universe into existence with a mere word now washes feet, even those of Judas who was about to betray him. A task normally relegated for a household servant becomes the joyful task of the Divine King.

Jesus came to serve, both in daily practice and with finality in his death. Not only are his disciples to serve and love one another in the same way, but by doing so, they demonstrate that they are true followers of Christ (v. 35).

Throughout his ministry on earth, Jesus displayed an extraordinary humility and love. Notably, this character of the Son of God wasn't unique to his humanity, as if these qualities were suddenly inherited when he took on human flesh. No, this is and always has been the very character and nature of the eternal God. Jesus simply made God's nature visible.

Chapter 14

John 14:1–31

> [1] "Do not let your heart be troubled; believe in God, believe also in Me. [2] "In My Father's house are many dwelling places; if it were not so, I would have told you; for I go to prepare a place for you. [3] "If I go and prepare a place for you, I will come again and receive you to Myself, that where I am, *there* you may be also. [4] "And you know the way where I am going." [5] Thomas said to Him, "Lord, we do not know where You are going, how do we know the way?" [6] Jesus said to him, "I am the way, and the truth, and the life; no one comes to the Father but through Me. [7] "If you had known Me, you would have known My Father also; from now on you know Him, and have seen Him."
>
> [8] Philip said to Him, "Lord, show us the Father, and it is enough for us." [9] Jesus said to him, "Have I been so long with you, and *yet* you have not come to know Me, Philip? He who has seen Me has seen the Father; how *can* you say, 'Show us the Father'? [10] "Do you not believe that I am in the Father, and the Father is in Me? The words that I say to you I do not speak on My own initiative, but the Father abiding in Me does His works. [11] "Believe Me that I am in the Father and the Father is in Me; otherwise believe because of the works themselves. [12] "Truly, truly, I say to you, he who believes in Me, the works that I do, he will do also; and greater *works* than these he will do; because I go to the Father. [13] "Whatever you ask in My name, that will I do, so that the Father may be glorified in the Son. [14] "If you ask Me anything in My name, I will do *it*.
>
> [15] "If you love Me, you will keep My commandments. [16] "I will ask the Father, and He will give you another Helper, that

He may be with you forever; **17** *that is* the Spirit of truth, whom the world cannot receive, because it does not see Him or know Him, *but* you know Him because He abides with you and will be in you.

18 "I will not leave you as orphans; I will come to you. **19** "After a little while the world will no longer see Me, but you *will* see Me; because I live, you will live also. **20** "In that day you will know that I am in My Father, and you in Me, and I in you. **21** "He who has My commandments and keeps them is the one who loves Me; and he who loves Me will be loved by My Father, and I will love him and will disclose Myself to him." **22** Judas (not Iscariot) said to Him, "Lord, what then has happened that You are going to disclose Yourself to us and not to the world?" **23** Jesus answered and said to him, "If anyone loves Me, he will keep My word; and My Father will love him, and We will come to him and make Our abode with him. **24** "He who does not love Me does not keep My words; and the word which you hear is not Mine, but the Father's who sent Me.

25 "These things I have spoken to you while abiding with you. **26** "But the Helper, the Holy Spirit, whom the Father will send in My name, He will teach you all things, and bring to your remembrance all that I said to you. **27** "Peace I leave with you; My peace I give to you; not as the world gives do I give to you. Do not let your heart be troubled, nor let it be fearful. **28** "You heard that I said to you, 'I go away, and I will come to you.' If you loved Me, you would have rejoiced because I go to the Father, for the Father is greater than I. **29** "Now I have told you before it happens, so that when it happens, you may believe. **30** "I will not speak much more with you, for the ruler of the world is coming, and he has nothing in Me; **31** but so that the world may know that I love the Father, I do exactly as the Father commanded Me. Get up, let us go from here.

Consider . . .

The world seeks peace. Yet, at every corner, it only finds chaos, wars, and hatred. To compound the problem, every human being struggles to find peace in his own soul. Man lives with a perpetual discomfort with himself, plagued by pervasive and unrelenting guilt and unrest which tells him something is deeply wrong. Something is profoundly amiss.

The turmoil in the heart of man due to his own sin can only be replaced with the rest and peace found through the forgiveness of sins. Jesus makes it plain that he is the giver of peace (v. 27) and that he is the only one who can provide this peace. "I am the way, and the truth, and the life; no one comes to the Father but through Me." (v. 6).

Jesus is the only gateway to eternal life and eternal peace. Many would say that all religious roads lead to heaven. Jesus says there is only one. Him. And those who follow him are marked by obedience to his will (v. 15). Thus, to be a disciple of Christ is believe in him. To believe in him is to surrender to his authority. And to surrender to him is to seek to obey him. This is the exclusive path to life and peace.

Chapter 15

John 15:1–27

> **1** "I am the true vine, and My Father is the vinedresser. **2** "Every branch in Me that does not bear fruit, He takes away; and every *branch* that bears fruit, He prunes it so that it may bear more fruit. **3** "You are already clean because of the word which I have spoken to you. **4** "Abide in Me, and I in you. As the branch cannot bear fruit of itself unless it abides in the vine, so neither *can* you unless you abide in Me. **5** "I am the vine, you are the branches; he who abides in Me and I in him, he bears much fruit, for apart from Me you can do nothing. **6** "If anyone does not abide in Me, he is thrown away as a branch and dries up; and they gather them, and cast them into the fire and they are burned. **7** "If you abide in Me, and My words abide in you, ask whatever you wish, and it will be done for you. **8** "My Father is glorified by this, that you bear much fruit, and *so* prove to be My disciples. **9** "Just as the Father has loved Me, I have also loved you; abide in My love. **10** "If you keep My commandments, you will abide in My love; just as I have kept My Father's commandments and abide in His love. **11** "These things I have spoken to you so that My joy may be in you, and *that* your joy may be made full.
>
> **12** "This is My commandment, that you love one another, just as I have loved you. **13** "Greater love has no one than this, that one lay down his life for his friends. **14** "You are My friends if you do what I command you. **15** "No longer do I call you slaves, for the slave does not know what his master is doing; but I have called you friends, for all things that I have heard from

My Father I have made known to you. ¹⁶ "You did not choose Me but I chose you, and appointed you that you would go and bear fruit, and *that* your fruit would remain, so that whatever you ask of the Father in My name He may give to you. ¹⁷ "This I command you, that you love one another.

¹⁸ "If the world hates you, you know that it has hated Me before *it hated* you. ¹⁹ "If you were of the world, the world would love its own; but because you are not of the world, but I chose you out of the world, because of this the world hates you. ²⁰ "Remember the word that I said to you, 'A slave is not greater than his master.' If they persecuted Me, they will also persecute you; if they kept My word, they will keep yours also. ²¹ "But all these things they will do to you for My name's sake, because they do not know the One who sent Me. ²² "If I had not come and spoken to them, they would not have sin, but now they have no excuse for their sin. ²³ "He who hates Me hates My Father also. ²⁴ "If I had not done among them the works which no one else did, they would not have sin; but now they have both seen and hated Me and My Father as well. ²⁵ "But *they have done this* to fulfill the word that is written in their Law, 'THEY HATED ME WITHOUT A CAUSE.'

²⁶ "When the Helper comes, whom I will send to you from the Father, *that is* the Spirit of truth who proceeds from the Father, He will testify about Me, ²⁷ and you *will* testify also, because you have been with Me from the beginning.

Consider . . .

What does it mean to be a Christian? Many have rightly asked this question, and as Jesus continues to teach his disciples on the night before his death, he provides the answer with clarity. To be a Christian is to remain or abide in him.

Using a vine analogy, Jesus illustrates that being a Christian is not sprinkling some religion into your life. Instead, to be one with Christ is like the branch which is one with the vine. To be "in" Christ is to love him by obeying him (v. 10). This obedience is evidenced by spiritual fruit such as peace, joy, kindness, and self-control (Gal 5:22–24).

There is great joy in being in Christ. God is not a cosmic kill-joy seeking to squash man's happiness. Instead, he is the giver of true and lasting joy—not a flippant happiness derived from some passing pleasure, but a joy rooted in his saving and preserving love, a joy which only comes when man lives as he was created to be: in a loving relationship with his Creator.

In this analogy, Jesus presents a graphic warning. Any branch not truly of the vine is pruned and thrown into the fire and burned (v. 6). For the "fake branch" who does not wholly follow Christ in genuine and obedient faith, destruction and eternal judgment is his end.

Chapter 16

John 16:1–33

1 "These things I have spoken to you so that you may be kept from stumbling. 2 "They will make you outcasts from the synagogue, but an hour is coming for everyone who kills you to think that he is offering service to God. 3 "These things they will do because they have not known the Father or Me. 4 "But these things I have spoken to you, so that when their hour comes, you may remember that I told you of them. These things I did not say to you at the beginning, because I was with you.

5 "But now I am going to Him who sent Me; and none of you asks Me, 'Where are You going?' 6 "But because I have said these things to you, sorrow has filled your heart. 7 "But I tell you the truth, it is to your advantage that I go away; for if I do not go away, the Helper will not come to you; but if I go, I will send Him to you. 8 "And He, when He comes, will convict the world concerning sin and righteousness and judgment; 9 concerning sin, because they do not believe in Me; 10 and concerning righteousness, because I go to the Father and you no longer see Me; 11 and concerning judgment, because the ruler of this world has been judged.

12 "I have many more things to say to you, but you cannot bear *them* now. 13 "But when He, the Spirit of truth, comes, He will guide you into all the truth; for He will not speak on His own initiative, but whatever He hears, He will speak; and He will disclose to you what is to come. 14 "He will glorify Me, for He will take of Mine and will disclose *it* to you. 15 "All things that the Father has are Mine; therefore I said that He takes of Mine and will disclose *it* to you.

16 "A little while, and you will no longer see Me; and again a little while, and you will see Me." 17 *Some* of His disciples then said to one another, "What is this thing He is telling us, 'A little while, and you will not see Me; and again a little while, and you

will see Me'; and, 'because I go to the Father'?" **18** So they were saying, "What is this that He says, 'A little while'? We do not know what He is talking about." **19** Jesus knew that they wished to question Him, and He said to them, "Are you deliberating together about this, that I said, 'A little while, and you will not see Me, and again a little while, and you will see Me'? **20** "Truly, truly, I say to you, that you will weep and lament, but the world will rejoice; you will grieve, but your grief will be turned into joy. **21** "Whenever a woman is in labor she has pain, because her hour has come; but when she gives birth to the child, she no longer remembers the anguish because of the joy that a child has been born into the world. **22** "Therefore you too have grief now; but I will see you again, and your heart will rejoice, and no one *will* take your joy away from you. **23** "In that day you will not question Me about anything. Truly, truly, I say to you, if you ask the Father for anything in My name, He will give it to you. **24** "Until now you have asked for nothing in My name; ask and you will receive, so that your joy may be made full.

25 "These things I have spoken to you in figurative language; an hour is coming when I will no longer speak to you in figurative language, but will tell you plainly of the Father. **26** "In that day you will ask in My name, and I do not say to you that I will request of the Father on your behalf; **27** for the Father Himself loves you, because you have loved Me and have believed that I came forth from the Father. **28** "I came forth from the Father and have come into the world; I am leaving the world again and going to the Father."

29 His disciples said, "Lo, now You are speaking plainly and are not using a figure of speech. **30** "Now we know that You know all things, and have no need for anyone to question You; by this we believe that You came from God." **31** Jesus answered them, "Do you now believe? **32** "Behold, an hour is coming, and has *already* come, for you to be scattered, each to his own *home,* and to leave Me alone; and *yet* I am not alone, because the Father is with Me. **33** "These things I have spoken to you, so that in Me you may have peace. In the world you have tribulation, but take courage; I have overcome the world."

Consider . . .

Jesus teaches the disciples a critical consequence of following him: you will suffer (v. 33). Too many today teach a false gospel which says Jesus wants to give you a rich and materially prosperous life of ease that you can seize with the right amount of faith. Jesus says, follow me and the world will hate you (15:19); follow me and you will suffer (16:1–2); follow me and you will have tribulation (v. 33).

Jesus declares in no uncertain terms that there is a cost to following him. But the cost is confined to this world. In return, the Christian gains the love of God (v. 27), the forgiveness of sins, and the eternal, unfading riches of heaven. There is glorious victory in the end for the disciple of Christ, for he follows the One who has "overcome the world" (v. 33).

Chapter 17

John 17:1–26

> ¹ Jesus spoke these things; and lifting up His eyes to heaven, He said, "Father, the hour has come; glorify Your Son, that the Son may glorify You, ² even as You gave Him authority over all flesh, that to all whom You have given Him, He may give eternal life. ³ "This is eternal life, that they may know You, the only true God, and Jesus Christ whom You have sent. ⁴ "I glorified You on the earth, having accomplished the work which You have given Me to do. ⁵ "Now, Father, glorify Me together with Yourself, with the glory which I had with You before the world was.
> ⁶ "I have manifested Your name to the men whom You gave Me out of the world; they were Yours and You gave them to Me, and they have kept Your word. ⁷ "Now they have come to know that everything You have given Me is from You; ⁸ for the words which You gave Me I have given to them; and they received *them* and truly understood that I came forth from You, and they believed that You sent Me. ⁹ "I ask on their behalf; I do not ask on behalf of the world, but of those whom You have given Me; for they are Yours; ¹⁰ and all things that are Mine are Yours, and Yours are Mine; and I have been glorified in them. ¹¹ "I am no longer in the world; and *yet* they themselves are in the world, and I come to You. Holy Father, keep them in Your name, *the name* which You have given Me, that they may be one even as We *are*. ¹² "While I was with them, I was keeping them in Your name which You have given Me; and I guarded them and not one of them perished but the son of perdition, so that the Scripture would be fulfilled. ¹³ "But now I come to You; and these things I speak in the world so that they may have My joy

made full in themselves. [14] "I have given them Your word; and the world has hated them, because they are not of the world, even as I am not of the world. [15] "I do not ask You to take them out of the world, but to keep them from the evil *one.* [16] "They are not of the world, even as I am not of the world. [17] "Sanctify them in the truth; Your word is truth. [18] "As You sent Me into the world, I also have sent them into the world. [19] "For their sakes I sanctify Myself, that they themselves also may be sanctified in truth.

[20] "I do not ask on behalf of these alone, but for those also who believe in Me through their word; [21] that they may all be one; even as You, Father, *are* in Me and I in You, that they also may be in Us, so that the world may believe that You sent Me. [22] "The glory which You have given Me I have given to them, that they may be one, just as We are one; [23] I in them and You in Me, that they may be perfected in unity, so that the world may know that You sent Me, and loved them, even as You have loved Me. [24] "Father, I desire that they also, whom You have given Me, be with Me where I am, so that they may see My glory which You have given Me, for You loved Me before the foundation of the world.

[25] "O righteous Father, although the world has not known You, yet I have known You; and these have known that You sent Me; [26] and I have made Your name known to them, and will make it known, so that the love with which You loved Me may be in them, and I in them."

Consider . . .

John records this intimate prayer of Jesus to the Father. Through this prayer we discover rich truths:

1. Jesus, the Son of God, has enjoyed a perfect fellowship in unity with the Father from eternity past (v. 24).

2. Jesus seeks to glorify the Father by making him known to the world (vv. 4, 6).

3. The Father has given Jesus, whose desire is to bring people to himself, authority to save (vv. 2, 24).

4. Jesus intercedes on behalf of believers (v. 9).

5. God's desire is sanctification for believers—to become more like him as his truth is known and lived (vv. 17–19).

6. The world is governed by hatred for truth and followers of truth (v. 14).

7. Believers are filled with joy that comes from Jesus (v. 13).

8. Jesus doesn't promise ease in this lifetime (v. 15), but he does promise future glory (v. 22).

9. Salvation brings believers into an eternal fellowship of love with the Father and Son (vv. 22–23, 26).

10. This joyful fellowship shows the love of God to the world (vv. 21, 23).

Chapter 18

John 18:1–40

1 When Jesus had spoken these words, He went forth with His disciples over the ravine of the Kidron, where there was a garden, in which He entered with His disciples. **2** Now Judas also, who was betraying Him, knew the place, for Jesus had often met there with His disciples. **3** Judas then, having received the *Roman* cohort and officers from the chief priests and the Pharisees, came there with lanterns and torches and weapons. **4** So Jesus, knowing all the things that were coming upon Him, went forth and said to them, "Whom do you seek?" **5** They answered Him, "Jesus the Nazarene." He said to them, "I am *He.*" And Judas also, who was betraying Him, was standing with them. **6** So when He said to them, "I am *He,*" they drew back and fell to the ground. **7** Therefore He again asked them, "Whom do you seek?" And they said, "Jesus the Nazarene." **8** Jesus answered, "I told you that I am *He;* so if you seek Me, let these go their way," **9** to fulfill the word which He spoke, "Of those whom You have given Me I lost not one." **10** Simon Peter then, having a sword, drew it and struck the high priest's slave, and cut off his right ear; and the slave's name was Malchus. **11** So Jesus said to Peter, "Put the sword into the sheath; the cup which the Father has given Me, shall I not drink it?"

12 So the *Roman* cohort and the commander and the officers of the Jews, arrested Jesus and bound Him, **13** and led Him to Annas first; for he was father-in-law of Caiaphas, who was high priest that year. **14** Now Caiaphas was the one who had advised the Jews that it was expedient for one man to die on behalf of the people.

15 Simon Peter was following Jesus, and *so was* another disciple. Now that disciple was known to the high priest, and entered with Jesus into the court of the high priest, **16** but Peter was standing at the door outside. So the other disciple, who was known to the high priest, went out and spoke to the doorkeeper, and brought Peter in. **17** Then the slave-girl who kept the door said to Peter, "You are not also *one* of this man's disciples, are you?" He said, "I am not." **18** Now the slaves and the officers were standing *there,* having made a charcoal fire, for it was cold and they were warming themselves; and Peter was also with them, standing and warming himself.

19 The high priest then questioned Jesus about His disciples, and about His teaching. **20** Jesus answered him, "I have spoken openly to the world; I always taught in synagogues and in the temple, where all the Jews come together; and I spoke nothing in secret. **21** "Why do you question Me? Question those who have heard what I spoke to them; they know what I said." **22** When He had said this, one of the officers standing nearby struck Jesus, saying, "Is that the way You answer the high priest?" **23** Jesus answered him, "If I have spoken wrongly, testify of the wrong; but if rightly, why do you strike Me?" **24** So Annas sent Him bound to Caiaphas the high priest.

25 Now Simon Peter was standing and warming himself. So they said to him, "You are not also *one* of His disciples, are you?" He denied *it,* and said, "I am not." **26** One of the slaves of the high priest, being a relative of the one whose ear Peter cut off, said, "Did I not see you in the garden with Him?" **27** Peter then denied *it* again, and immediately a rooster crowed.

28 Then they led Jesus from Caiaphas into the Praetorium, and it was early; and they themselves did not enter into the Praetorium so that they would not be defiled, but might eat the Passover. **29** Therefore Pilate went out to them and said, "What accusation do you bring against this Man?" **30** They answered and said to him, "If this Man were not an evildoer, we would not have delivered Him to you." **31** So Pilate said to them, "Take Him yourselves, and judge Him according to your law." The Jews said to him, "We are not permitted to put anyone to death," **32** to fulfill the word of Jesus which He spoke, signifying by what kind of death He was about to die.

33 Therefore Pilate entered again into the Praetorium, and summoned Jesus and said to Him, "Are You the King of the Jews?" **34** Jesus answered, "Are you saying this on your own initiative, or did others tell you about Me?" **35** Pilate answered, "I am not a Jew, am I? Your own nation and the chief priests delivered You to me; what have You done?" **36** Jesus answered, "My kingdom is not of this world. If My kingdom were of this world, then My servants would be fighting so that I would not be handed over to the Jews; but as it is, My kingdom is not of this realm." **37** Therefore Pilate said to Him, "So You are a king?" Jesus answered, "You say *correctly* that I am a king. For this I have been born, and for this I have come into the world, to testify to the truth. Everyone who is of the truth hears My voice." **38** Pilate said to Him, "What is truth?"

And when he had said this, he went out again to the Jews and said to them, "I find no guilt in Him. **39** "But you have a custom that I release someone for you at the Passover; do you wish then that I release for you the King of the Jews?" **40** So they cried out again, saying, "Not this Man, but Barabbas." Now Barabbas was a robber.

Chapter 19

John 19:1–42

1 Pilate then took Jesus and scourged Him. **2** And the soldiers twisted together a crown of thorns and put it on His head, and put a purple robe on Him; **3** and they *began* to come up to Him and say, "Hail, King of the Jews!" and to give Him slaps *in the face.* **4** Pilate came out again and said to them, "Behold, I am bringing Him out to you so that you may know that I find no guilt in Him." **5** Jesus then came out, wearing the crown of thorns and the purple robe. *Pilate* said to them, "Behold, the Man!" **6** So when the chief priests and the officers saw Him, they cried out saying, "Crucify, crucify!" Pilate said to them, "Take Him yourselves and crucify Him, for I find no guilt in Him." **7** The Jews answered him, "We have a law, and by that law He ought to die because He made Himself out *to be* the Son of God."

8 Therefore when Pilate heard this statement, he was *even* more afraid; **9** and he entered into the Praetorium again and said to Jesus, "Where are You from?" But Jesus gave him no answer. **10** So Pilate said to Him, "You do not speak to me? Do You not know that I have authority to release You, and I have authority to crucify You?" **11** Jesus answered, "You would have no authority over Me, unless it had been given you from above; for this reason he who delivered Me to you has *the* greater sin." **12** As a result of this Pilate made efforts to release Him, but the Jews cried out saying, "If you release this Man, you are no friend of Caesar; everyone who makes himself out *to be* a king opposes Caesar."

13 Therefore when Pilate heard these words, he brought Jesus out, and sat down on the judgment seat at a place called The Pavement, but in Hebrew, Gabbatha. **14** Now it was the day of preparation for the Passover; it was about the sixth hour. And he said to the Jews, "Behold, your King!" **15** So they cried out, "Away with *Him,* away with *Him,* crucify Him!" Pilate said to them, "Shall I crucify your King?" The chief priests answered, "We have no king but Caesar." **16** So he then handed Him over to them to be crucified.

17 They took Jesus, therefore, and He went out, bearing His own cross, to the place called the Place of a Skull, which is called in Hebrew, Golgotha. **18** There they crucified Him, and with Him two other men, one on either side, and Jesus in between. **19** Pilate also wrote an inscription and put it on the cross. It was written, "JESUS THE NAZARENE, THE KING OF THE JEWS." **20** Therefore many of the Jews read this inscription, for the place where Jesus was crucified was near the city; and it was written in Hebrew, Latin *and* in Greek. **21** So the chief priests of the Jews were saying to Pilate, "Do not write, 'The King of the Jews'; but that He said, 'I am King of the Jews.'" **22** Pilate answered, "What I have written I have written."

23 Then the soldiers, when they had crucified Jesus, took His outer garments and made four parts, a part to every soldier and *also* the tunic; now the tunic was seamless, woven in one piece. **24** So they said to one another, "Let us not tear it, but cast lots for it, *to decide* whose it shall be"; *this was* to fulfill the Scripture: "THEY DIVIDED MY OUTER GARMENTS AMONG THEM, AND FOR MY CLOTHING THEY CAST LOTS." **25** Therefore the soldiers did these things.

But standing by the cross of Jesus were His mother, and His mother's sister, Mary the *wife* of Clopas, and Mary Magdalene. **26** When Jesus then saw His mother, and the disciple whom He loved standing nearby, He said to His mother, "Woman, behold, your son!" **27** Then He said to the disciple, "Behold, your mother!" From that hour the disciple took her into his own *household.*

28 After this, Jesus, knowing that all things had already been accomplished, to fulfill the Scripture, said, "I am thirsty." **29** A jar full of sour wine was standing there; so they put a sponge full of the sour wine upon *a branch of* hyssop and brought it up to

His mouth. **30** Therefore when Jesus had received the sour wine, He said, "It is finished!" And He bowed His head and gave up His spirit.

31 Then the Jews, because it was the day of preparation, so that the bodies would not remain on the cross on the Sabbath (for that Sabbath was a high day), asked Pilate that their legs might be broken, and *that* they might be taken away. **32** So the soldiers came, and broke the legs of the first man and of the other who was crucified with Him; **33** but coming to Jesus, when they saw that He was already dead, they did not break His legs. **34** But one of the soldiers pierced His side with a spear, and immediately blood and water came out. **35** And he who has seen has testified, and his testimony is true; and he knows that he is telling the truth, so that you also may believe. **36** For these things came to pass to fulfill the Scripture, "NOT A BONE OF HIM SHALL BE BROKEN." **37** And again another Scripture says, "THEY SHALL LOOK ON HIM WHOM THEY PIERCED."

38 After these things Joseph of Arimathea, being a disciple of Jesus, but a secret *one* for fear of the Jews, asked Pilate that he might take away the body of Jesus; and Pilate granted permission. So he came and took away His body. **39** Nicodemus, who had first come to Him by night, also came, bringing a mixture of myrrh and aloes, about a hundred pounds *weight*. **40** So they took the body of Jesus and bound it in linen wrappings with the spices, as is the burial custom of the Jews. **41** Now in the place where He was crucified there was a garden, and in the garden a new tomb in which no one had yet been laid. **42** Therefore because of the Jewish day of preparation, since the tomb was nearby, they laid Jesus there.

Chapter 20

John 20:1–31

1 Now on the first *day* of the week Mary Magdalene came early to the tomb, while it was still dark, and saw the stone *already* taken away from the tomb. **2** So she ran and came to Simon Peter and to the other disciple whom Jesus loved, and said to them, "They have taken away the Lord out of the tomb, and we do not know where they have laid Him." **3** So Peter and the other disciple went forth, and they were going to the tomb. **4** The two were running together; and the other disciple ran ahead faster than Peter and came to the tomb first; ⁵ and stooping and look-ing in, he saw the linen wrappings lying *there;* but he did not go in. ⁶ And so Simon Peter also came, following him, and entered the tomb; and he saw the linen wrappings lying *there,* ⁷ and the face-cloth which had been on His head, not lying with the linen wrappings, but rolled up in a place by itself. ⁸ So the other dis-ciple who had first come to the tomb then also entered, and he saw and believed. ⁹ For as yet they did not understand the Scrip-ture, that He must rise again from the dead. ¹⁰ So the disciples went away again to their own homes.

¹¹ But Mary was standing outside the tomb weeping; and so, as she wept, she stooped and looked into the tomb; ¹² and she saw two angels in white sitting, one at the head and one at the feet, where the body of Jesus had been lying. ¹³ And they said to her, "Woman, why are you weeping?" She said to them, "Because they have taken away my Lord, and I do not know where they have laid Him." ¹⁴ When she had said this, she turned around and saw Jesus standing *there,* and did not know that it was Jesus. ¹⁵ Jesus said to her, "Woman, why are you weeping? Whom are you seeking?" Supposing Him to be the gardener, she said to Him, "Sir, if you have carried Him away, tell me where you have laid Him, and I will take Him away." ¹⁶ Jesus said to her, "Mary!" She turned and said to Him in Hebrew, "Rabboni!" (which means, Teacher). ¹⁷ Jesus said to her, "Stop clinging to Me, for I have not yet ascended to the Father; but go to My brethren and say to them, 'I ascend to My Father and your Father, and My God and your God.'" ¹⁸ Mary Magdalene came, announcing to the disciples, "I have seen the Lord," and *that* He had said these things to her.

¹⁹ So when it was evening on that day, the first *day* of the week, and when the doors were shut where the disciples were, for fear of the Jews, Jesus came and stood in their midst and said to them, "Peace *be* with you." ²⁰ And when He had said this, He showed them both His hands and His side. The disciples then rejoiced when they saw the Lord. ²¹ So Jesus said to them again, "Peace *be* with you; as the Father has sent Me, I also send you." ²² And when He had said this, He breathed on them and said to them, "Receive the Holy Spirit. ²³ "If you forgive the sins of any, *their sins* have been forgiven them; if you retain the *sins* of any, they have been retained."

²⁴ But Thomas, one of the twelve, called Didymus, was not with them when Jesus came. ²⁵ So the other disciples were saying to him, "We have seen the Lord!" But he said to them, "Unless I see in His hands the imprint of the nails, and put my

finger into the place of the nails, and put my hand into His side, I will not believe."

26 After eight days His disciples were again inside, and Thomas with them. Jesus came, the doors having been shut, and stood in their midst and said, "Peace *be* with you." **27** Then He said to Thomas, "Reach here with your finger, and see My hands; and reach here your hand and put it into My side; and do not be unbelieving, but believing." **28** Thomas answered and said to Him, "My Lord and my God!" **29** Jesus said to him, "Because you have seen Me, have you believed? Blessed *are* they who did not see, and *yet* believed."

30 Therefore many other signs Jesus also performed in the presence of the disciples, which are not written in this book; **31** but these have been written so that you may believe that Jesus is the Christ, the Son of God; and that believing you may have life in His name.

Chapter 21

The Eighth Sign: The Miraculous Catch
John 21:1–25

1 After these things Jesus manifested Himself again to the disciples at the Sea of Tiberias, and He manifested *Himself* in this way. **2** Simon Peter, and Thomas called Didymus, and Nathanael of Cana in Galilee, and the *sons* of Zebedee, and two others of His disciples were together. **3** Simon Peter said to them, "I am going fishing." They said to him, "We will also come with you." They went out and got into the boat; and that night they caught nothing.

4 But when the day was now breaking, Jesus stood on the beach; yet the disciples did not know that it was Jesus. **5** So Jesus said to them, "Children, you do not have any fish, do you?" They answered Him, "No." **6** And He said to them, "Cast the net on the right-hand side of the boat and you will find *a catch*." So they cast, and then they were not able to haul it in because of the great number of fish. **7** Therefore that disciple whom Jesus loved said to Peter, "It is the Lord." So when Simon Peter heard that it was the Lord, he put his outer garment on (for he was stripped *for work*), and threw himself into the sea. **8** But the other disciples came in the little boat, for they were not far from the land, but about one hundred yards away, dragging the net *full* of fish.

9 So when they got out on the land, they saw a charcoal fire *already* laid and fish placed on it, and bread. **10** Jesus said to them, "Bring some of the fish which you have now caught." **11** Simon Peter went up and drew the net to land, full of large fish, a hundred and fifty-three; and although there were so many, the net was not torn. **12** Jesus said to them, "Come *and* have breakfast." None of the disciples ventured to question Him, "Who are You?" knowing that it was the Lord. **13** Jesus came and took the bread and gave *it* to them, and the fish likewise. **14** This is now the third time that Jesus was manifested to the disciples, after He was raised from the dead.

15 So when they had finished breakfast, Jesus said to Simon Peter, "Simon, *son* of John, do you love Me more than these?" He said to Him, "Yes, Lord; You know that I love You." He said to him, "Tend My lambs." **16** He said to him again a second time, "Simon, *son* of John, do you love Me?" He said to Him, "Yes, Lord; You know that I love You." He said to him, "Shepherd My sheep." **17** He said to him the third time, "Simon, *son* of John, do you love Me?" Peter was grieved because He said to him the third time, "Do you love Me?" And he said to Him, "Lord, You know all things; You know that I love You." Jesus said to him, "Tend My sheep. **18** "Truly, truly, I say to you, when you were younger, you used to gird yourself and walk wherever you wished; but when you grow old, you will stretch out your hands and someone else will gird you, and bring you where you do not wish to *go*." **19** Now this He said, signifying by what kind of death he would glorify God. And when He had spoken this, He said to him, "Follow Me!"

20 Peter, turning around, saw the disciple whom Jesus loved following *them;* the one who also had leaned back on His bosom at the supper and said, "Lord, who is the one who betrays You?" **21** So Peter seeing him said to Jesus, "Lord, and what about this man?" **22** Jesus said to him, "If I want him to remain until I come, what *is that* to you? You follow Me!" **23** Therefore this saying went out among the brethren that that disciple would not die; yet Jesus did not say to him that he would not die, but *only,* "If I want him to remain until I come, what *is that* to you?"

24 This is the disciple who is testifying to these things and wrote these things, and we know that his testimony is true.

25 And there are also many other things which Jesus did, which if they were written in detail, I suppose that even the world itself would not contain the books that would be written.

Consider . . .

During the unjust trial of Jesus, Pilate asks a piercing question which rules all other questions in significance: "What is truth?" (18:38). Indeed, this is *the* question. To answer this question, there are only two possible approaches. Either man defines truth, or God defines truth. It's all or nothing. You can't have it both ways.

If man defines truth, then the problems are immediately evident. Truth becomes arbitrary, up to the whim of man. Man might say, "I only believe the facts." Yet facts must be interpreted, and we often find one man's "fact" is another man's lie.

Our Only Hope

The "gospel" is the good news about Christ and what he has done and is doing for mankind. In a stunning act of humility and love, Christ suffered and died for man, man who is evil and wicked (Rom 5:8).

As the Lamb of God, he became the perfect sacrifice, dying in man's place. While sinless, he took on man's sin and was punished by the Father on the cross as *if* he were a sinner. Jesus, thus, became the substitute for man. By dying in our place, he satisfied the required judgment for sin—eternal death (1 Pet 3:18). His resurrection then validated the sacrifice and vindicated his divinity.

The gospel, therefore, is the message of how God saves man from himself to himself—from his wrath to his eternal, saving love. As John has laid out in this gospel, the path to salvation and eternal life is through Christ and Christ alone by the following means:

1. Believe

To be a Christian means to believe in the person and work of Jesus (Eph 2:8–9). It is a cry for mercy from a sinner who knows he is hopelessly lost and condemned. However, such belief is not just an acknowledgment of the facts about Jesus. Even the demons believe, but they are not saved because, in rebellion to his authority, they refuse to submit to Christ (Jas 2:19). For them, there is no real repentance.

2. Repent

To repent is to turn away from sin and turn toward Christ (2 Cor 7:10). It requires acknowledgment of personal sin and the just condemnation of hell and wrath from a holy God (Rom 3:10–18; Heb 9:27). To repent is to reject one's sinful life lived for self and embrace a life lived exclusively for Christ according to his ways.

3. Surrender

True repentance involves surrender to Christ. He is King. One does not make Christ king of his life, he acknowledges the fact and submits to him as King. Instead of living for self and according to one's own will, the true believer now lives for Christ and seeks Christ's will. Surrendering to the lordship of Christ is a rejection of personal autonomy and a joyful submission to Christ's authority (Matt 10:37–39).

4. Obey

To submit to Christ's authority is to seek to obey him. The life of a Christian is one of obedience. To be clear, obedience does not save, for no one can do enough good deeds to earn salvation. But a life governed by a pattern of and desire for obedience is the evidence of true belief and repentance to the Lord Jesus Christ (John 14:15).

If man made up this story about a savior, he certainly wouldn't have created the Jesus John presents—a meek, humble, sacrificial lamb who willingly gets killed by the bad guys. But this is God's story. It's his extraordinary plan of redemption.

Two thousand years ago, Jesus asked a question which echos into the present: *Who do you say I am?*

The Pharisees claimed he was demon-possessed.

His persecutors mocked him.

John says: You are King. You are God. You are Savior. And you are the only path to eternal life and joy.

Jesus now asks you: *Who do you say I am?*

www.ingramcontent.com/pod-product-compliance
Lightning Source LLC
Chambersburg PA
CBHW052025020726
47501CB00004B/1253

* 9 7 8 1 6 6 6 7 4 5 3 9 9 *